DINO MIGHTY!

BY **DOUG PALEO**

ILLUSTRATED BY **AARON BLECHA**

HOUGHTON MIFFLIN HARCOURT

BOSTON   NEW YORK

ALL RIGHTS RESERVED. FOR INFORMATION ABOUT PERMISSION
TO REPRODUCE SELECTIONS FROM THIS BOOK, WRITE TO
TRADE.PERMISSIONS@HMHCO.COM OR TO PERMISSIONS,
HOUGHTON MIFFLIN HARCOURT PUBLISHING COMPANY,
3 PARK AVENUE, 19TH FLOOR, NEW YORK, NEW YORK 10016.

ETCH IS AN IMPRINT OF HOUGHTON MIFFLIN HARCOURT
PUBLISHING COMPANY.

HMHBOOKS.COM

ILLUSTRATED BY AARON BLECHA
THE ILLUSTRATIONS IN THIS BOOK WERE SKETCHED
IN PENCIL AND THEN CREATED DIGITALLY.
THE TEXT WAS SET IN FENNARIO AND KIDPRINT.
THE DISPLAY TYPE WAS SET IN GRANDSTANDER.
COVER DESIGN BY AARON BLECHA AND PHIL CAMINITI
INTERIOR DESIGN BY PHIL CAMINITI

THE LIBRARY OF CONGRESS CATALOGING-IN-PUBLICATION
DATA IS ON FILE.

ISBN: 978-0-358-33156-8

MANUFACTURED IN CHINA
SCP 10 9 8 7 6 5 4 3 2 1
4500800229

CHAPTERS

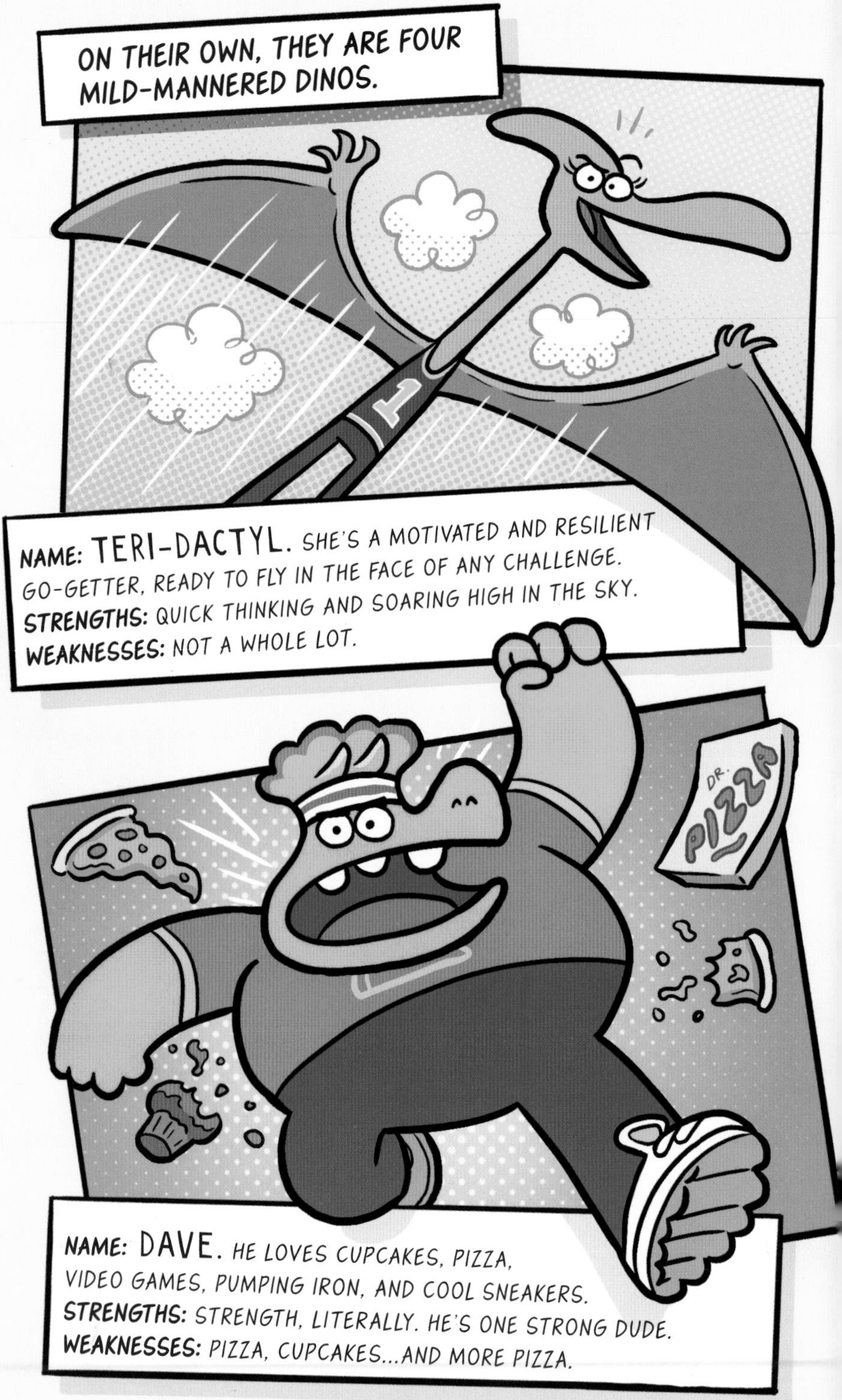
ON THEIR OWN, THEY ARE FOUR MILD-MANNERED DINOS.
1
NAME: TERI-DACTYL. SHE'S A MOTIVATED AND RESILIENT GO-GETTER, READY TO FLY IN THE FACE OF ANY CHALLENGE.
STRENGTHS: QUICK THINKING AND SOARING HIGH IN THE SKY.
WEAKNESSES: NOT A WHOLE LOT.
DR. PIZZA
NAME: DAVE. HE LOVES CUPCAKES, PIZZA, VIDEO GAMES, PUMPING IRON, AND COOL SNEAKERS.
STRENGTHS: STRENGTH, LITERALLY. HE'S ONE STRONG DUDE.
WEAKNESSES: PIZZA, CUPCAKES...AND MORE PIZZA.

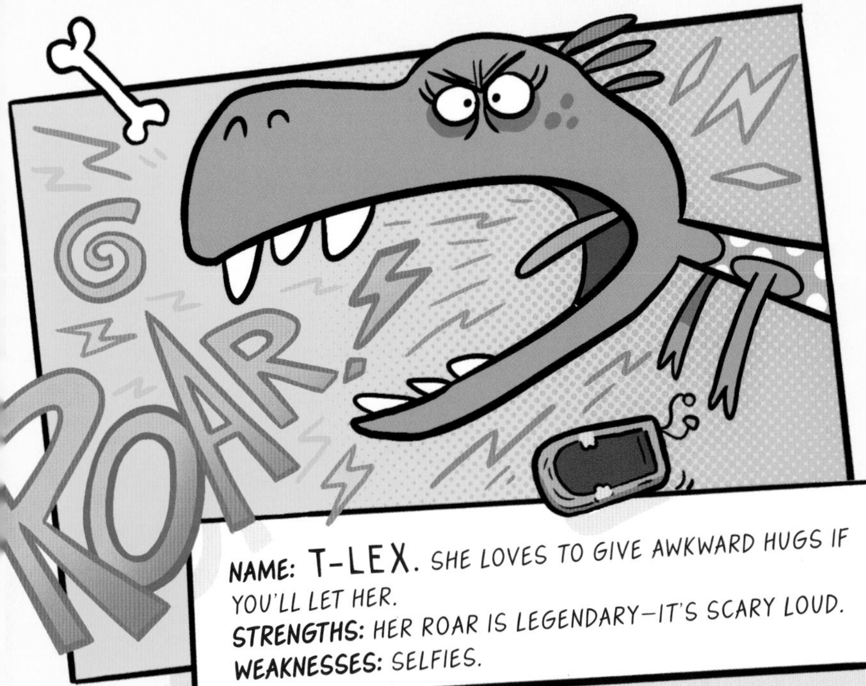
ROAR!

NAME: T-LEX. SHE LOVES TO GIVE AWKWARD HUGS IF YOU'LL LET HER.
STRENGTHS: HER ROAR IS LEGENDARY—IT'S SCARY LOUD.
WEAKNESSES: SELFIES.

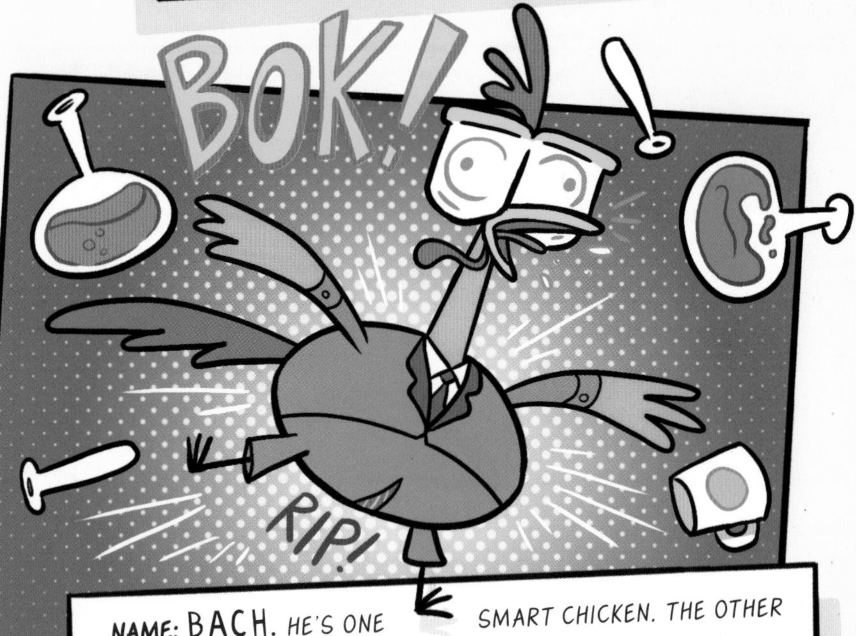
BOK!
RIP!

NAME: BACH. HE'S ONE SMART CHICKEN. THE OTHER DINOMIGHTIES FOUND HIM CROSSING THE ROAD.
STRENGTHS: EGGSELLENT INTELLIGENCE.
WEAKNESSES: HE ONLY WRITES IN CHICKEN SCRATCHES AND SAYS ONE WORD: BOK. THIS GENIUS IS OFTEN MISUNDERSTOOD.

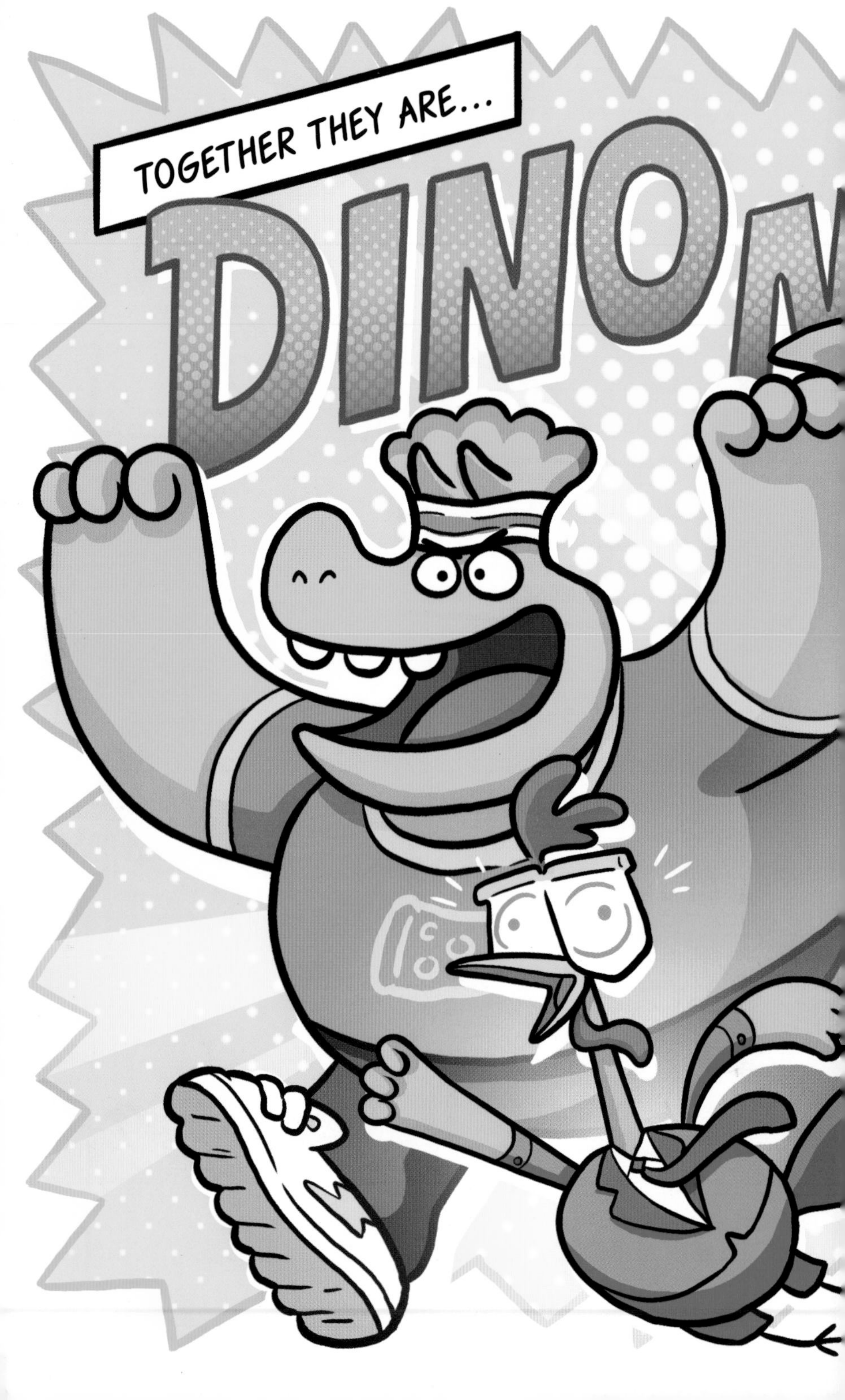
TOGETHER THEY ARE...
DINO

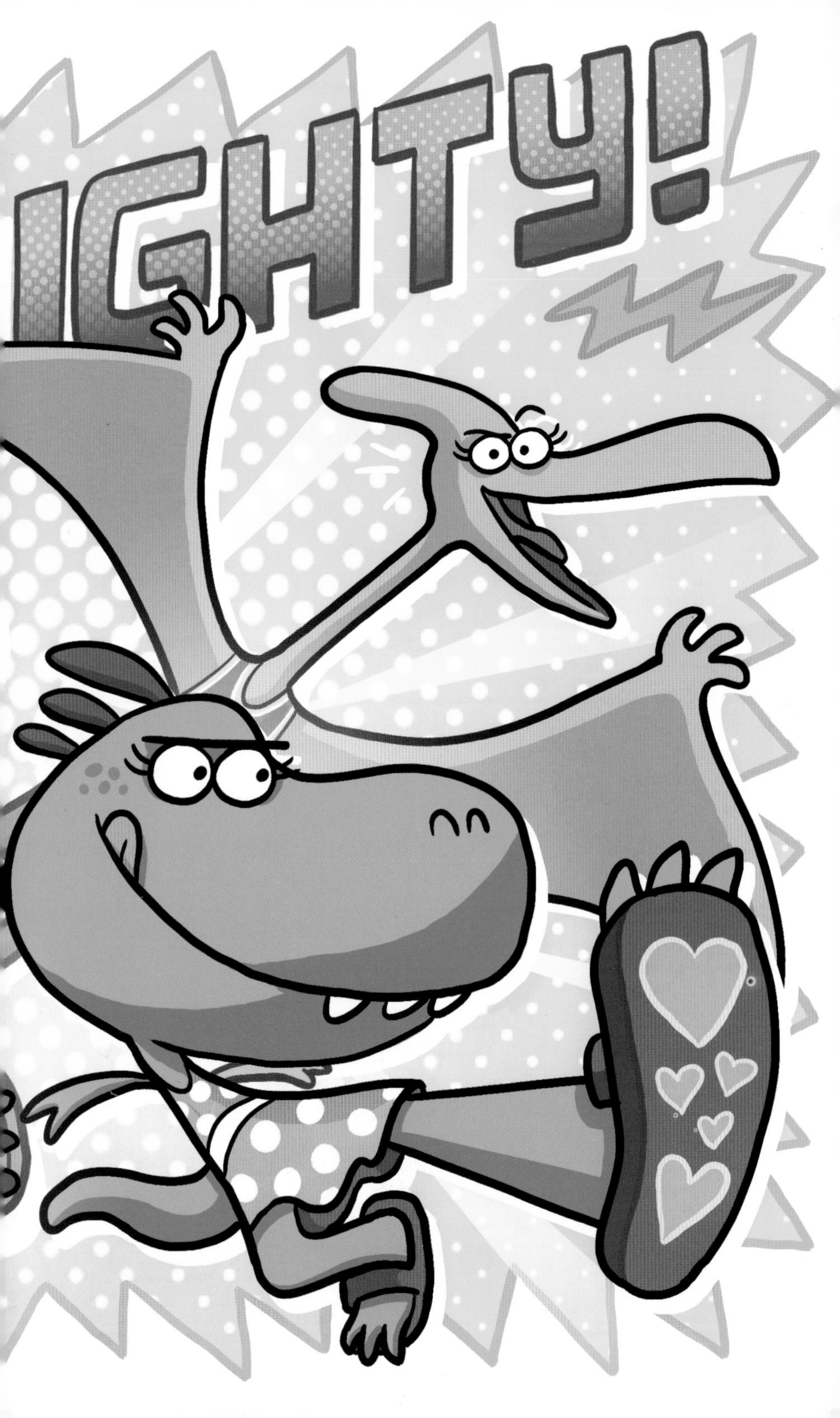
IGHTY!

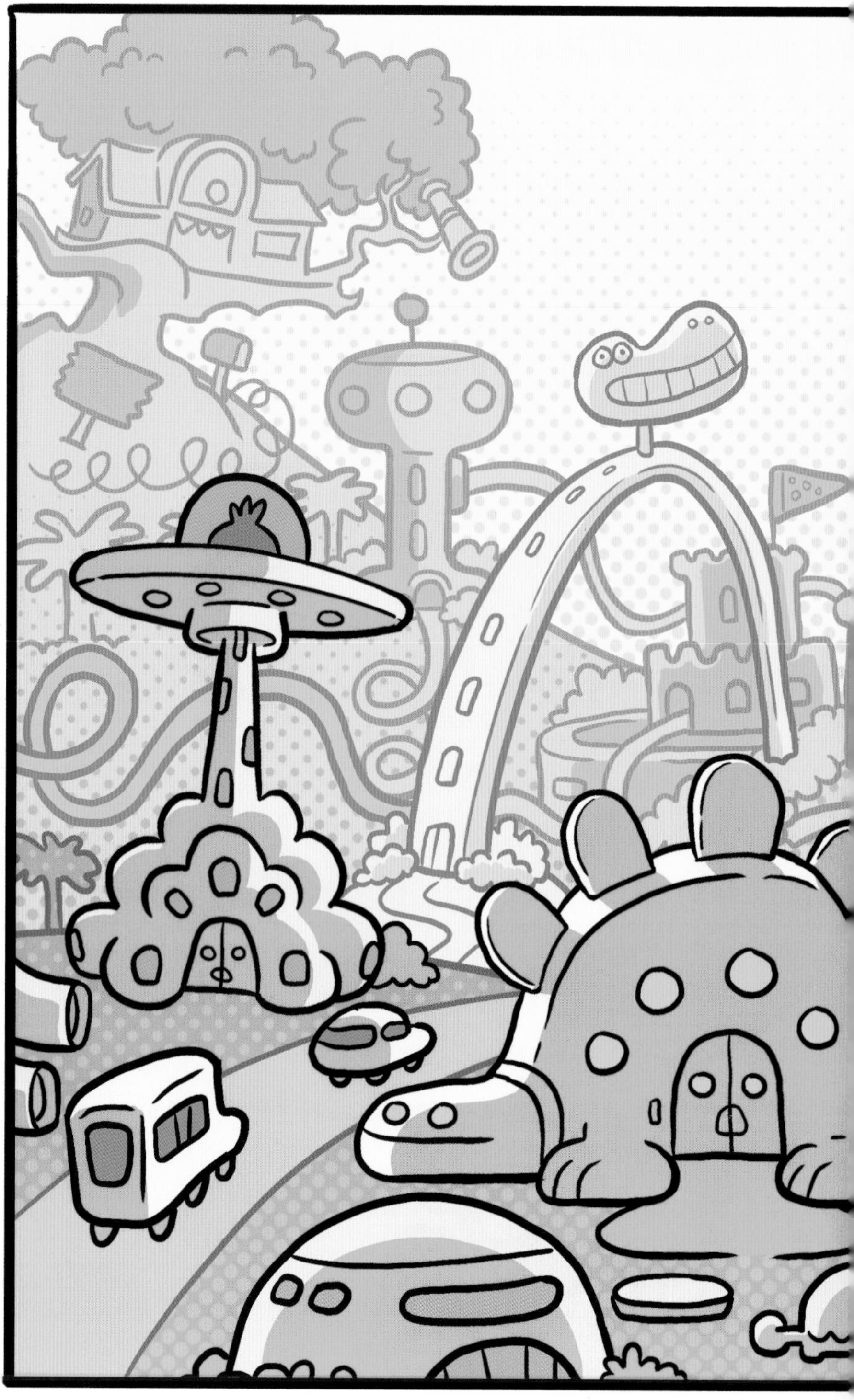

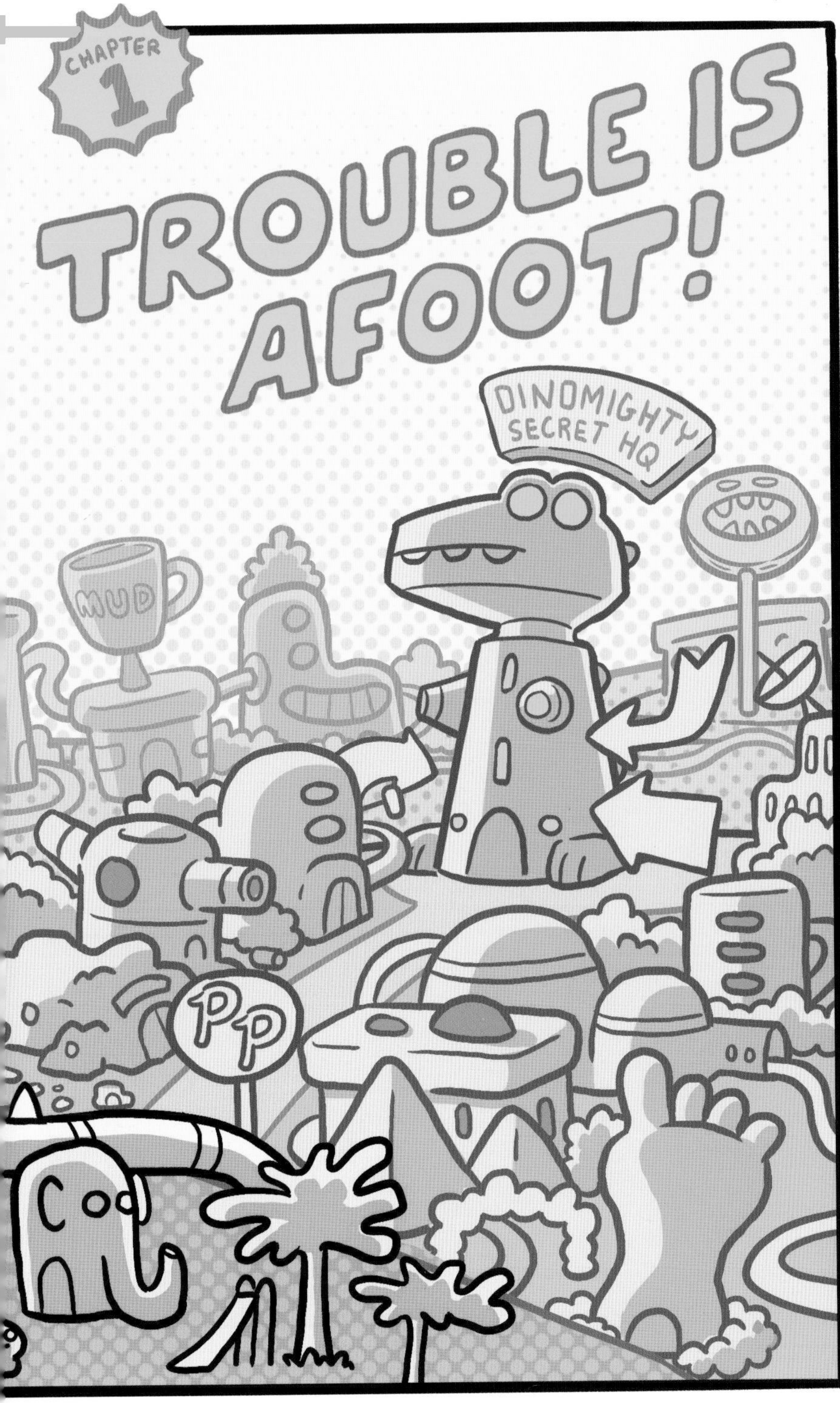
CHAPTER
1
TROUBLE IS
AFOOT!
DINOMIGHTY
SECRET HQ
MUD
Pp

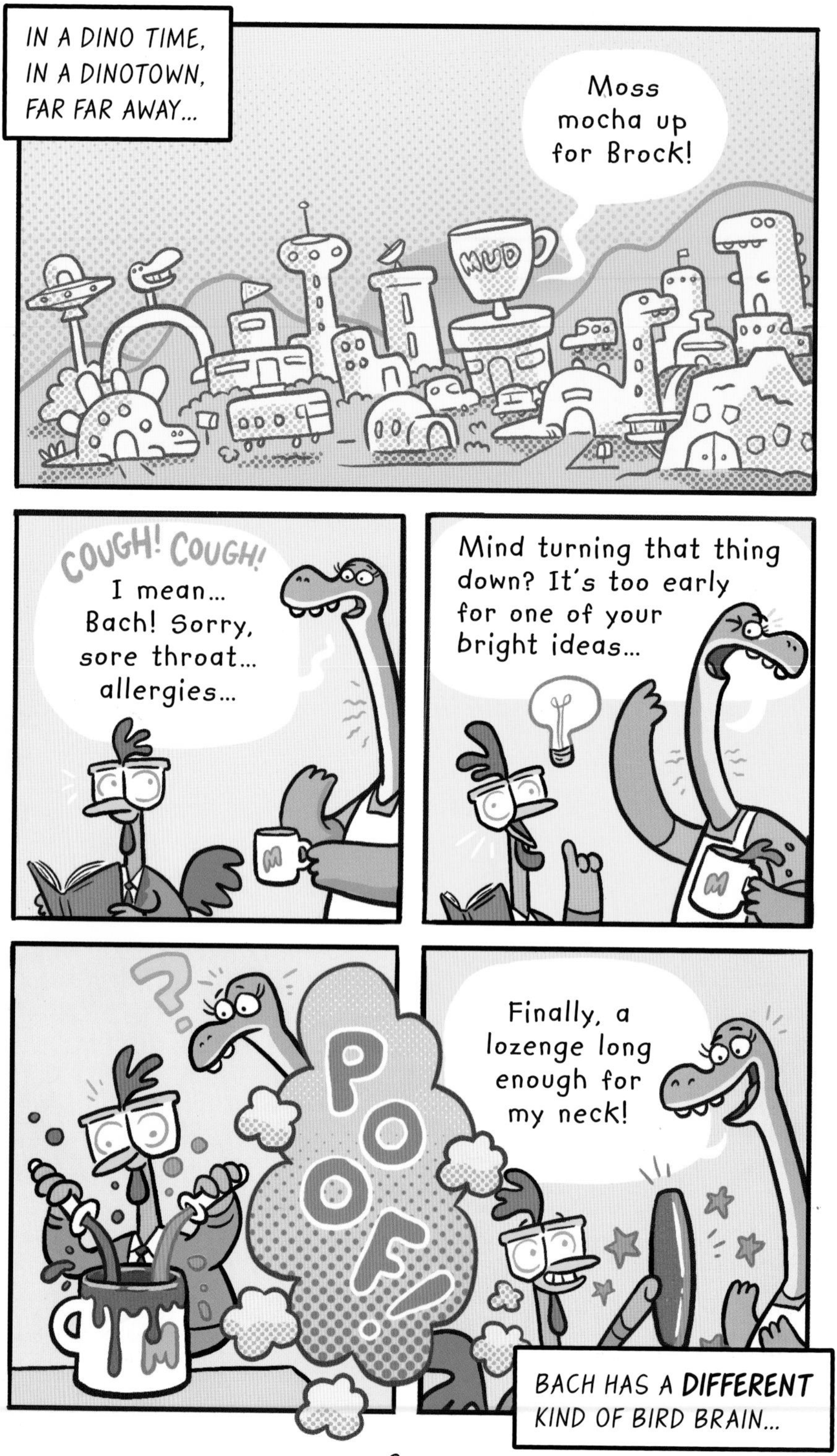
IN A DINO TIME,
IN A DINOTOWN,
FAR FAR AWAY...
Moss mocha up for Brock!
MUD
COUGH! COUGH!
I mean... Bach! Sorry, sore throat... allergies...
Mind turning that thing down? It's too early for one of your bright ideas...
?
POOF!
Finally, a lozenge long enough for my neck!
BACH HAS A **DIFFERENT** KIND OF BIRD BRAIN...

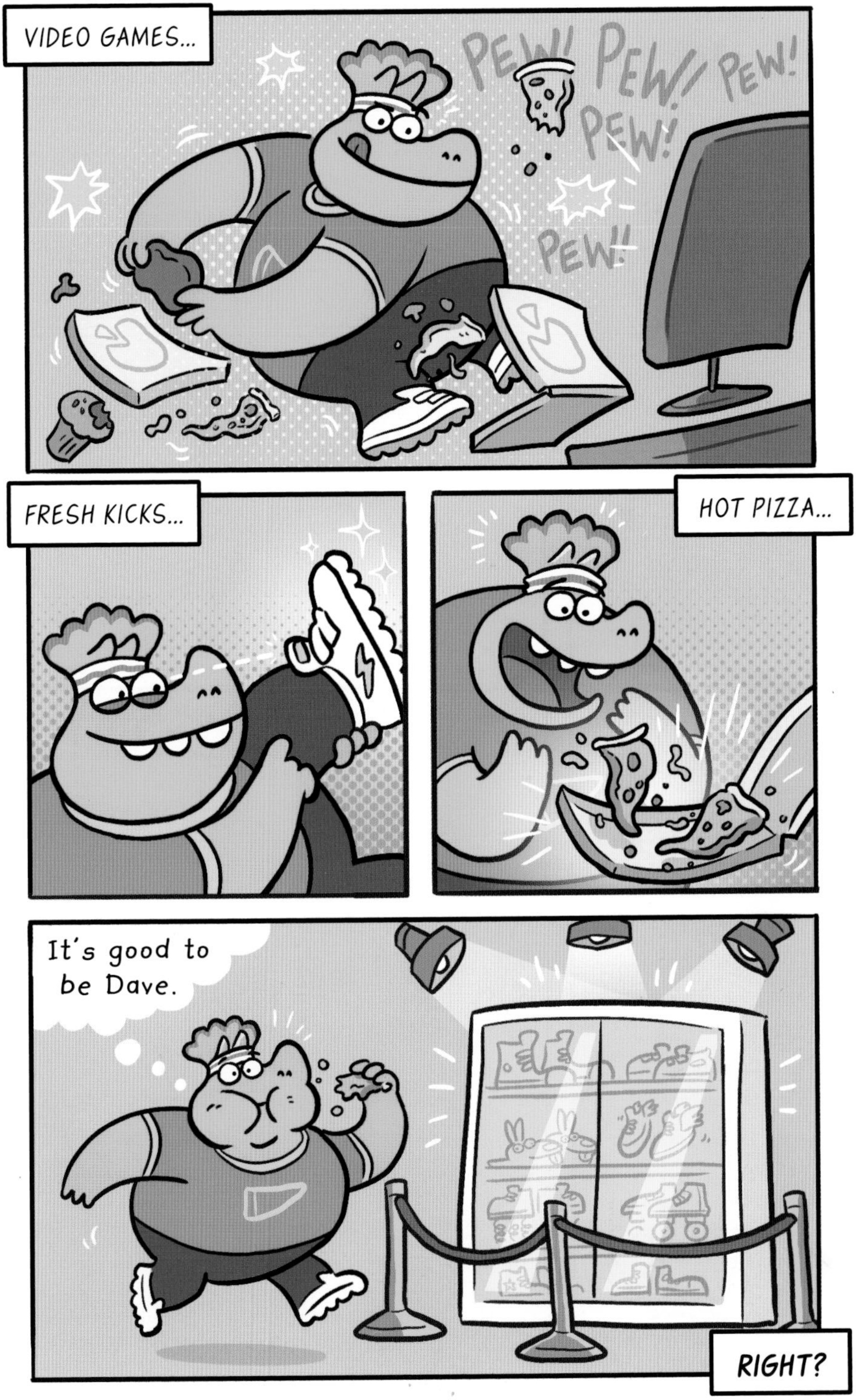
VIDEO GAMES...
PEW! PEW! PEW!
PEW!
PEW!
FRESH KICKS...
HOT PIZZA...
It's good to be Dave.
RIGHT?

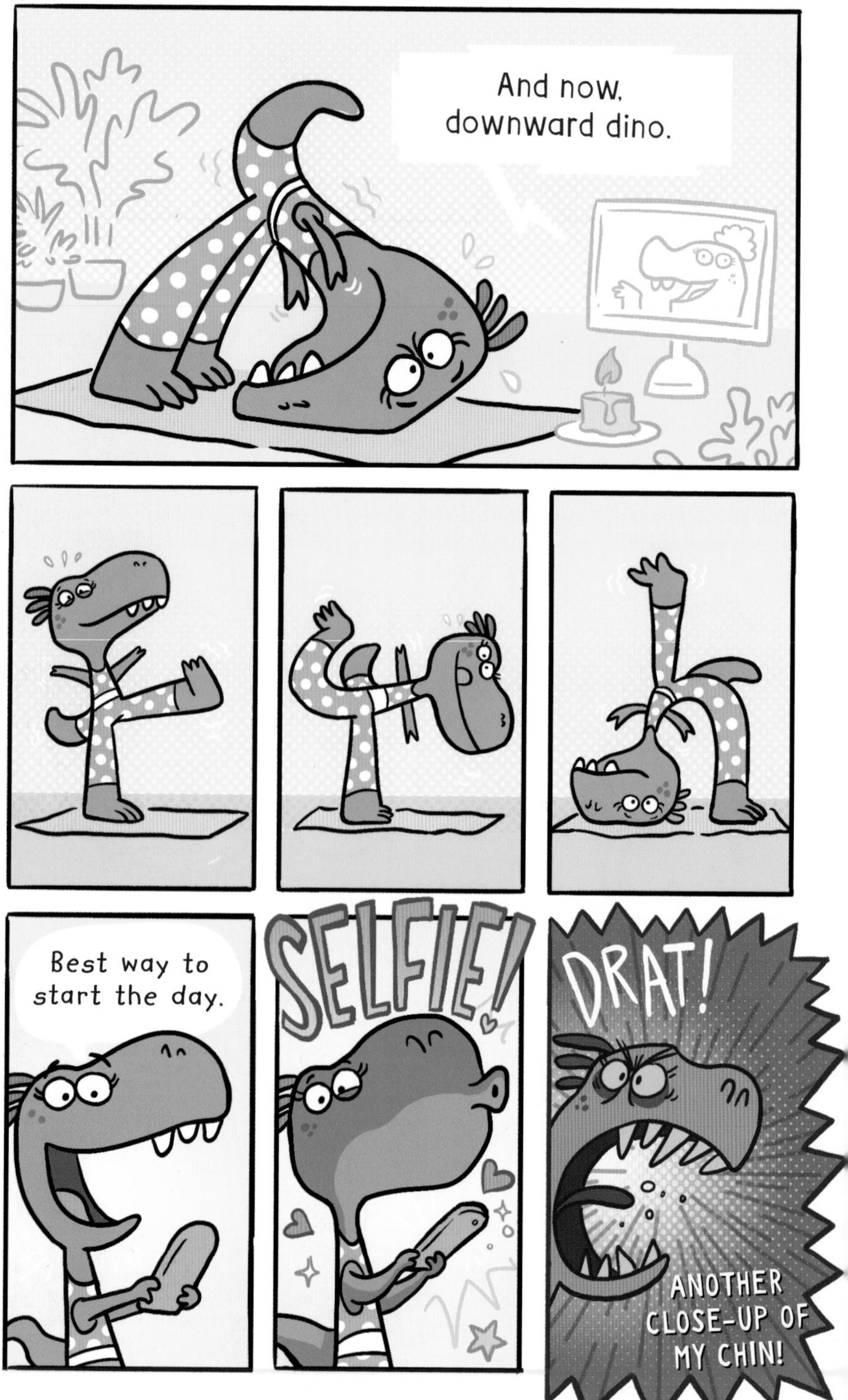
And now, downward dino.
Best way to start the day.
SELFIE!
DRAT!
ANOTHER CLOSE-UP OF MY CHIN!

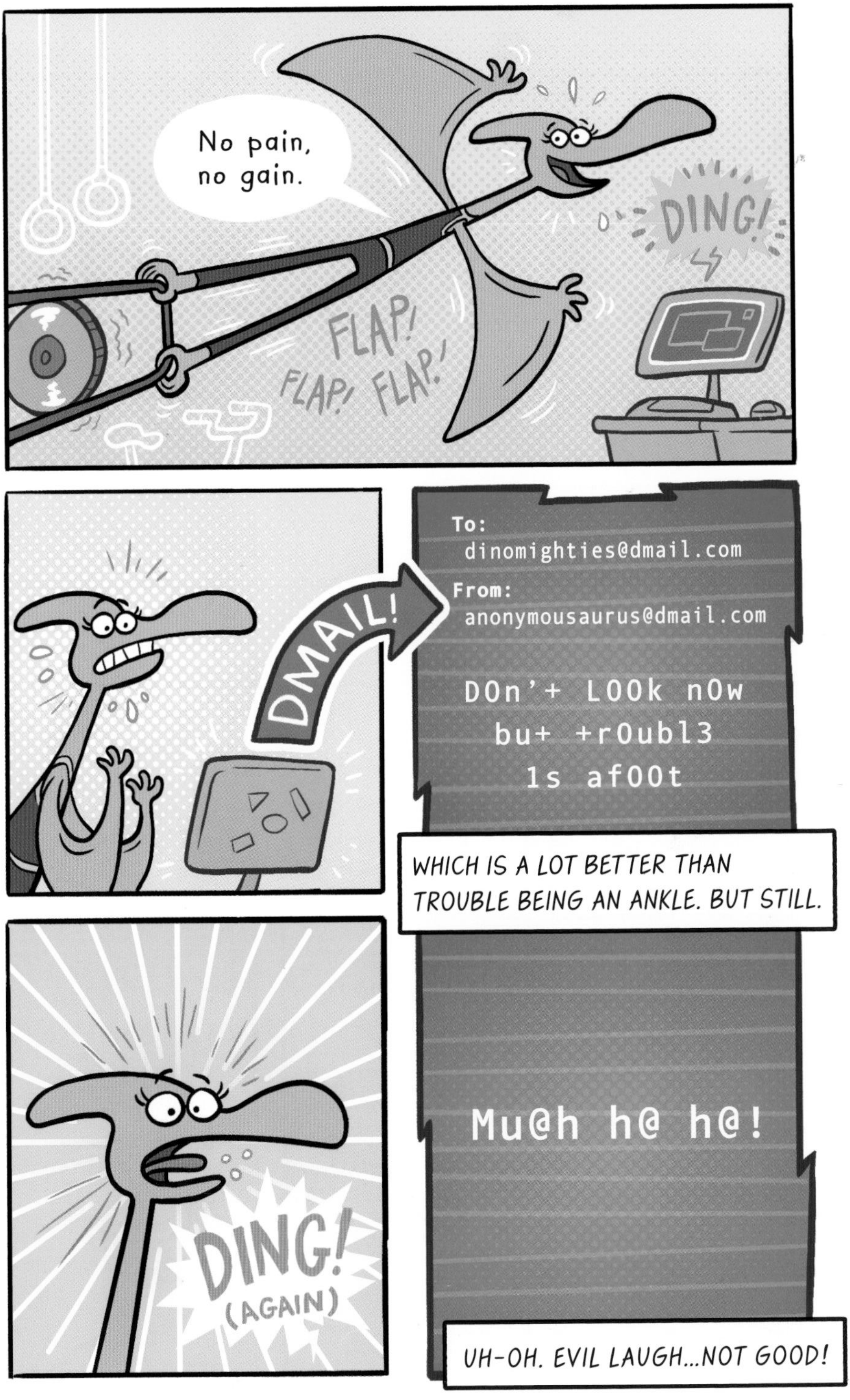
No pain, no gain.
DING!
FLAP! FLAP! FLAP!
DMAIL!
To:
dinomighties@dmail.com
From:
anonymousaurus@dmail.com
D0n'+ L00k n0w
bu+ +r0ubl3
1s af00t
WHICH IS A LOT BETTER THAN TROUBLE BEING AN ANKLE. BUT STILL.
DING! (AGAIN)
Mu@h h@ h@!
UH-OH. EVIL LAUGH...NOT GOOD!

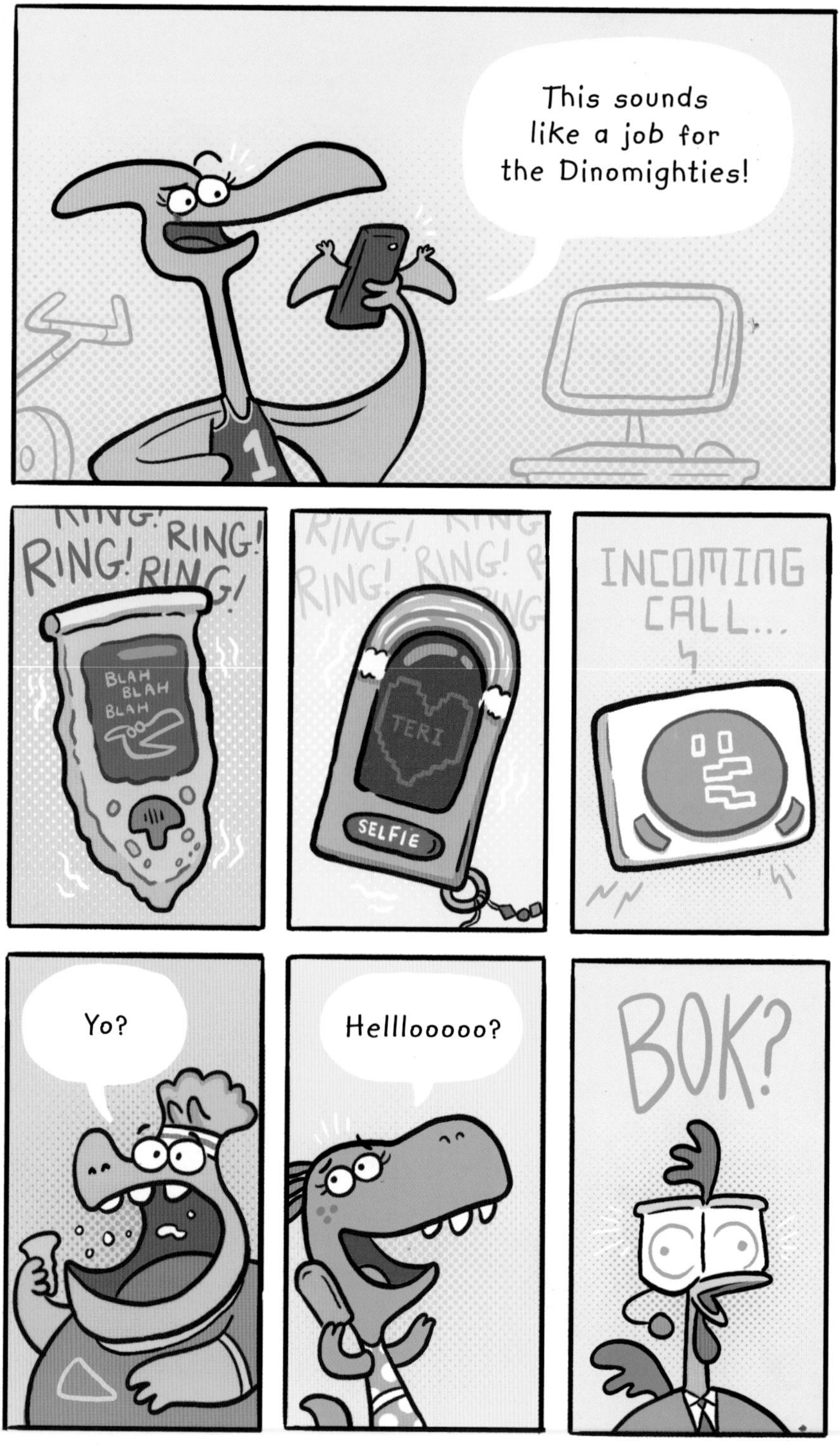
This sounds like a job for the Dinomighties!
RING! RING! RING!
BLAH BLAH BLAH
RING! RING!
TERI
SELFIE
INCOMING CALL...
Yo?
Hellloooooo?
BOK?

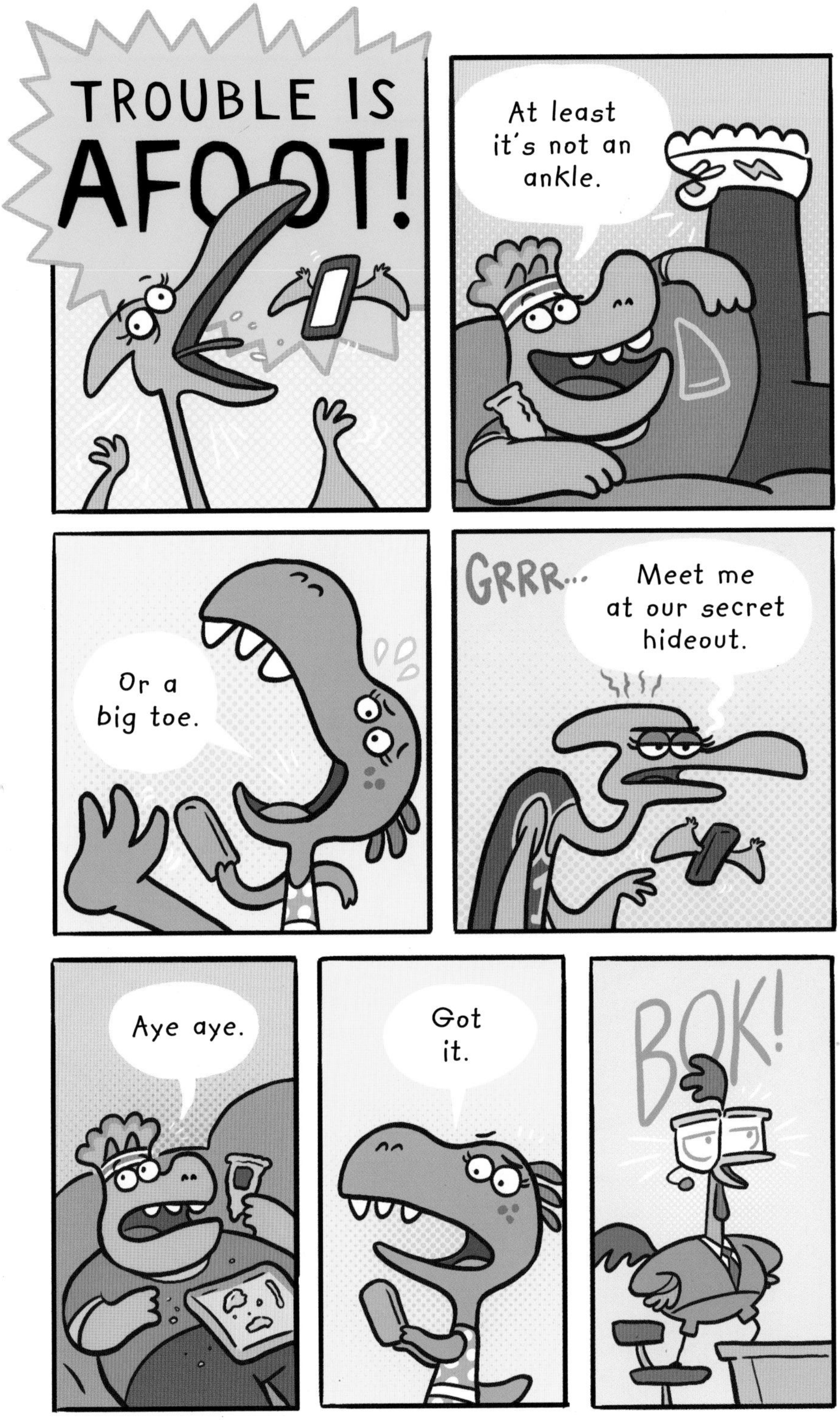
TROUBLE IS AFOOT!
At least it's not an ankle.
Or a big toe.
GRRR...
Meet me at our secret hideout.
Aye aye.
Got it.
BOK!

IN DINOTOWN, THE DINOMIGHTIES TRAVEL BY—YOU GUESSED IT—WATERSLIDE.

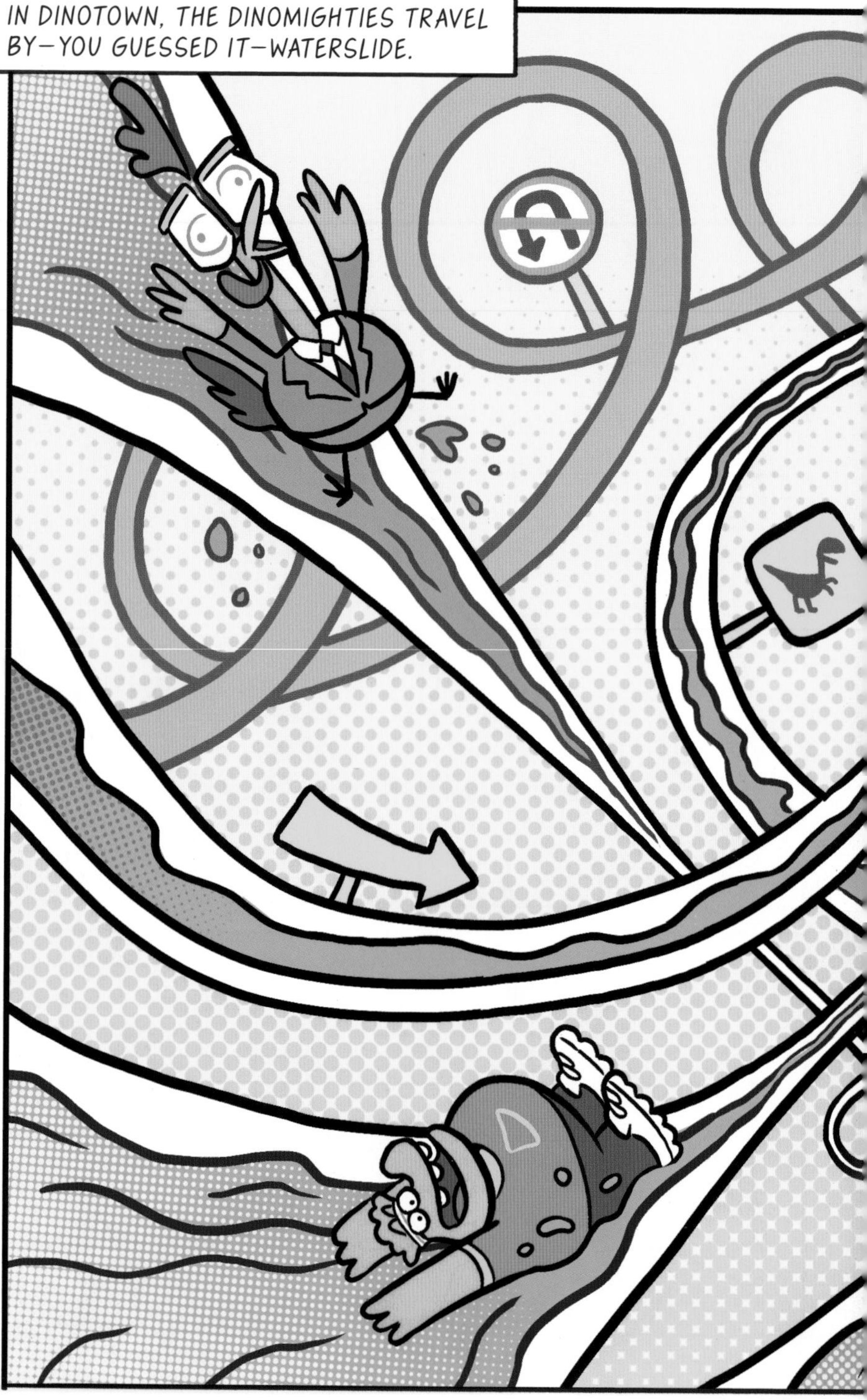

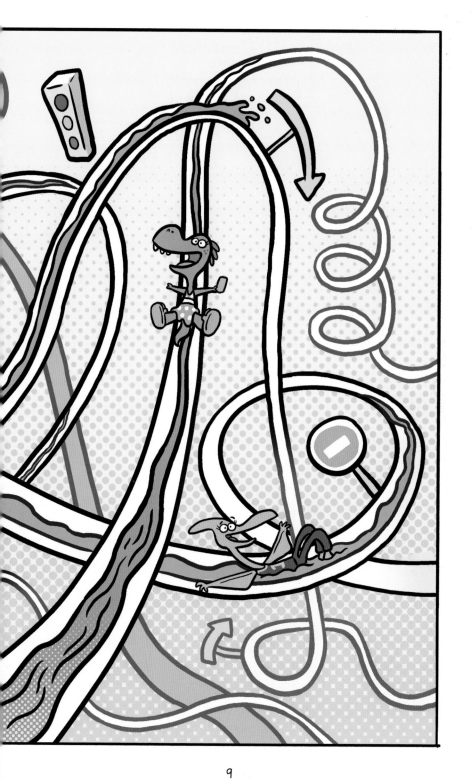

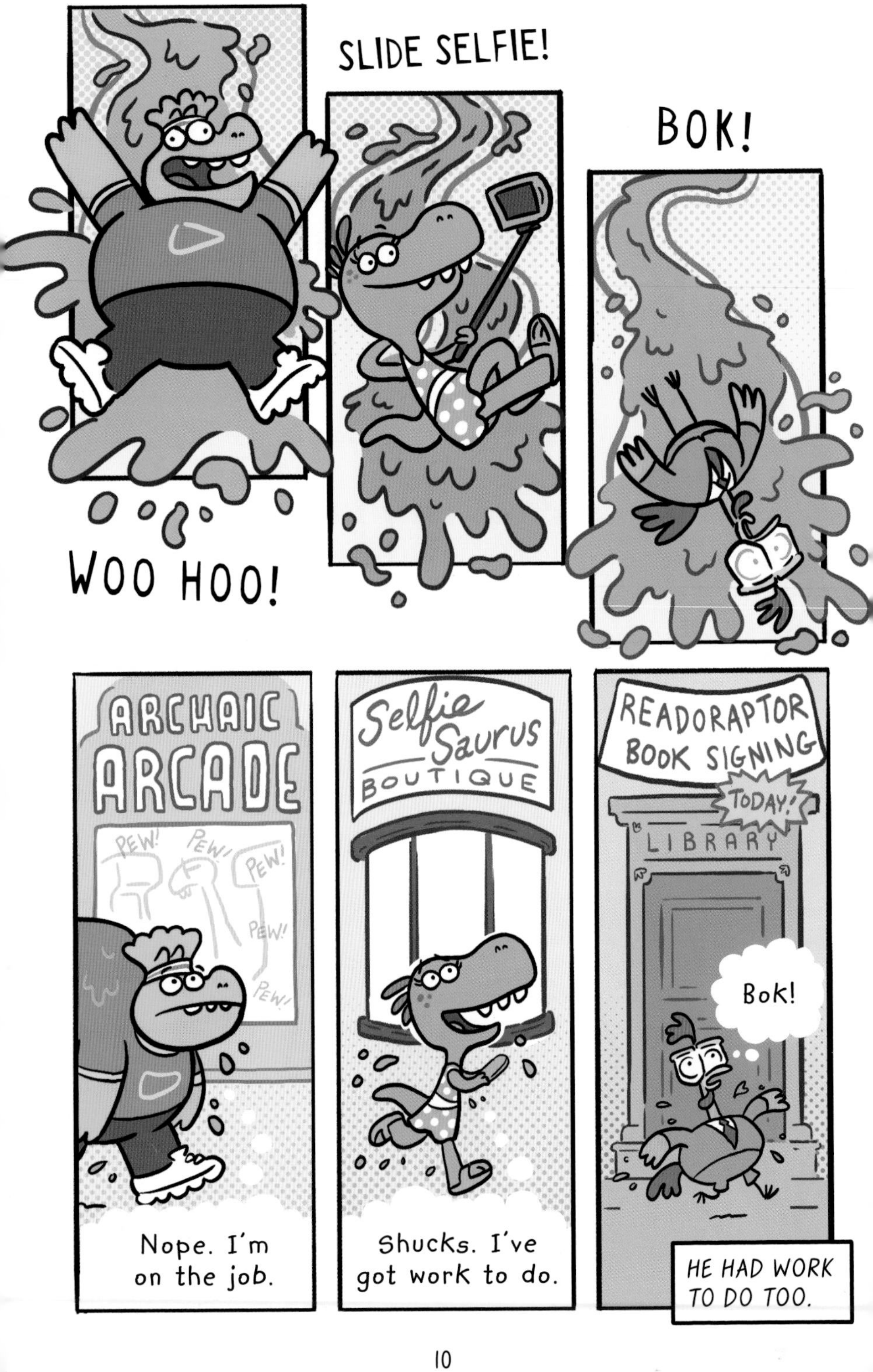
WOO HOO!
SLIDE SELFIE!
BOK!
ARCHAIC ARCADE
PEW!
PEW!
PEW!
PEW!
PEW!
Nope. I'm on the job.
Selfie Saurus BOUTIQUE
Shucks. I've got work to do.
READORAPTOR BOOK SIGNING
TODAY!
LIBRARY
Bok!
HE HAD WORK TO DO TOO.

BEHOLD...THE DINOMIGHTIES' SECRET HIDEOUT!

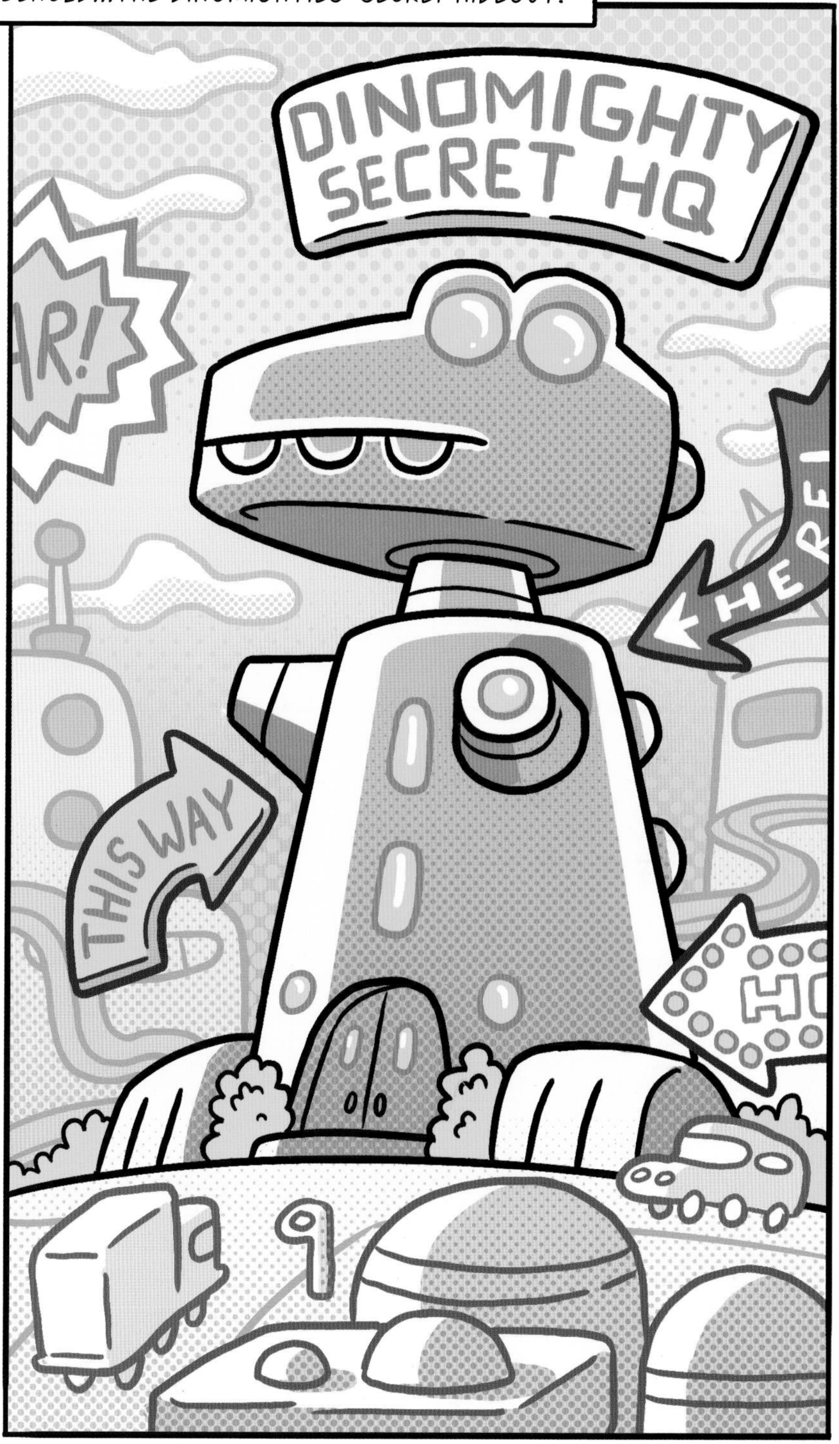
DINOMIGHTY SECRET HQ
AR!
THIS WAY
HERE

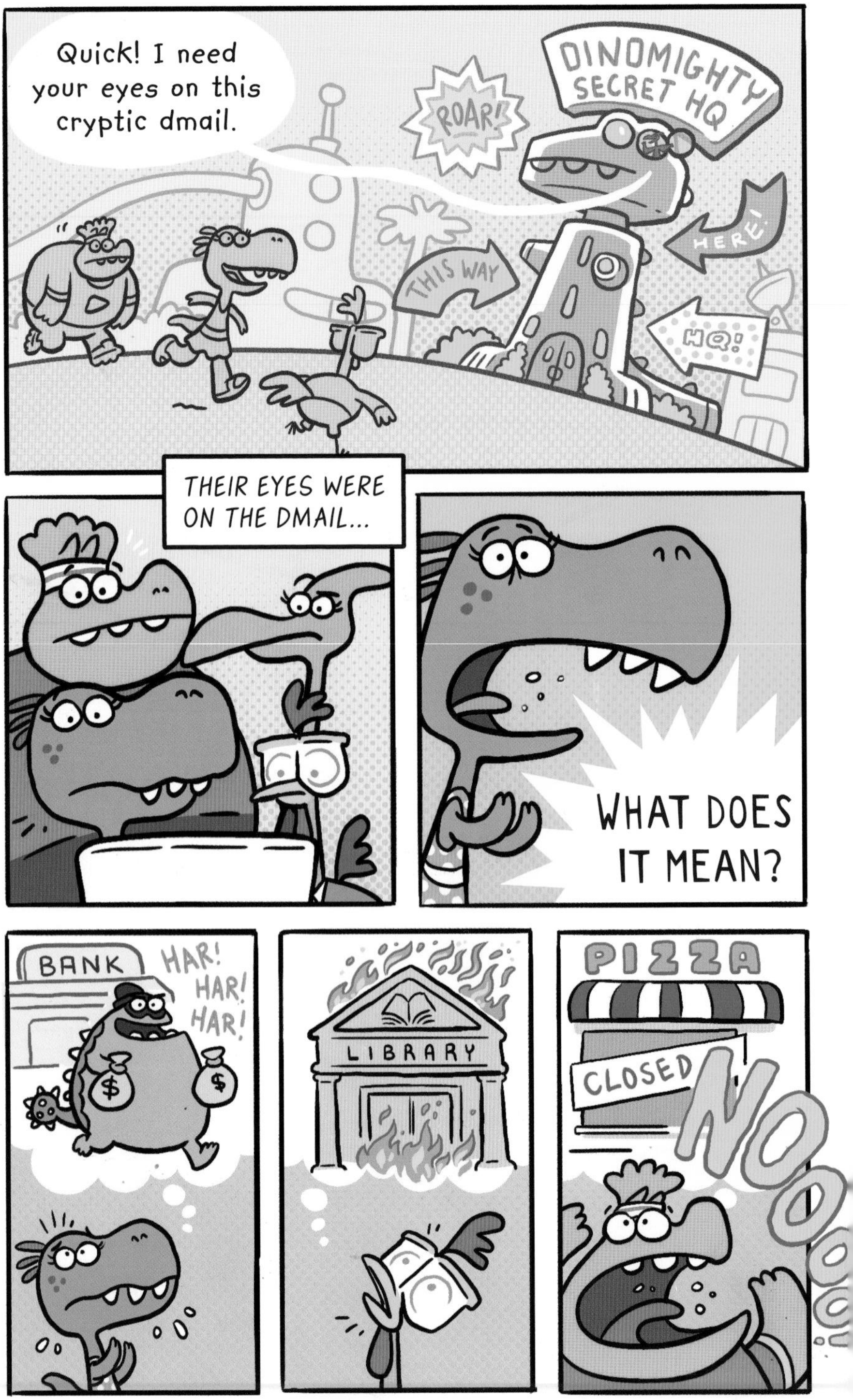
Quick! I need your eyes on this cryptic dmail.
ROAR!
DINOMIGHTY SECRET HQ
HERE!
THIS WAY
HQ!
THEIR EYES WERE ON THE DMAIL...
WHAT DOES IT MEAN?
BANK
HAR! HAR! HAR!
$
$
LIBRARY
PIZZA
CLOSED
NOOOOO!

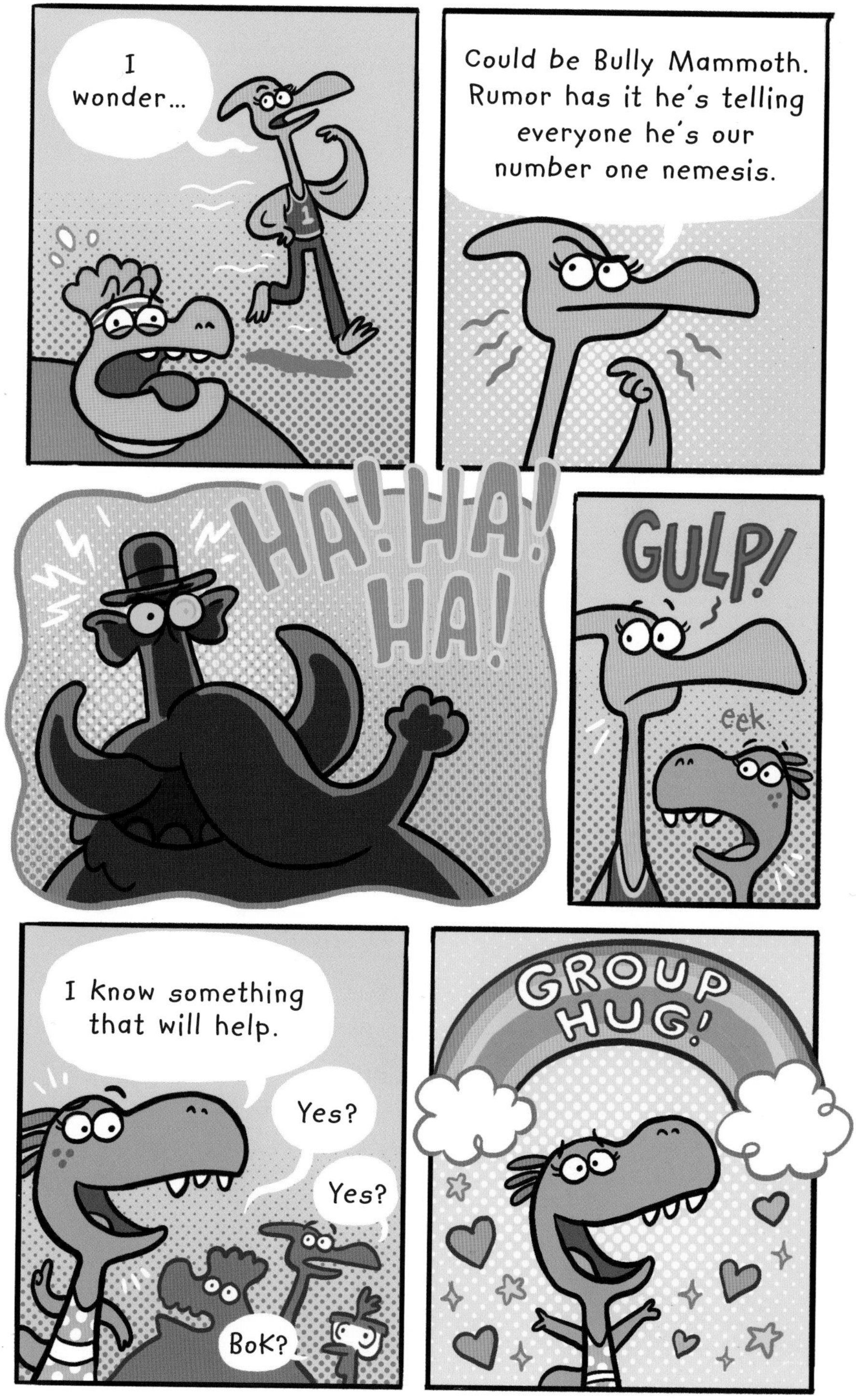
I wonder...
Could be Bully Mammoth. Rumor has it he's telling everyone he's our number one nemesis.
HA! HA! HA!
GULP!
eek
I know something that will help.
Yes?
Yes?
BOK?
GROUP HUG!

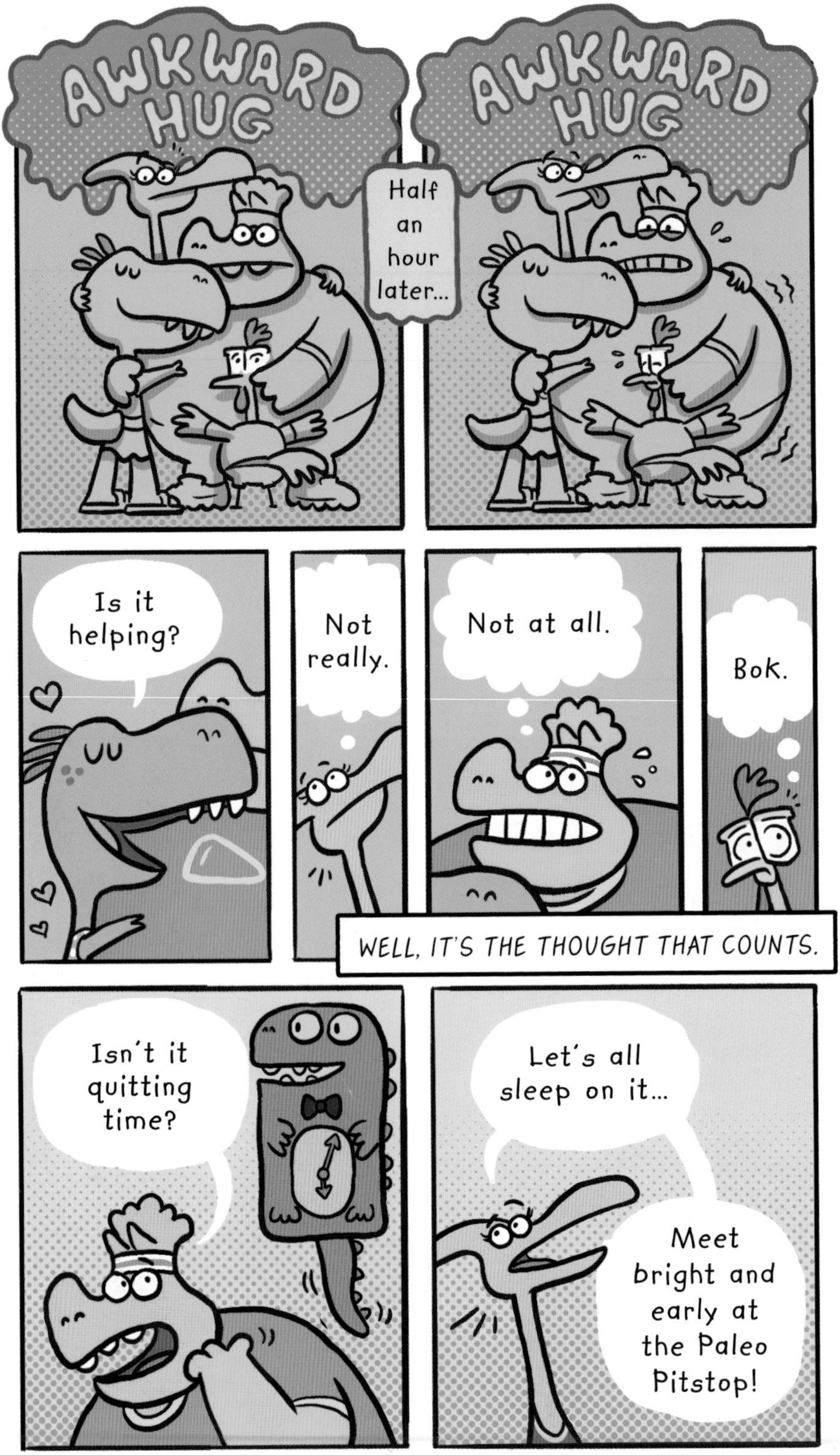
AWKWARD HUG
Half an hour later...
AWKWARD HUG
Is it helping?
Not really.
Not at all.
Bok.
WELL, IT'S THE THOUGHT THAT COUNTS.
Isn't it quitting time?
Let's all sleep on it...
Meet bright and early at the Paleo Pitstop!

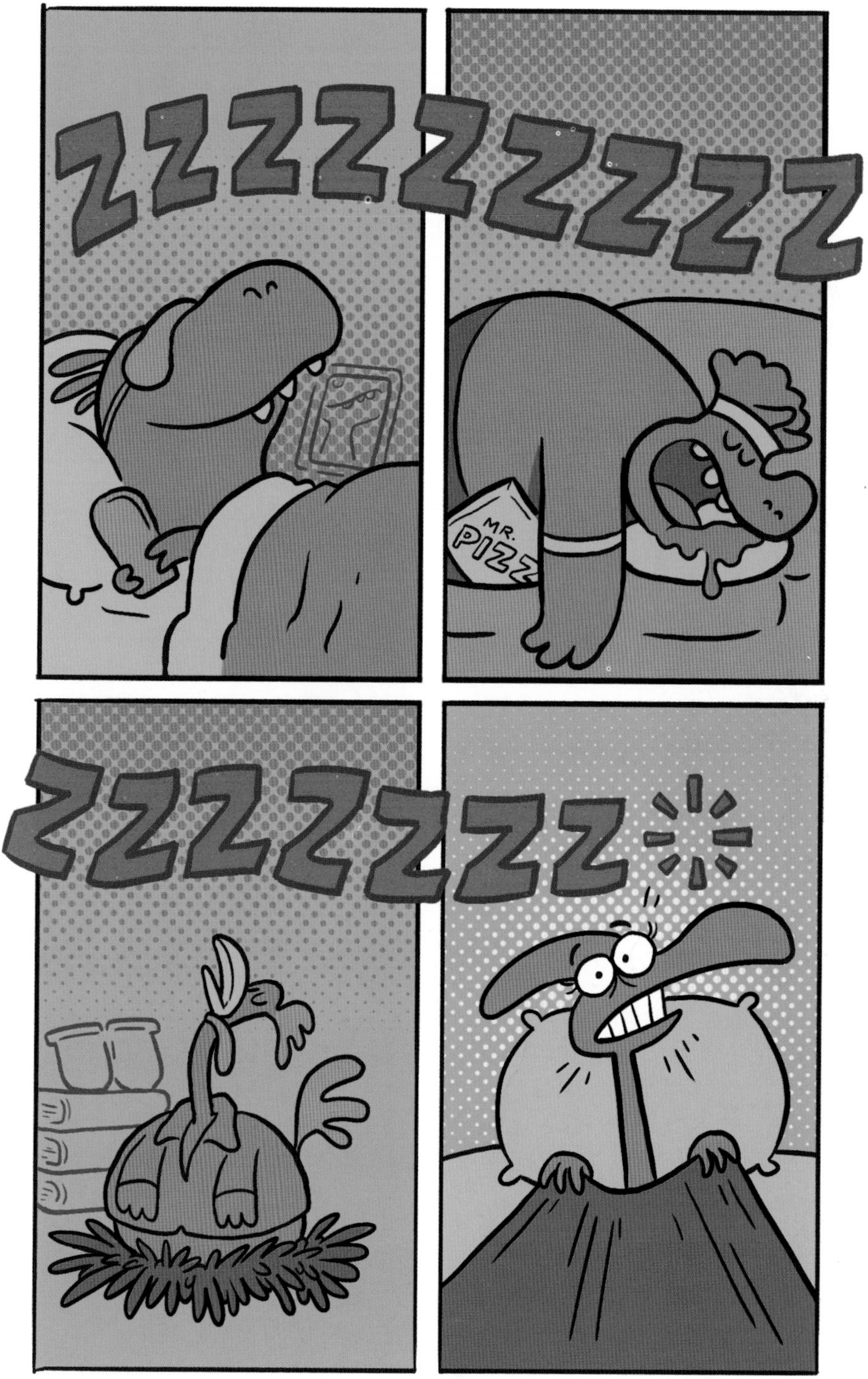
ZZZZZZZZZZZZZ
MR. PIZZ
ZZZZZZZZZZ

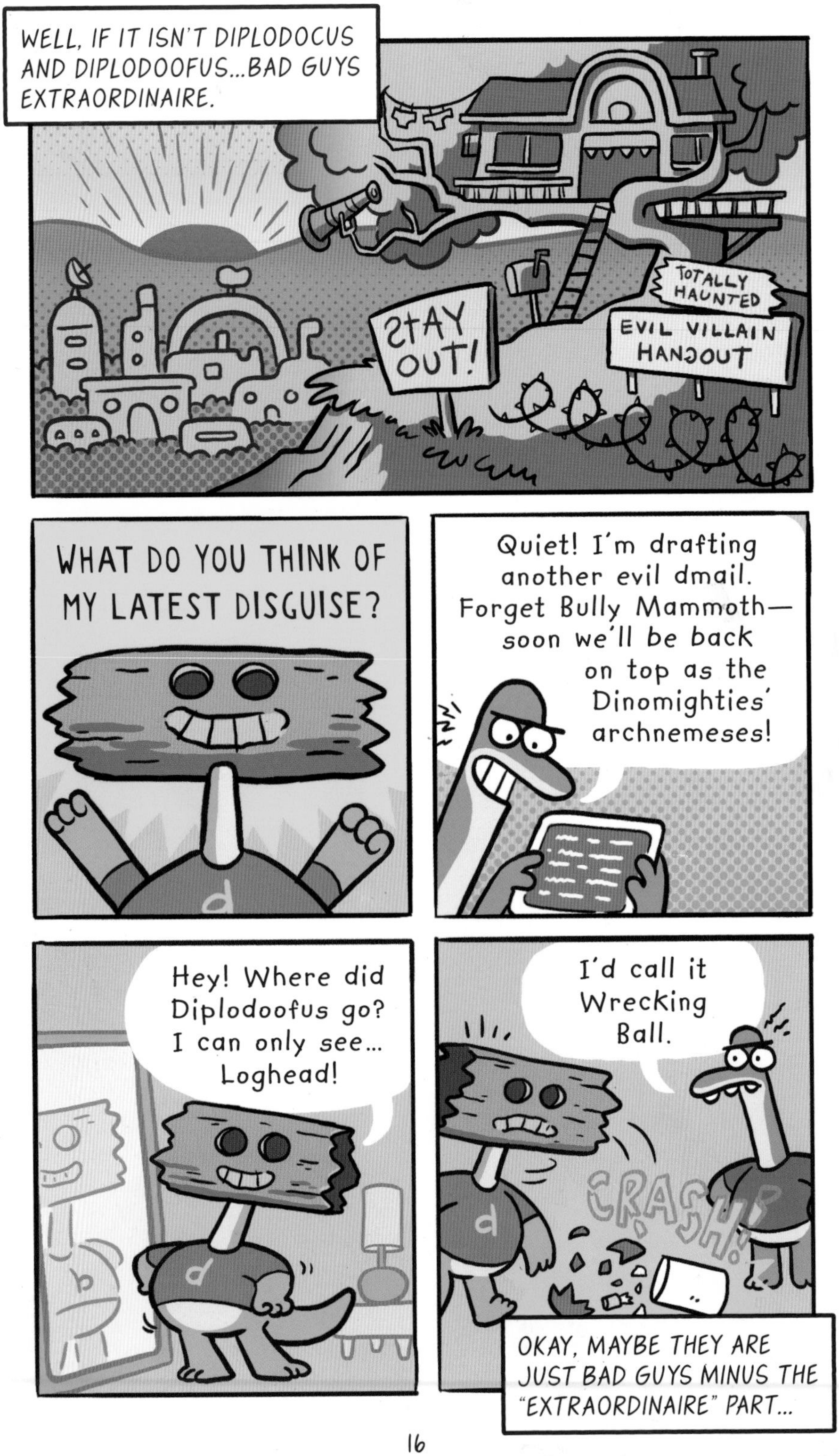
WELL, IF IT ISN'T DIPLODOCUS AND DIPLODOOFUS...BAD GUYS EXTRAORDINAIRE.
STAY OUT!
TOTALLY HAUNTED
EVIL VILLAIN HANGOUT
WHAT DO YOU THINK OF MY LATEST DISGUISE?
Quiet! I'm drafting another evil dmail. Forget Bully Mammoth— soon we'll be back on top as the Dinomighties' archnemeses!
Hey! Where did Diplodoofus go? I can only see... Loghead!
I'd call it Wrecking Ball.
CRASH!
OKAY, MAYBE THEY ARE JUST BAD GUYS MINUS THE "EXTRAORDINAIRE" PART...

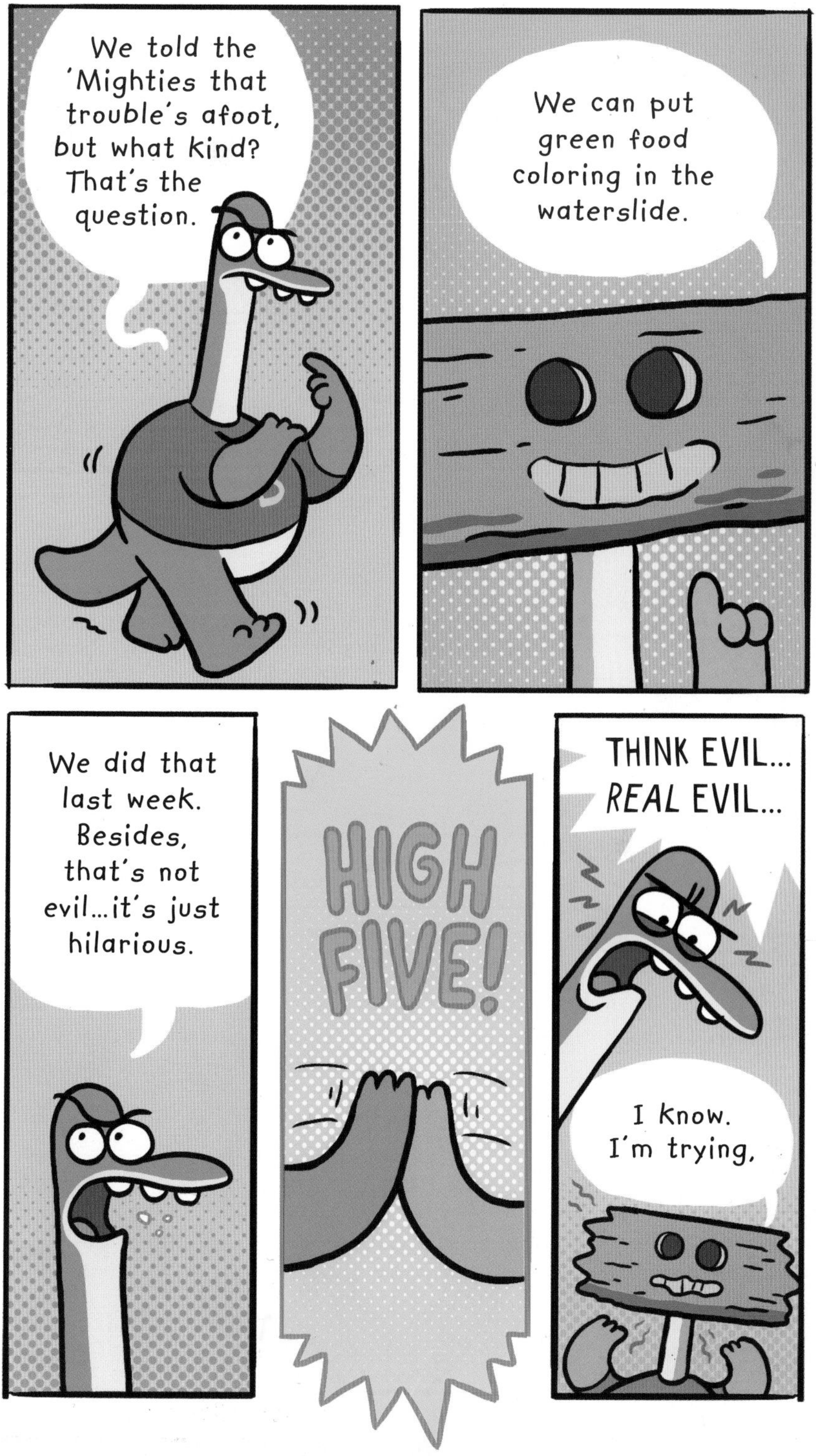
We told the 'Mighties that trouble's afoot, but what kind? That's the question.
We can put green food coloring in the waterslide.
We did that last week. Besides, that's not evil...it's just hilarious.
HIGH FIVE!
THINK EVIL... *REAL* EVIL...
I know. I'm trying.

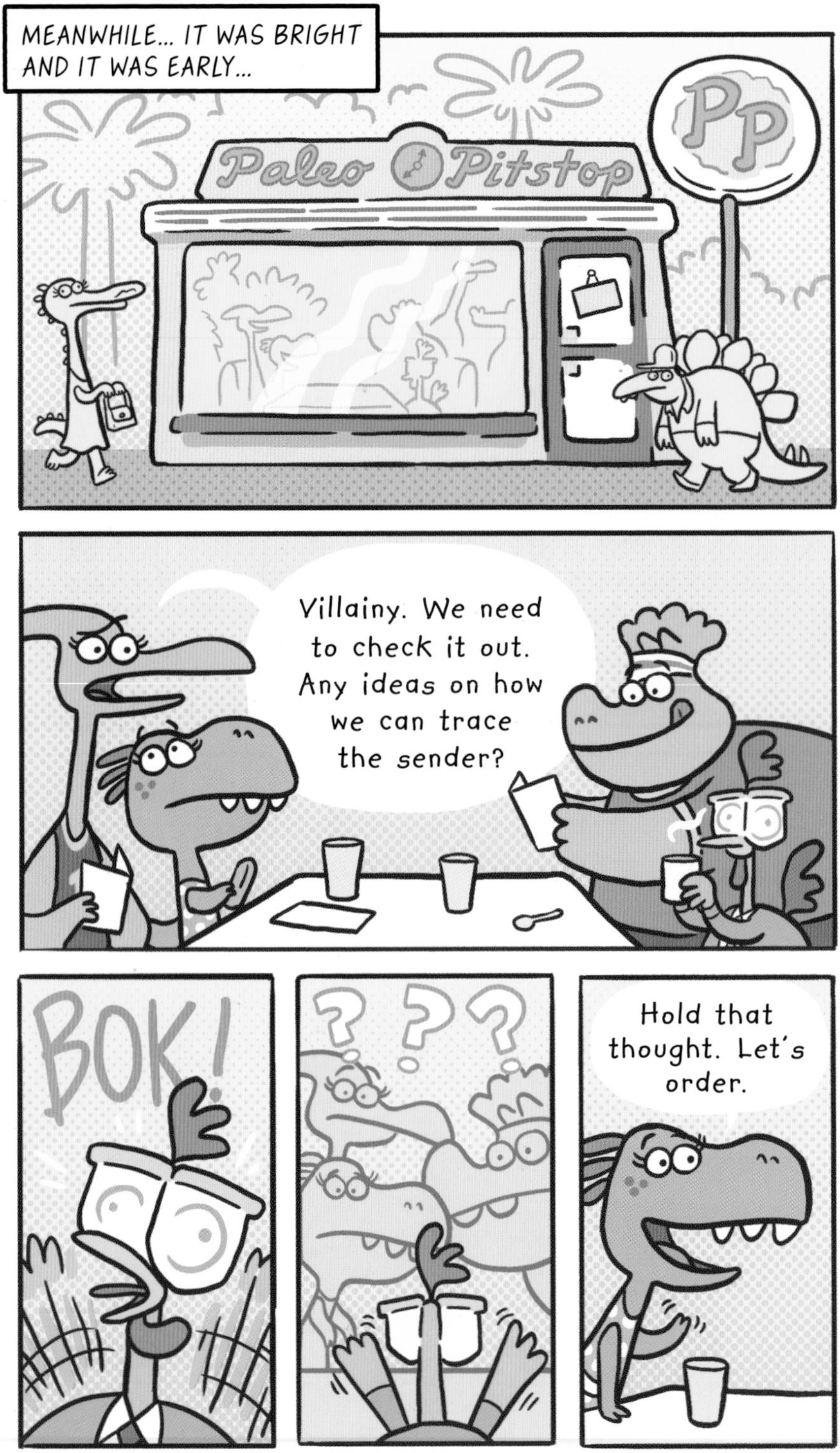
MEANWHILE... IT WAS BRIGHT AND IT WAS EARLY...
Paleo Pitstop
PP
Villainy. We need to check it out. Any ideas on how we can trace the sender?
BOK!
? ? ?
Hold that thought. Let's order.

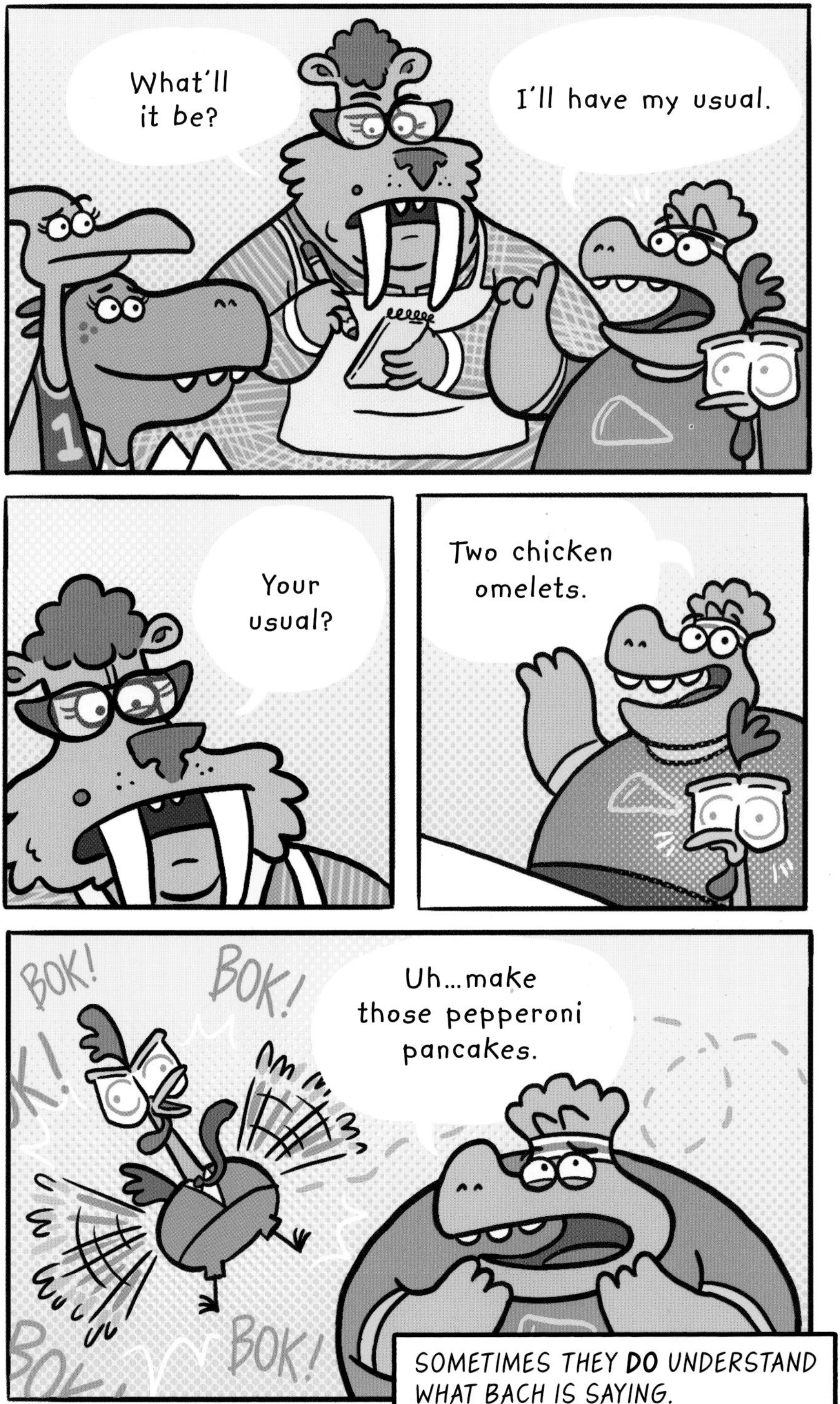
What'll it be?
I'll have my usual.
Your usual?
Two chicken omelets.
BOK! BOK!
Uh...make those pepperoni pancakes.
BOK!
SOMETIMES THEY **DO** UNDERSTAND WHAT BACH IS SAYING.

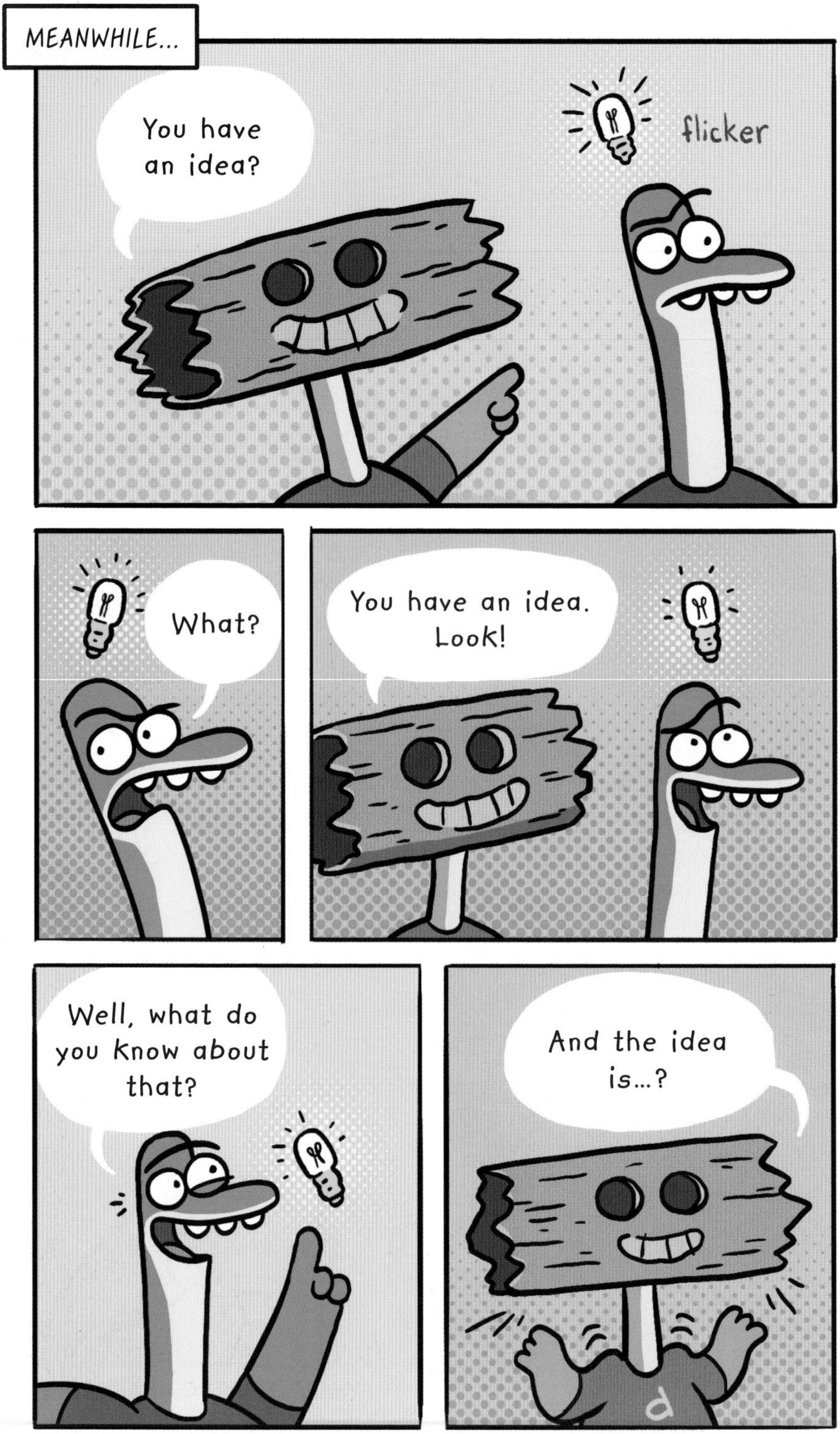
MEANWHILE...
You have an idea?
flicker
What?
You have an idea. Look!
Well, what do you know about that?
And the idea is...?

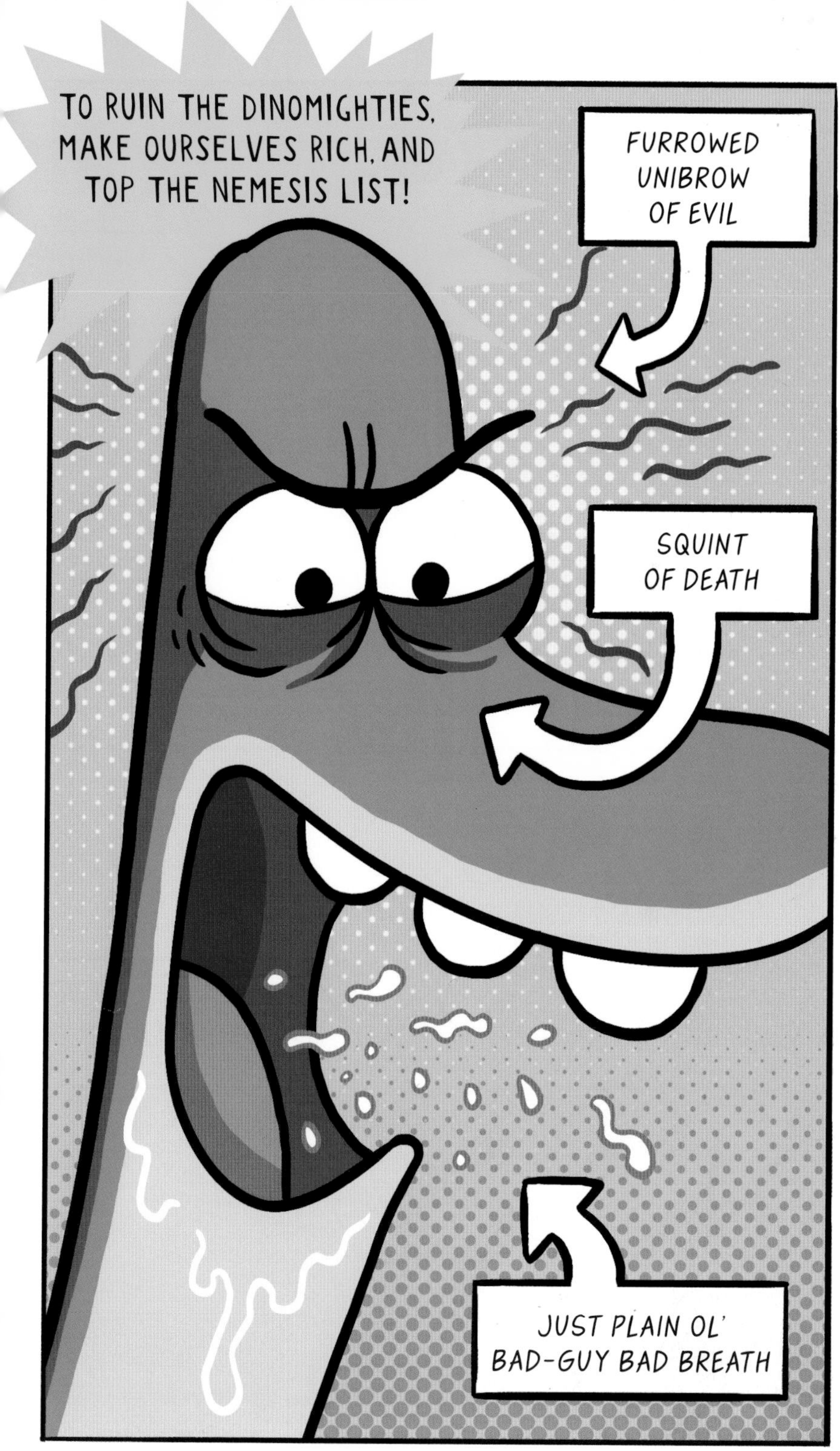
TO RUIN THE DINOMIGHTIES, MAKE OURSELVES RICH, AND TOP THE NEMESIS LIST!
FURROWED UNIBROW OF EVIL
SQUINT OF DEATH
JUST PLAIN OL' BAD-GUY BAD BREATH

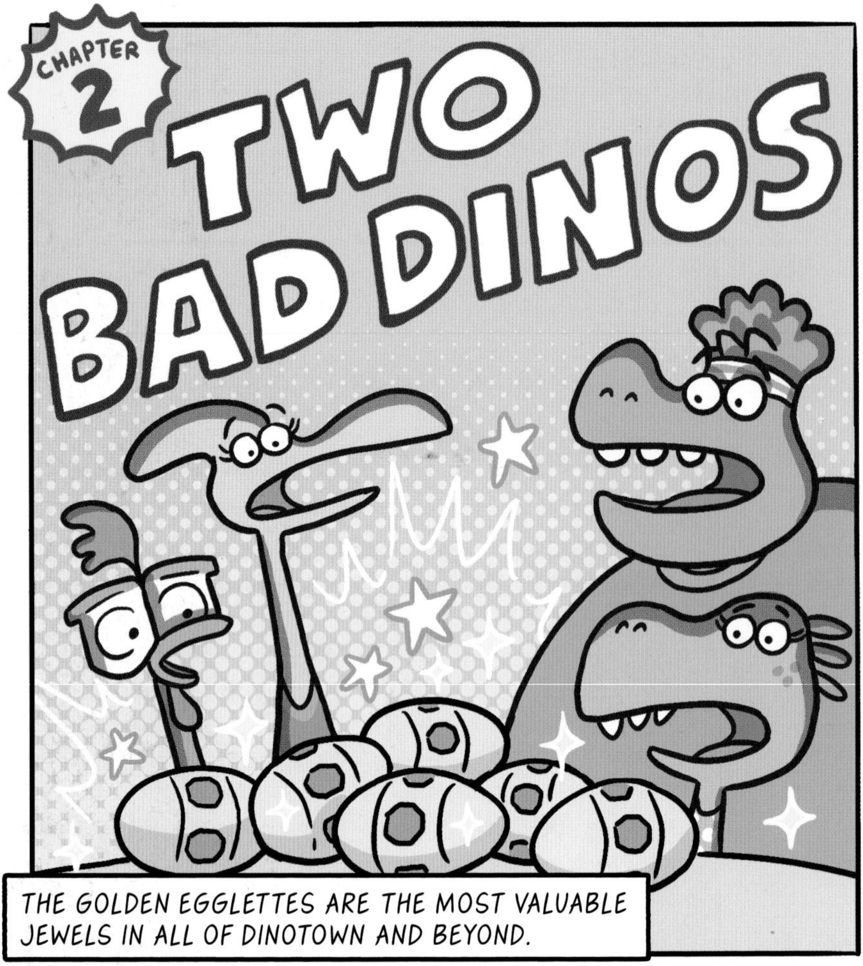
CHAPTER 2
TWO BAD DINOS
THE GOLDEN EGGLETTES ARE THE MOST VALUABLE JEWELS IN ALL OF DINOTOWN AND BEYOND.

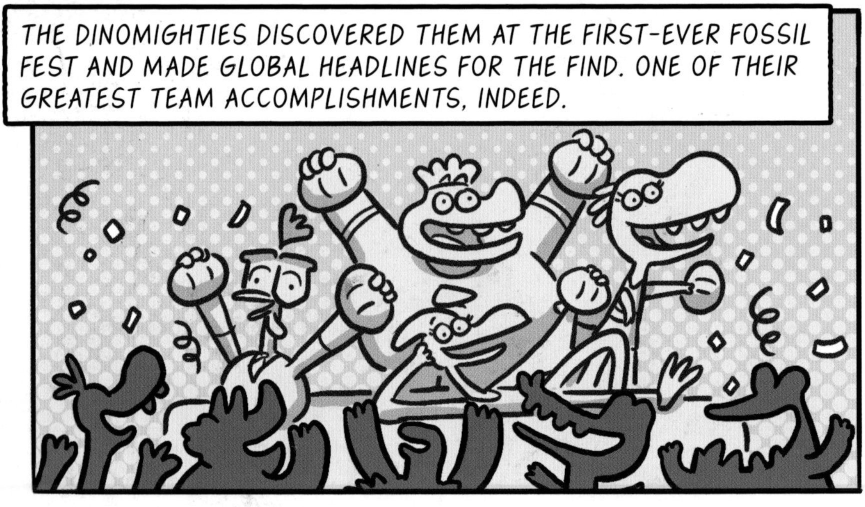
THE DINOMIGHTIES DISCOVERED THEM AT THE FIRST-EVER FOSSIL FEST AND MADE GLOBAL HEADLINES FOR THE FIND. ONE OF THEIR GREATEST TEAM ACCOMPLISHMENTS, INDEED.

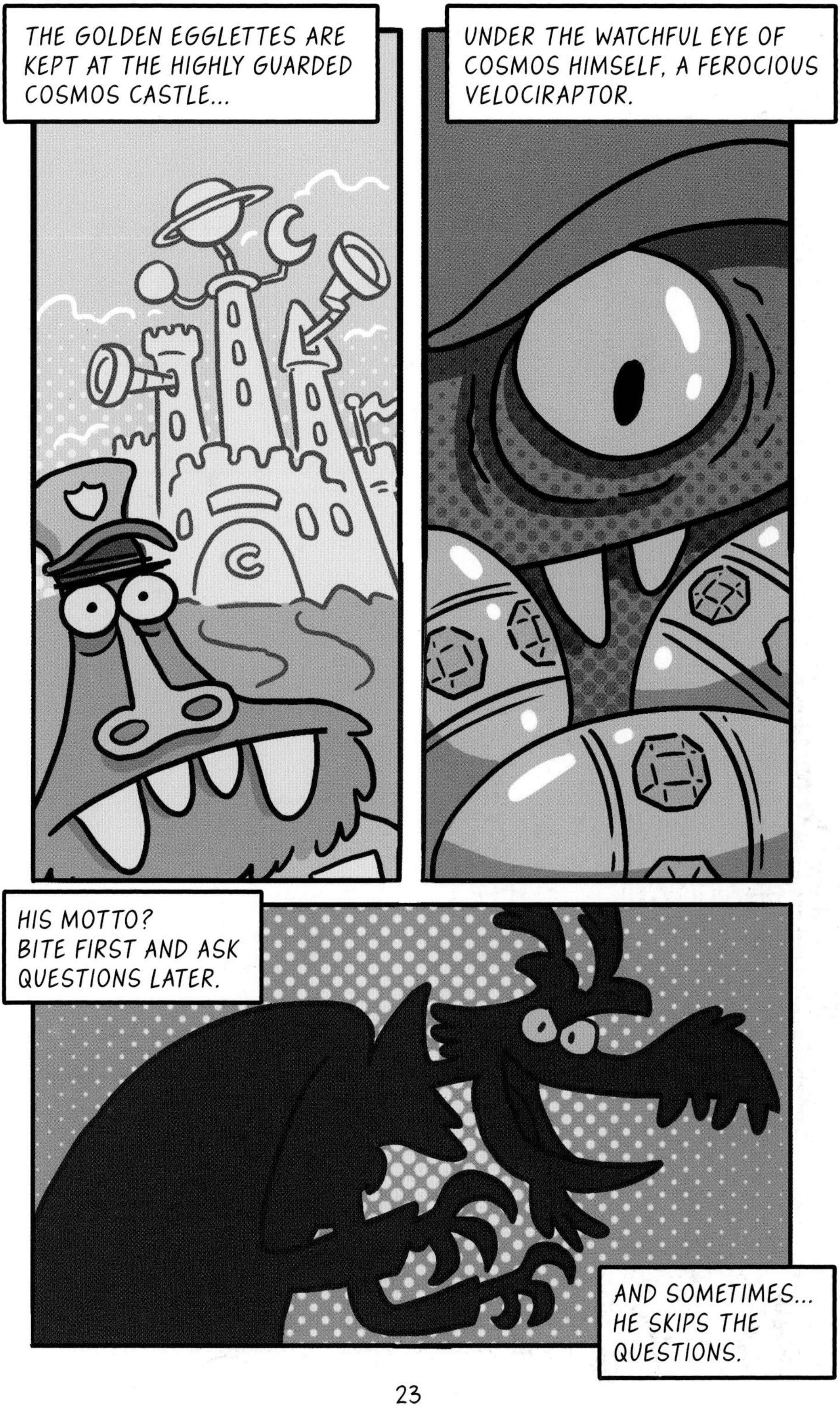
THE GOLDEN EGGLETTES ARE KEPT AT THE HIGHLY GUARDED COSMOS CASTLE...
UNDER THE WATCHFUL EYE OF COSMOS HIMSELF, A FEROCIOUS VELOCIRAPTOR.
HIS MOTTO? BITE FIRST AND ASK QUESTIONS LATER.
AND SOMETIMES... HE SKIPS THE QUESTIONS.

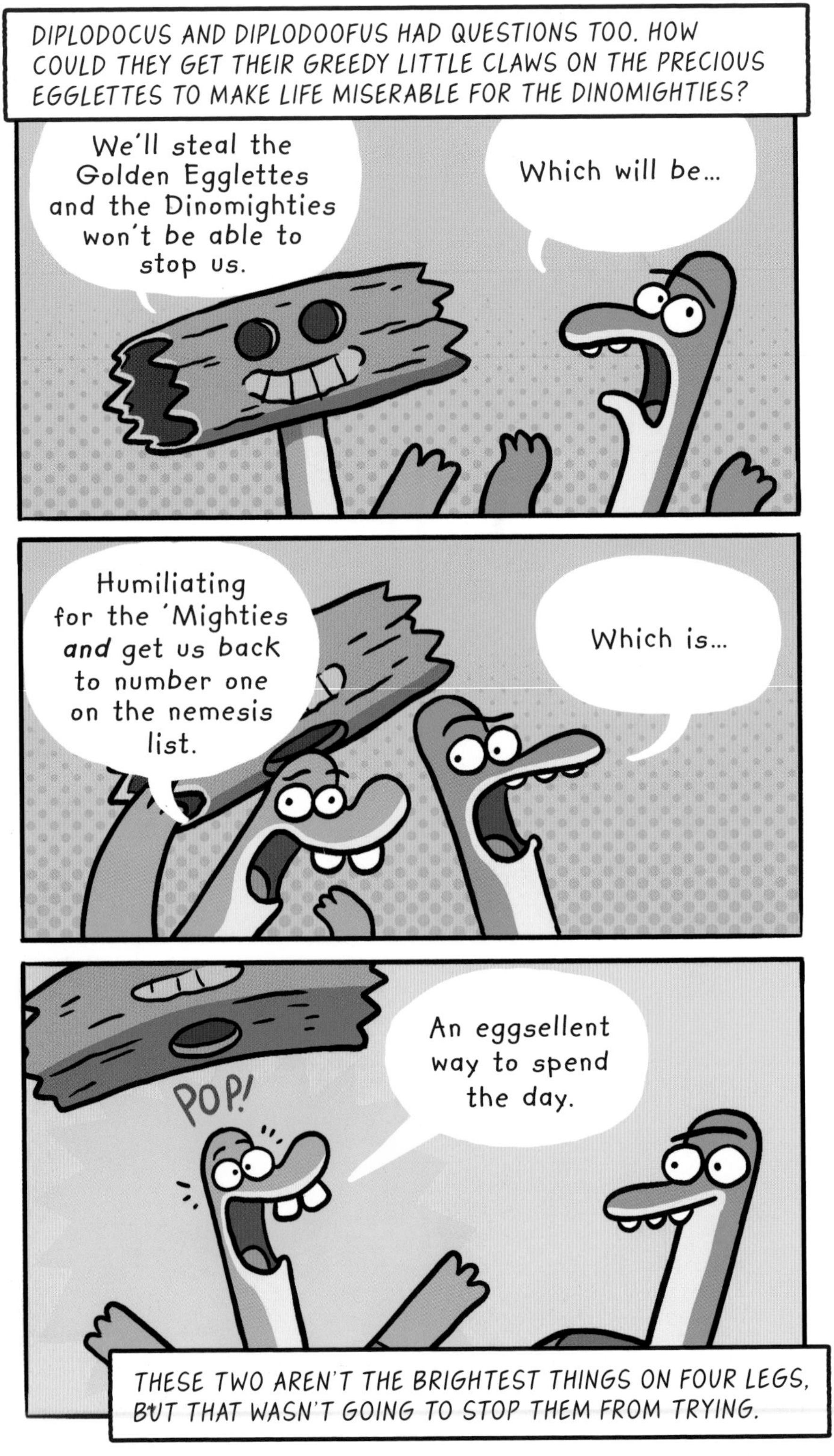
DIPLODOCUS AND DIPLODOOFUS HAD QUESTIONS TOO. HOW COULD THEY GET THEIR GREEDY LITTLE CLAWS ON THE PRECIOUS EGGLETTES TO MAKE LIFE MISERABLE FOR THE DINOMIGHTIES?
We'll steal the Golden Egglettes and the Dinomighties won't be able to stop us.
Which will be...
Humiliating for the 'Mighties *and* get us back to number one on the nemesis list.
Which is...
An eggsellent way to spend the day.
POP!
THESE TWO AREN'T THE BRIGHTEST THINGS ON FOUR LEGS, BUT THAT WASN'T GOING TO STOP THEM FROM TRYING.

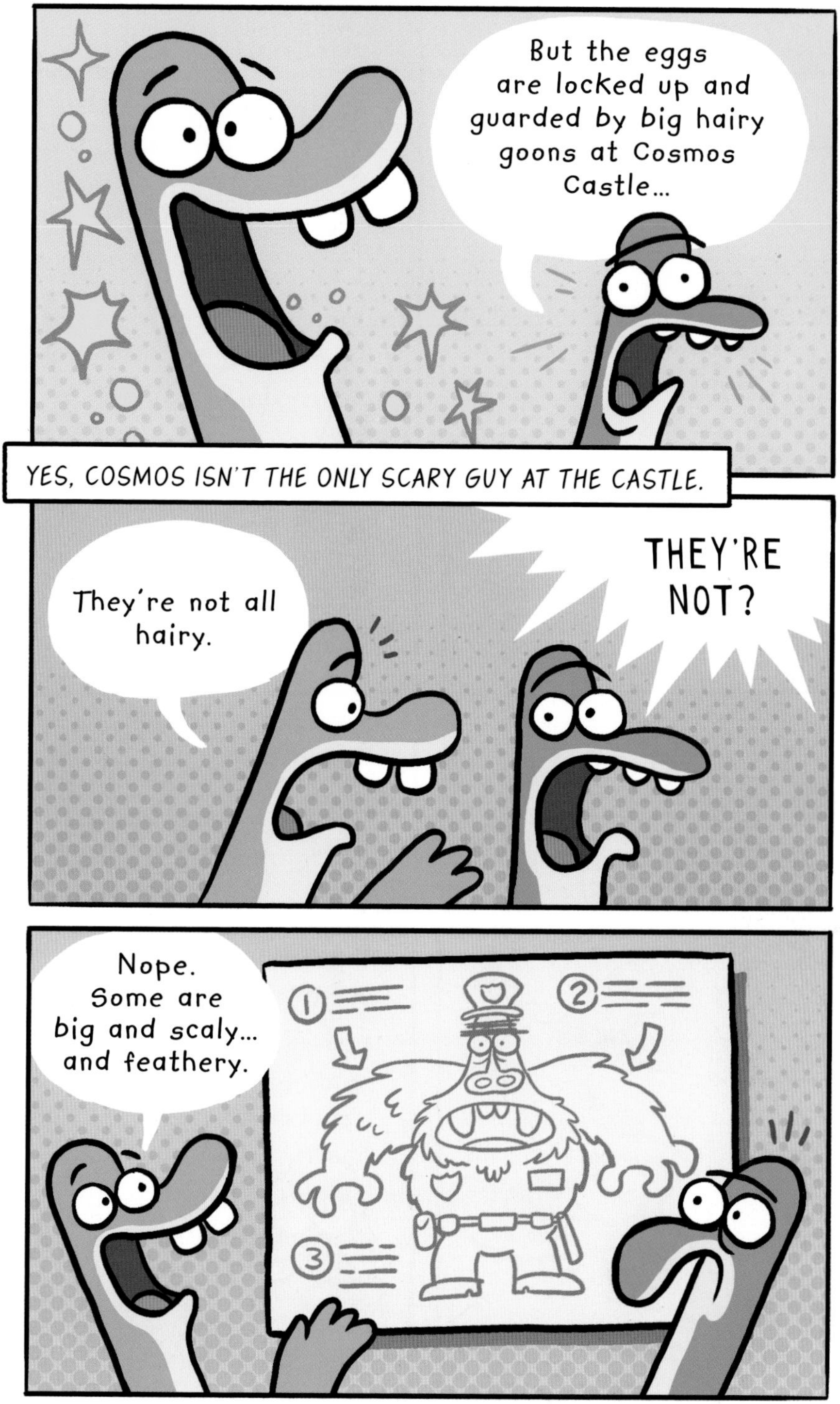
But the eggs are locked up and guarded by big hairy goons at Cosmos Castle...
YES, COSMOS ISN'T THE ONLY SCARY GUY AT THE CASTLE.
They're not all hairy.
THEY'RE NOT?
Nope. Some are big and scaly... and feathery.
1
2
3

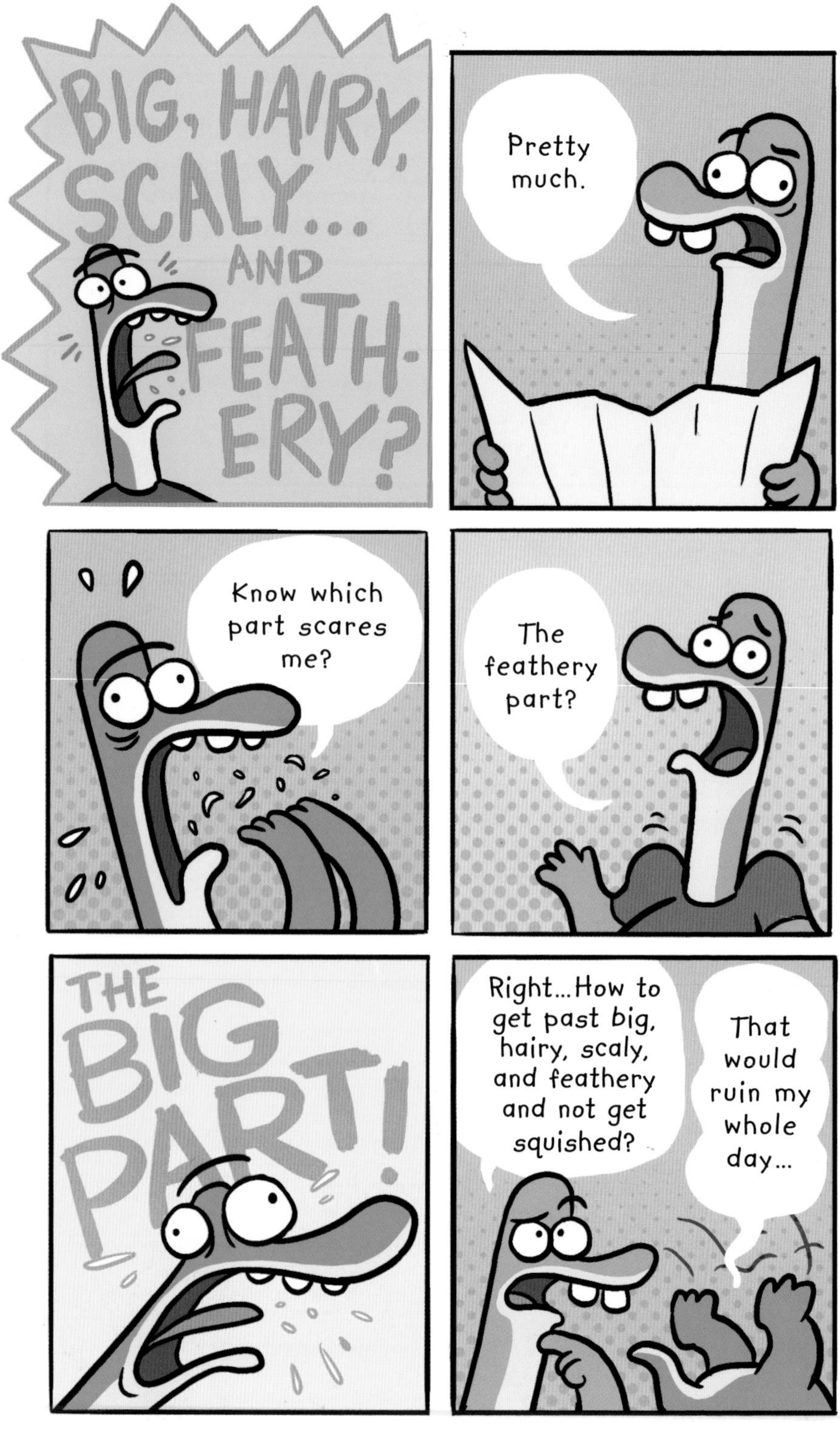
BIG, HAIRY, SCALY... AND FEATH-ERY?
Pretty much.
Know which part scares me?
The feathery part?
THE BIG PART!
Right... How to get past big, hairy, scaly, and feathery and not get squished?
That would ruin my whole day...

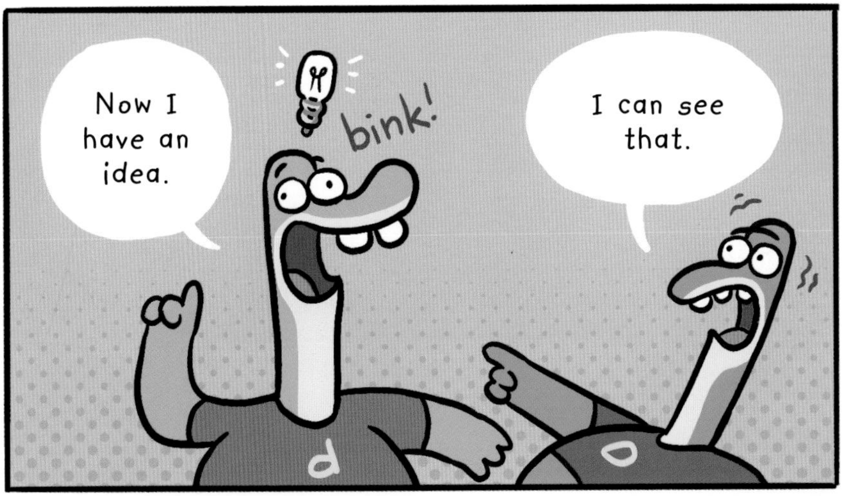
Now I have an idea.
bink!
I can see that.

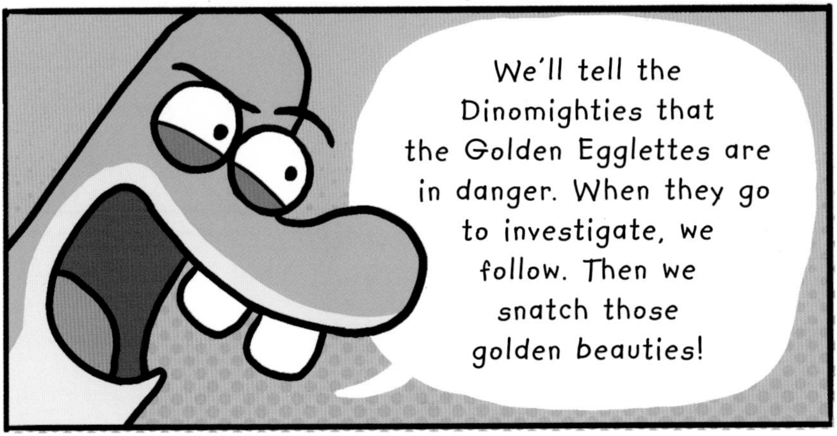
We'll tell the Dinomighties that the Golden Egglettes are in danger. When they go to investigate, we follow. Then we snatch those golden beauties!

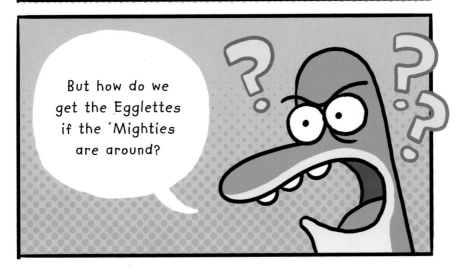

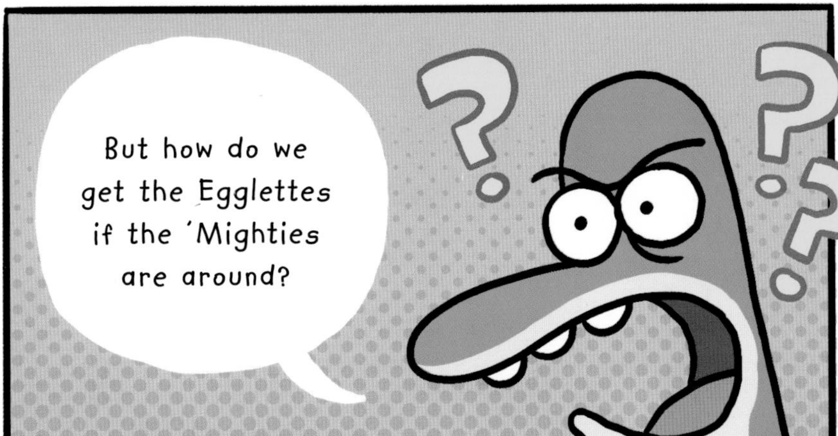
But how do we get the Egglettes if the 'Mighties are around?

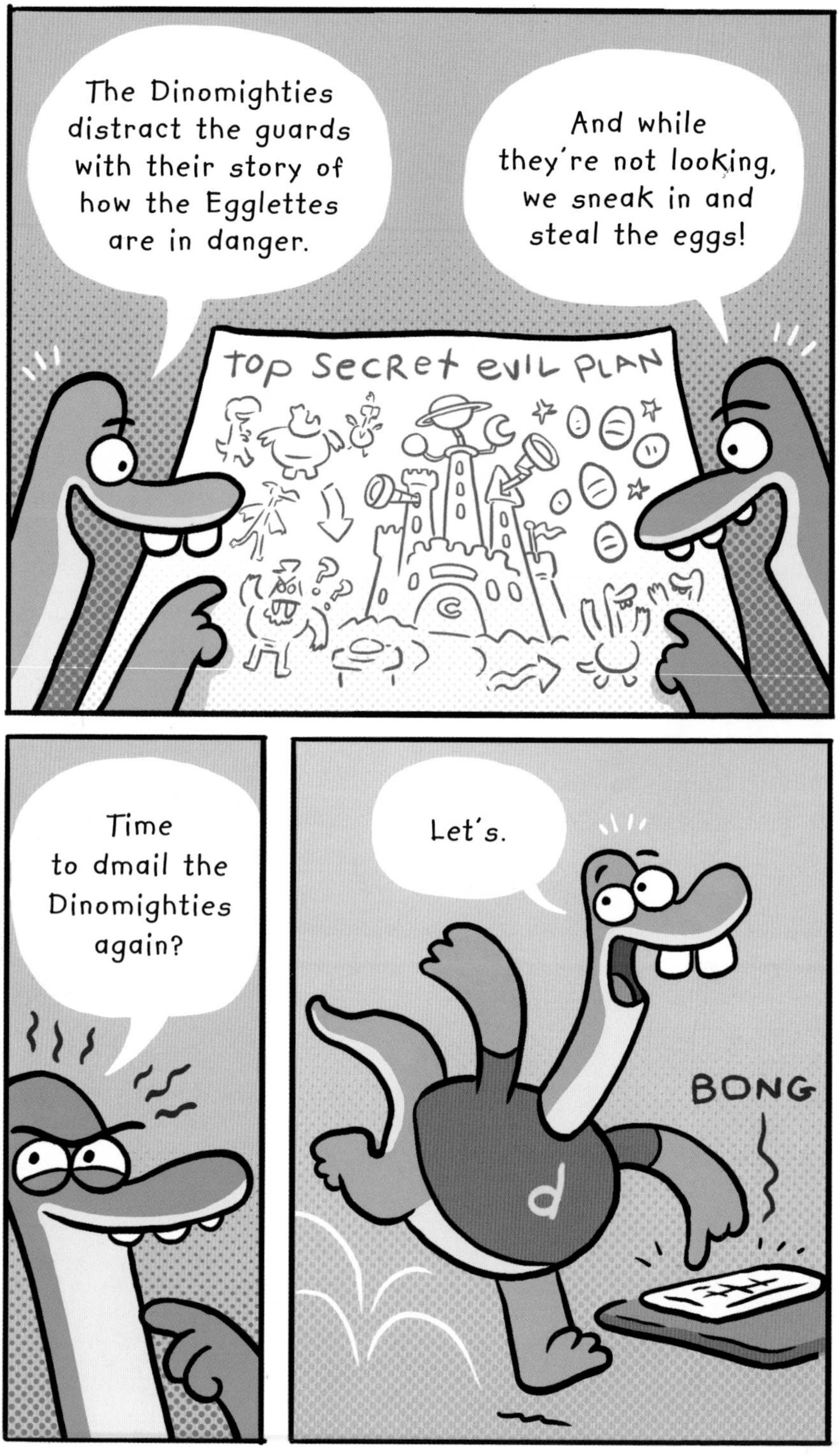
The Dinomighties distract the guards with their story of how the Egglettes are in danger.
And while they're not looking, we sneak in and steal the eggs!
TOP SECRET EVIL PLAN
Time to dmail the Dinomighties again?
Let's.
BONG

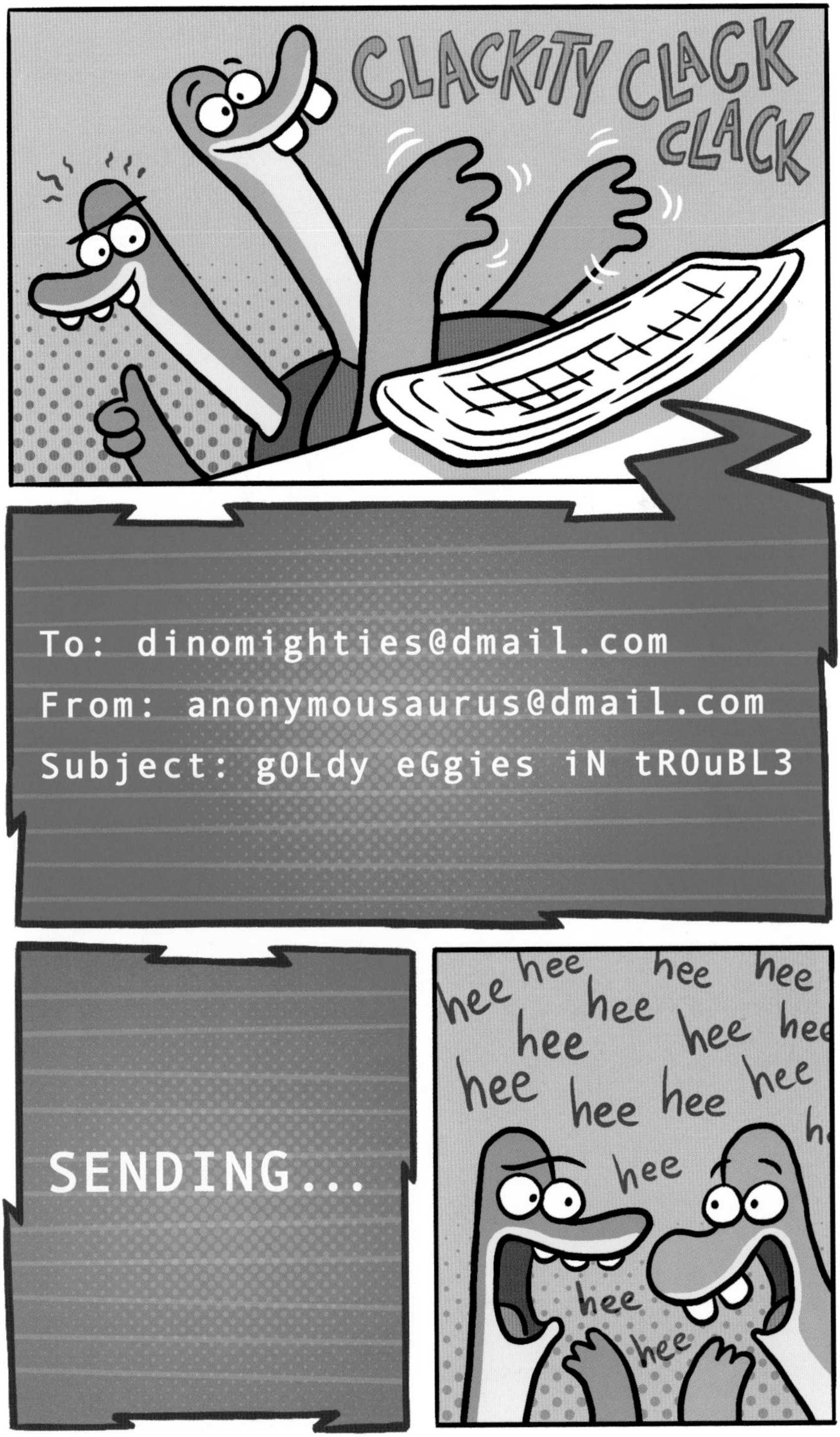

CLACKITY CLACK CLACK
To: dinomighties@dmail.com
From: anonymousaurus@dmail.com
Subject: gOLdy eGgies iN tROuBL3
SENDING...
hee hee hee hee
hee hee
hee hee
hee hee hee hee
hee
hee
hee

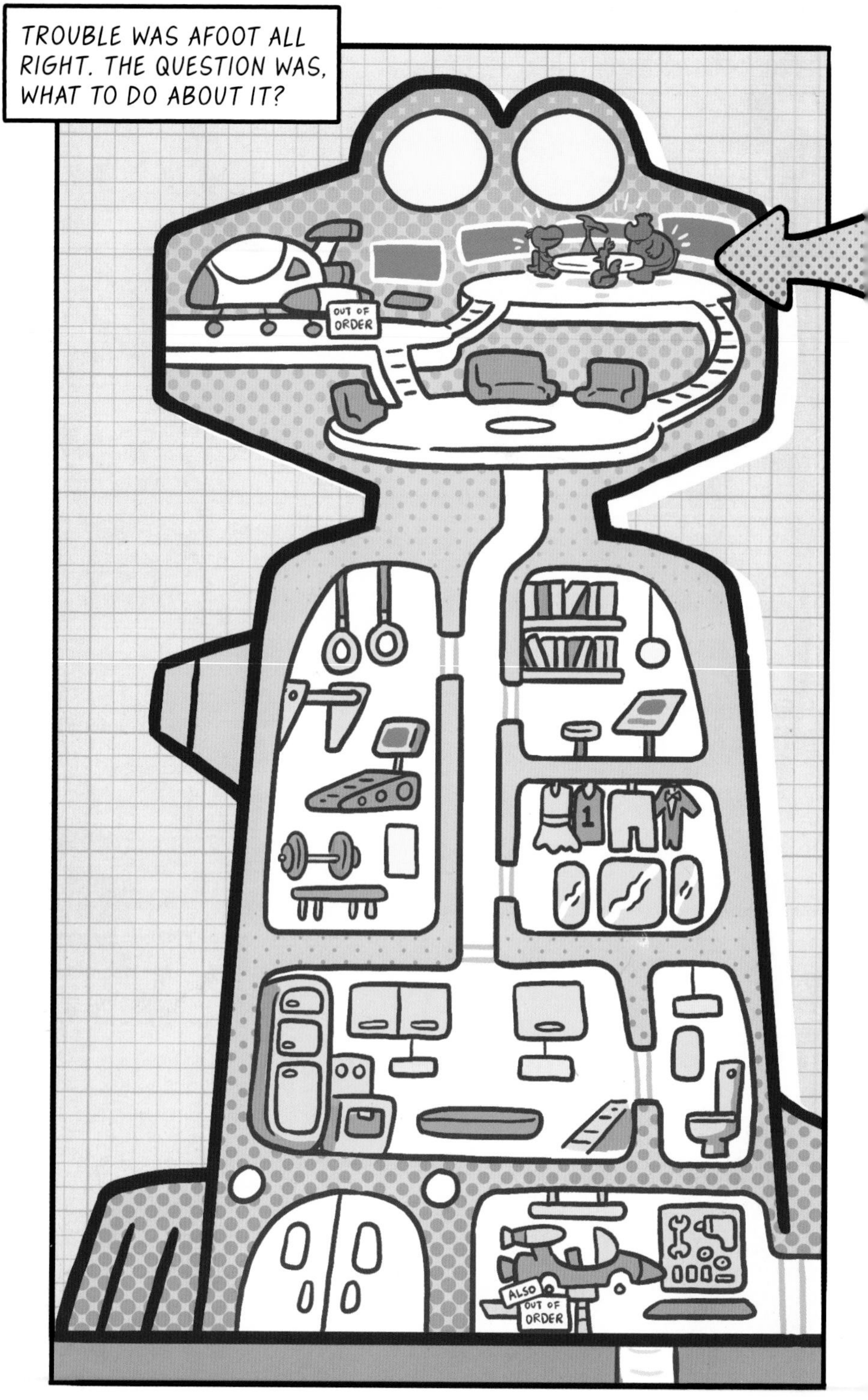
TROUBLE WAS AFOOT ALL RIGHT. THE QUESTION WAS, WHAT TO DO ABOUT IT?
OUT OF ORDER
1
ALSO
OUT OF ORDER

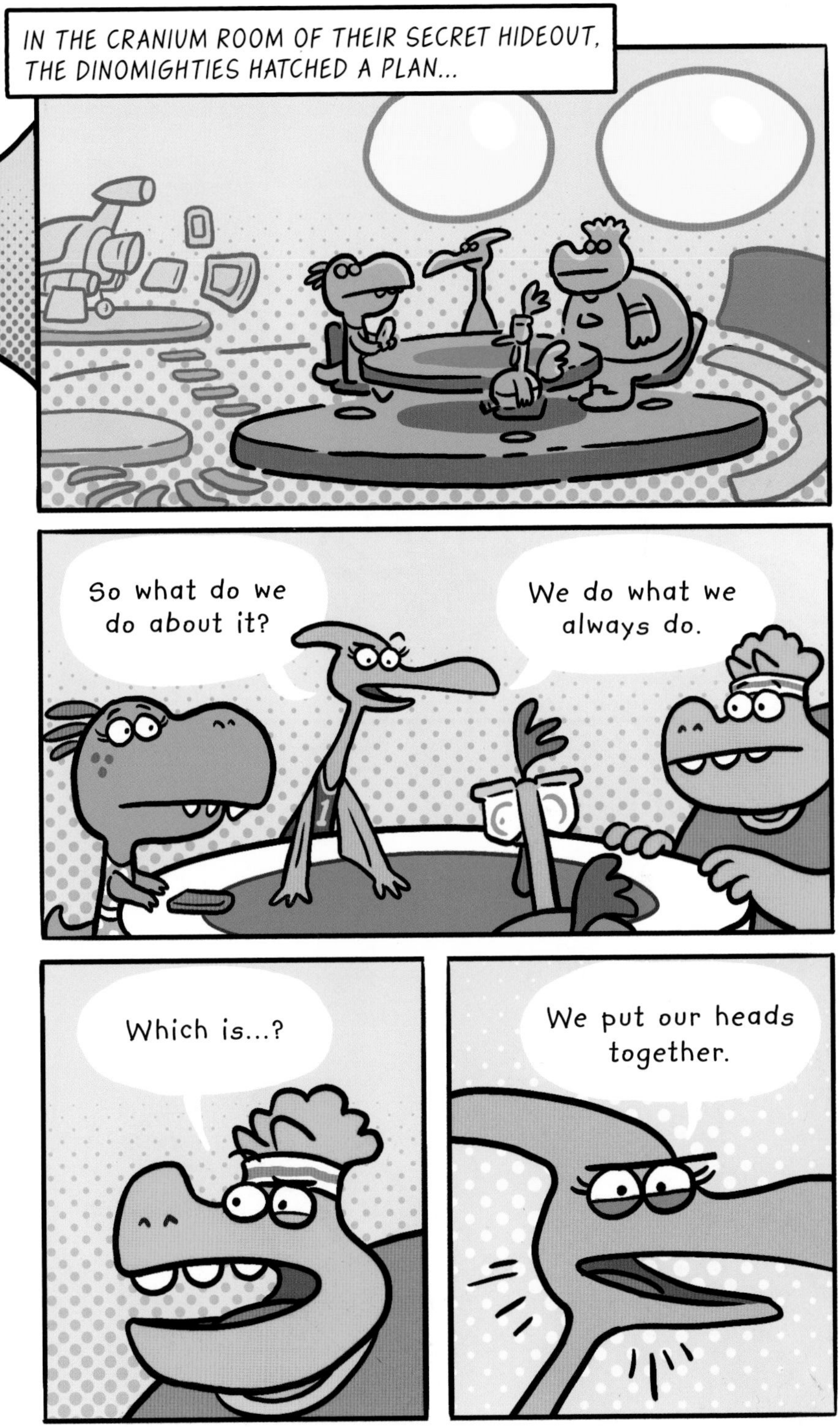
IN THE CRANIUM ROOM OF THEIR SECRET HIDEOUT, THE DINOMIGHTIES HATCHED A PLAN...
So what do we do about it?
We do what we always do.
Which is...?
We put our heads together.

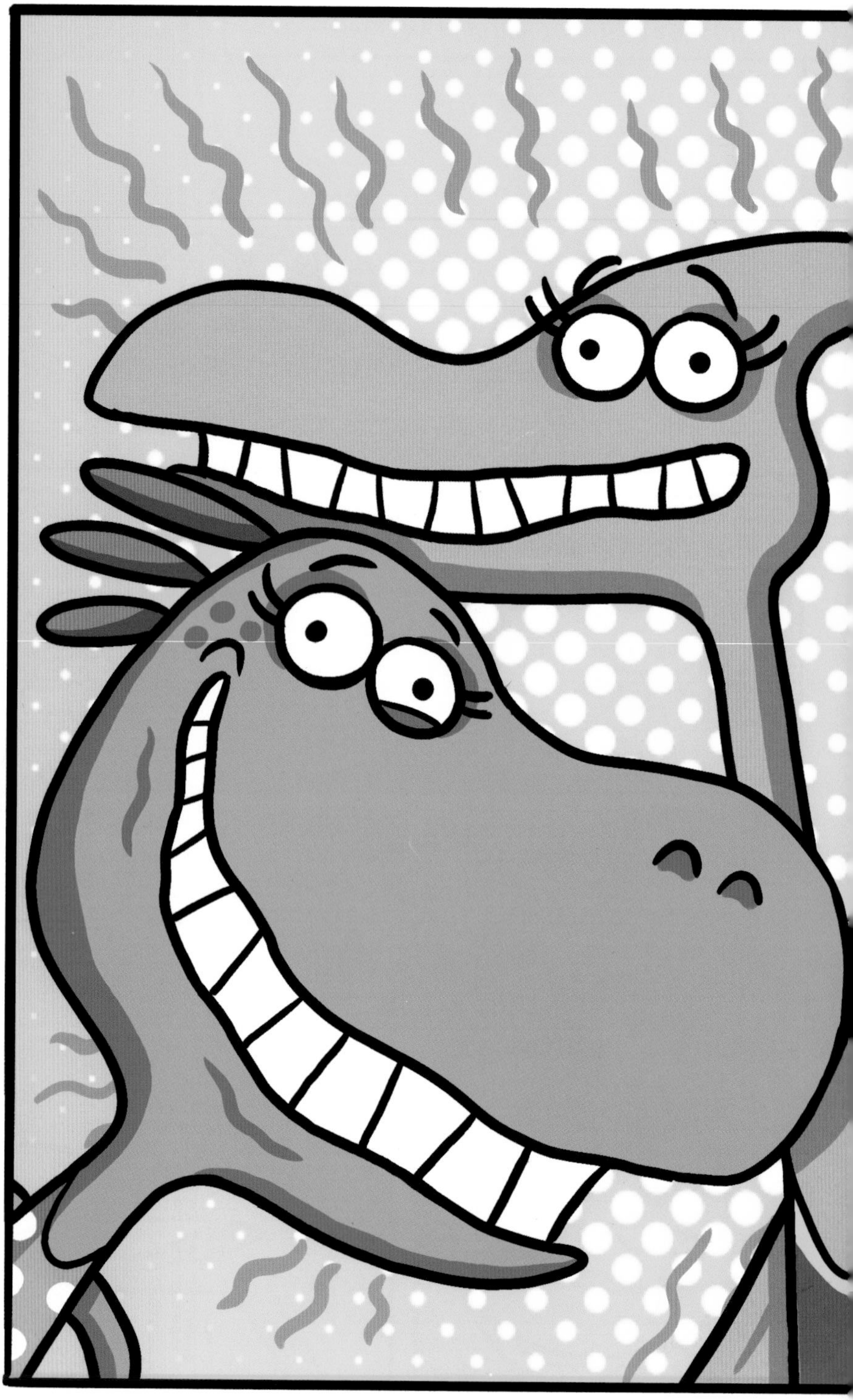

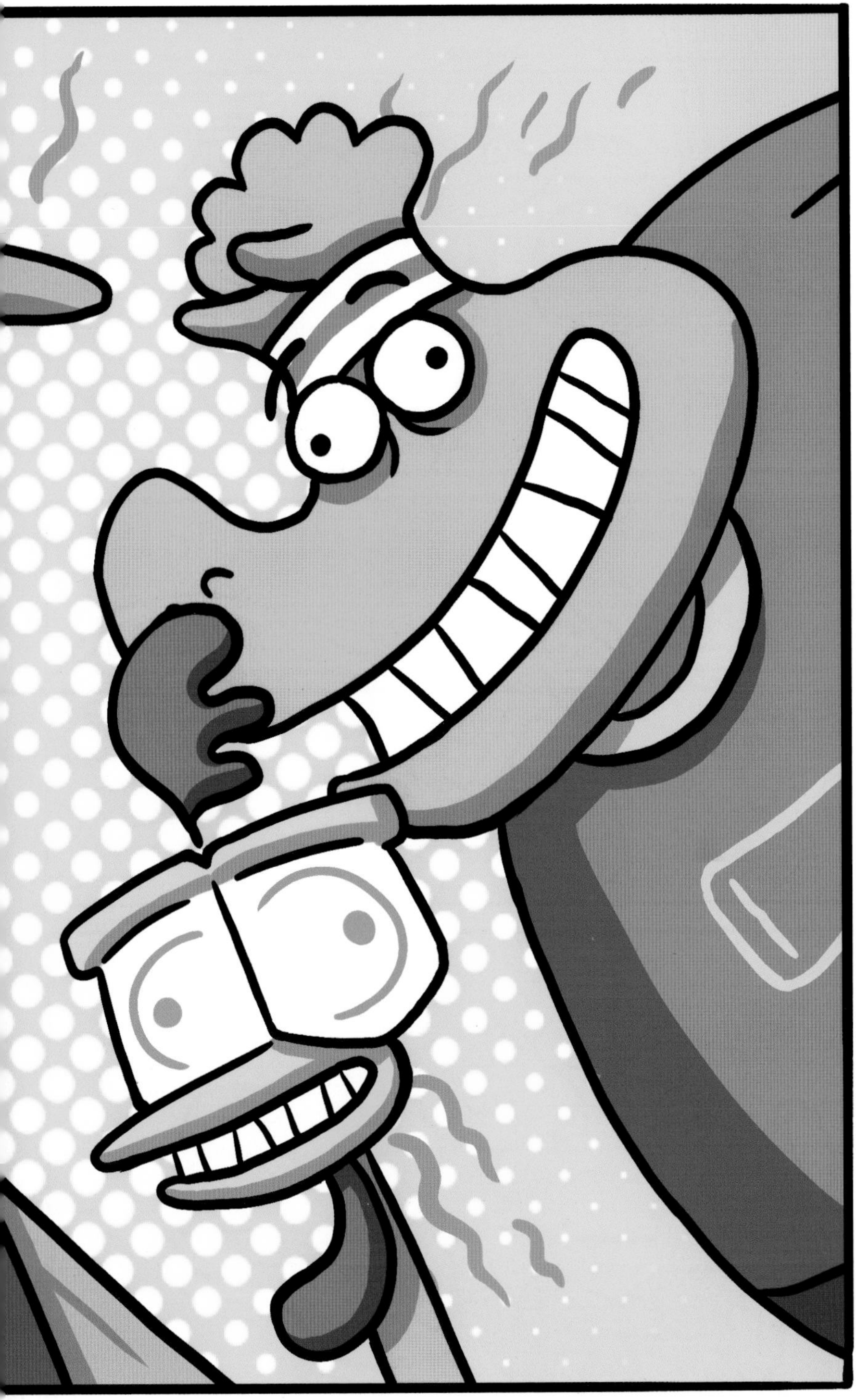

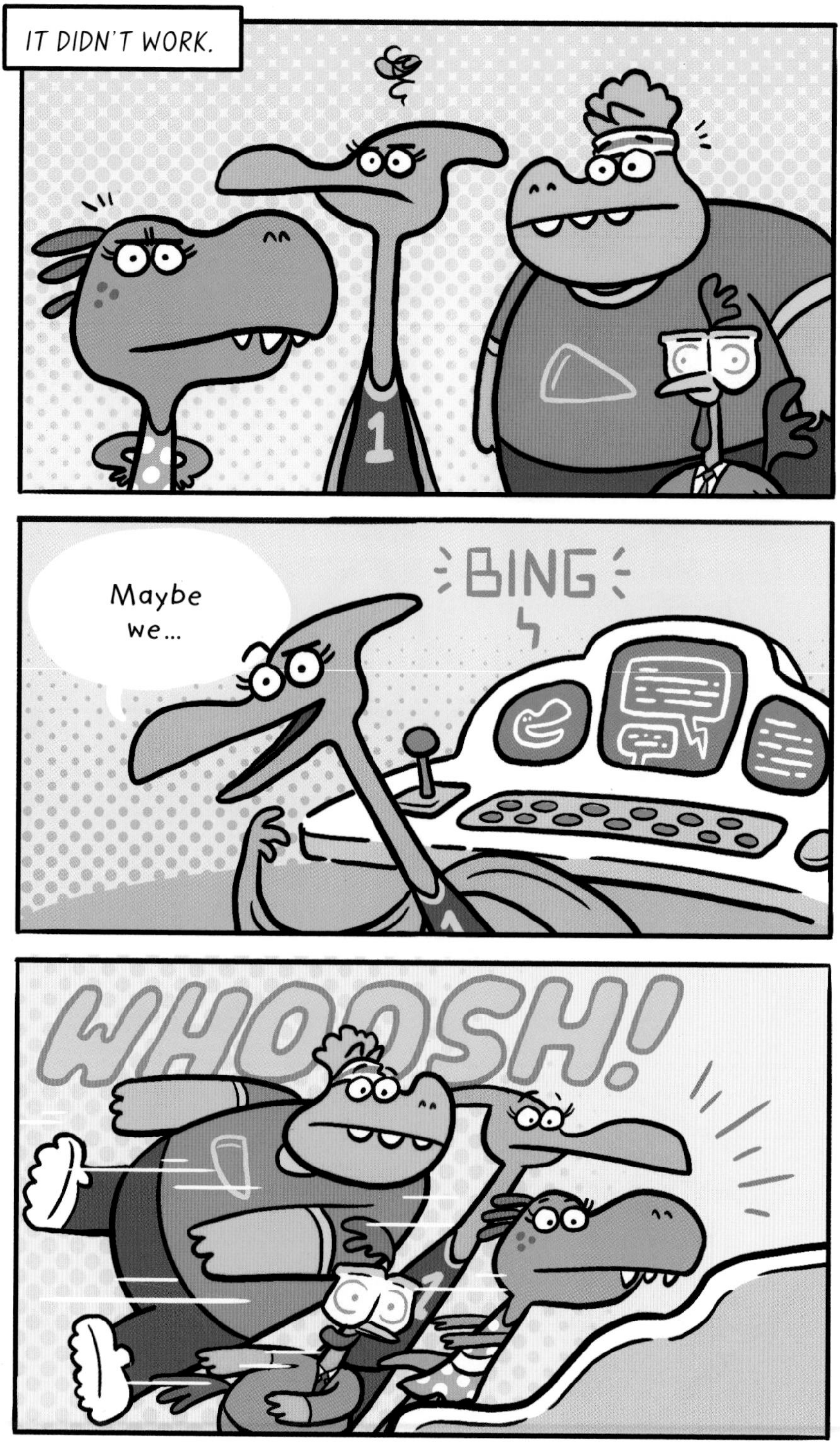
IT DIDN'T WORK.
1
Maybe we...
BING
1
WHOOSH!
1

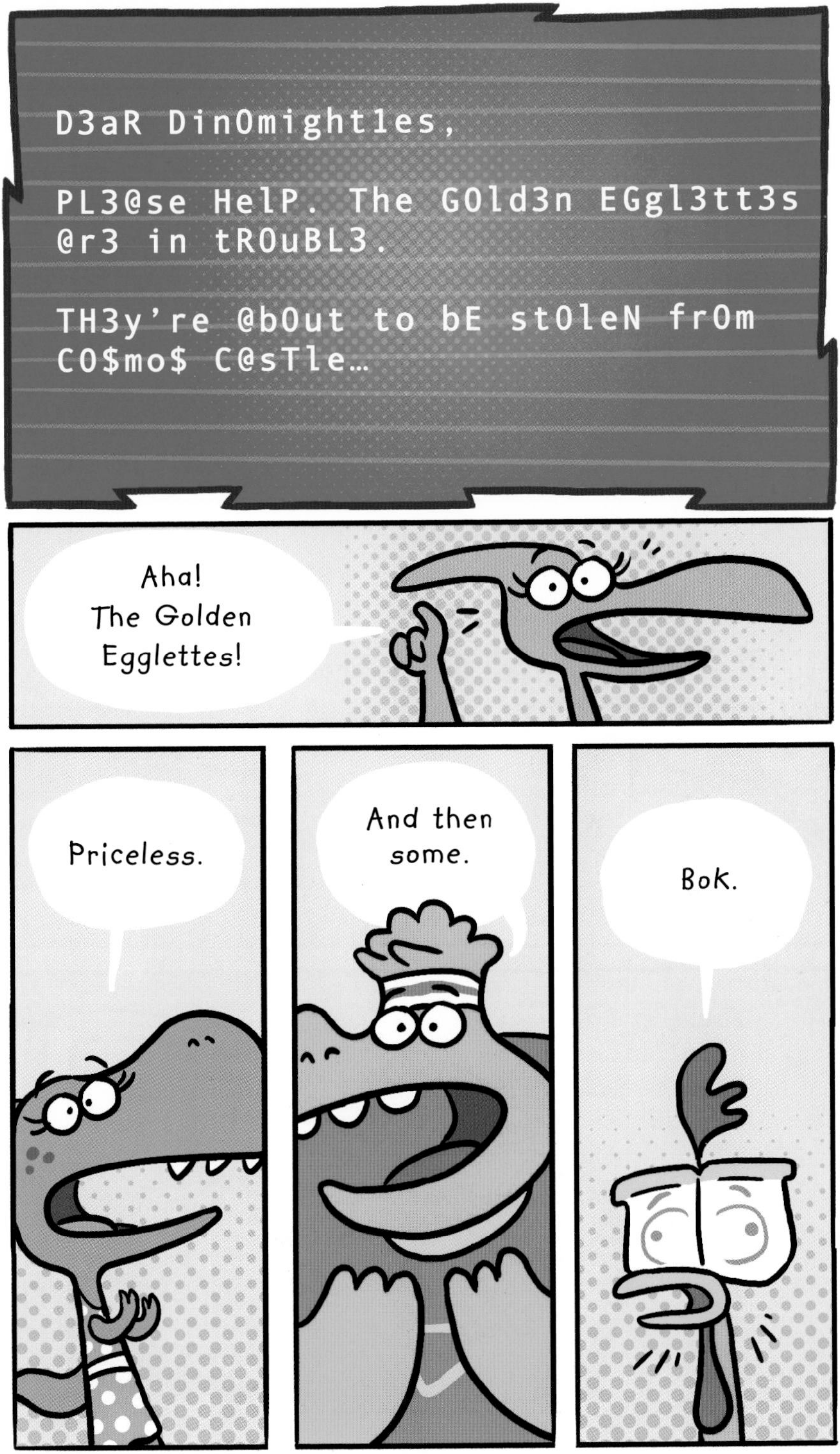
D3aR DinOmightles,
PL3@se HelP. The GOld3n EGgl3tt3s @r3 in tROuBL3.
TH3y're @bOut to bE stOleN frOm COmo C@sTle…
Aha! The Golden Egglettes!
Priceless.
And then some.
Bok.

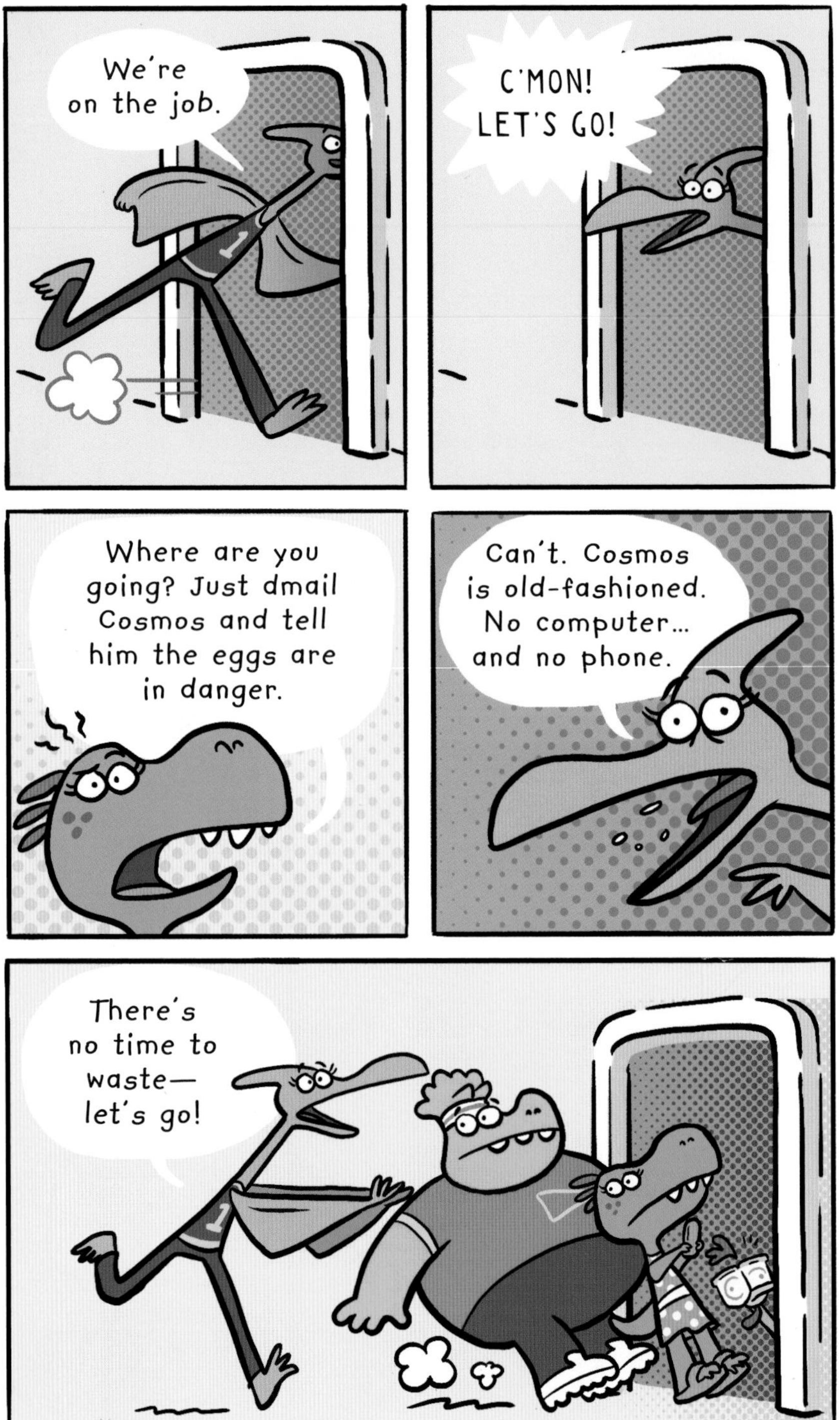
We're on the job.
C'MON! LET'S GO!
Where are you going? Just dmail Cosmos and tell him the eggs are in danger.
Can't. Cosmos is old-fashioned. No computer... and no phone.
There's no time to waste— let's go!

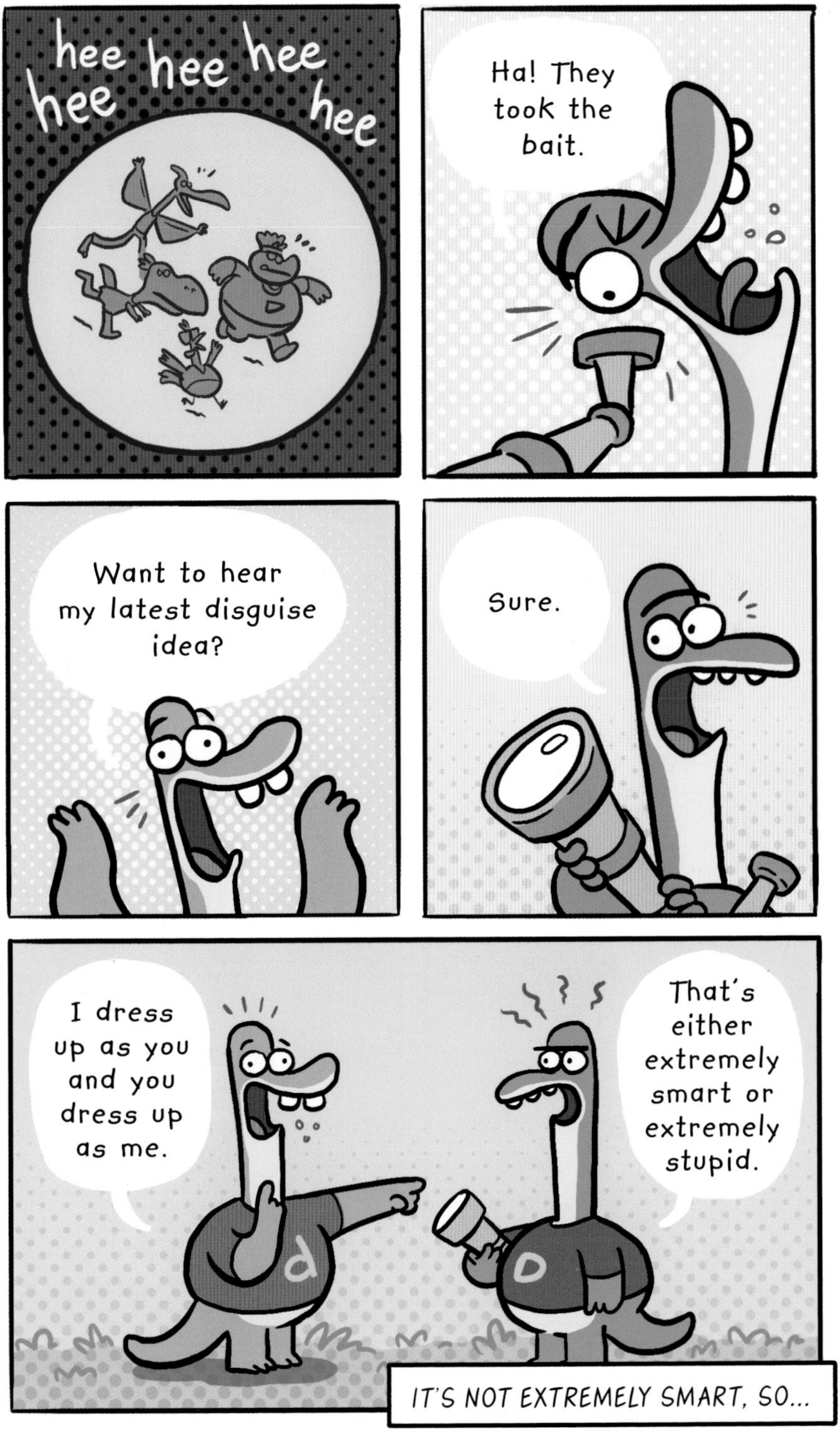
hee hee hee hee hee
Ha! They took the bait.
Want to hear my latest disguise idea?
Sure.
I dress up as you and you dress up as me.
That's either extremely smart or extremely stupid.
IT'S NOT EXTREMELY SMART, SO...

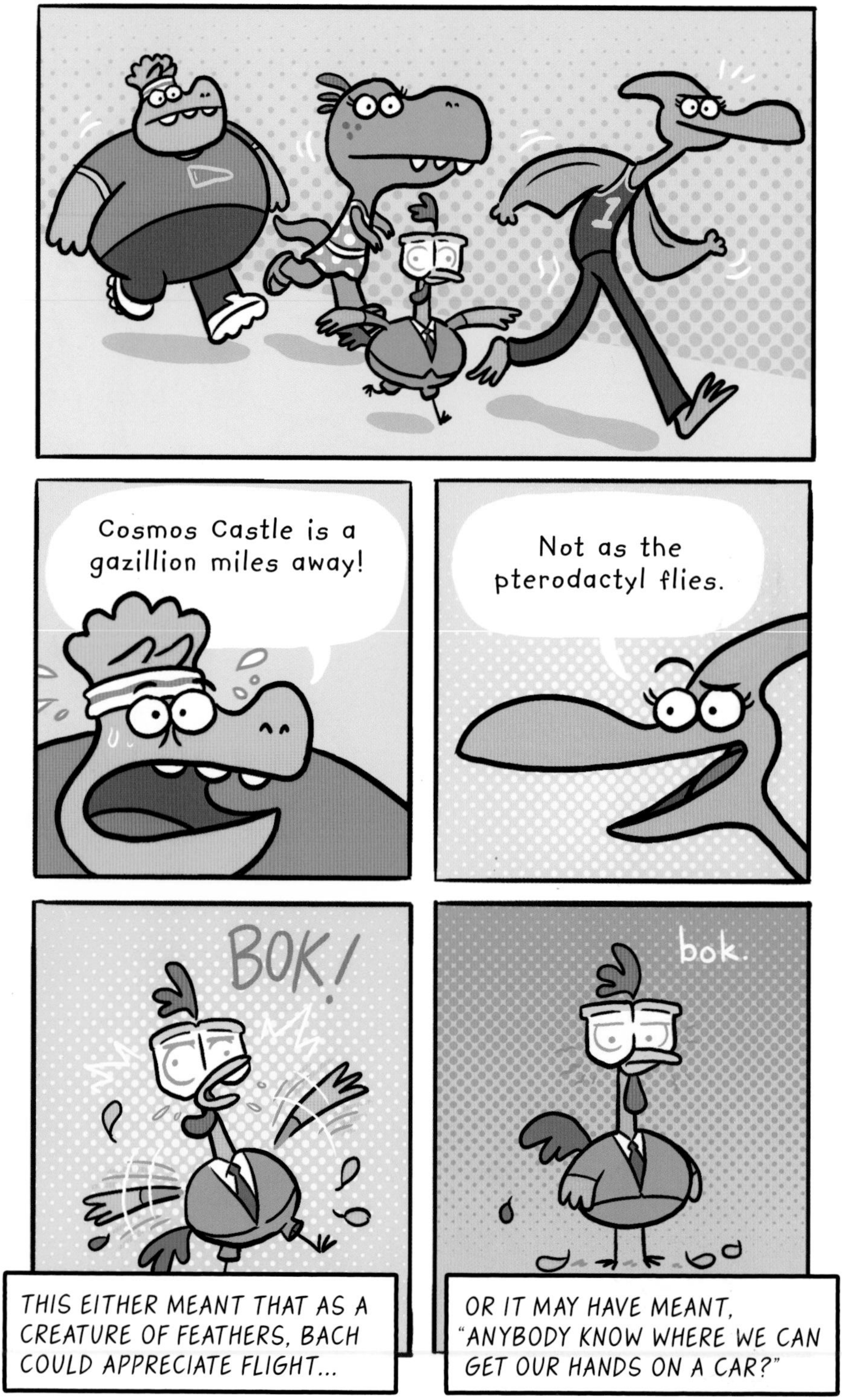
Cosmos Castle is a gazillion miles away!
Not as the pterodactyl flies.
BOK!
bok.
THIS EITHER MEANT THAT AS A CREATURE OF FEATHERS, BACH COULD APPRECIATE FLIGHT...
OR IT MAY HAVE MEANT, "ANYBODY KNOW WHERE WE CAN GET OUR HANDS ON A CAR?"

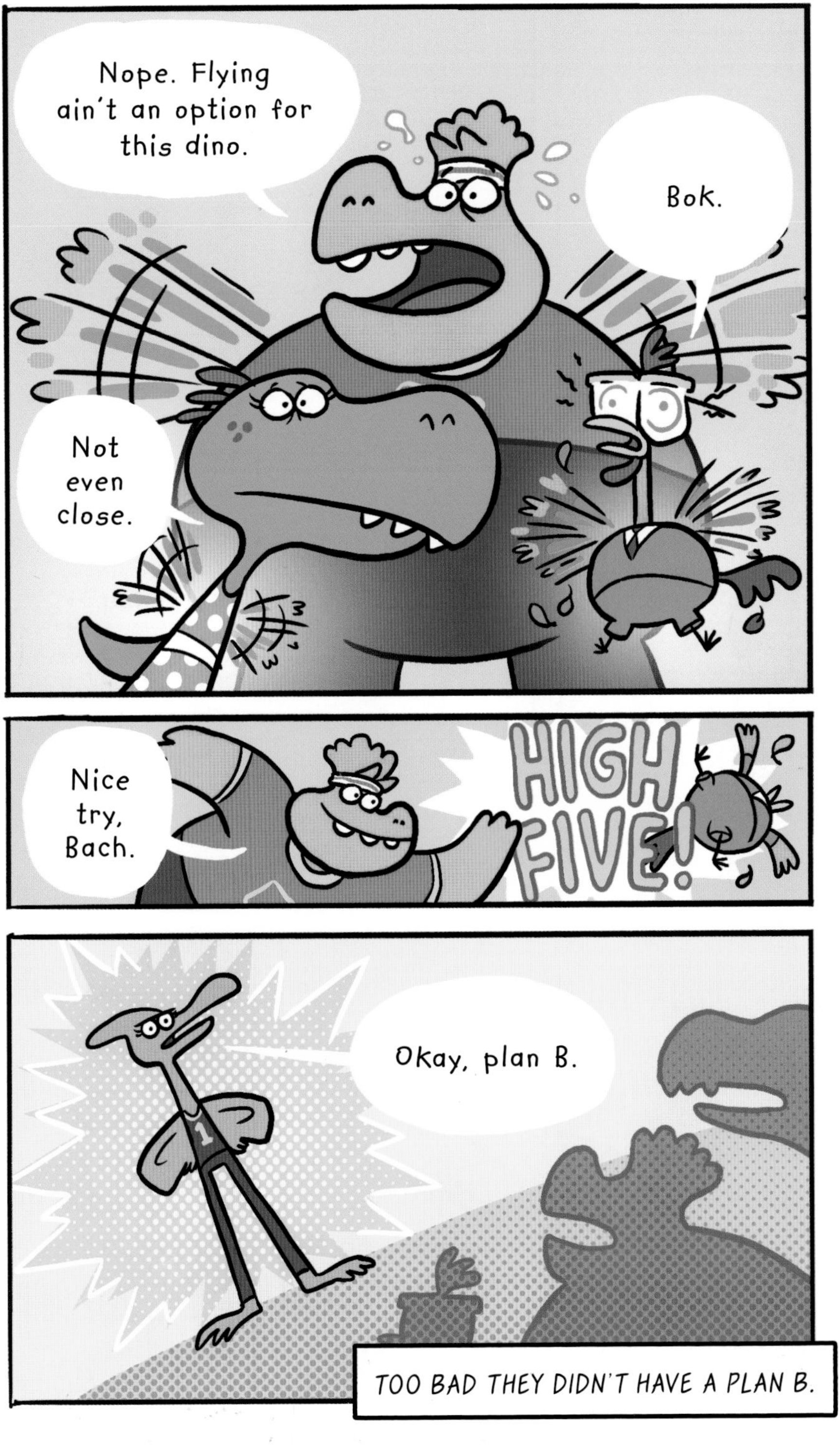
Nope. Flying ain't an option for this dino.
Bok.
Not even close.
Nice try, Bach.
HIGH FIVE!
Okay, plan B.
TOO BAD THEY DIDN'T HAVE A PLAN B.

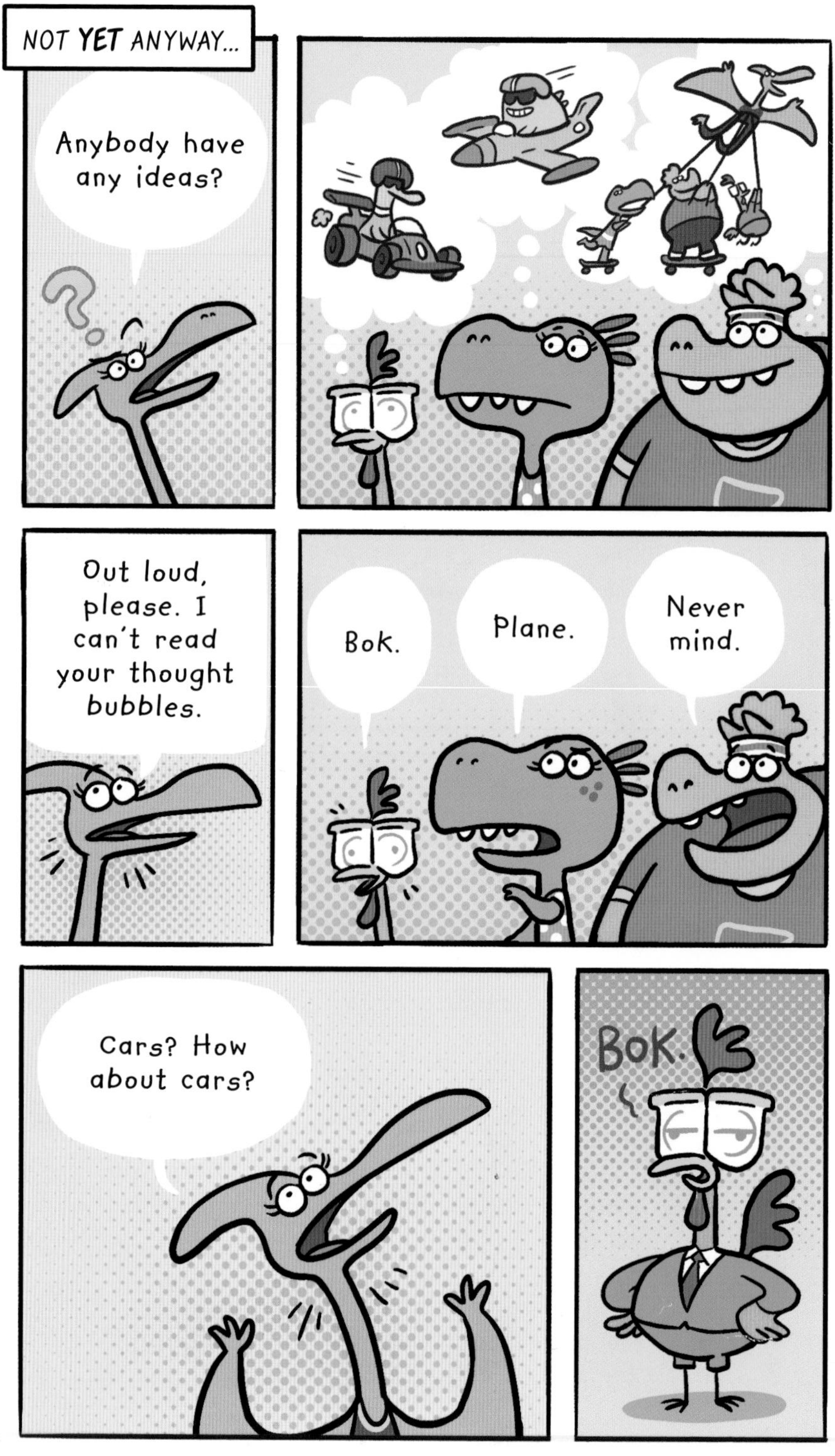
NOT **YET** ANYWAY...
Anybody have any ideas?
Out loud, please. I can't read your thought *bubbles*.
Bok.
Plane.
Never mind.
Cars? How about cars?
BOK.

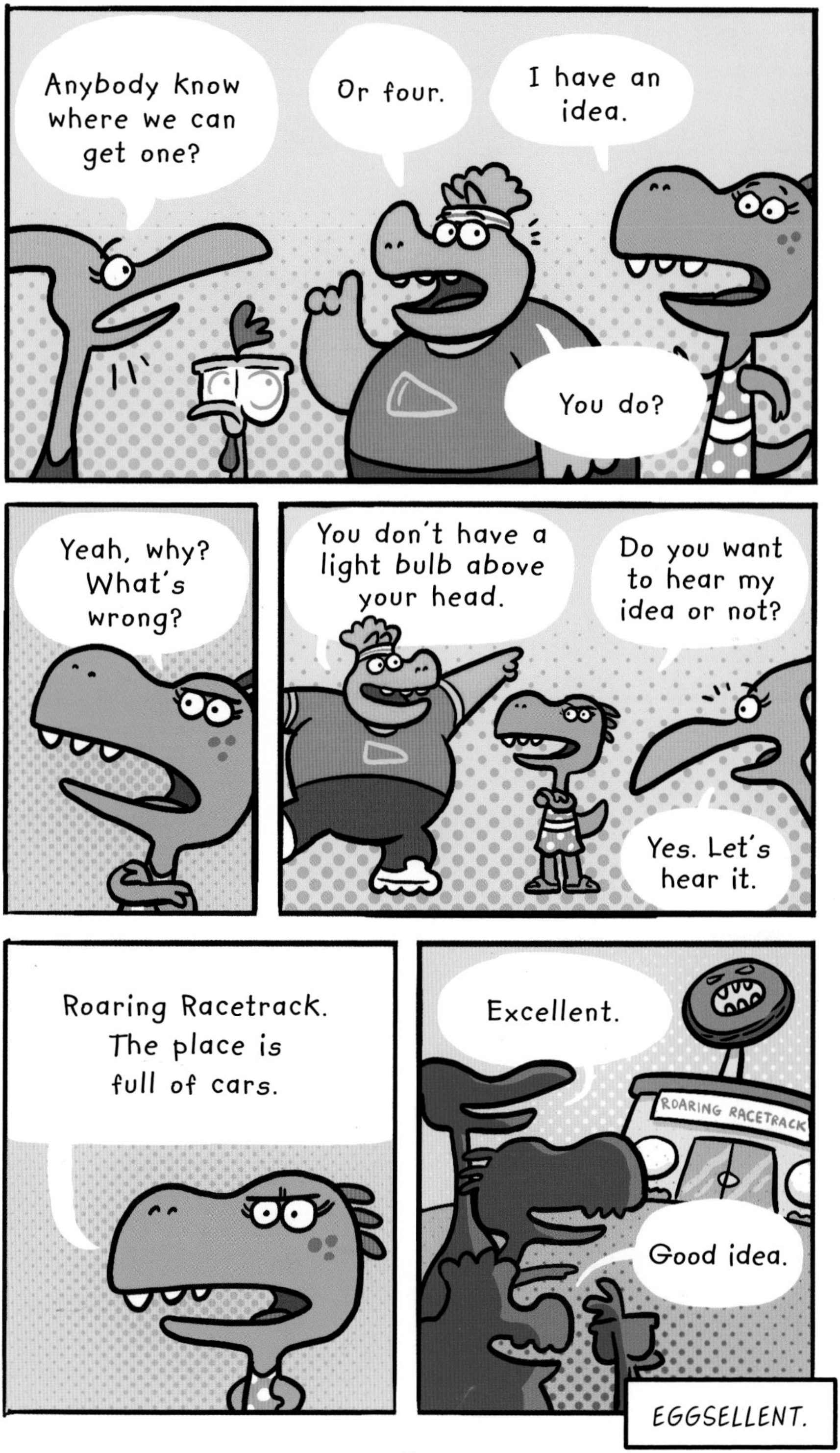
Anybody know where we can get one?
Or four.
I have an idea.
You do?
Yeah, why? What's wrong?
You don't have a light *bulb* above your head.
Do you want to hear my idea or not?
Yes. Let's hear it.
Roaring Racetrack. The place is full of cars.
Excellent.
ROARING RACETRACK
Good idea.
EGGSELLENT.

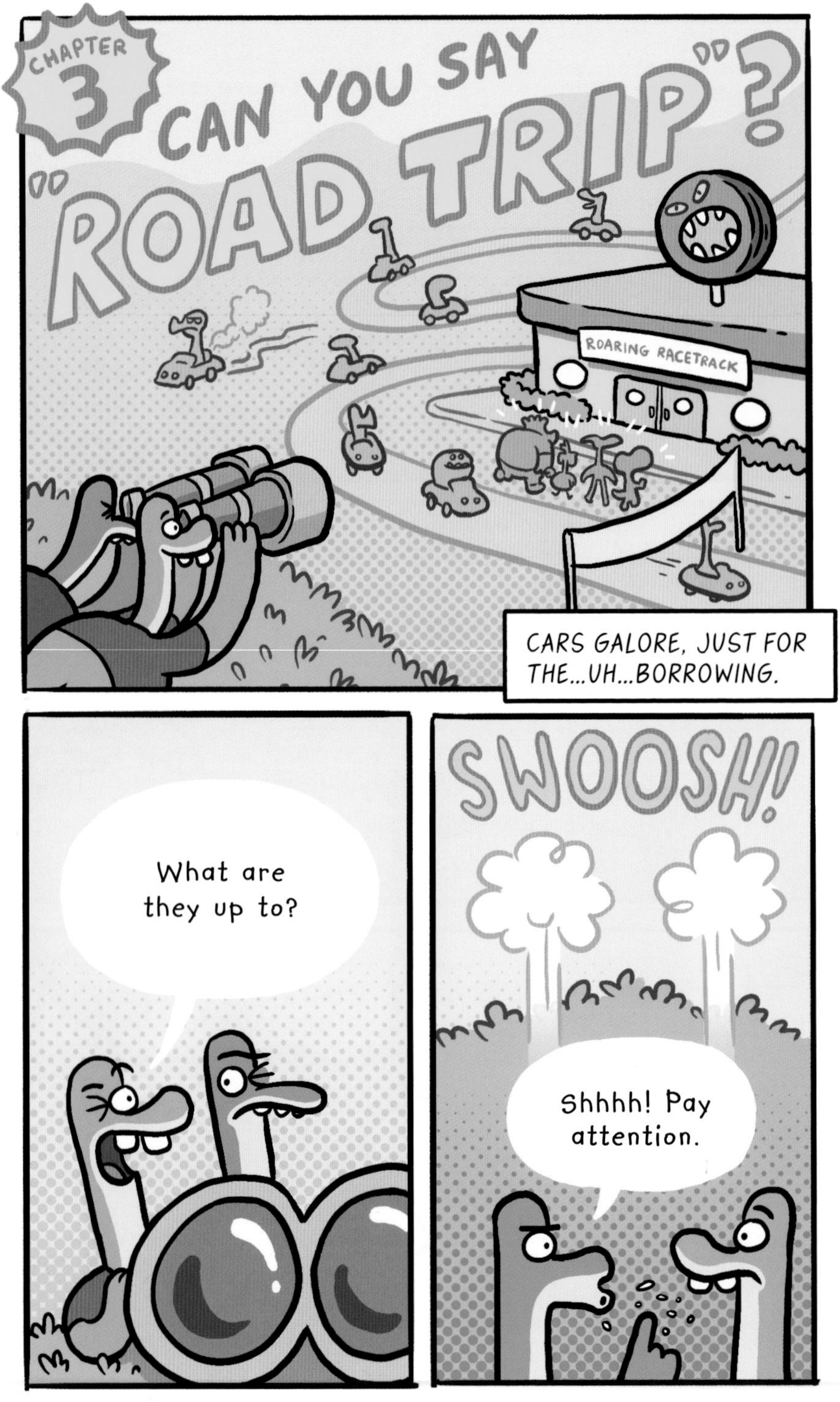
CHAPTER 3
CAN YOU SAY "ROAD TRIP"?
ROARING RACETRACK
CARS GALORE, JUST FOR THE...UH...BORROWING.
What are they up to?
SWOOSH!
Shhhh! Pay attention.

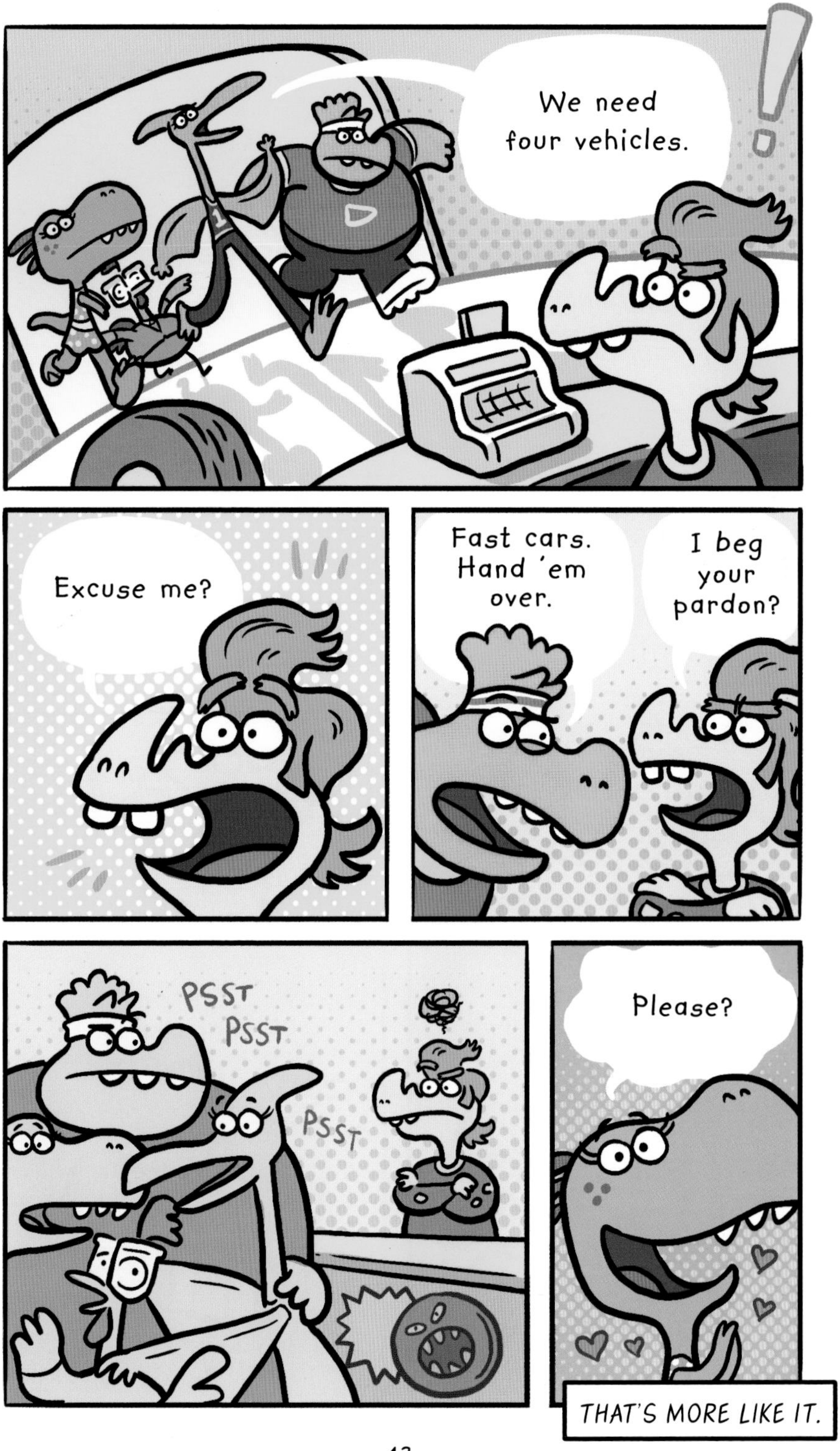
We need four vehicles.
Excuse me?
Fast cars. Hand 'em over.
I beg your pardon?
PSST
PSST
PSST
Please?
THAT'S MORE LIKE IT.

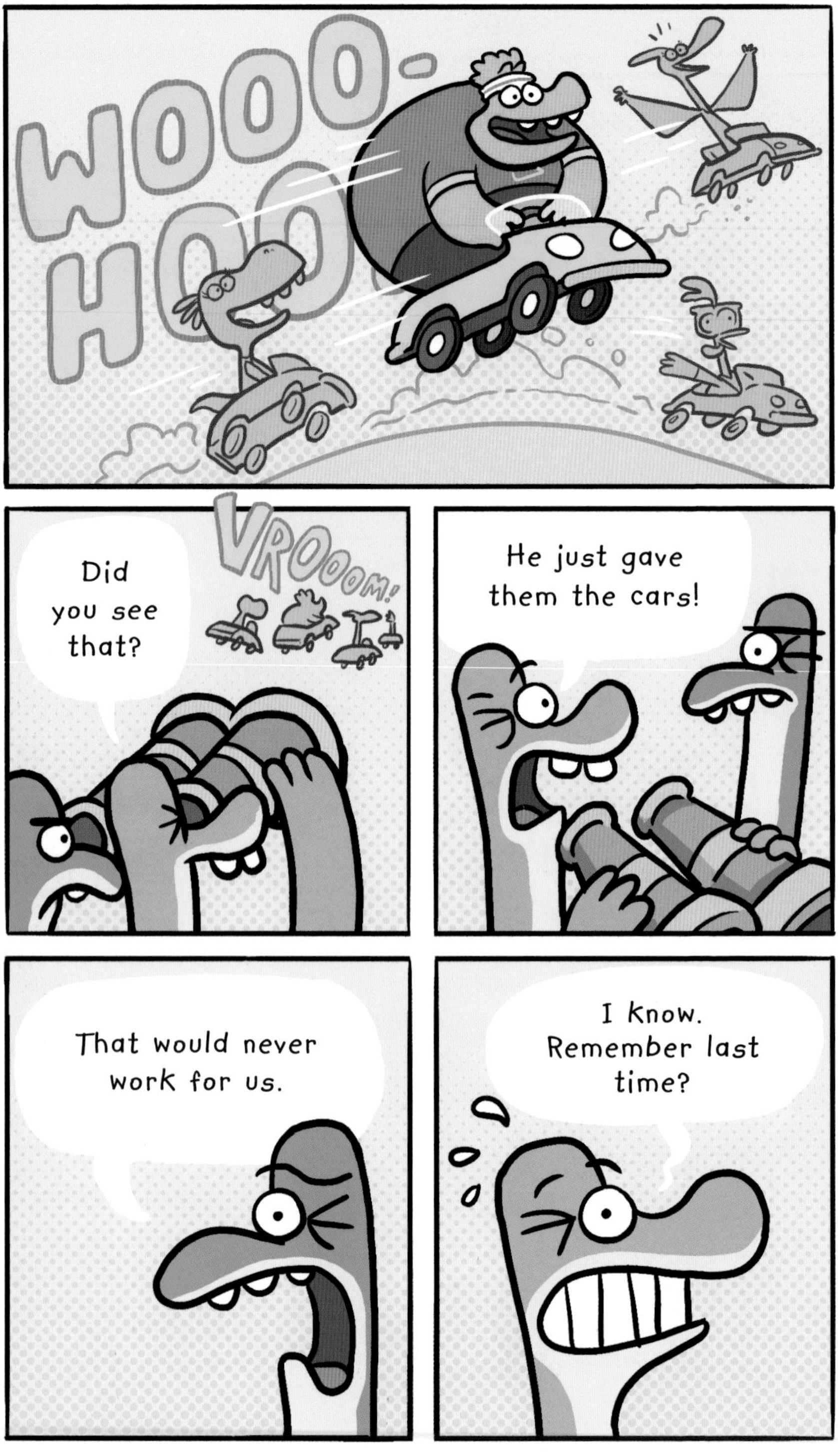
WOOO-HOO
Did you see that?
VROOOM!
He just gave them the cars!
That would never work for us.
I know. Remember last time?

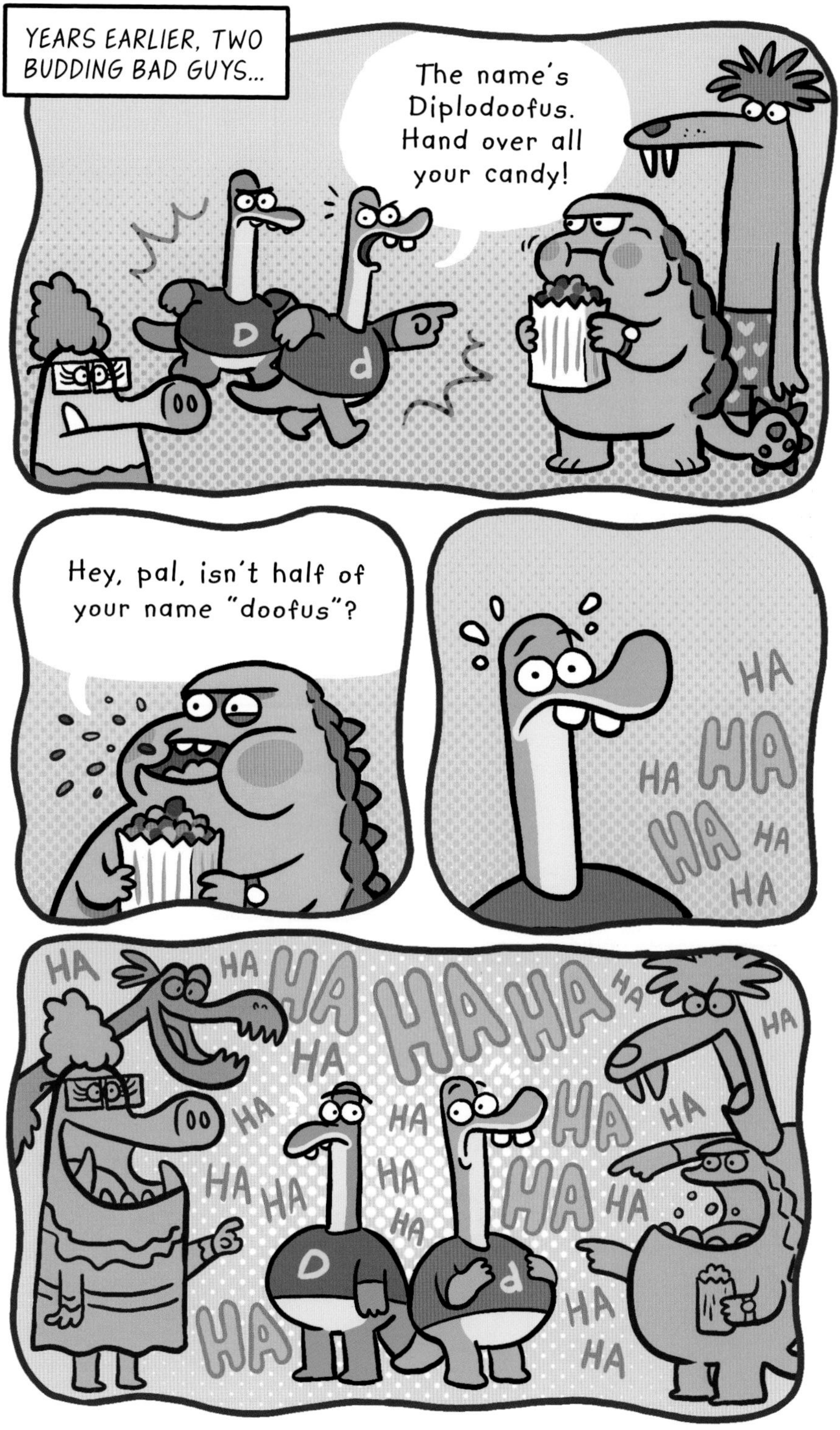
YEARS EARLIER, TWO BUDDING BAD GUYS...
The name's Diplodoofus. Hand over all your candy!
Hey, pal, isn't half of your name "doofus"?
HA HA HA HA HA HA
HA HA HA HA HA HA HA HA HA HA HA HA HA HA HA HA HA HA HA HA HA HA HA

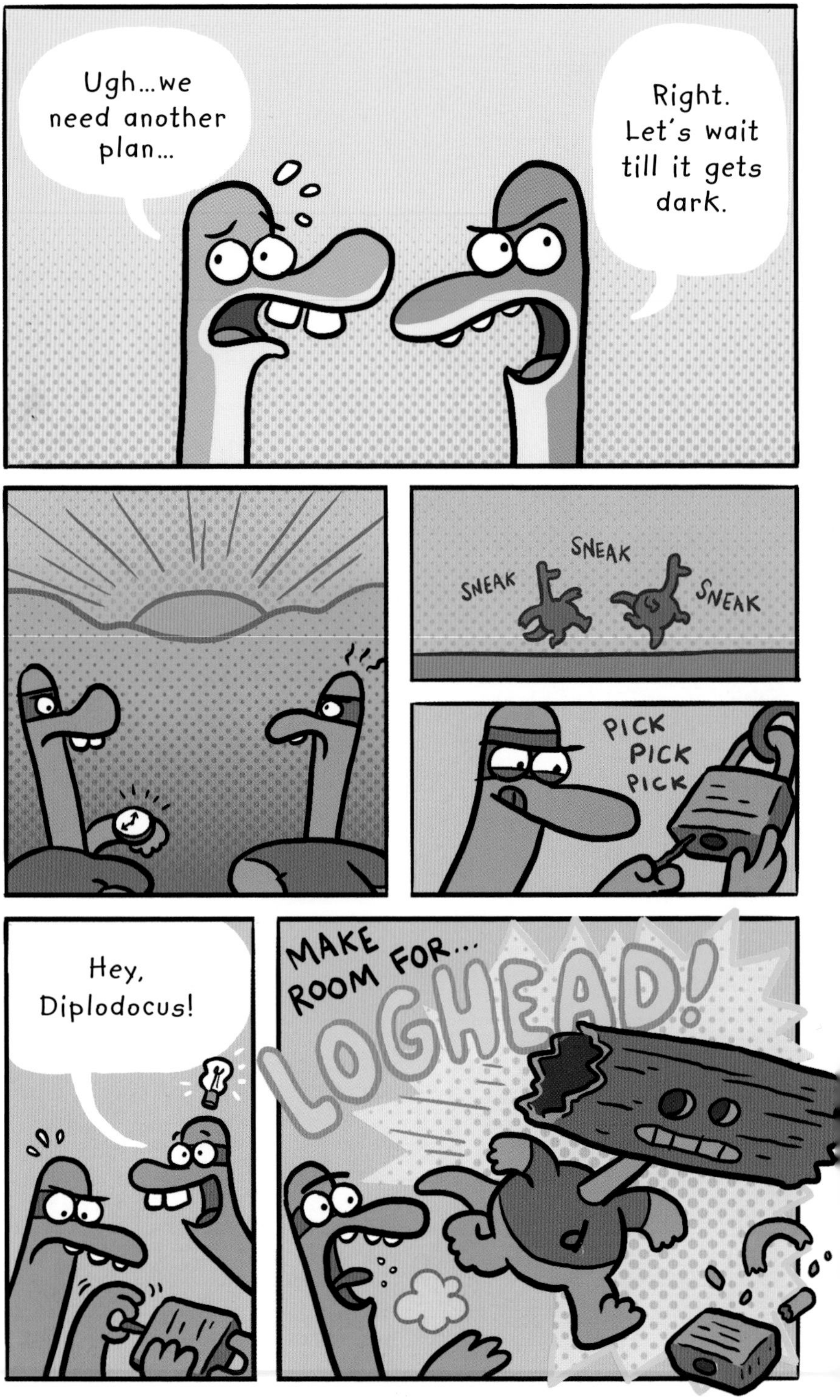
Ugh...we need another plan...
Right. Let's wait till it gets dark.
SNEAK
SNEAK
SNEAK
PICK
PICK
PICK
Hey, Diplodocus!
MAKE ROOM FOR...
LOGHEAD!

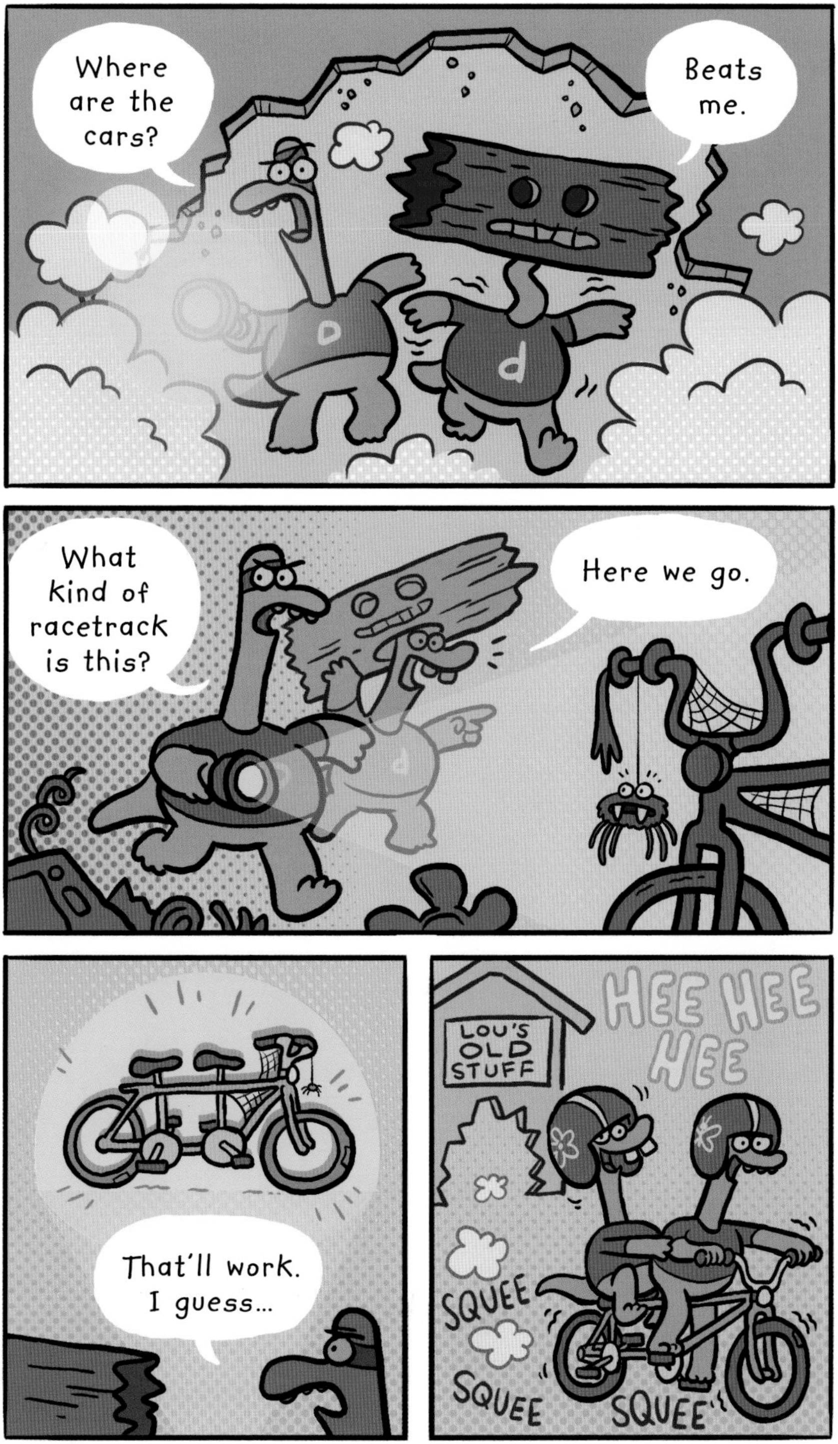
Where are the cars?
Beats me.
What kind of racetrack is this?
Here we go.
That'll work. I guess...
LOU'S OLD STUFF
HEE HEE HEE
SQUEE
SQUEE
SQUEE

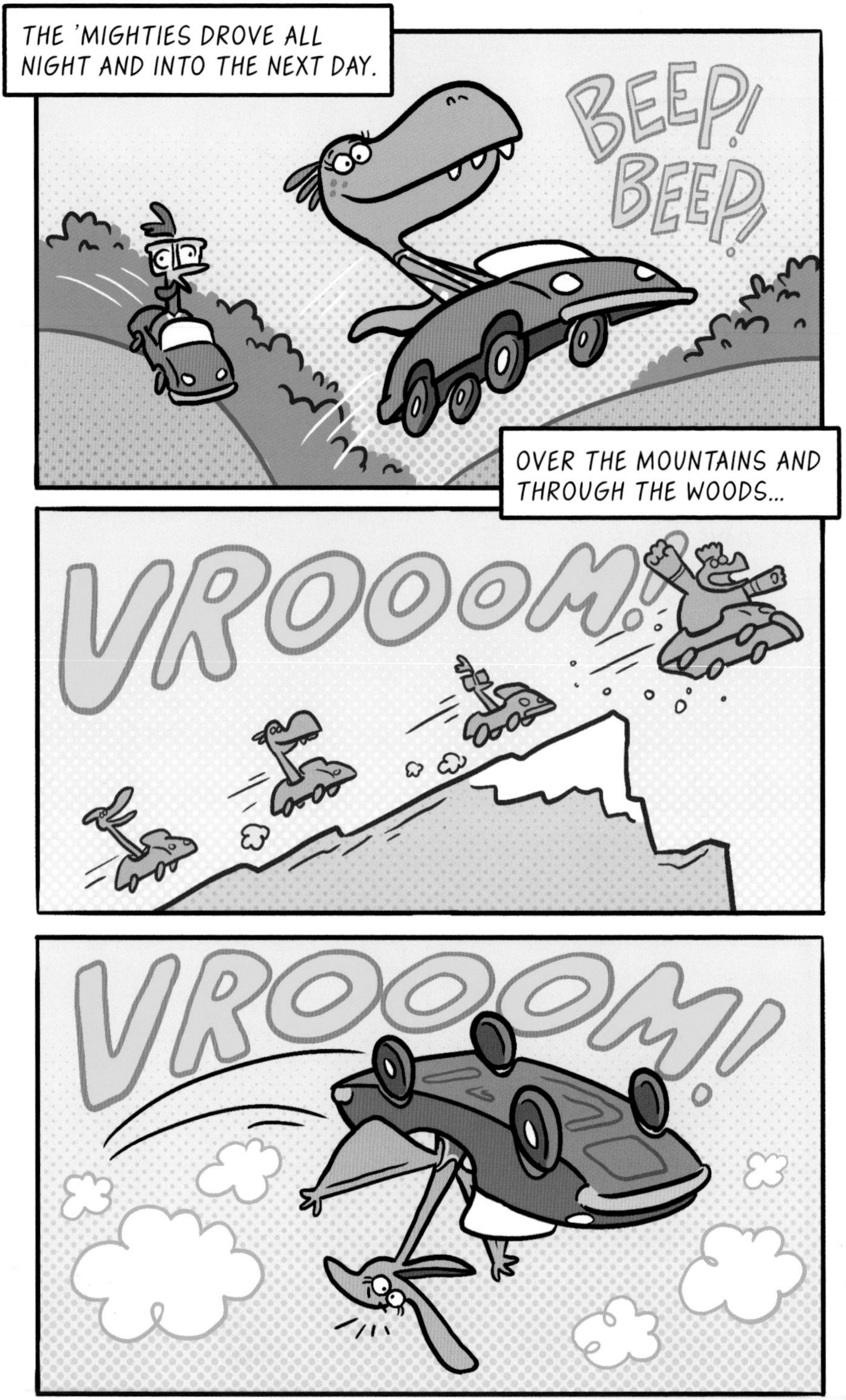
THE 'MIGHTIES DROVE ALL NIGHT AND INTO THE NEXT DAY.
BEEP! BEEP!
OVER THE MOUNTAINS AND THROUGH THE WOODS...
VROOOM!
VROOOM!

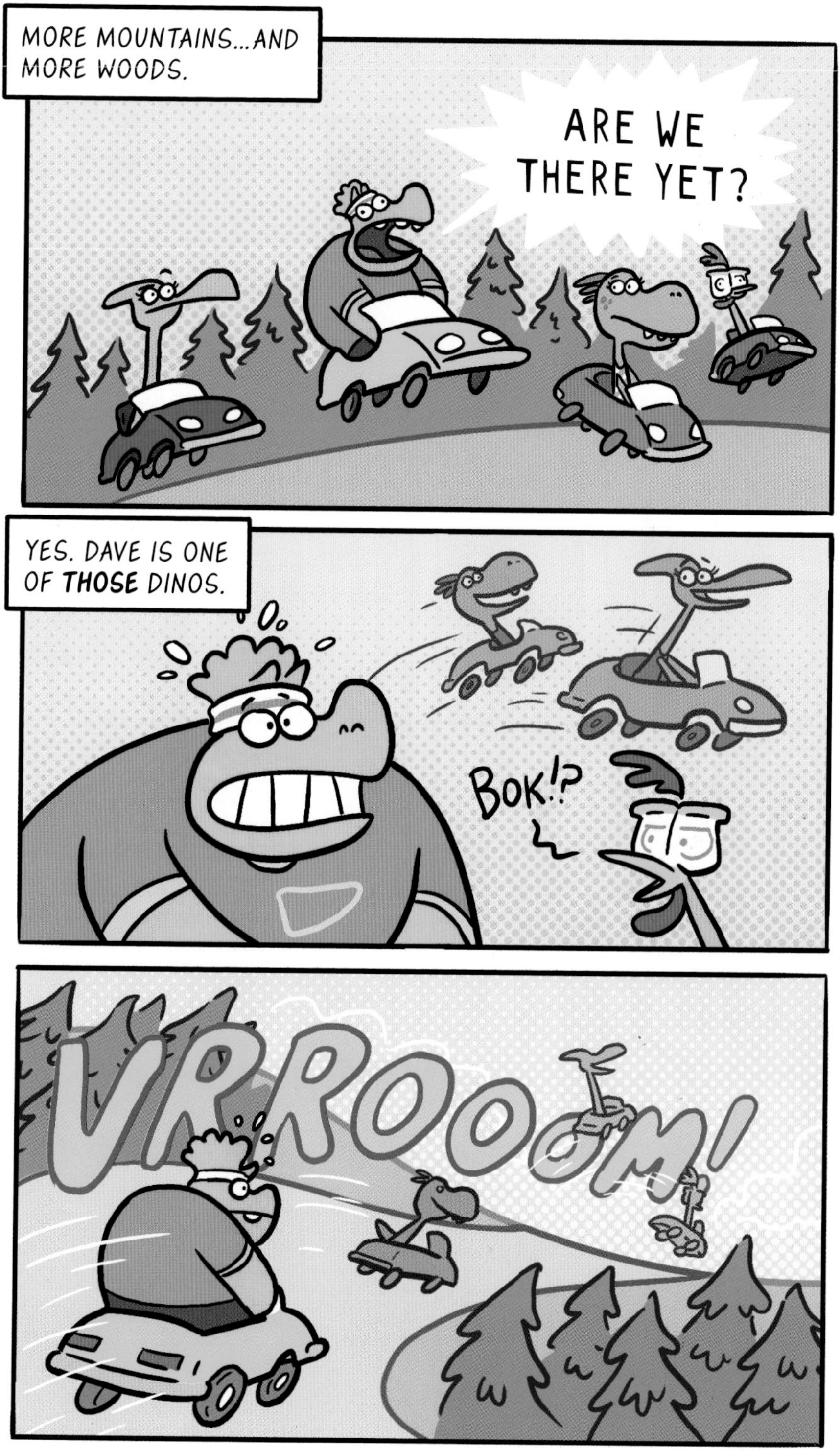
MORE MOUNTAINS...AND MORE WOODS.
ARE WE THERE YET?
YES. DAVE IS ONE OF **THOSE** DINOS.
BOK!?
VRROOOM!

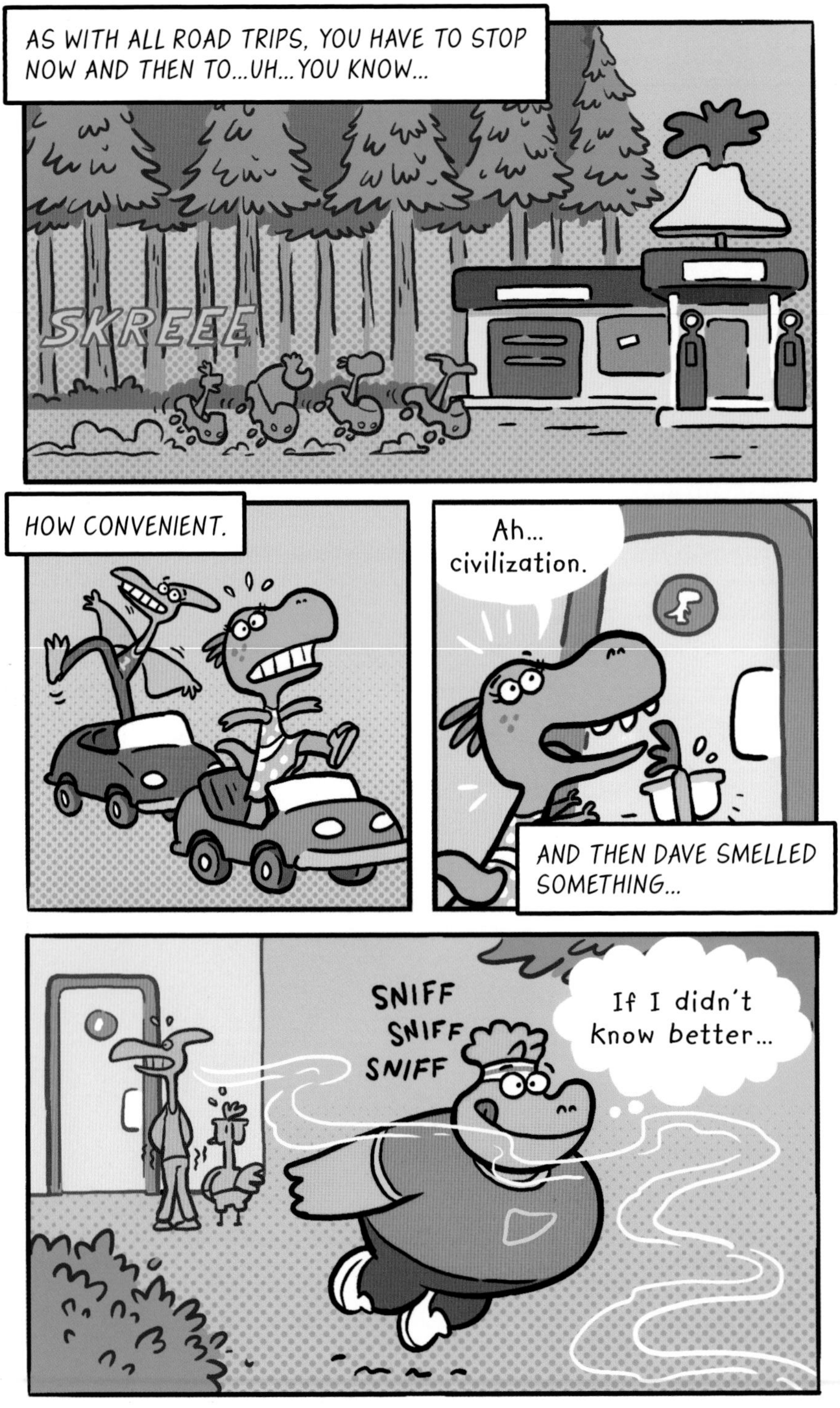
AS WITH ALL ROAD TRIPS, YOU HAVE TO STOP NOW AND THEN TO...UH...YOU KNOW...
SKREEE
HOW CONVENIENT.
Ah... civilization.
AND THEN DAVE SMELLED SOMETHING...
SNIFF
SNIFF
SNIFF
If I didn't know better...

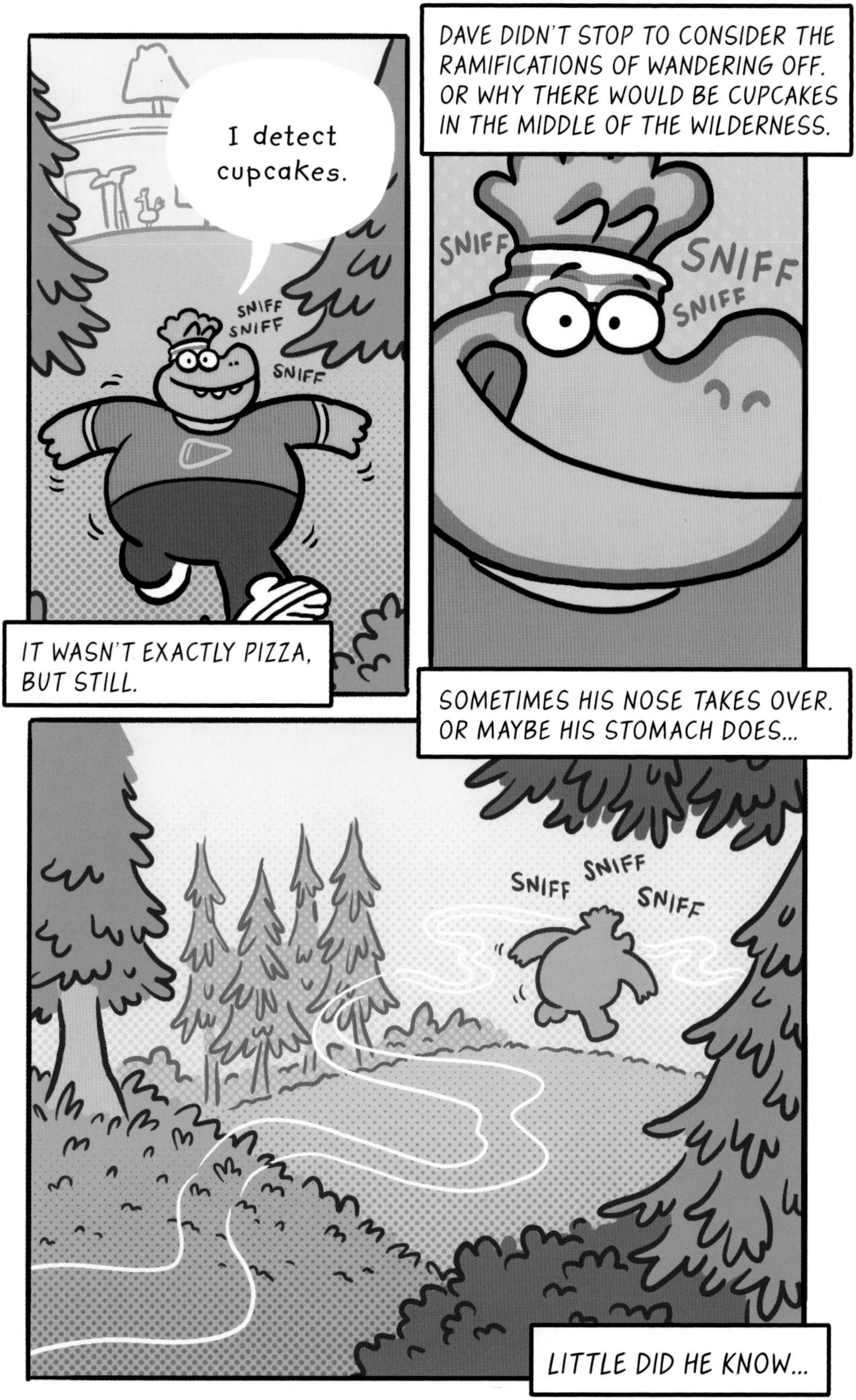
I detect cupcakes.
SNIFF
SNIFF
SNIFF
IT WASN'T EXACTLY PIZZA, BUT STILL.
DAVE DIDN'T STOP TO CONSIDER THE RAMIFICATIONS OF WANDERING OFF. OR WHY THERE WOULD BE CUPCAKES IN THE MIDDLE OF THE WILDERNESS.
SNIFF
SNIFF
SNIFF
SOMETIMES HIS NOSE TAKES OVER. OR MAYBE HIS STOMACH DOES...
SNIFF
SNIFF
SNIFF
LITTLE DID HE KNOW...

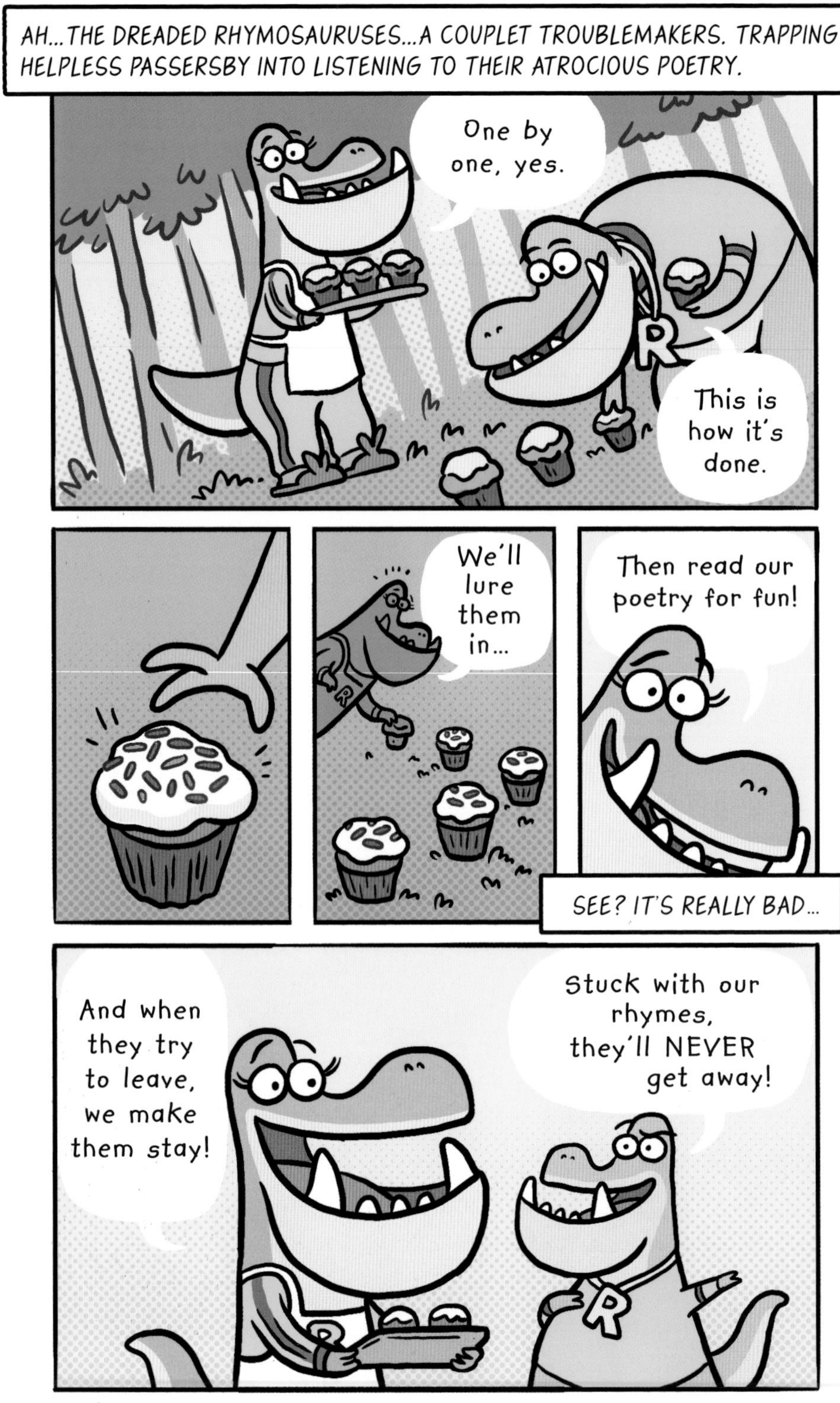
AH...THE DREADED RHYMOSAURUSES...A COUPLET TROUBLEMAKERS. TRAPPING HELPLESS PASSERSBY INTO LISTENING TO THEIR ATROCIOUS POETRY.
One by one, yes.
This is how it's done.
We'll lure them in...
Then read our poetry for fun!
SEE? IT'S REALLY BAD...
And when they try to leave, we make them stay!
Stuck with our rhymes, they'll NEVER get away!

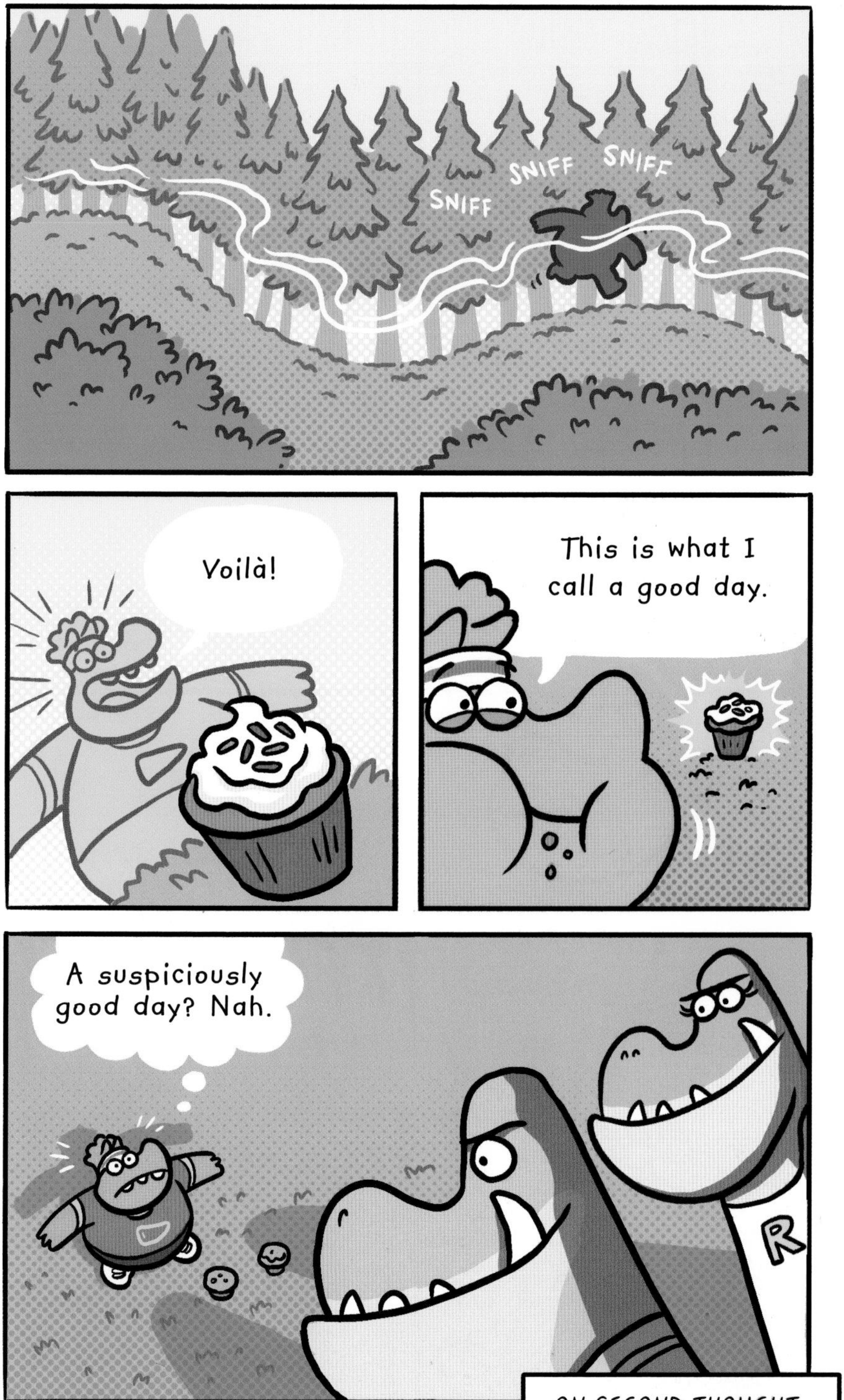
SNIFF
SNIFF
SNIFF
Voilà!
This is what I call a good day.
A suspiciously good day? Nah.
R
ON SECOND THOUGHT...

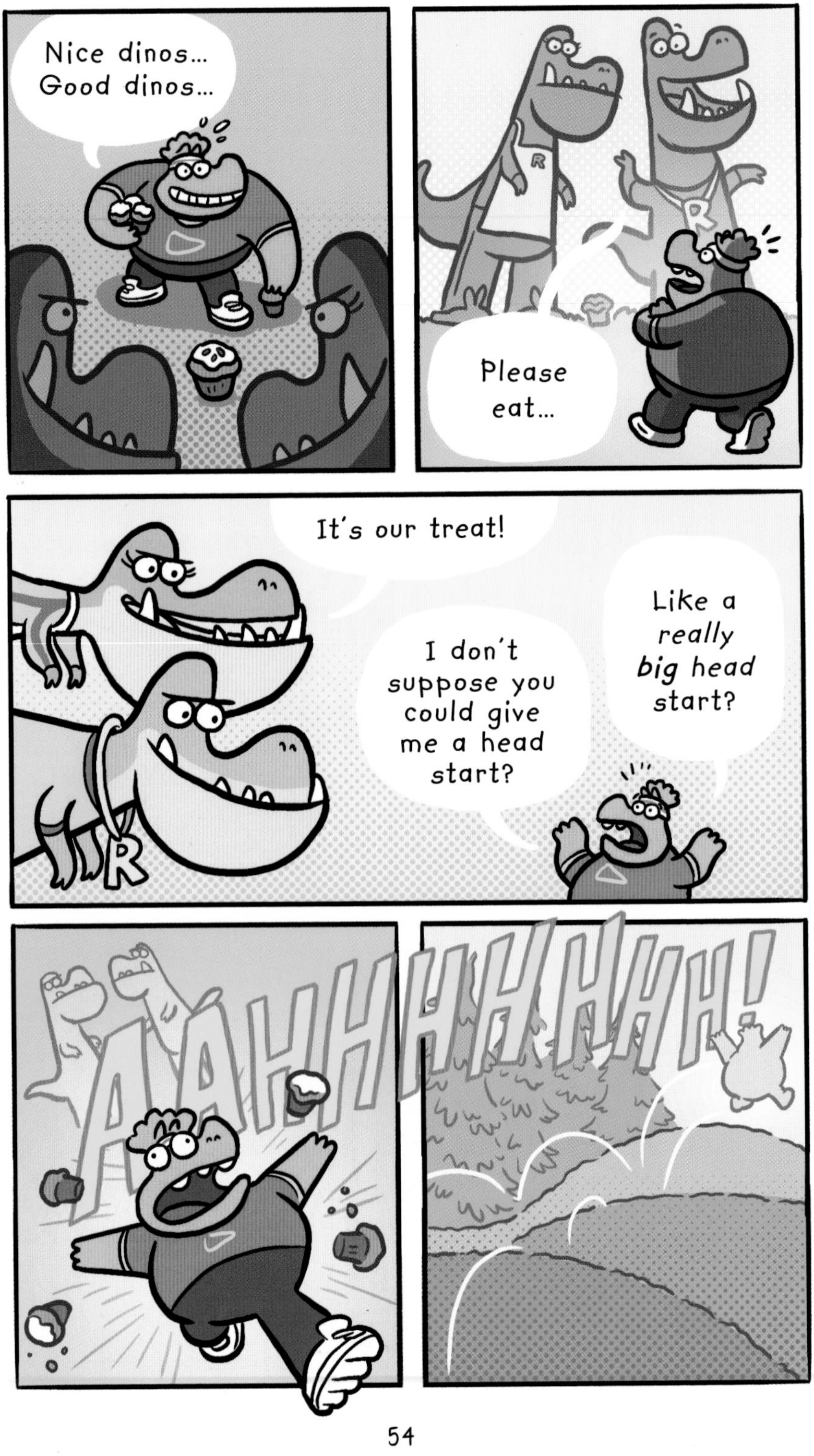
Nice dinos... Good dinos...
Please eat...
It's our treat!
I don't suppose you could give me a head start?
Like a *really big* head start?
AAHHHHHHHHH!

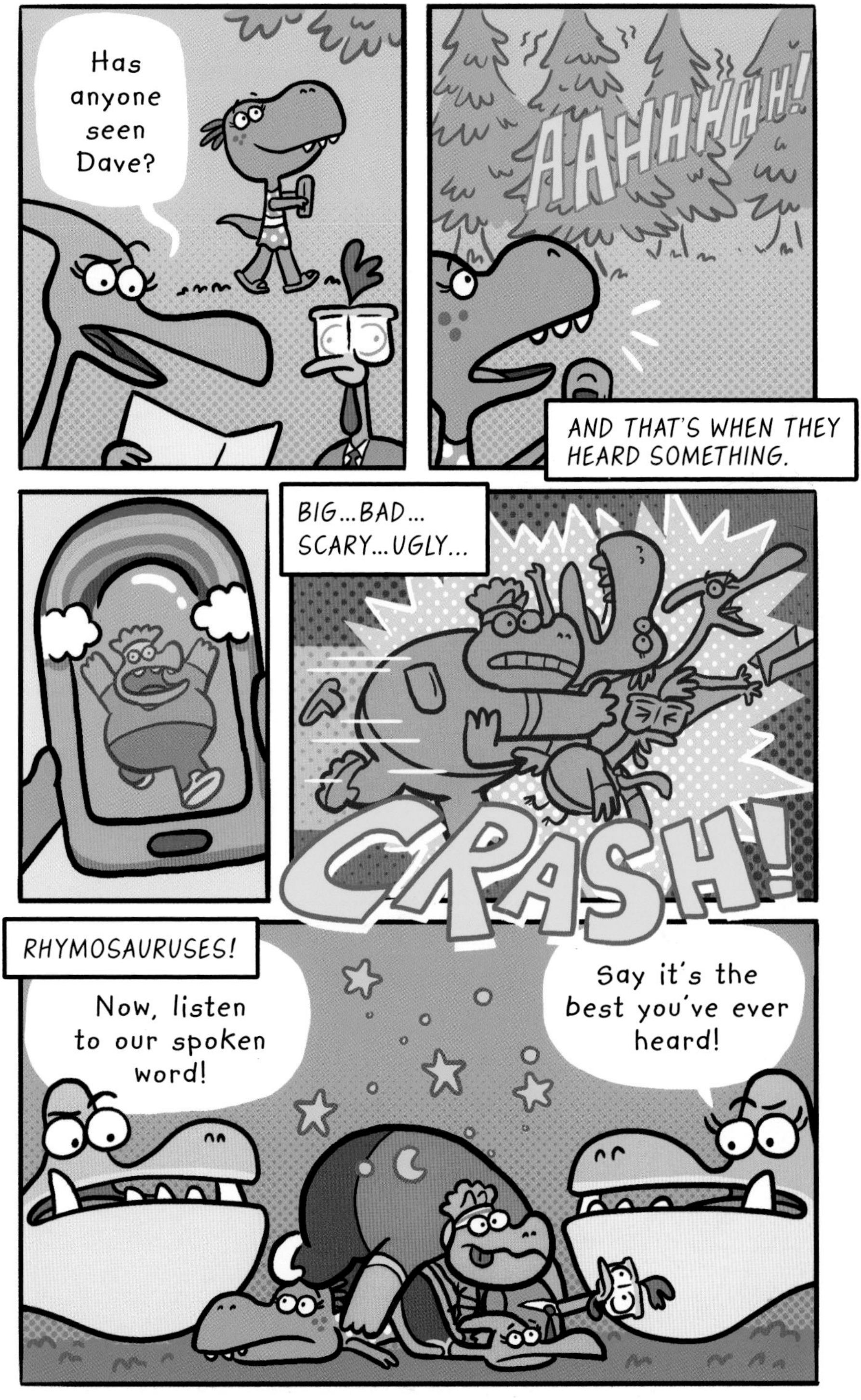
Has anyone seen Dave?
AAHHHHHH!
AND THAT'S WHEN THEY HEARD SOMETHING.
BIG...BAD... SCARY...UGLY...
CRASH!
RHYMOSAURUSES!
Now, listen to our spoken word!
Say it's the best you've ever heard!

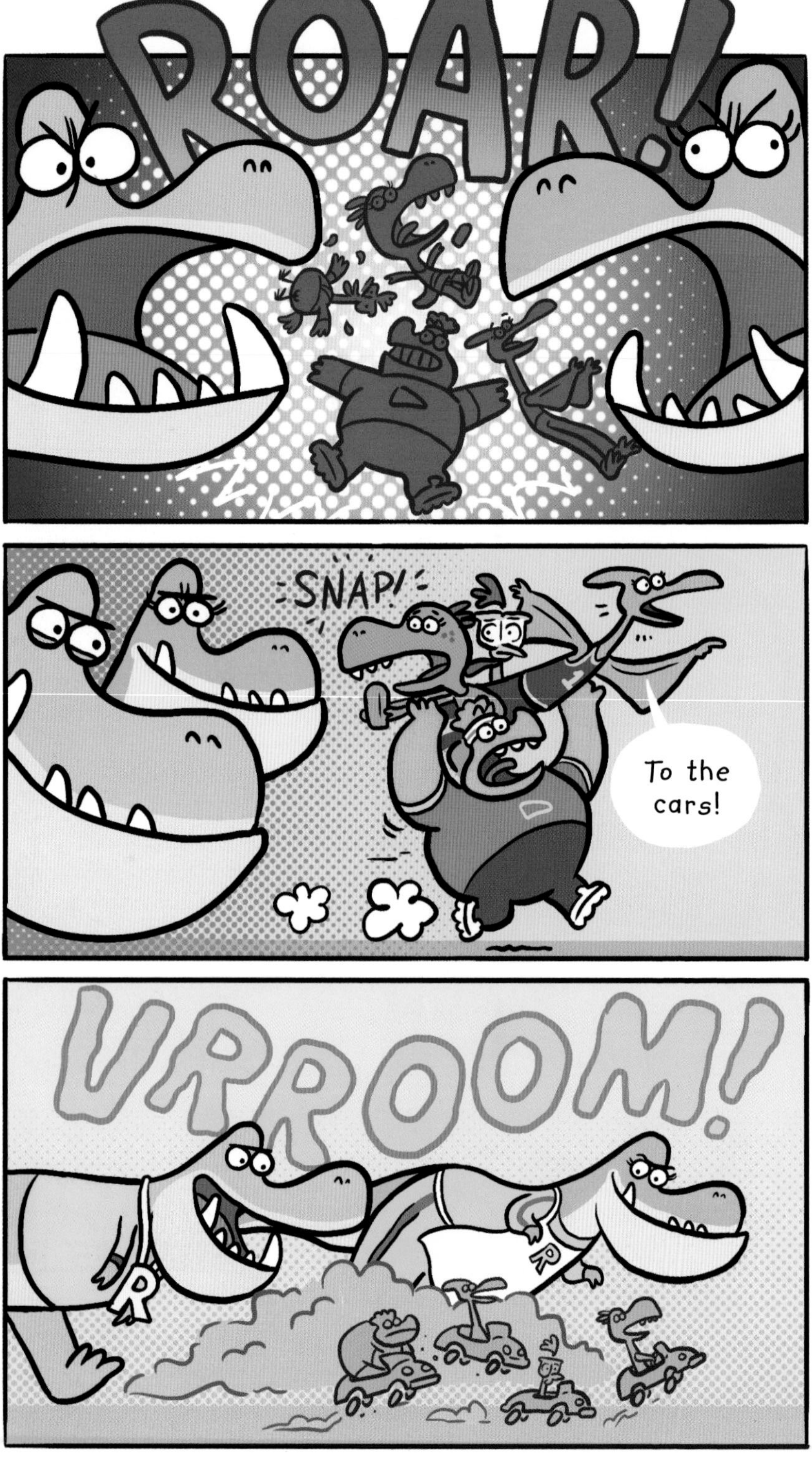
ROAR!
SNAP!
To the cars!
VRROOM!

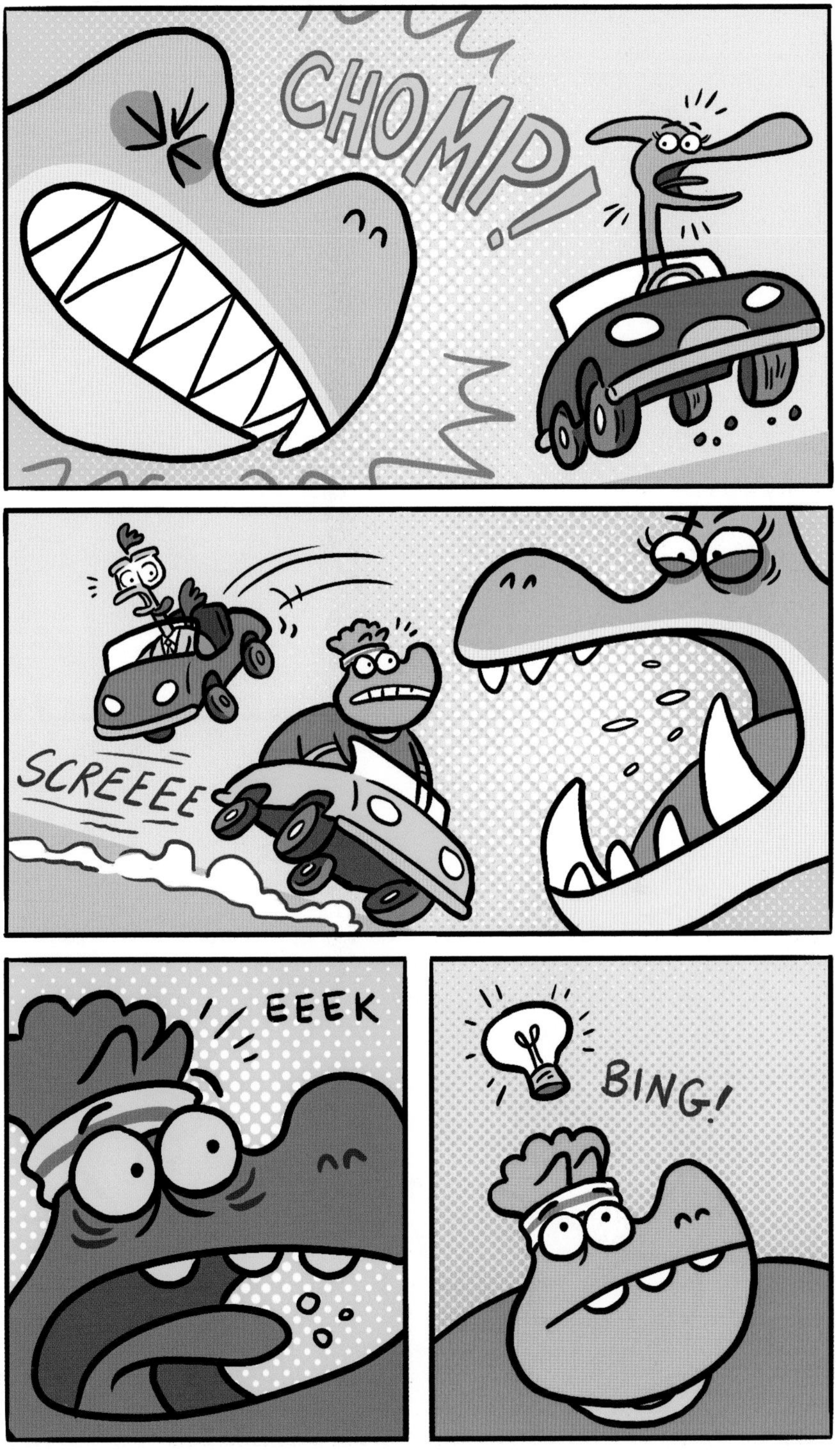
CHOMP!
SCREEEEE
EEEK
BING!

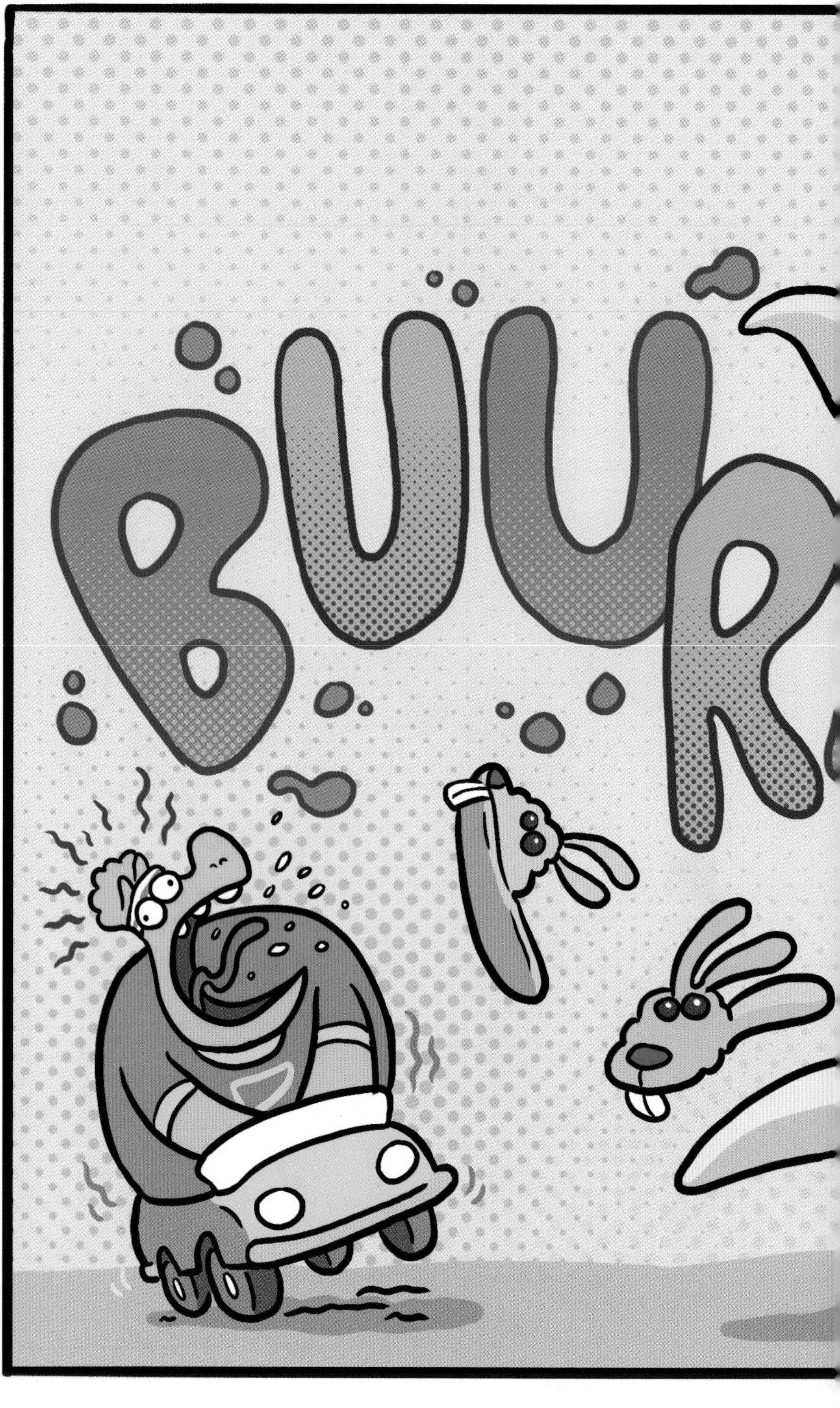
BUUR

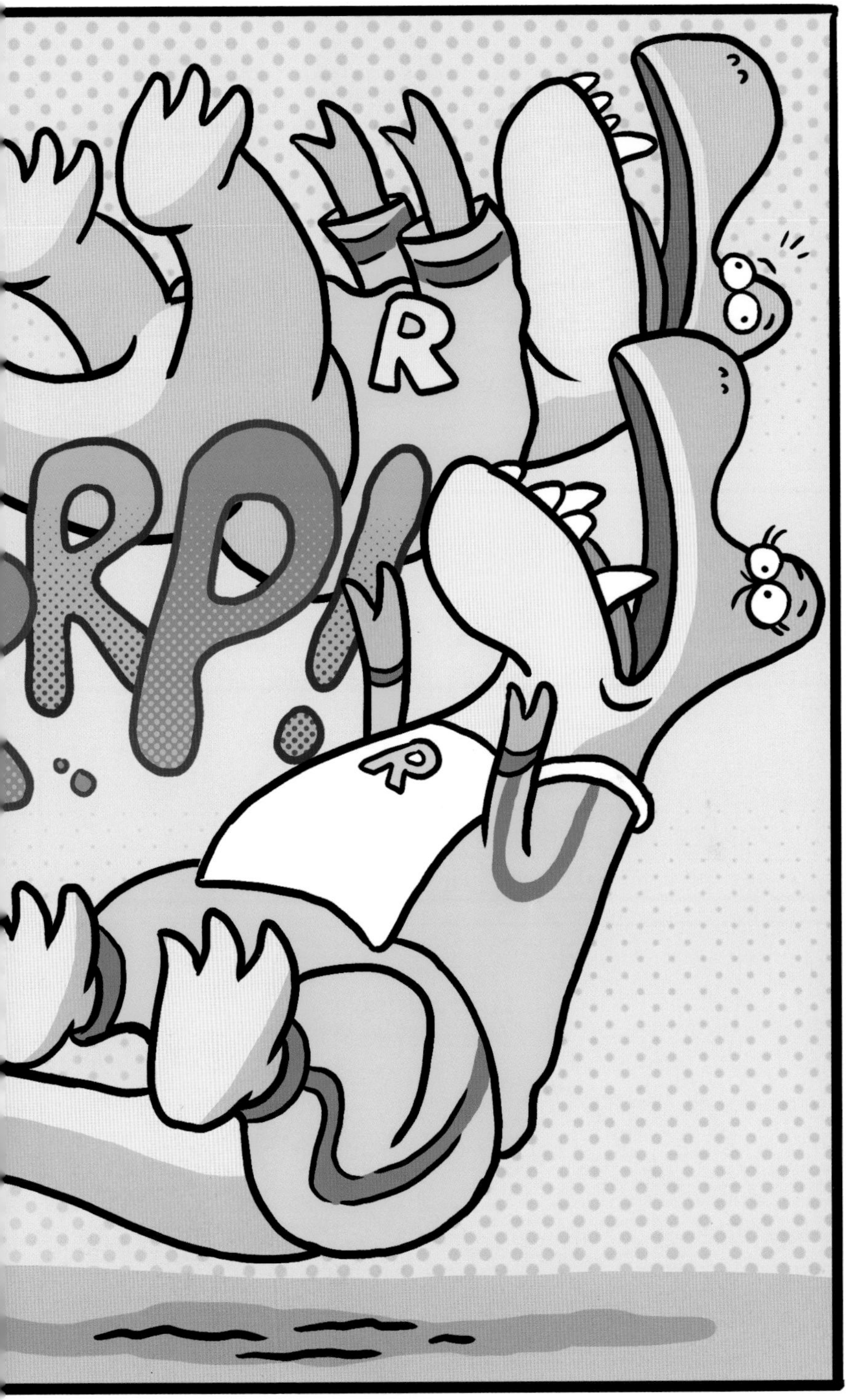
RP!

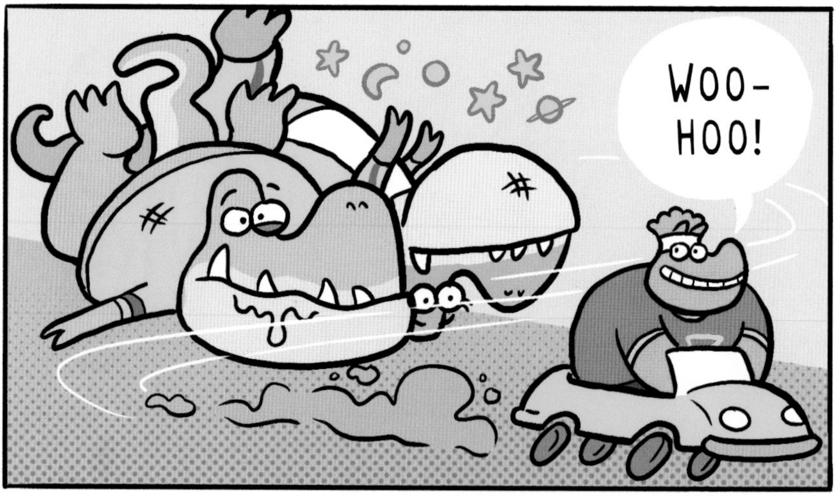
WOO-
HOO!

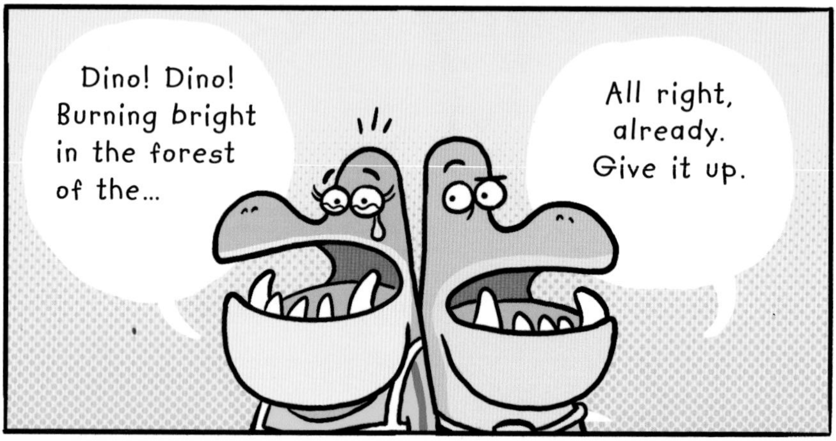
Dino! Dino! Burning bright in the forest of the...
All right, already. Give it up.

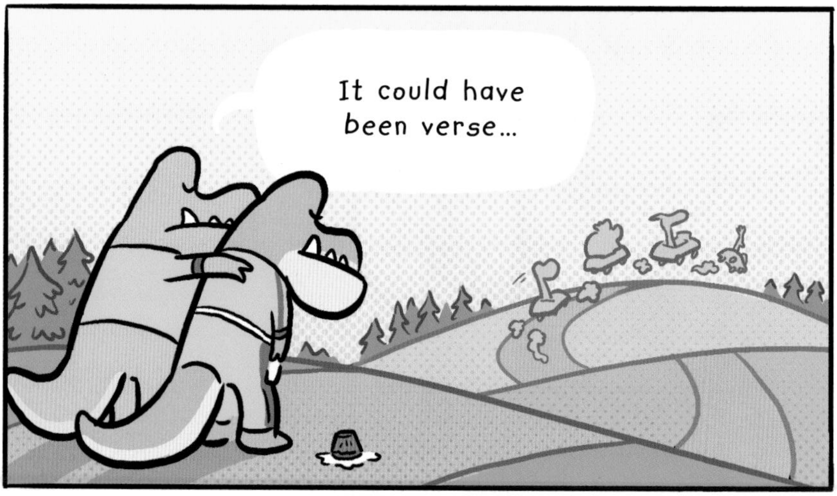
It could have been verse...

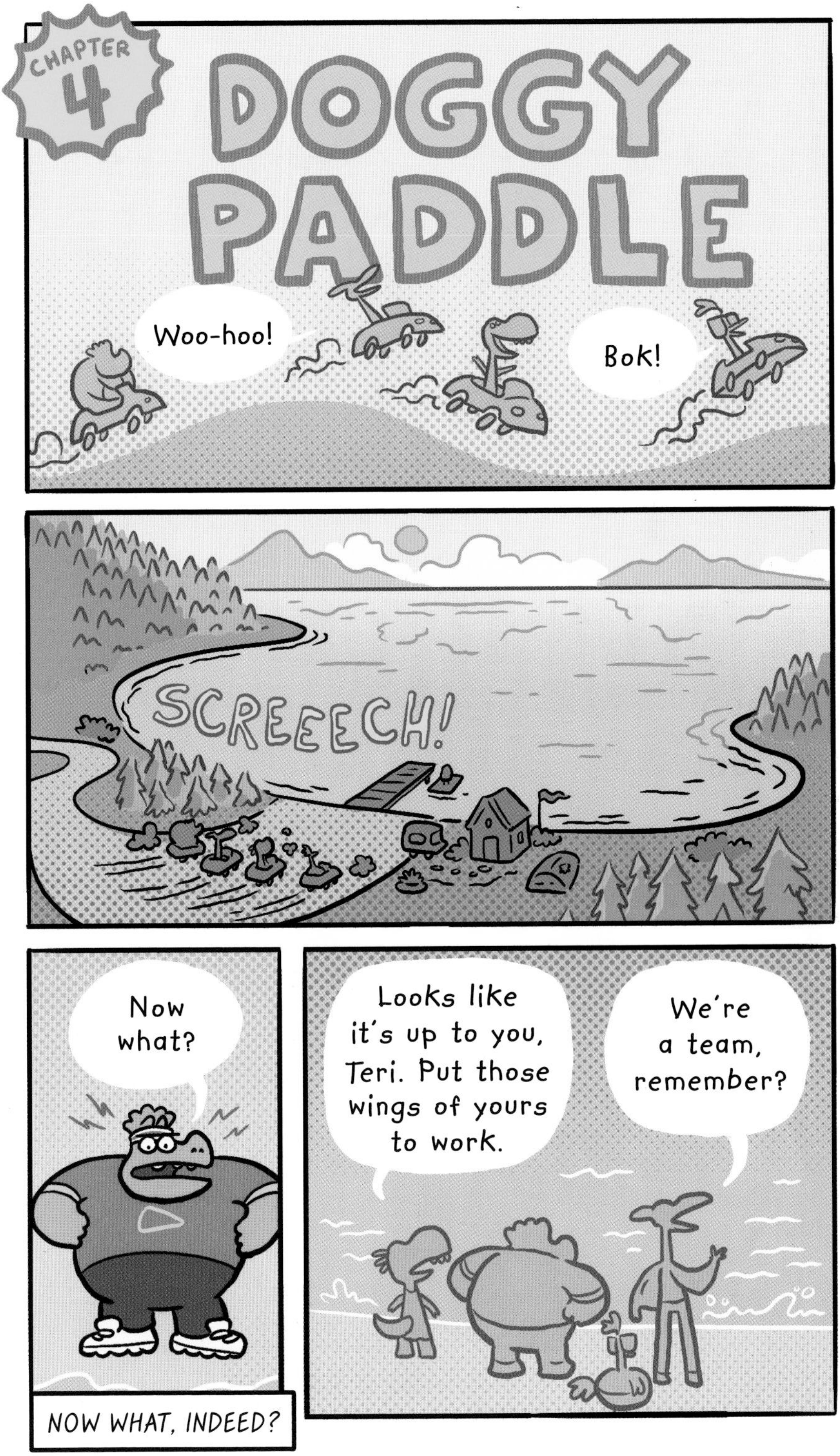
CHAPTER 4
DOGGY PADDLE
Woo-hoo!
Bok!
SCREEECH!
Now what?
Looks like it's up to you, Teri. Put those wings of yours to work.
We're a team, remember?
NOW WHAT, INDEED?

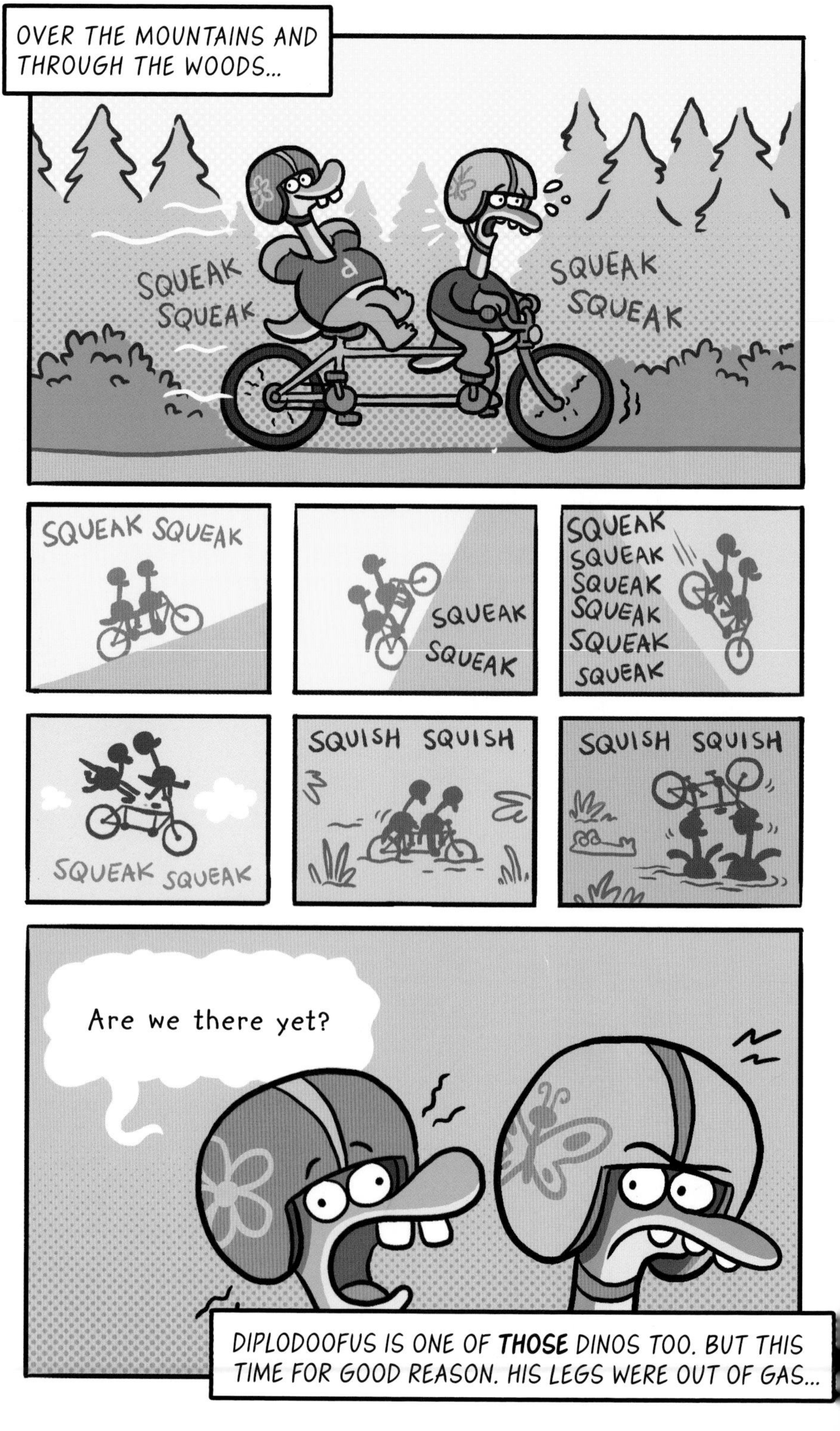
OVER THE MOUNTAINS AND THROUGH THE WOODS...
SQUEAK SQUEAK
SQUEAK SQUEAK
SQUEAK SQUEAK
SQUEAK SQUEAK
SQUEAK SQUEAK SQUEAK SQUEAK SQUEAK SQUEAK
SQUEAK SQUEAK
SQUISH SQUISH
SQUISH SQUISH
Are we there yet?
DIPLODOOFUS IS ONE OF **THOSE** DINOS TOO. BUT THIS TIME FOR GOOD REASON. HIS LEGS WERE OUT OF GAS...

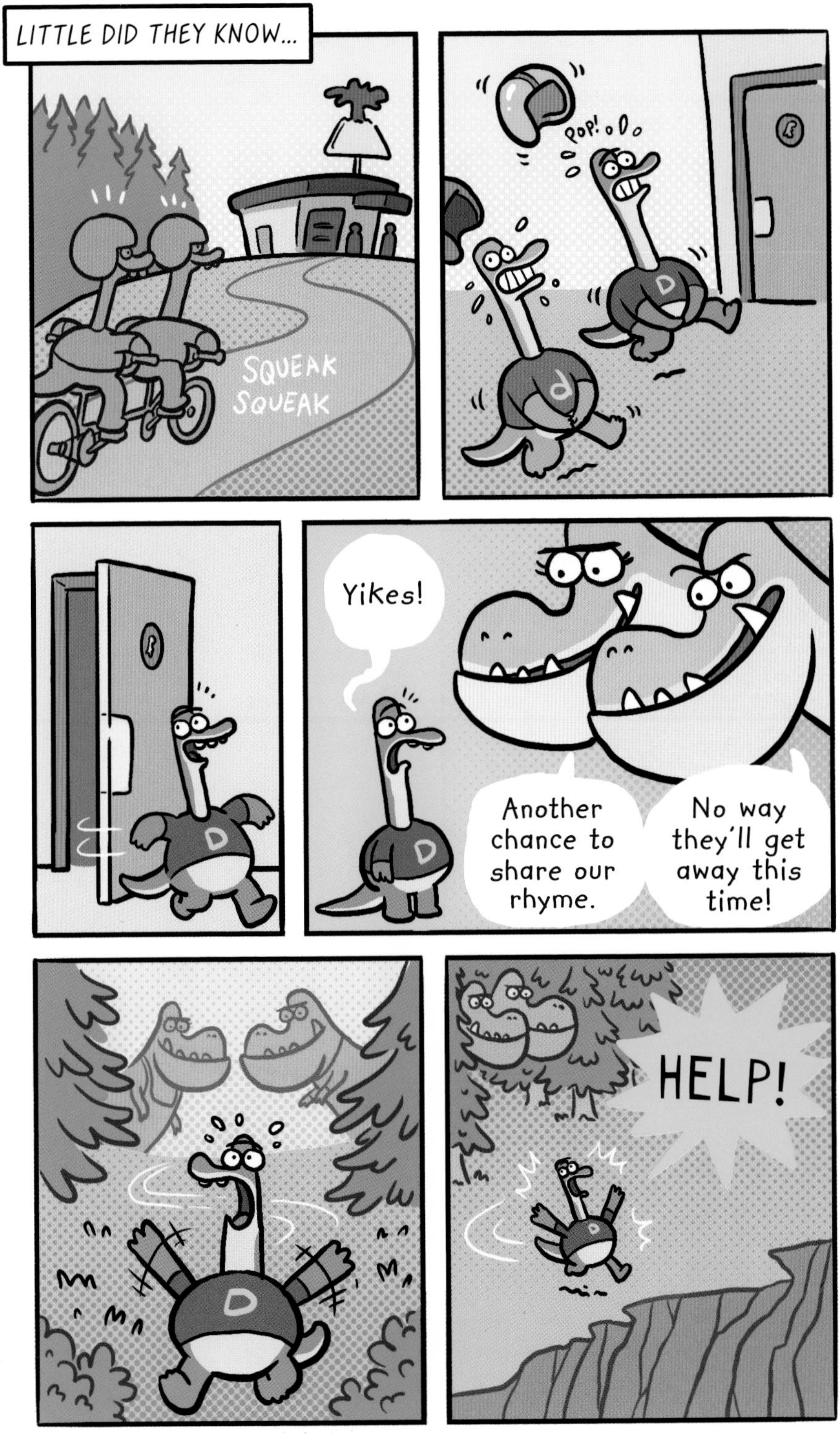
LITTLE DID THEY KNOW...
SQUEAK
SQUEAK
POP!
Yikes!
Another chance to share our rhyme.
No way they'll get away this time!
HELP!

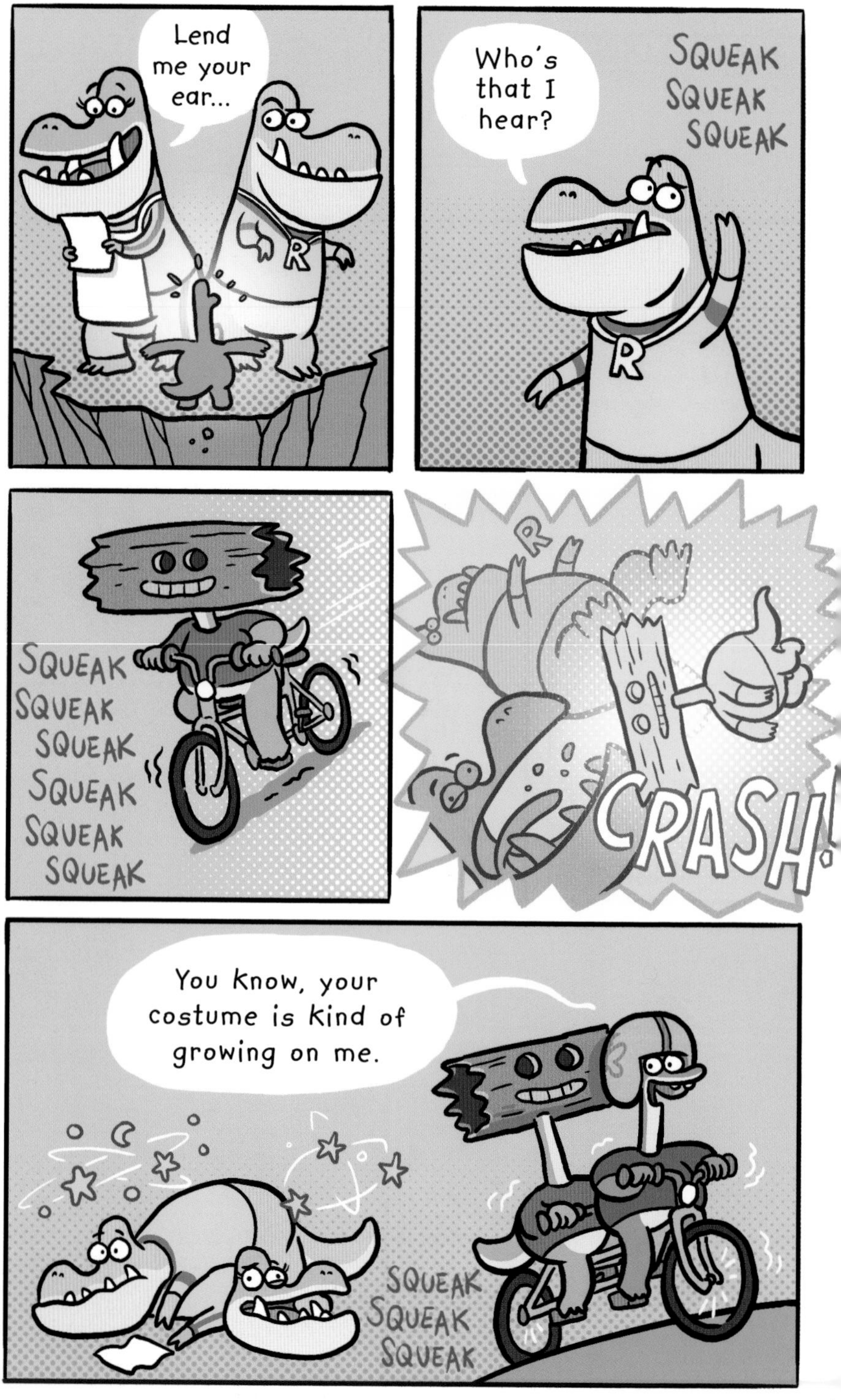
Lend me your ear...
Who's that I hear?
SQUEAK SQUEAK SQUEAK
SQUEAK SQUEAK SQUEAK SQUEAK SQUEAK SQUEAK
CRASH!
You know, your costume is kind of growing on me.
SQUEAK SQUEAK SQUEAK

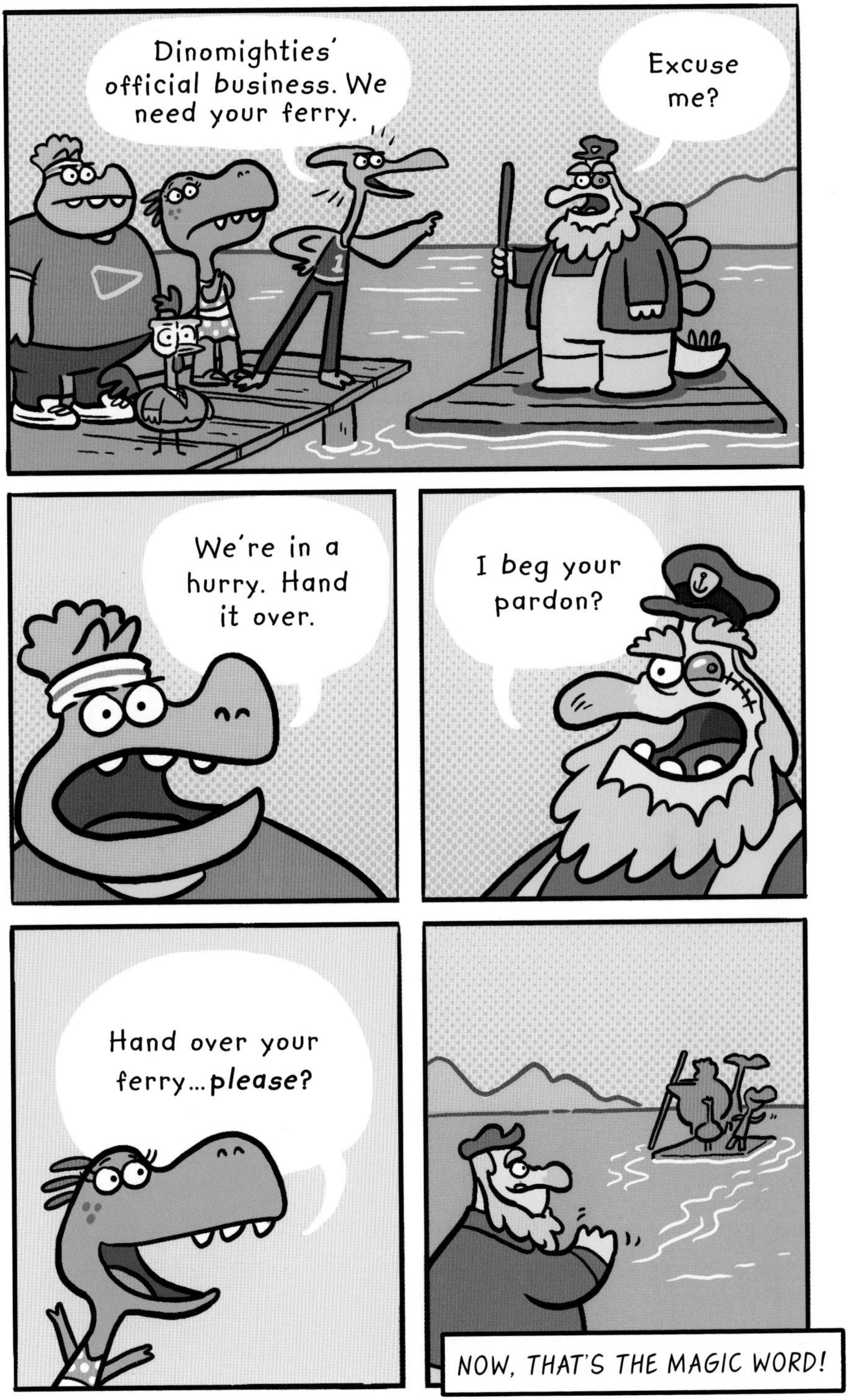

Dinomighties' official business. We need your ferry.
Excuse me?
We're in a hurry. Hand it over.
I beg your pardon?
Hand over your ferry...*please*?
NOW, THAT'S THE MAGIC WORD!

Great. How do we get across?

How's your doggy paddle?

Better than my butterfly stroke.

WHICH ISN'T SAYING A WHOLE LOT.

I've always wanted to learn to snorkel.

That's a long way to snorkel.

You got a better idea?

Sure... Yacht, cruise ship, canoe, air mattress.

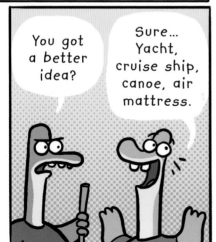

Something we can use now!

I got nothin'.

WELL THEN...

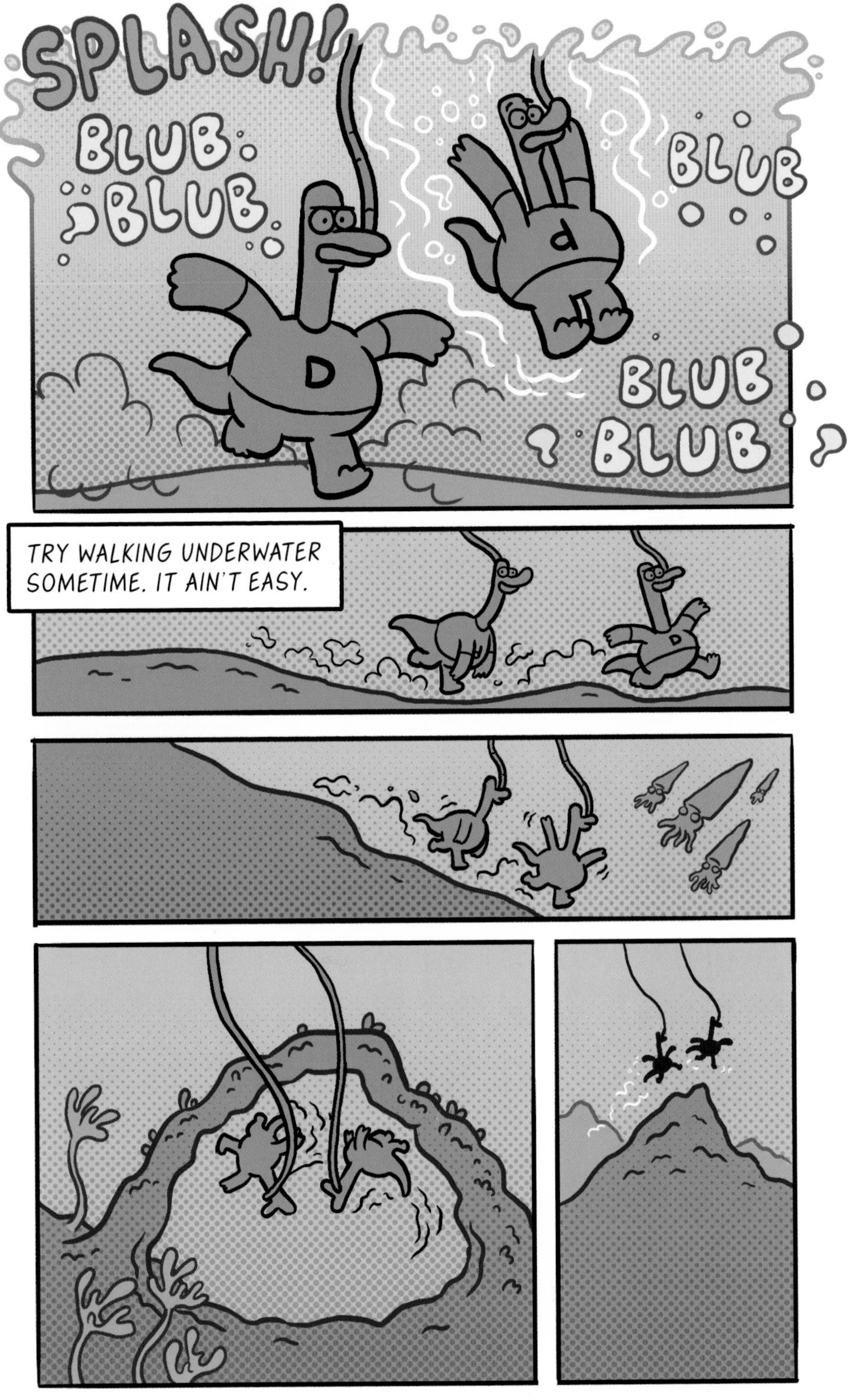
SPLASH!
BLUB BLUB
BLUB
BLUB BLUB
TRY WALKING UNDERWATER SOMETIME. IT AIN'T EASY.

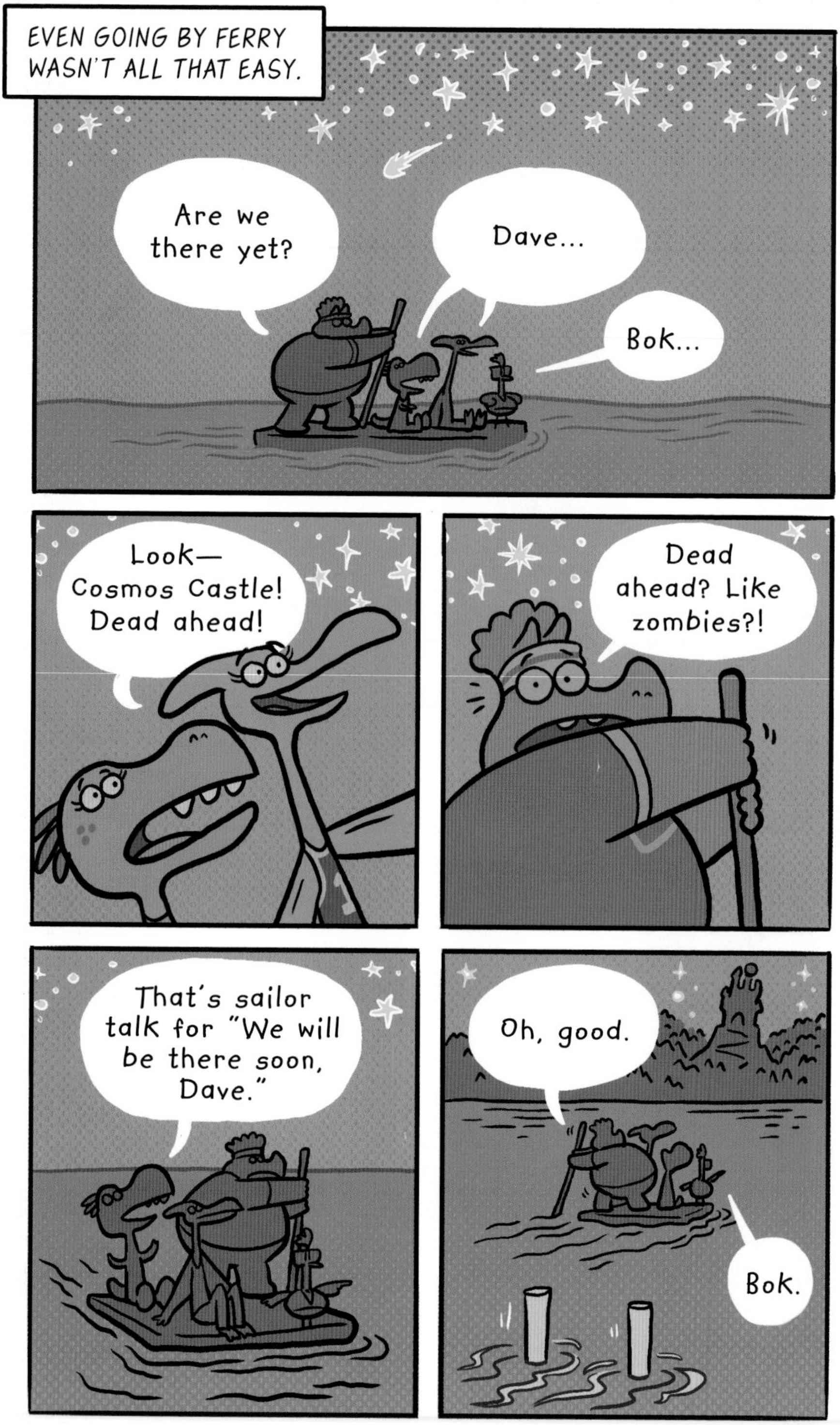
EVEN GOING BY FERRY WASN'T ALL THAT EASY.
Are we there yet?
Dave...
Bok...
Look— Cosmos Castle! Dead ahead!
Dead ahead? Like zombies?!
That's sailor talk for "We will be there soon, Dave."
Oh, good.
Bok.

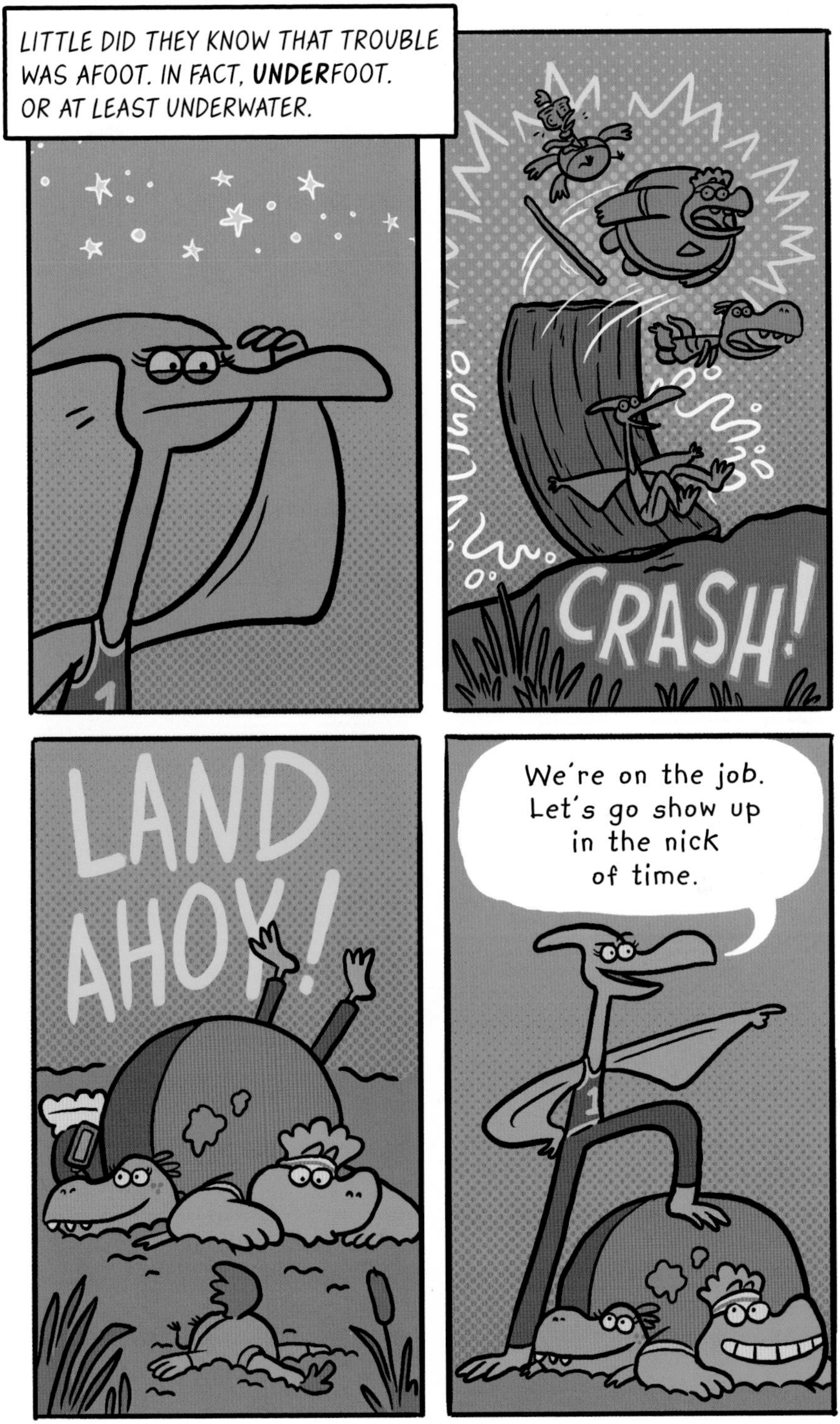

LITTLE DID THEY KNOW THAT TROUBLE WAS AFOOT. IN FACT, **UNDER**FOOT. OR AT LEAST UNDERWATER.
CRASH!
LAND AHOY!
We're on the job. Let's go show up in the nick of time.

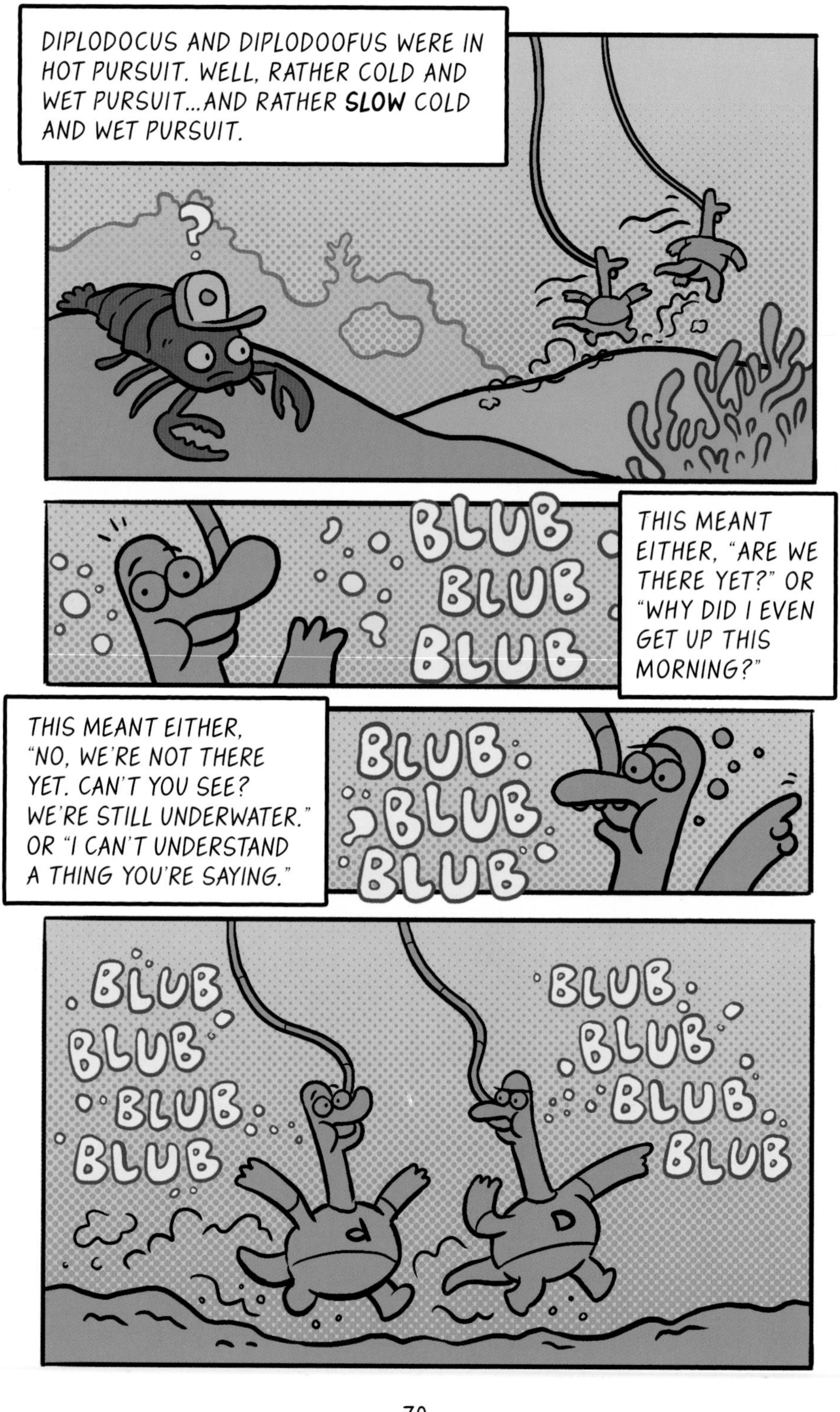
DIPLODOCUS AND DIPLODOOFUS WERE IN HOT PURSUIT. WELL, RATHER COLD AND WET PURSUIT...AND RATHER **SLOW** COLD AND WET PURSUIT.
?
BLUB BLUB BLUB
THIS MEANT EITHER, "ARE WE THERE YET?" OR "WHY DID I EVEN GET UP THIS MORNING?"
THIS MEANT EITHER, "NO, WE'RE NOT THERE YET. CAN'T YOU SEE? WE'RE STILL UNDERWATER." OR "I CAN'T UNDERSTAND A THING YOU'RE SAYING."
BLUB BLUB BLUB
BLUB BLUB BLUB BLUB
BLUB BLUB BLUB BLUB

BUT BACK TO THE DINOMIGHTIES...

Let's go.

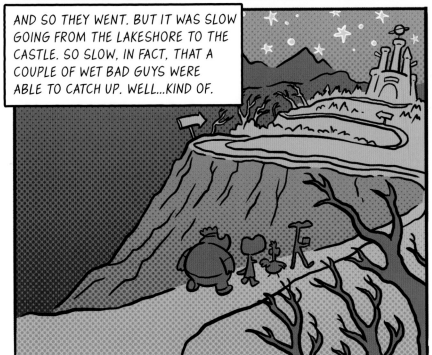

AND SO THEY WENT. BUT IT WAS SLOW GOING FROM THE LAKESHORE TO THE CASTLE. SO SLOW, IN FACT, THAT A COUPLE OF WET BAD GUYS WERE ABLE TO CATCH UP. WELL...KIND OF.

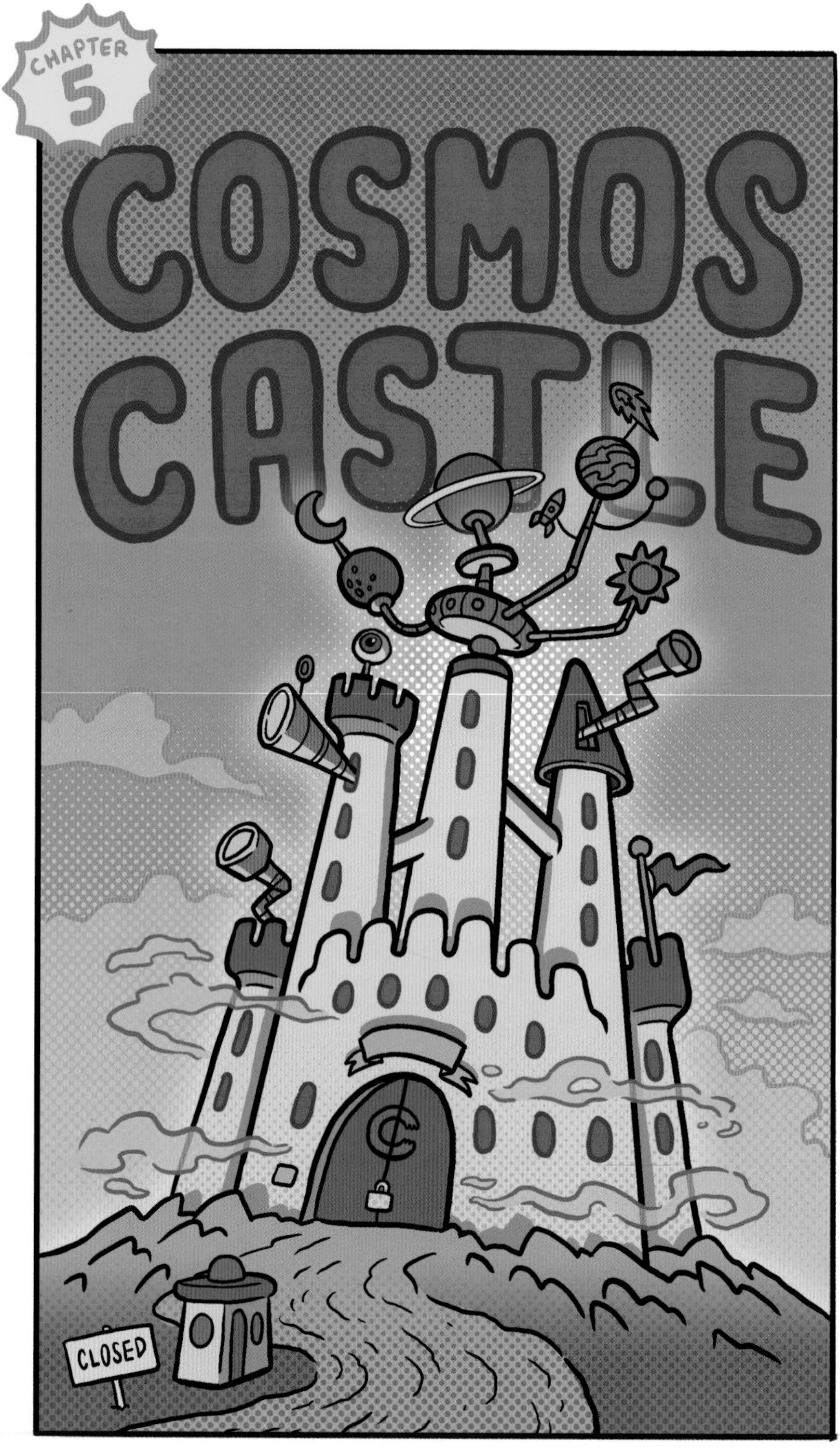
CHAPTER 5
COSMOS CASTLE
CLOSED

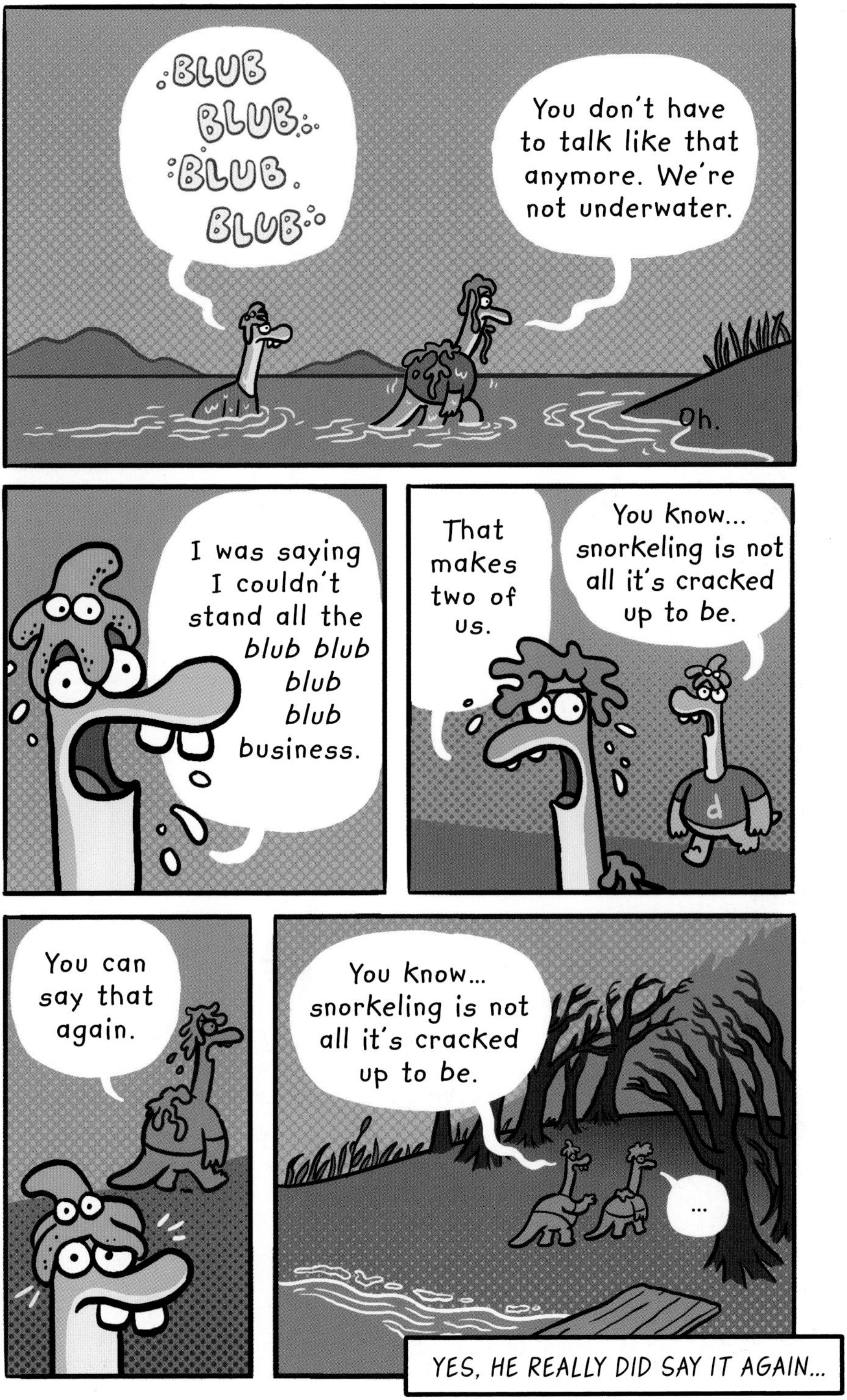
BLUB BLUB BLUB BLUB
You don't have to talk like that anymore. We're not underwater.
Oh.
I was saying I couldn't stand all the *blub blub blub blub* business.
That makes two of us.
You know... snorkeling is not all it's cracked up to be.
You can say that again.
You know... snorkeling is not all it's cracked up to be.
...
YES, HE REALLY DID SAY IT AGAIN...

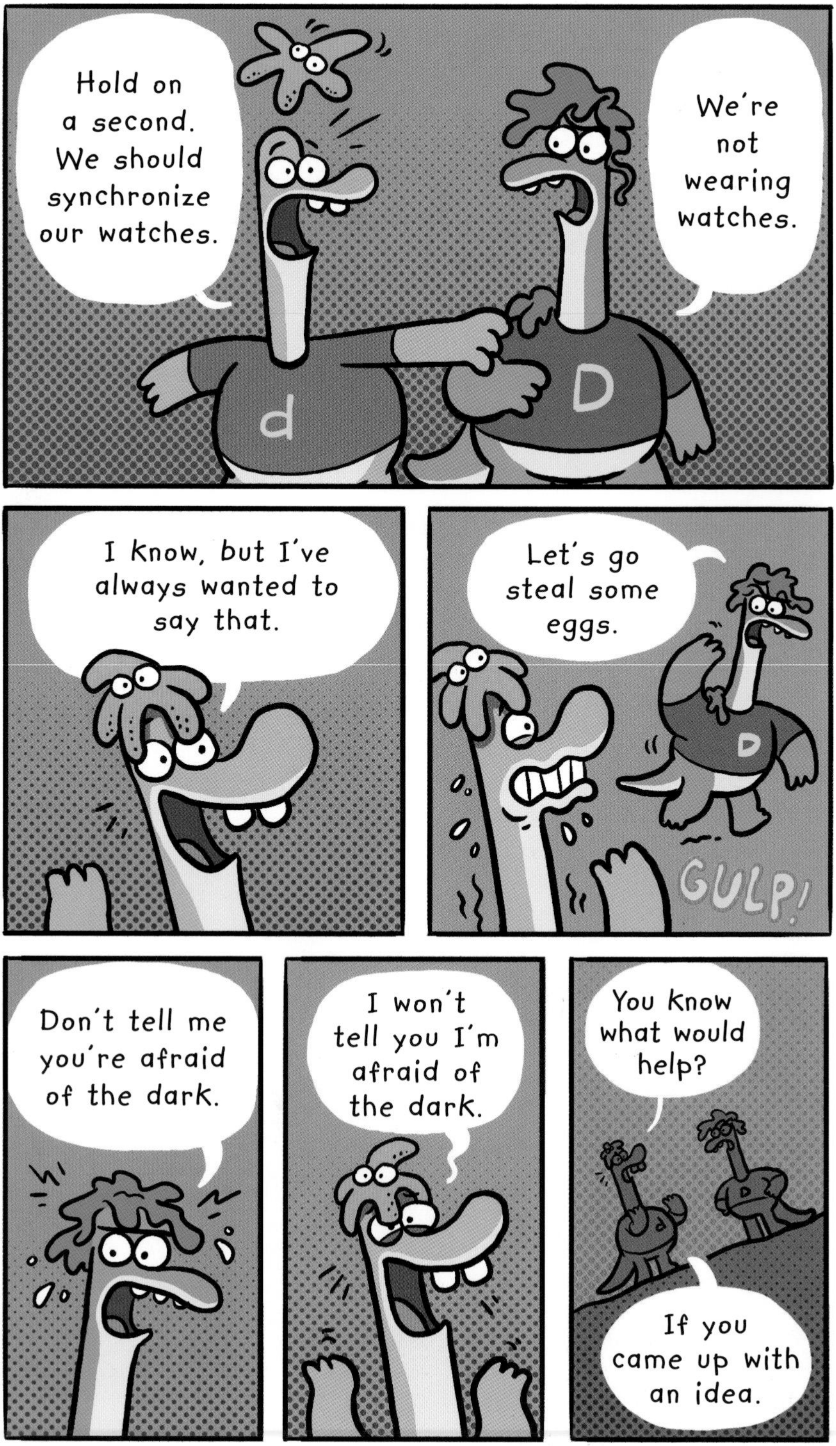
Hold on a second. We should synchronize our watches.
We're not wearing watches.
d
D
I know, but I've always wanted to say that.
Let's go steal some eggs.
D
GULP!
Don't tell me you're afraid of the dark.
I won't tell you I'm afraid of the dark.
You know what would help?
If you came up with an idea.

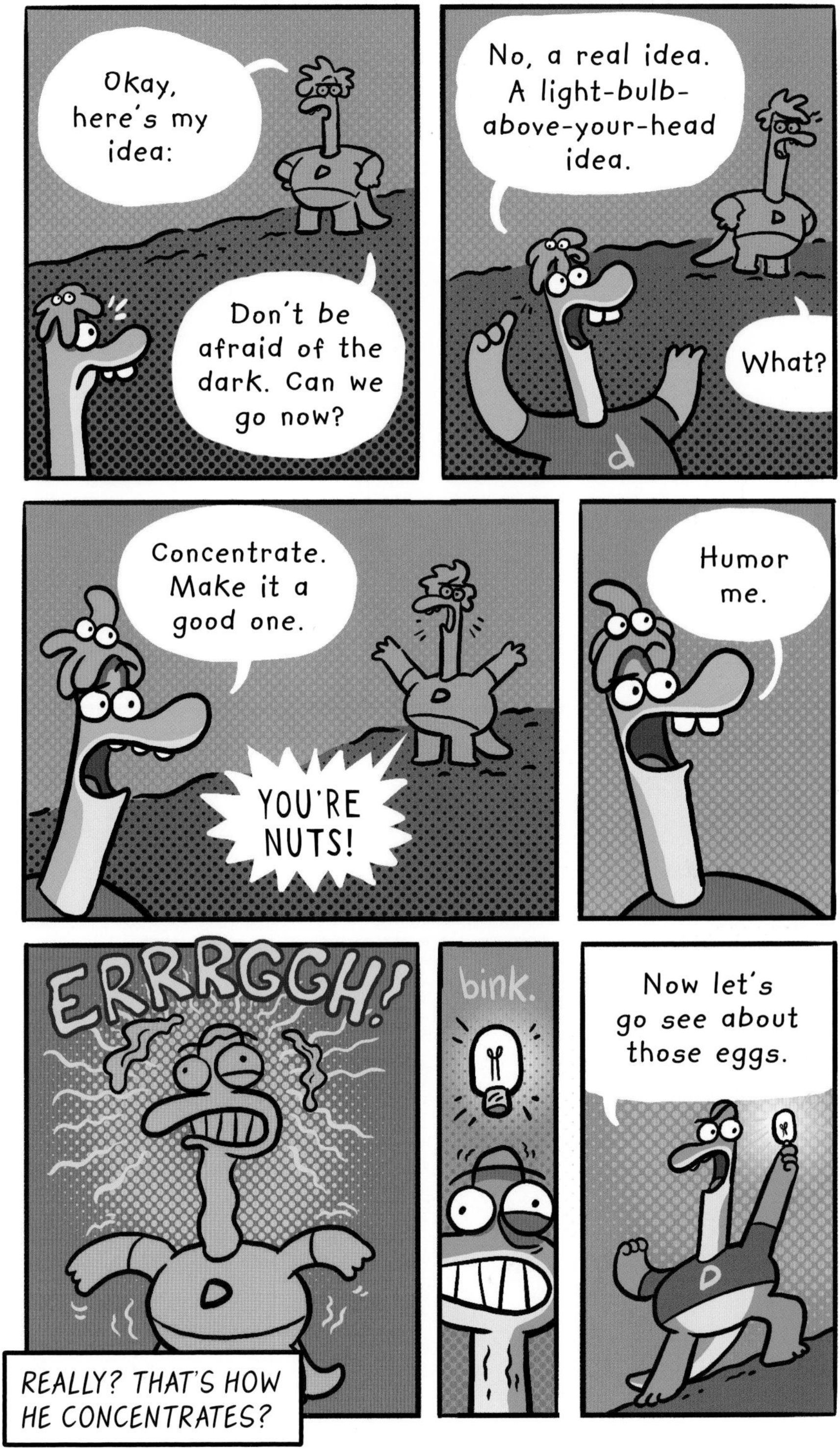
Okay, here's my idea:
Don't be afraid of the dark. Can we go now?
No, a real idea. A light-bulb-above-your-head idea.
What?
Concentrate. Make it a good one.
YOU'RE NUTS!
Humor me.
ERRRGGH!
REALLY? THAT'S HOW HE CONCENTRATES?
bink.
Now let's go see about those eggs.

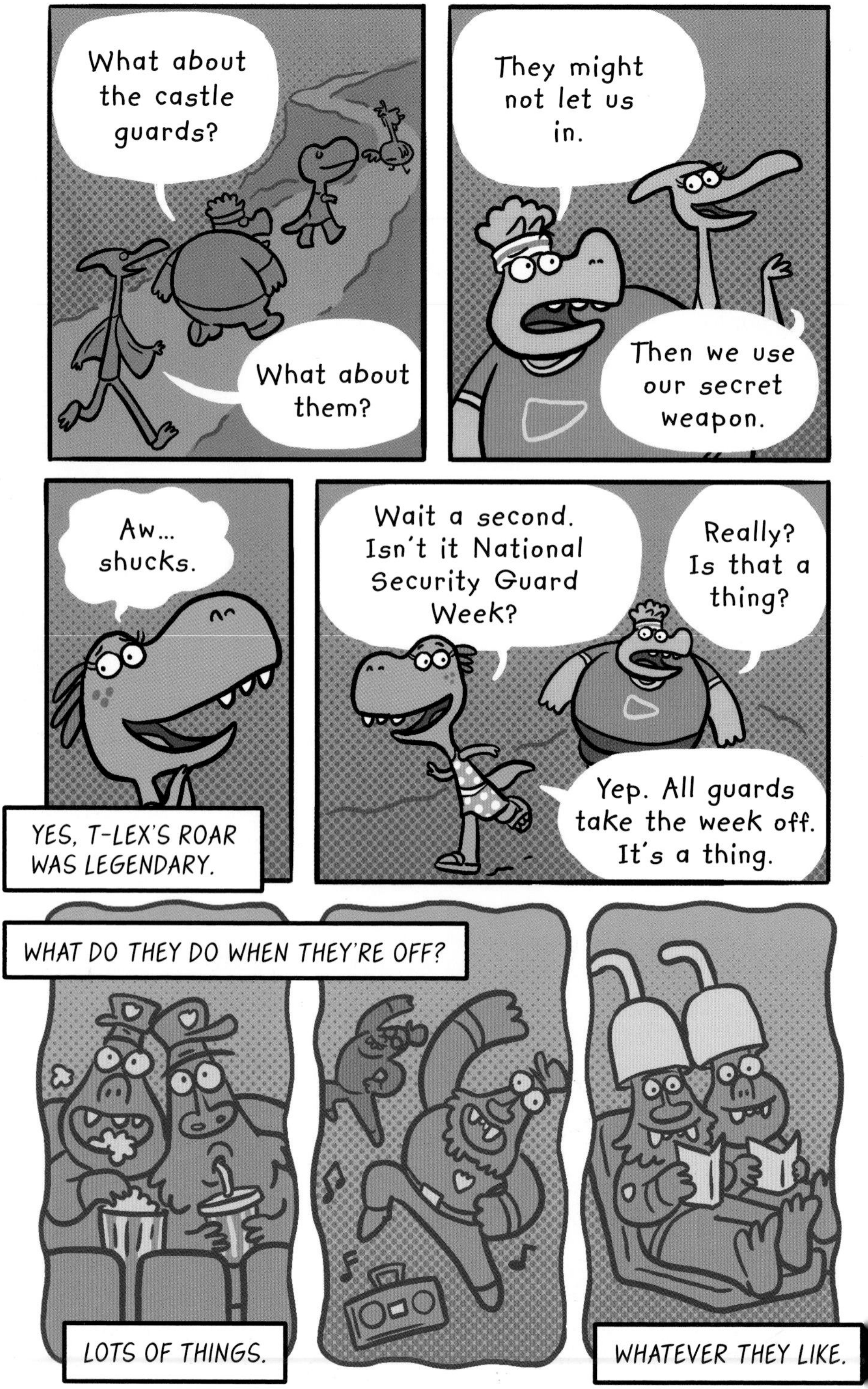
What about the castle guards?
What about them?
They might not let us in.
Then we use our secret weapon.
Aw... shucks.
YES, T-LEX'S ROAR WAS LEGENDARY.
Wait a second. Isn't it National Security Guard Week?
Really? Is that a thing?
Yep. All guards take the week off. It's a thing.
WHAT DO THEY DO WHEN THEY'RE OFF?
LOTS OF THINGS.
WHATEVER THEY LIKE.

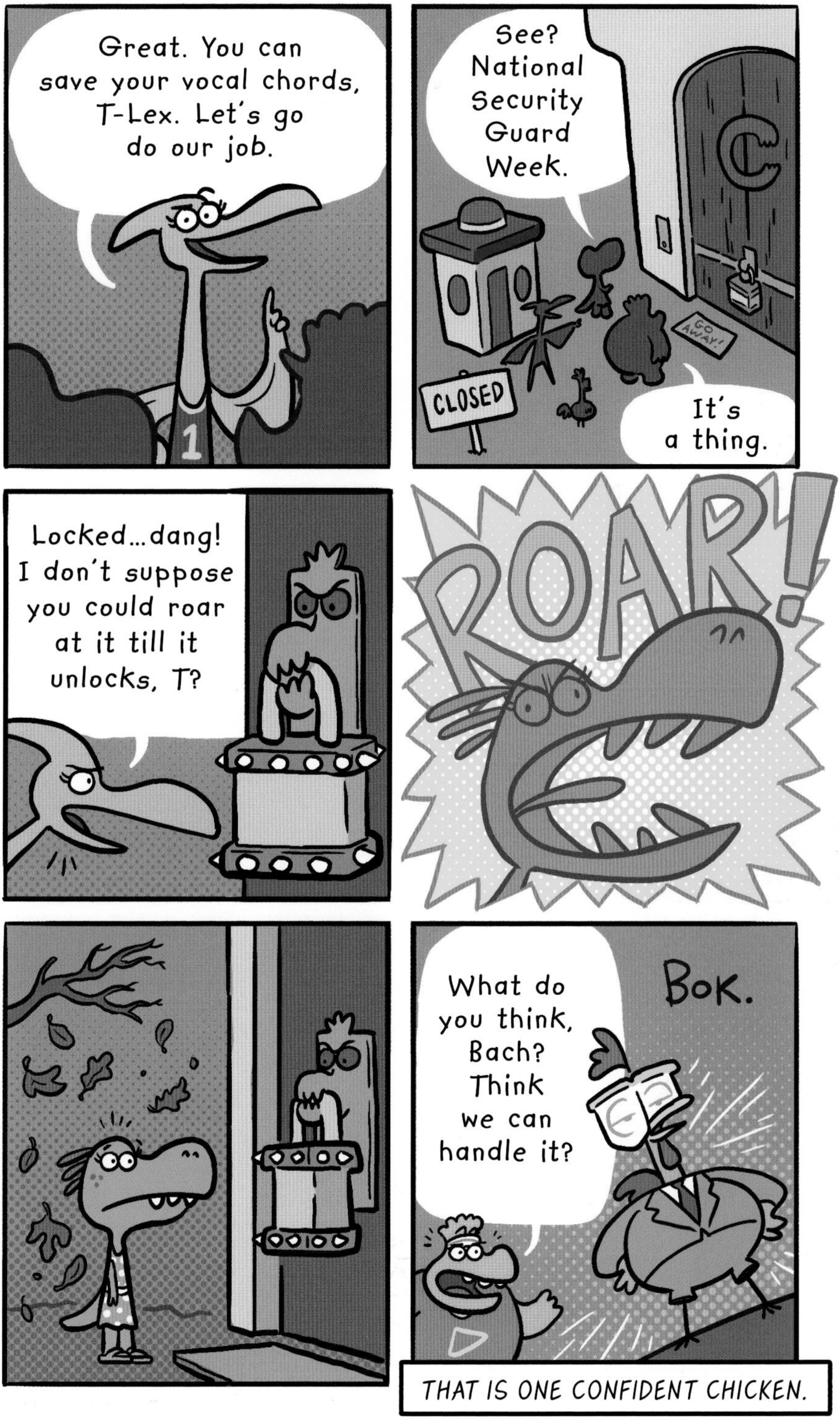
Great. You can save your vocal chords, T-Lex. Let's go do our job.
See? National Security Guard Week.
GO AWAY!
CLOSED
It's a thing.
Locked...dang! I don't suppose you could roar at it till it unlocks, T?
ROAR!
What do you think, Bach? Think we can handle it?
BOK.
THAT IS ONE CONFIDENT CHICKEN.

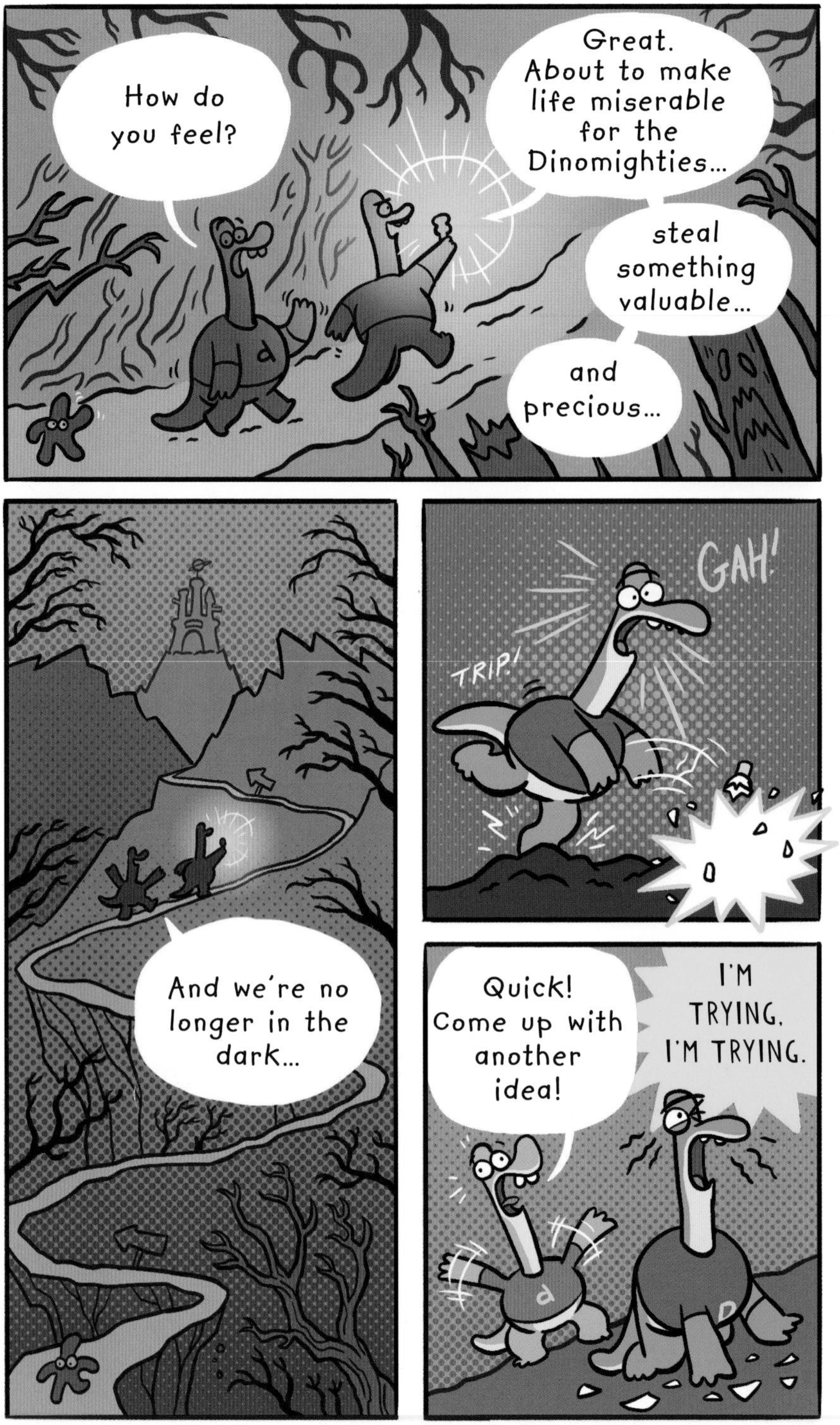
How do you feel?
Great. About to make life miserable for the Dinomighties...
steal something valuable...
and precious...
And we're no longer in the dark...
TRIP!
GAH!
Quick! Come up with another idea!
I'M TRYING. I'M TRYING.

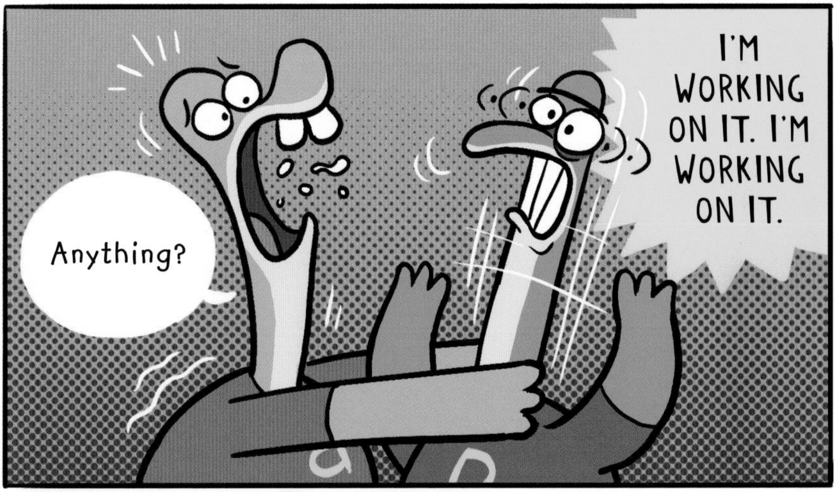
Anything?
I'M WORKING ON IT. I'M WORKING ON IT.

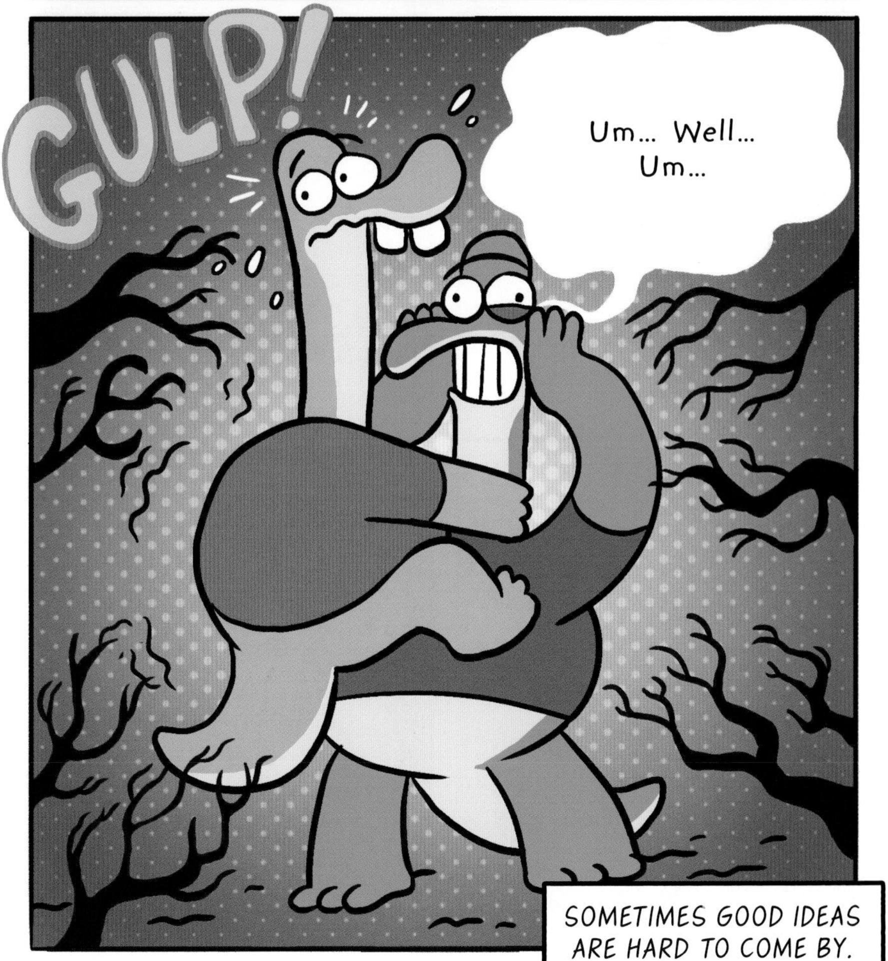
GULP!
Um... Well... Um...
SOMETIMES GOOD IDEAS ARE HARD TO COME BY.

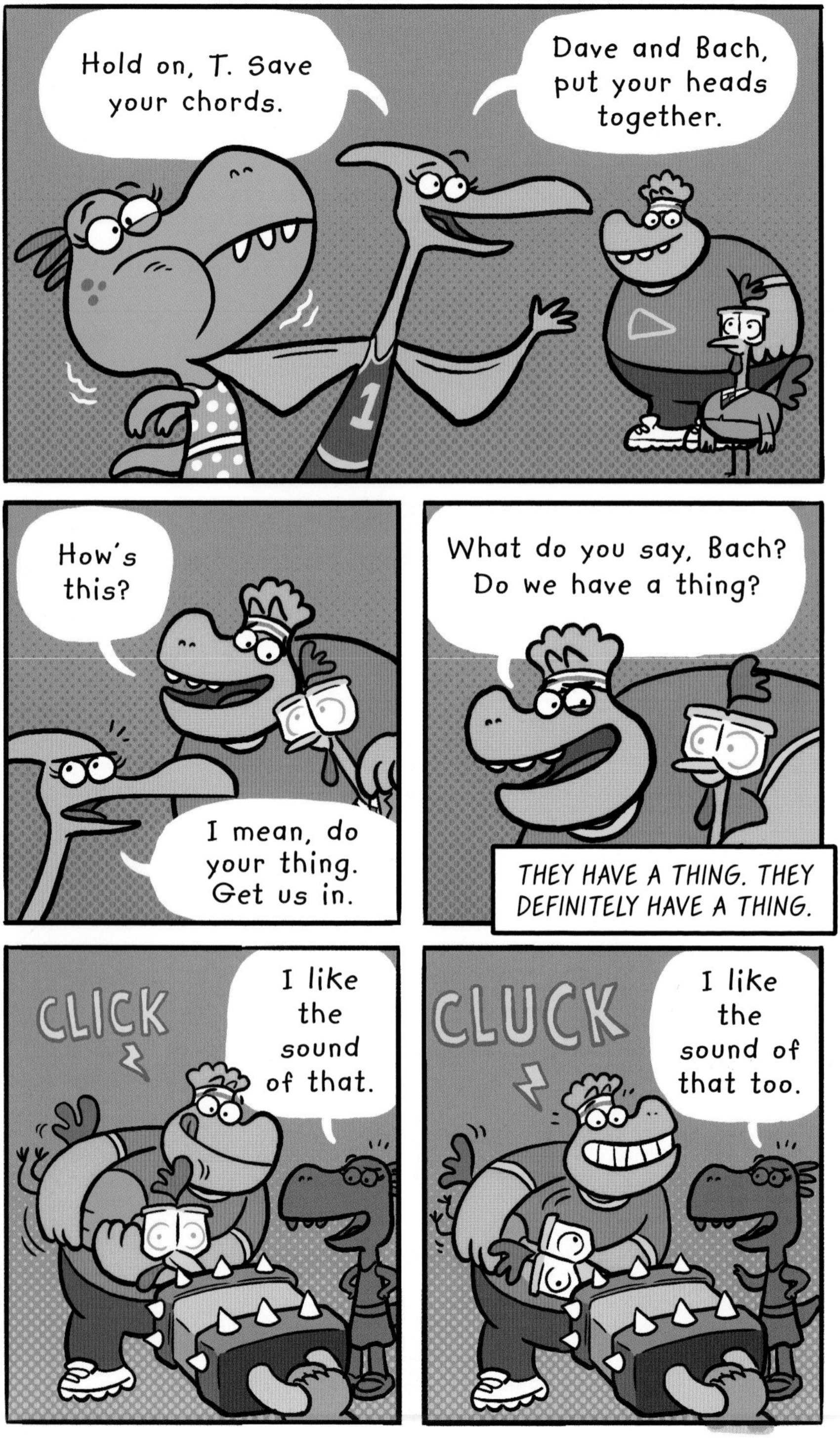
Hold on, T. Save your chords.
Dave and Bach, put your heads together.
How's this?
I mean, do your thing. Get us in.
What do you say, Bach? Do we have a thing?
THEY HAVE A THING. THEY DEFINITELY HAVE A THING.
CLICK
I like the sound of that.
CLUCK
I like the sound of that too.

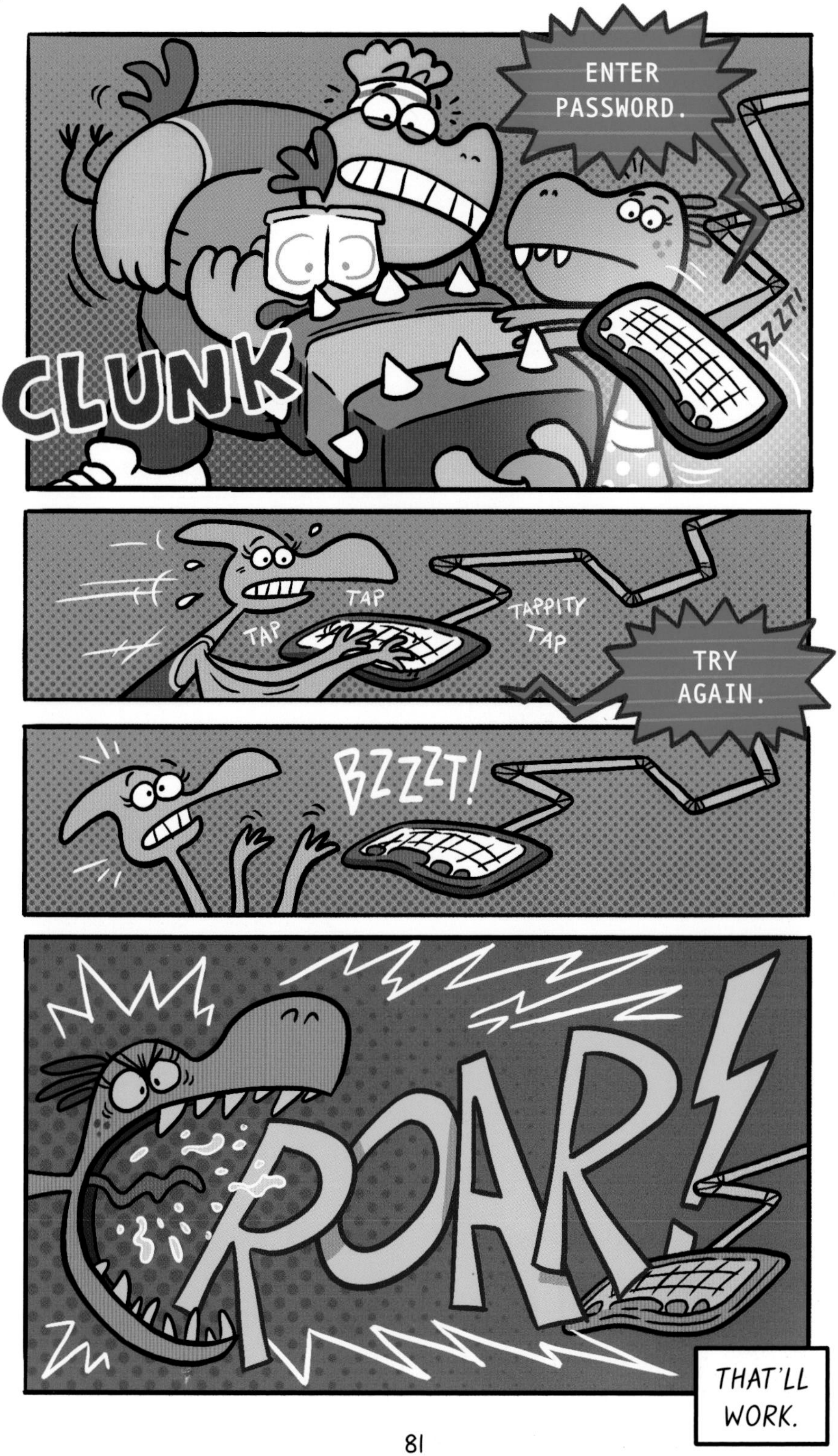
ENTER PASSWORD.
CLUNK
BZZT!
TAP
TAP
TAPPITY TAP
TRY AGAIN.
BZZZT!
ROAR!
THAT'LL WORK.

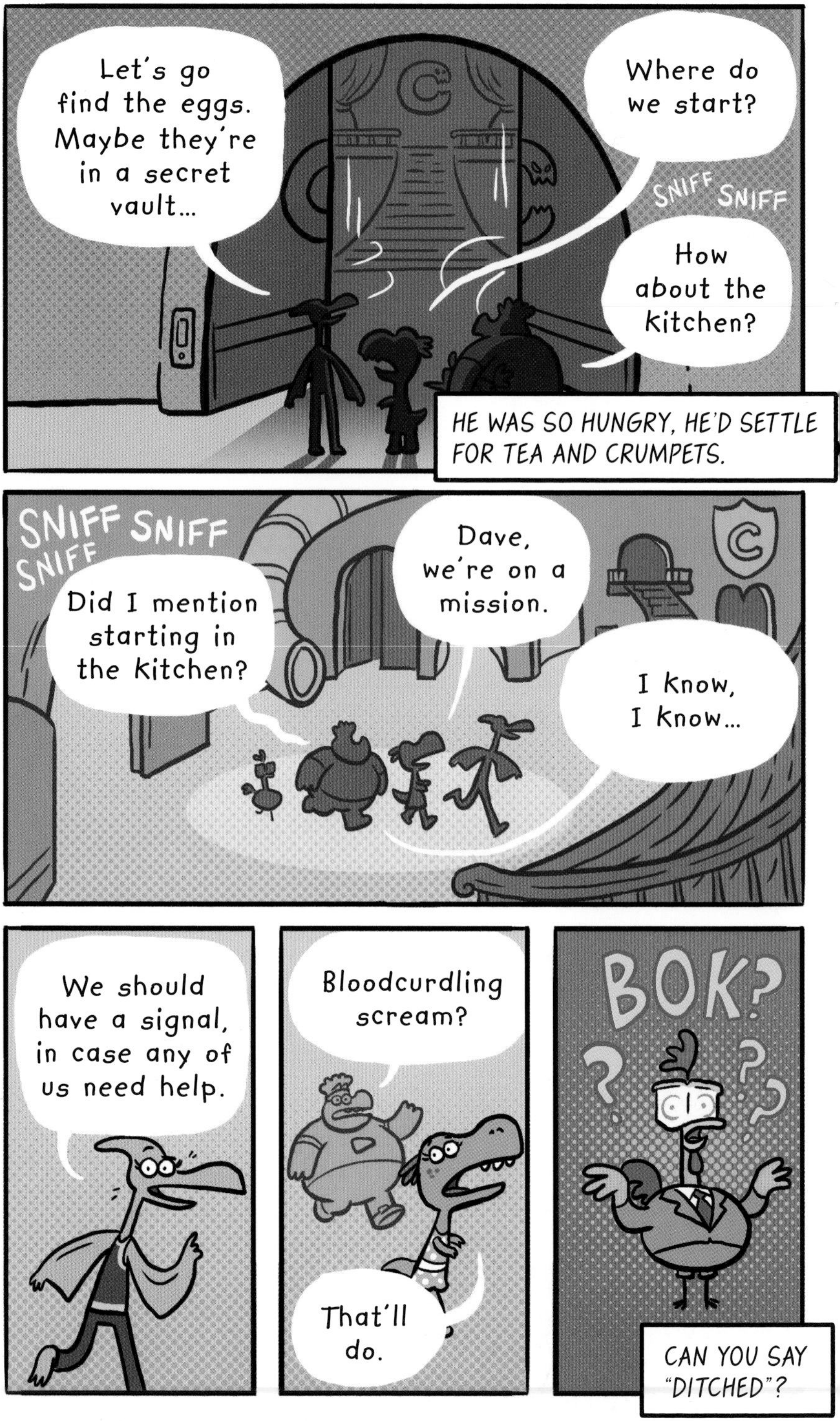
Let's go find the eggs. Maybe they're in a secret vault...
Where do we start?
SNIFF SNIFF
How about the kitchen?
HE WAS SO HUNGRY, HE'D SETTLE FOR TEA AND CRUMPETS.
SNIFF SNIFF SNIFF
Did I mention starting in the kitchen?
Dave, we're on a mission.
I know, I know...
We should have a signal, in case any of us need help.
Bloodcurdling scream?
That'll do.
BOK?
CAN YOU SAY "DITCHED"?

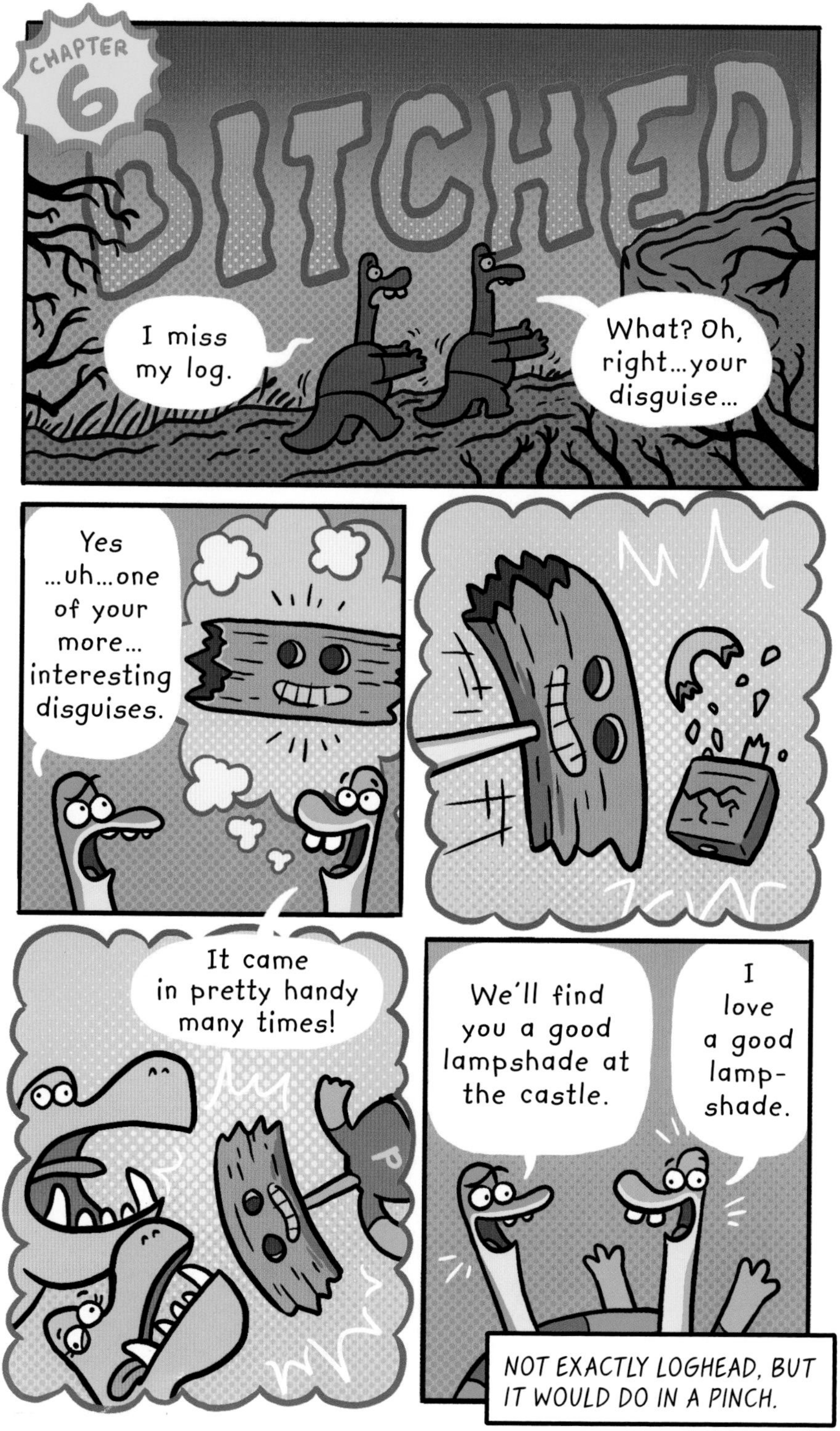
CHAPTER 6
DITCHED
I miss my log.
What? Oh, right...your disguise...
Yes ...uh...one of your more... interesting disguises.
It came in pretty handy many times!
P
We'll find you a good lampshade at the castle.
I love a good lamp-shade.
NOT EXACTLY LOGHEAD, BUT IT WOULD DO IN A PINCH.

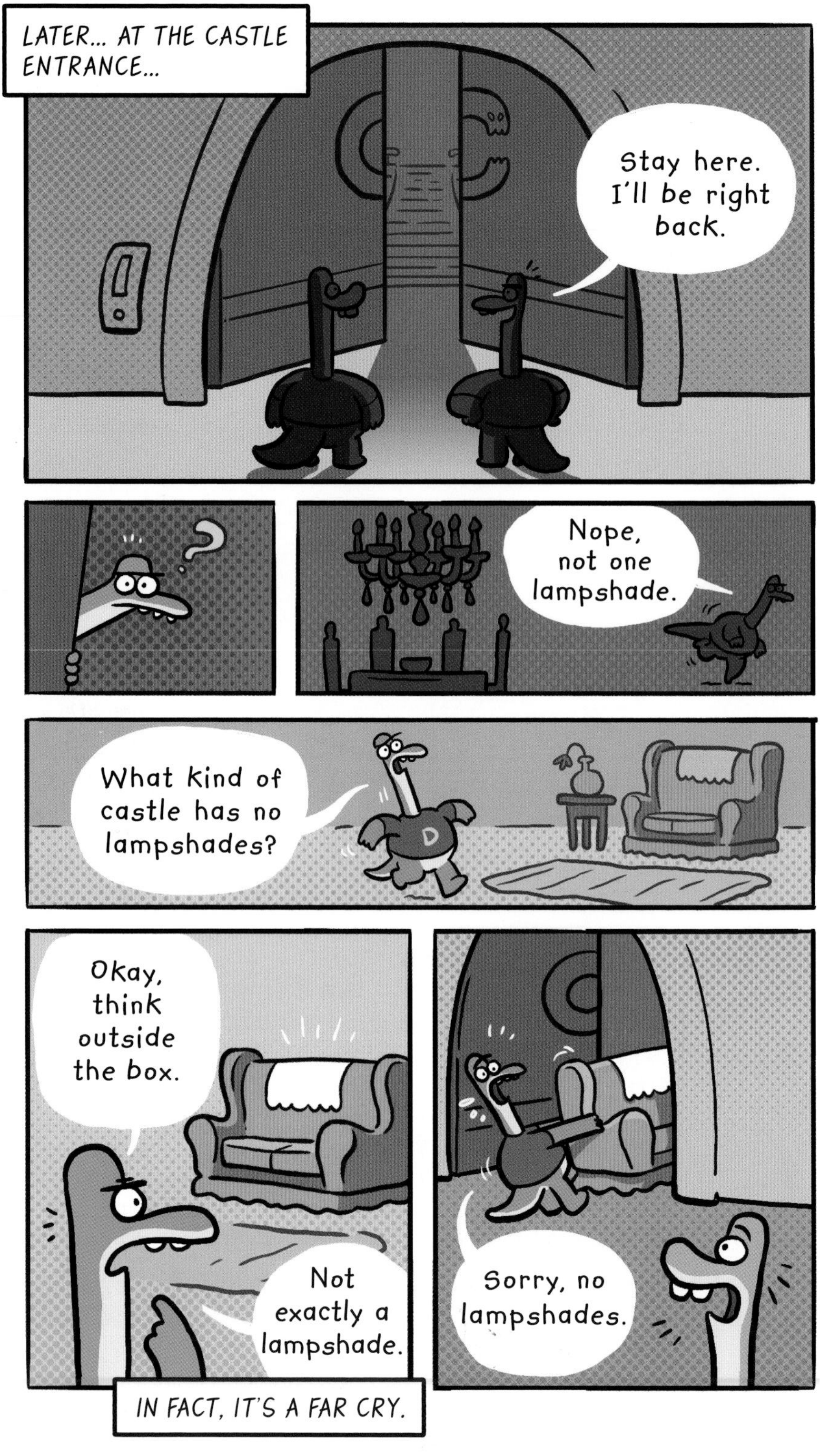
LATER... AT THE CASTLE ENTRANCE...
Stay here. I'll be right back.
Nope, not one lampshade.
What kind of castle has no lampshades?
Okay, think outside the box.
Not exactly a lampshade.
IN FACT, IT'S A FAR CRY.
Sorry, no lampshades.

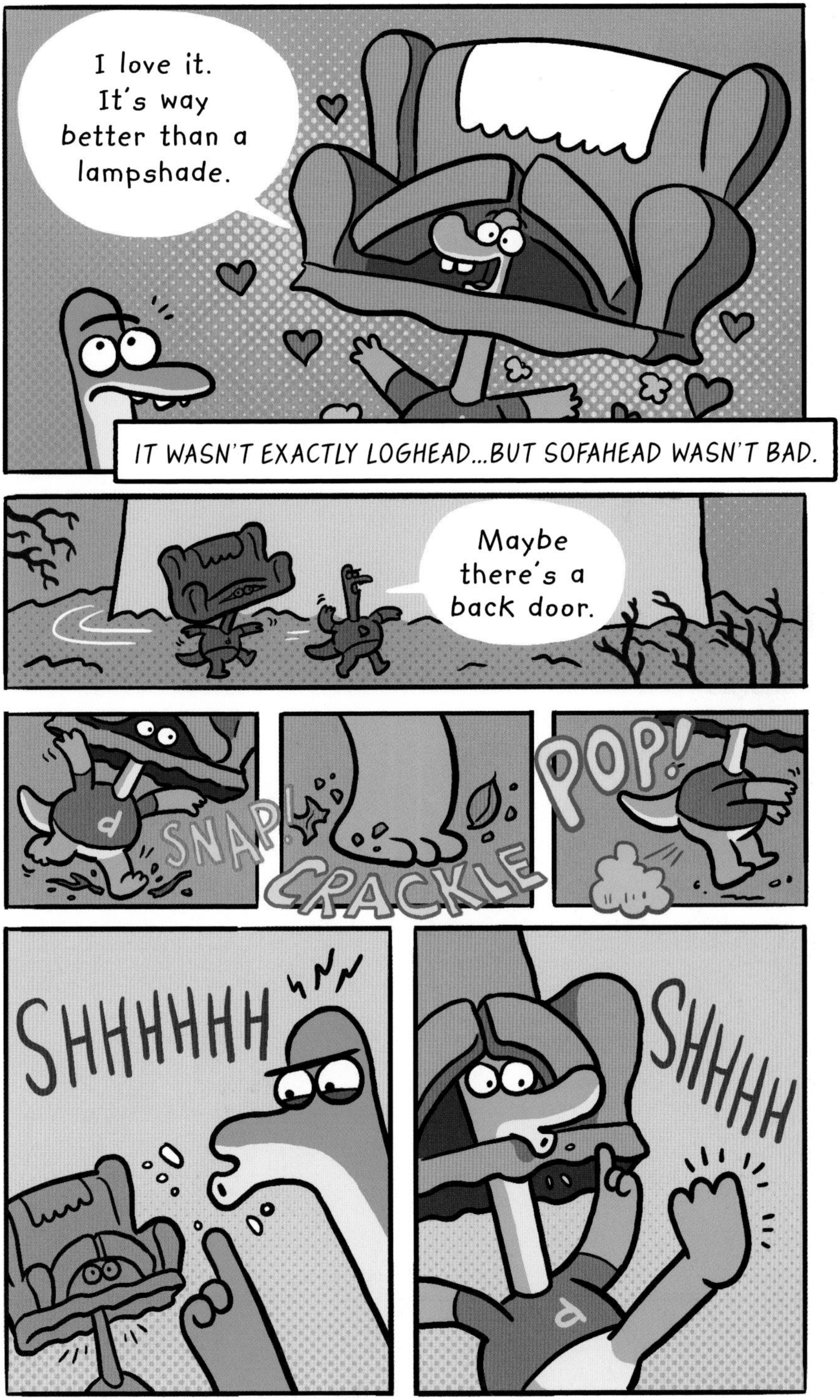
I love it.
It's way
better than a
lampshade.
IT WASN'T EXACTLY LOGHEAD...BUT SOFAHEAD WASN'T BAD.
Maybe
there's a
back door.
SNAP!
CRACKLE
POP!
SHHHHHH
SHHHH

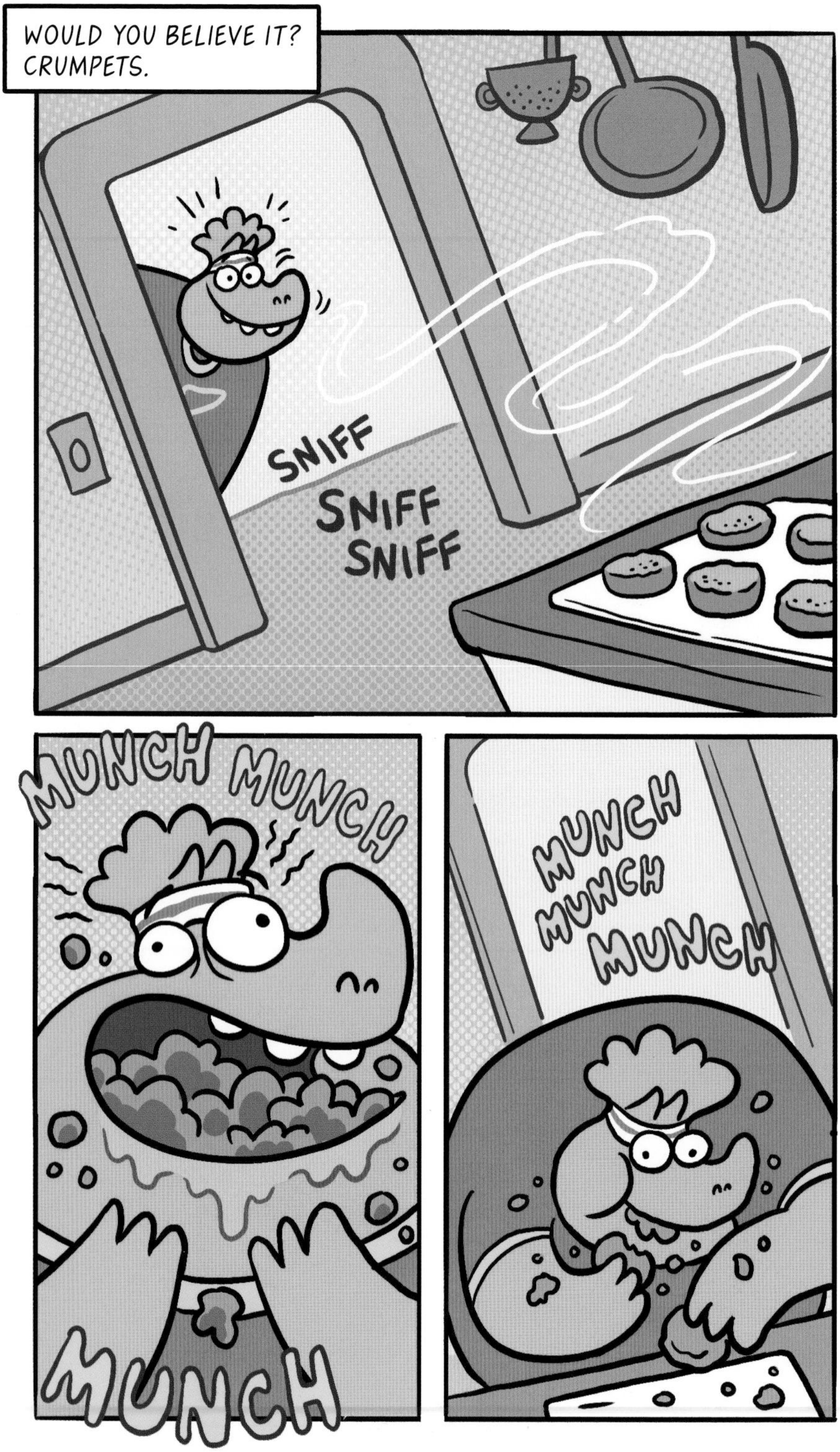
WOULD YOU BELIEVE IT? CRUMPETS.
SNIFF
SNIFF
SNIFF
MUNCH MUNCH
MUNCH
MUNCH
MUNCH
MUNCH

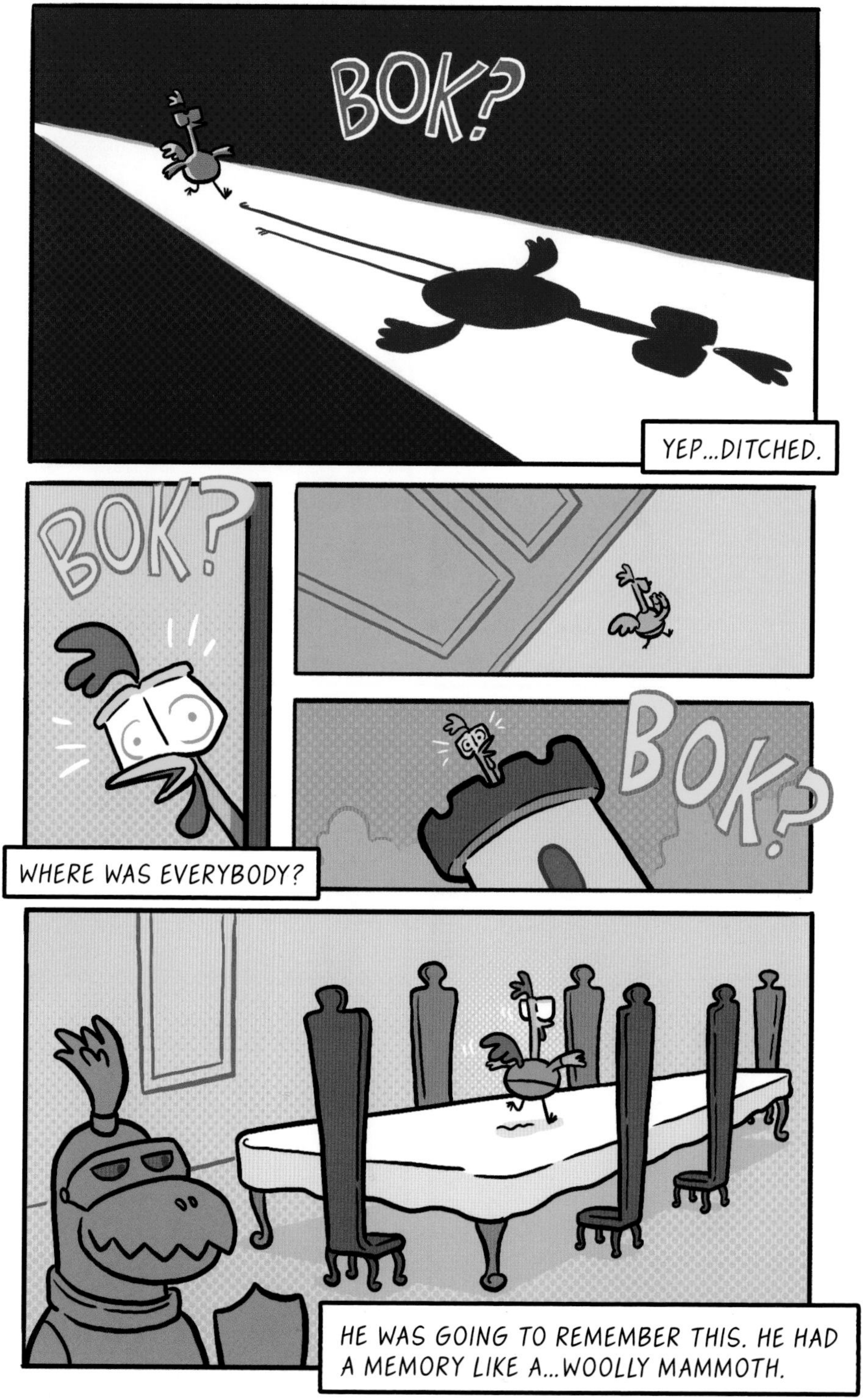
BOK?
YEP...DITCHED.
BOK?
BOK?
WHERE WAS EVERYBODY?
HE WAS GOING TO REMEMBER THIS. HE HAD A MEMORY LIKE A...WOOLLY MAMMOTH.

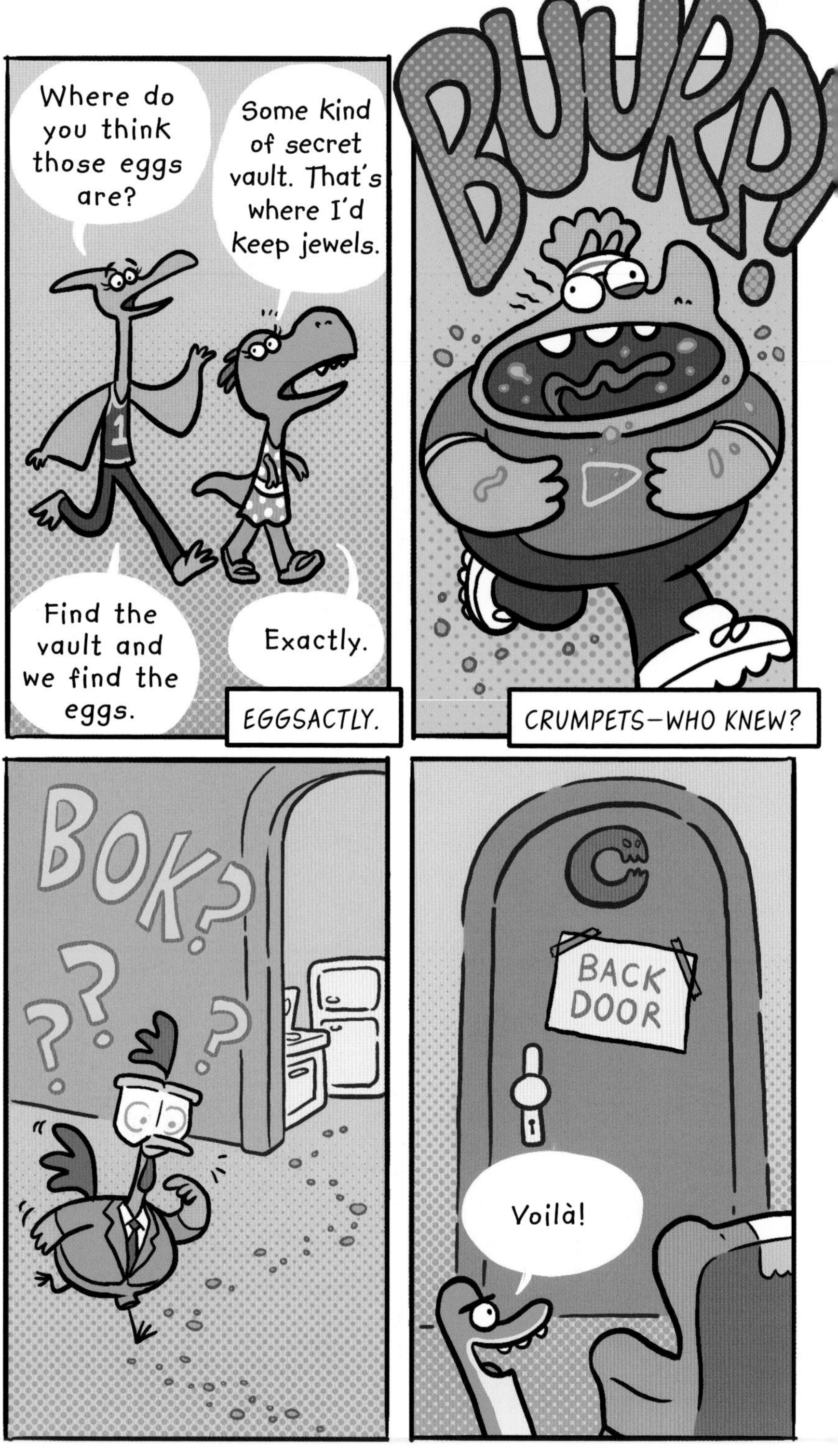
Where do you think those eggs are?
Some kind of secret vault. That's where I'd keep jewels.
Find the vault and we find the eggs.
Exactly.
EGGSACTLY.
BUURP!
CRUMPETS—WHO KNEW?
BOK?
Voilà!
BACK DOOR

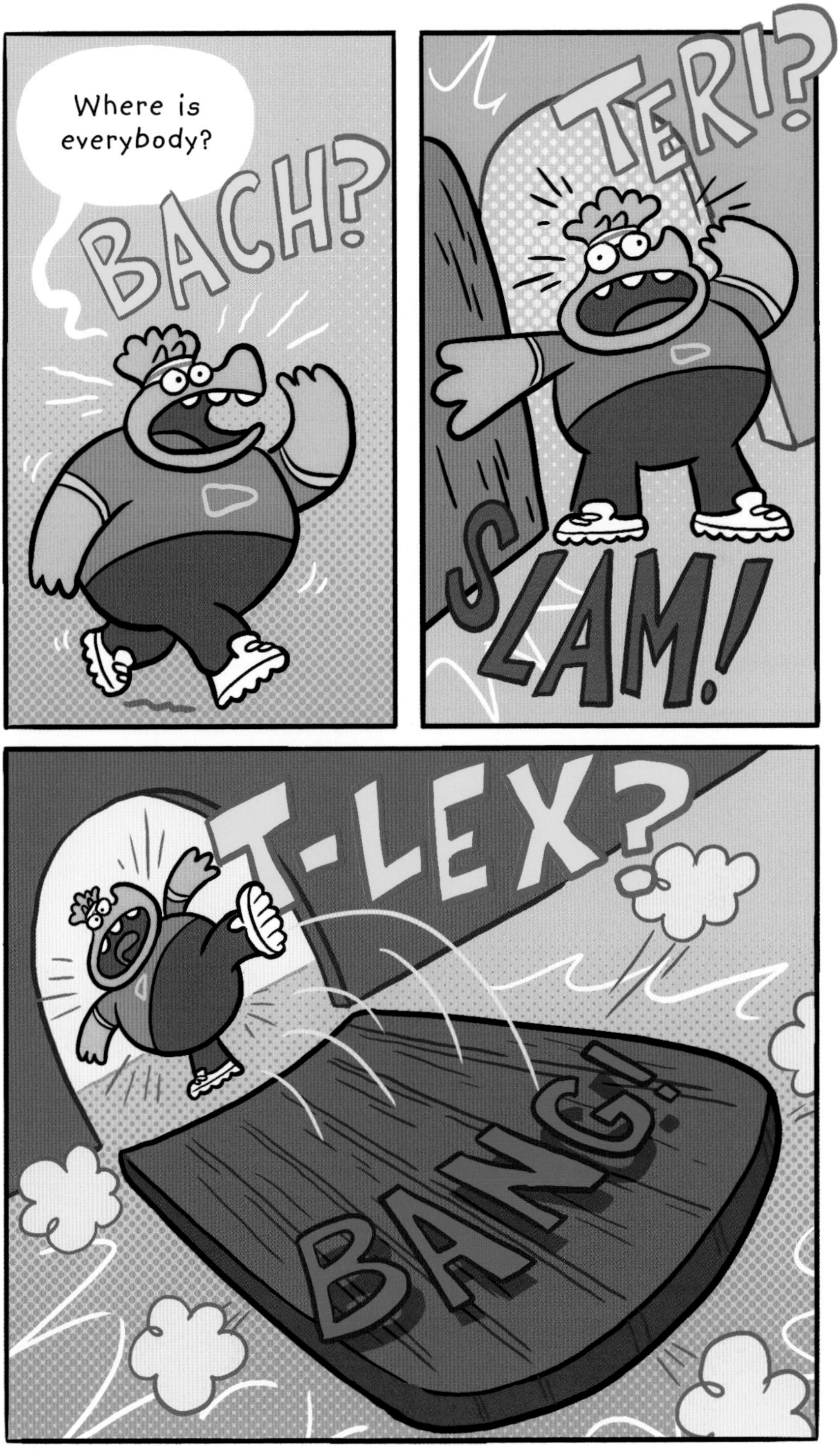
Where is everybody?
BACH?
TERI?
SLAM!
T-LEX?
BANG!

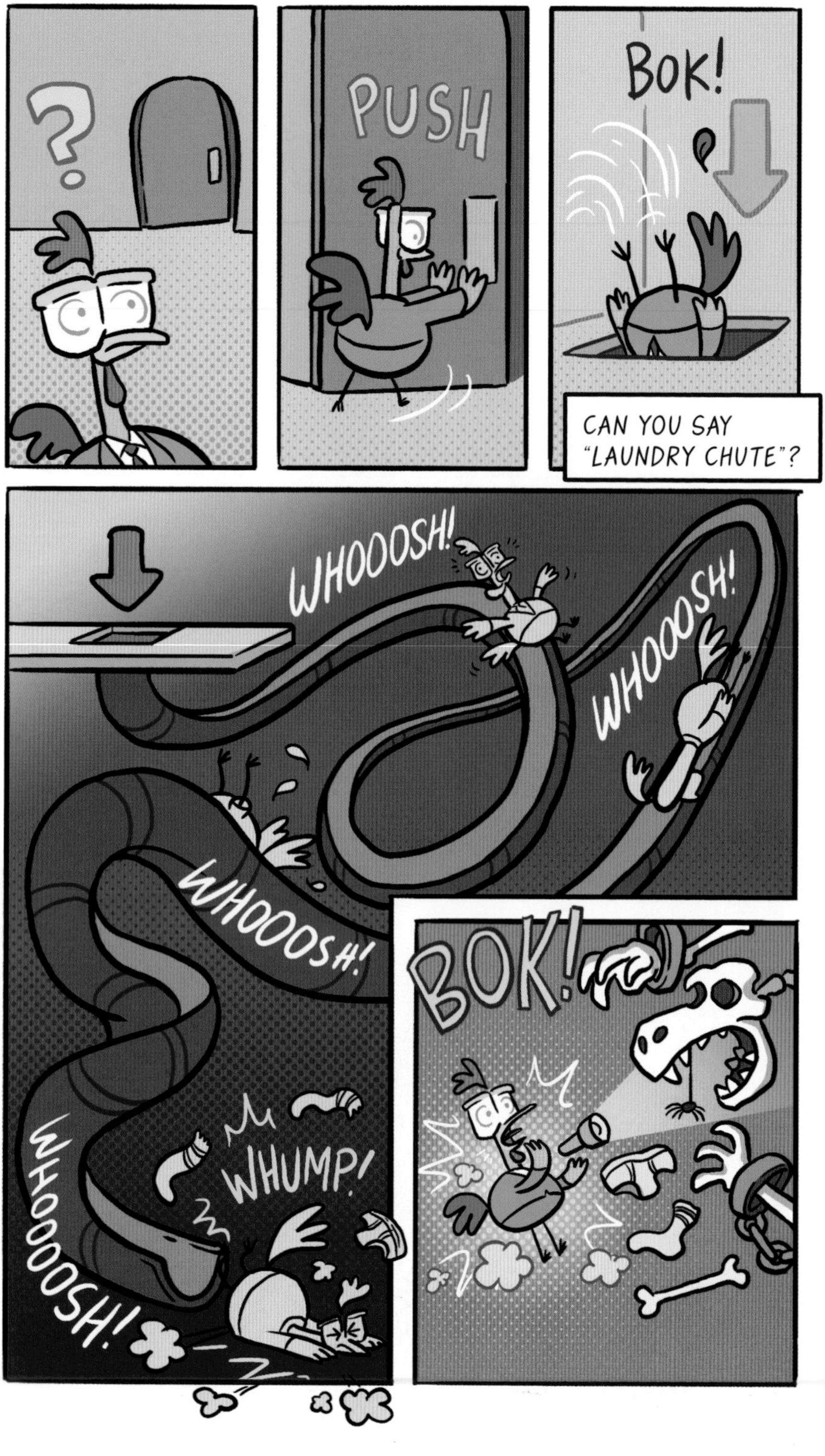
?
PUSH
BOK!
CAN YOU SAY "LAUNDRY CHUTE"?
WHOOOSH!
WHOOOSH!
WHOOOOSH!
WHOOOOOSH!
WHUMP!
BOK!

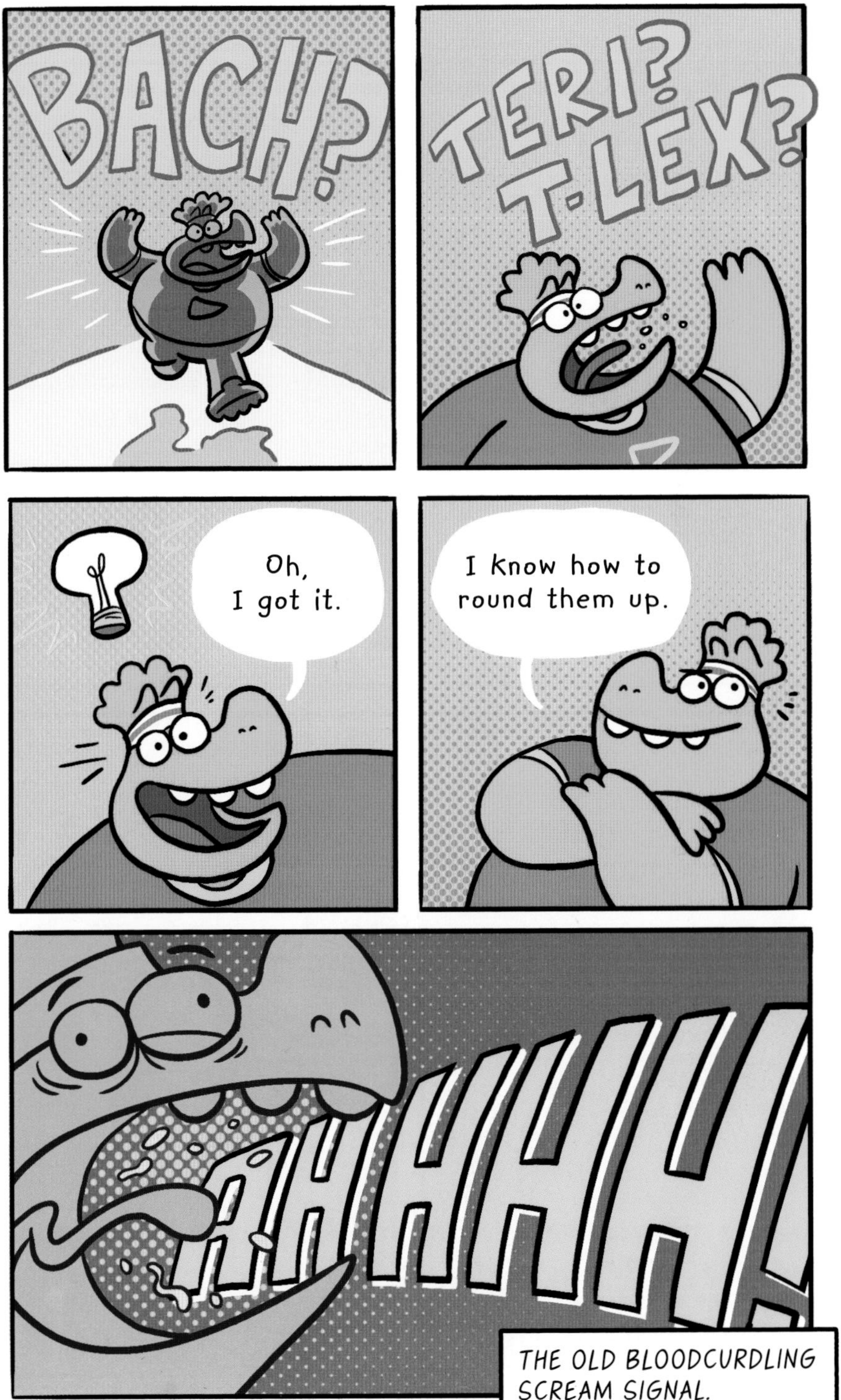
BACH?
TERI? T-LEX?
Oh, I got it.
I know how to round them up.
AHHHHHH!
THE OLD BLOODCURDLING SCREAM SIGNAL.

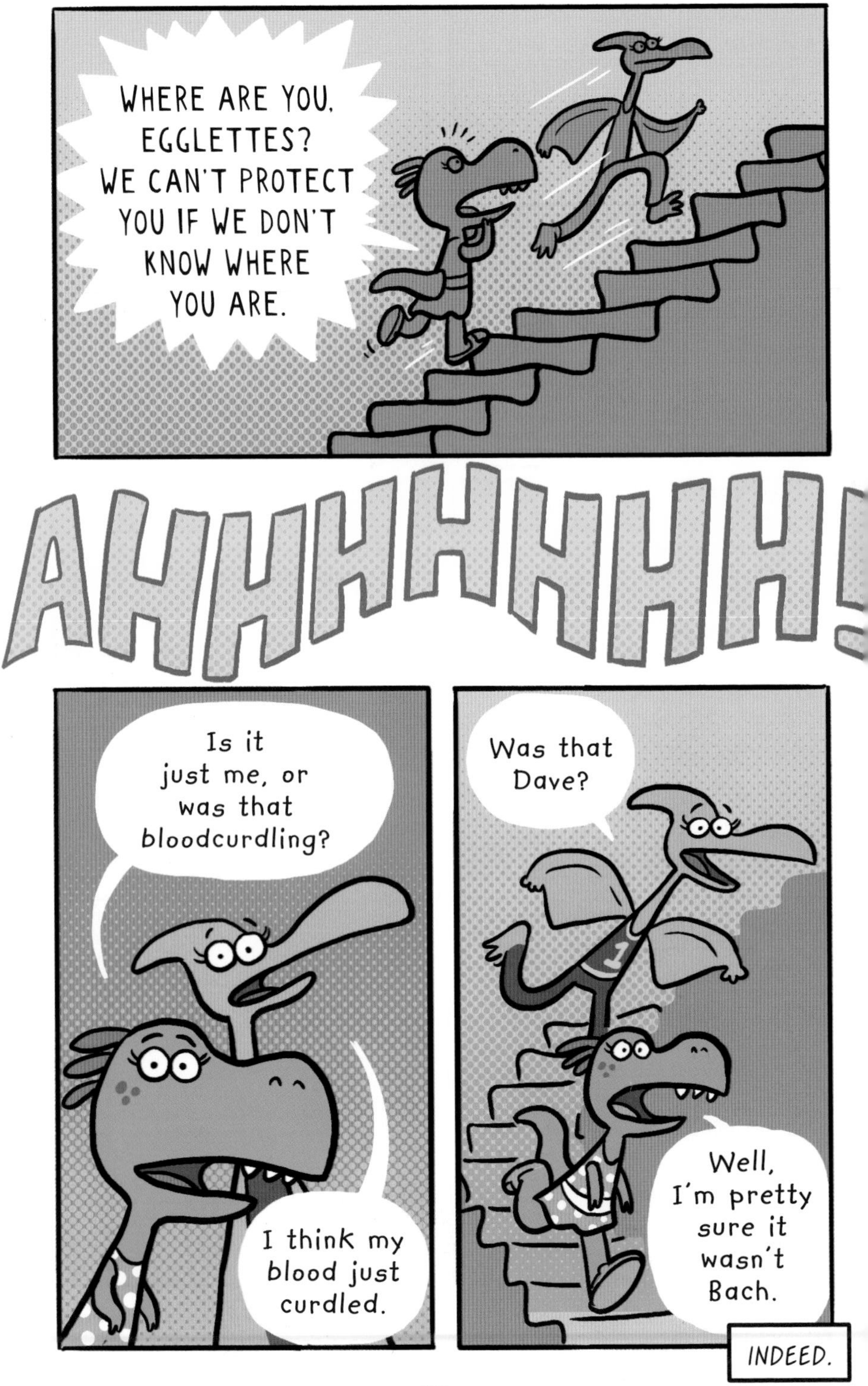
WHERE ARE YOU, EGGLETTES? WE CAN'T PROTECT YOU IF WE DON'T KNOW WHERE YOU ARE.
AHHHHHHHH!
Is it just me, or was that bloodcurdling?
I think my blood just curdled.
Was that Dave?
Well, I'm pretty sure it wasn't Bach.
INDEED.

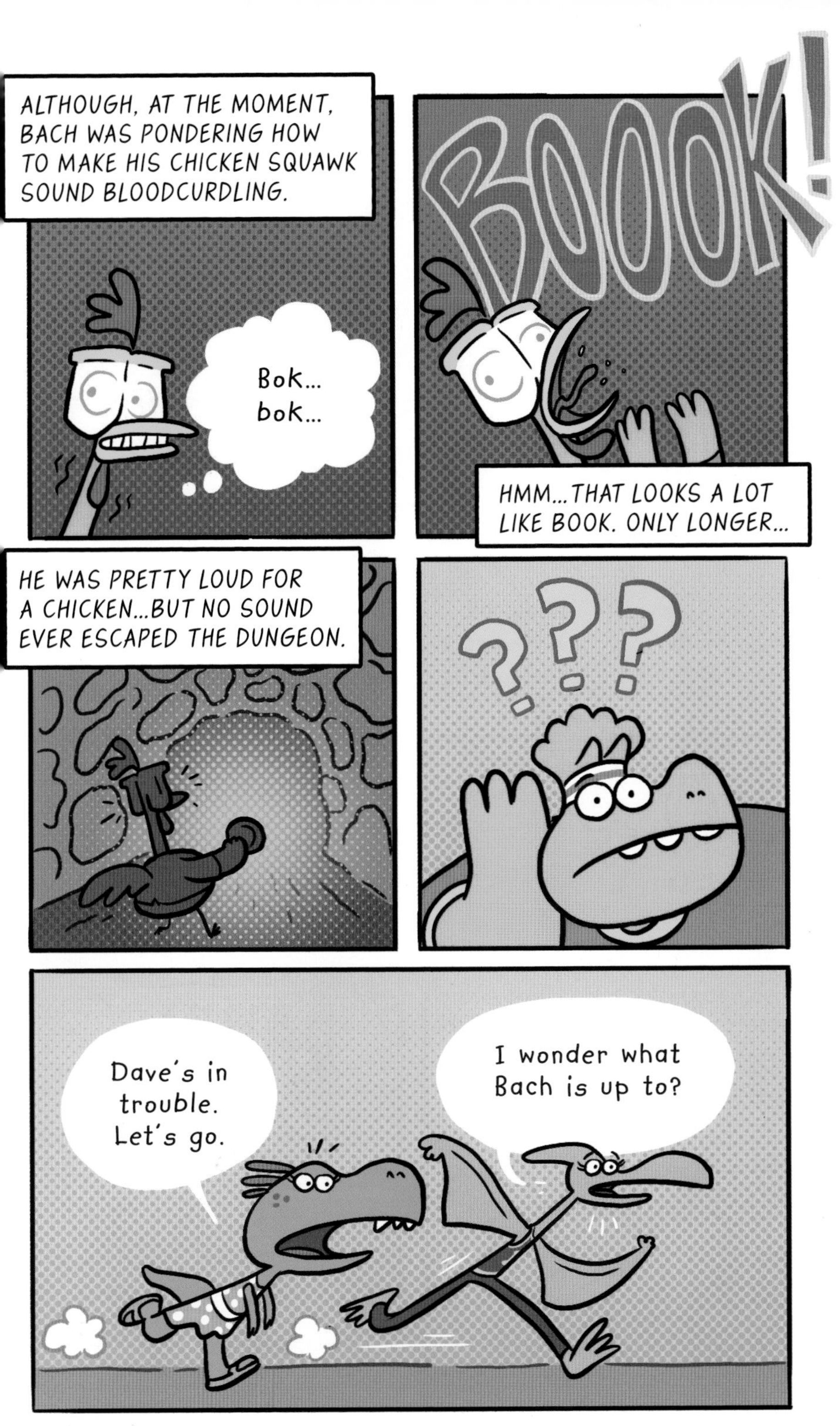
ALTHOUGH, AT THE MOMENT, BACH WAS PONDERING HOW TO MAKE HIS CHICKEN SQUAWK SOUND BLOODCURDLING.
Bok... bok...
BOOOK!
HMM...THAT LOOKS A LOT LIKE BOOK. ONLY LONGER...
HE WAS PRETTY LOUD FOR A CHICKEN...BUT NO SOUND EVER ESCAPED THE DUNGEON.
???
Dave's in trouble. Let's go.
I wonder what Bach is up to?

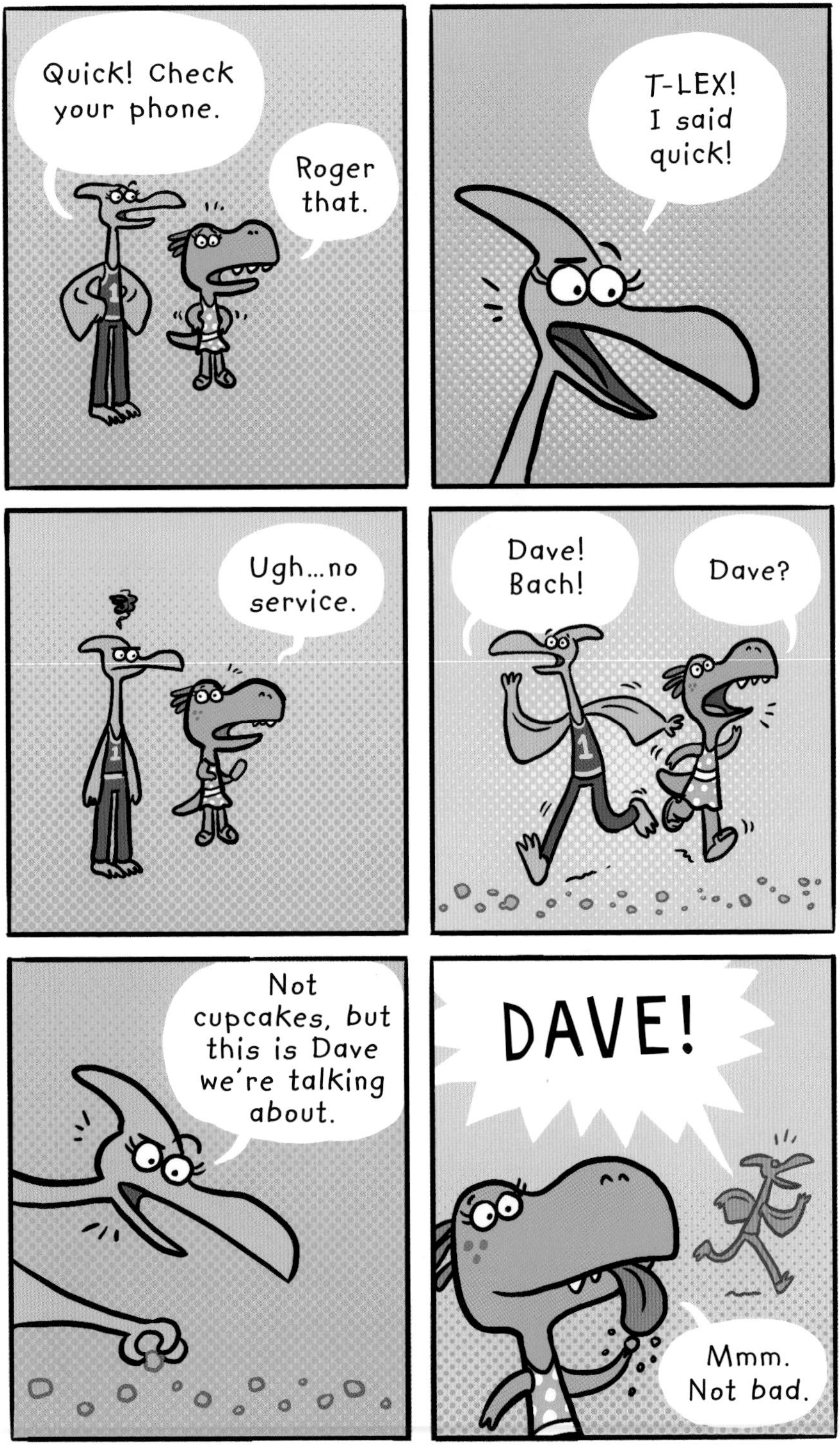
Quick! Check your phone.
Roger that.
T-LEX! I said quick!
Ugh...no service.
Dave! Bach!
Dave?
Not cupcakes, but this is Dave we're talking about.
DAVE!
Mmm. Not bad.

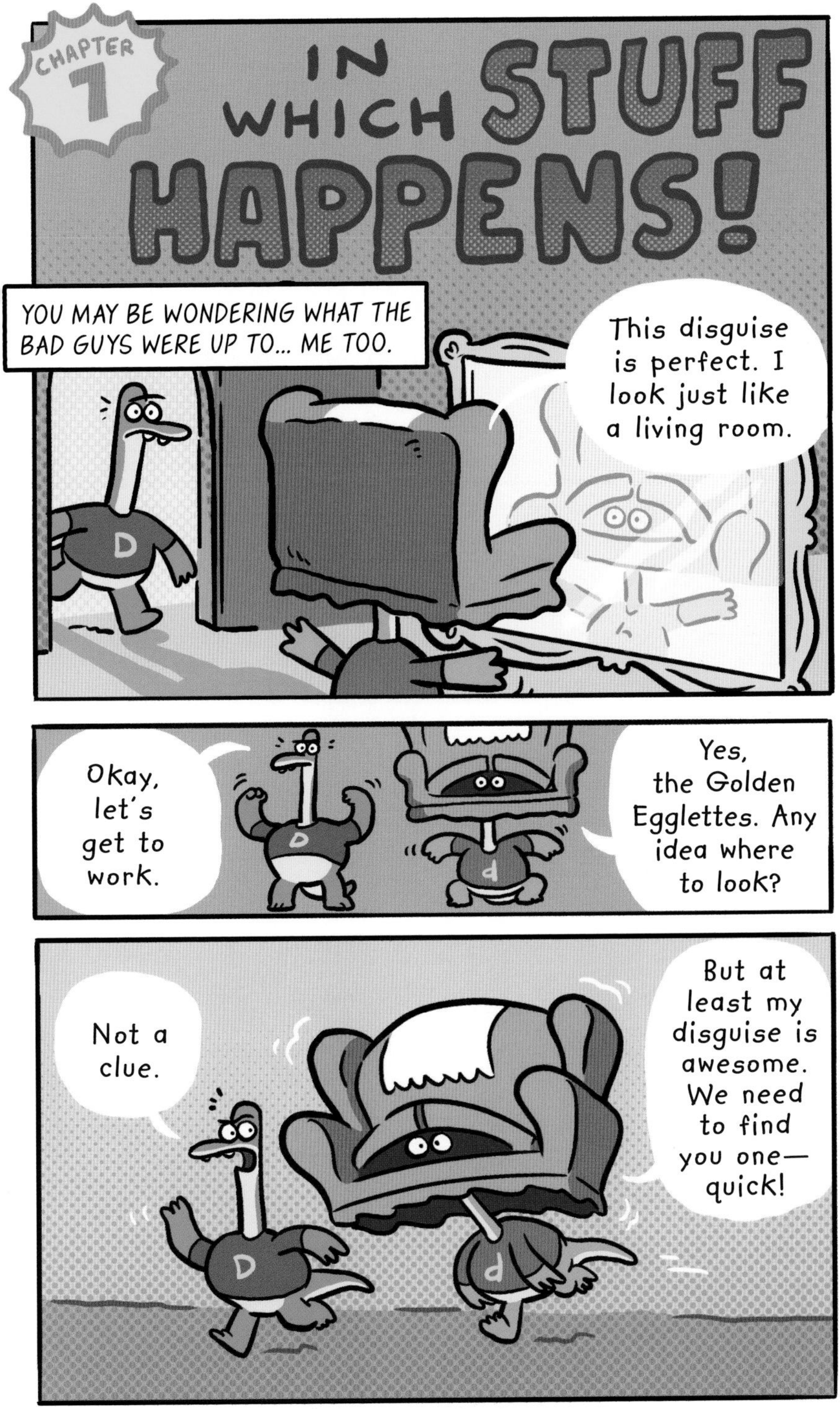
CHAPTER 7
IN WHICH STUFF HAPPENS!
YOU MAY BE WONDERING WHAT THE BAD GUYS WERE UP TO... ME TOO.
This disguise is perfect. I look just like a living room.
Okay, let's get to work.
Yes, the Golden Egglettes. Any idea where to look?
Not a clue.
But at least my disguise is awesome. We need to find you one—quick!

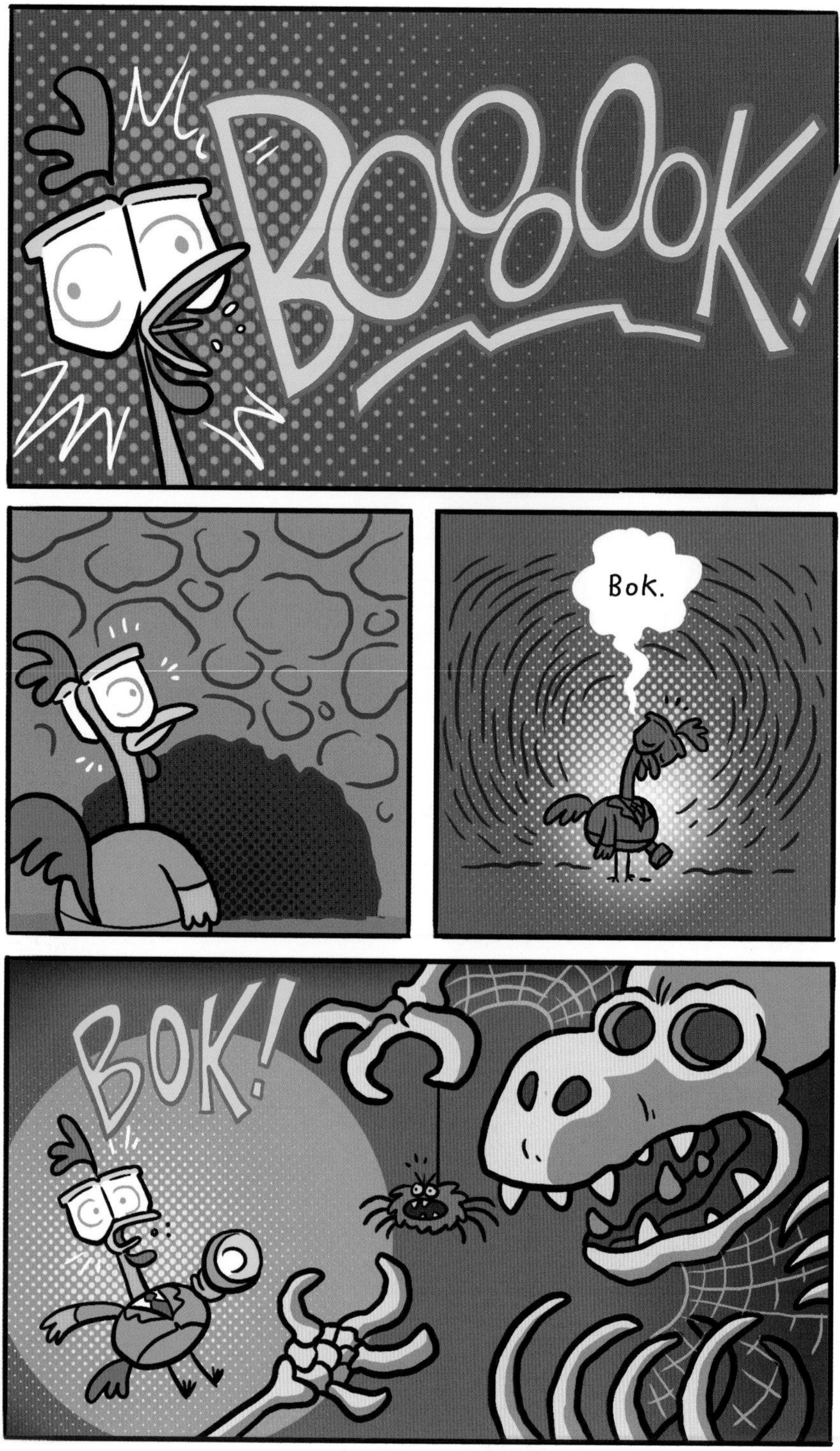
BOOOOOK!
Bok.
BOK!

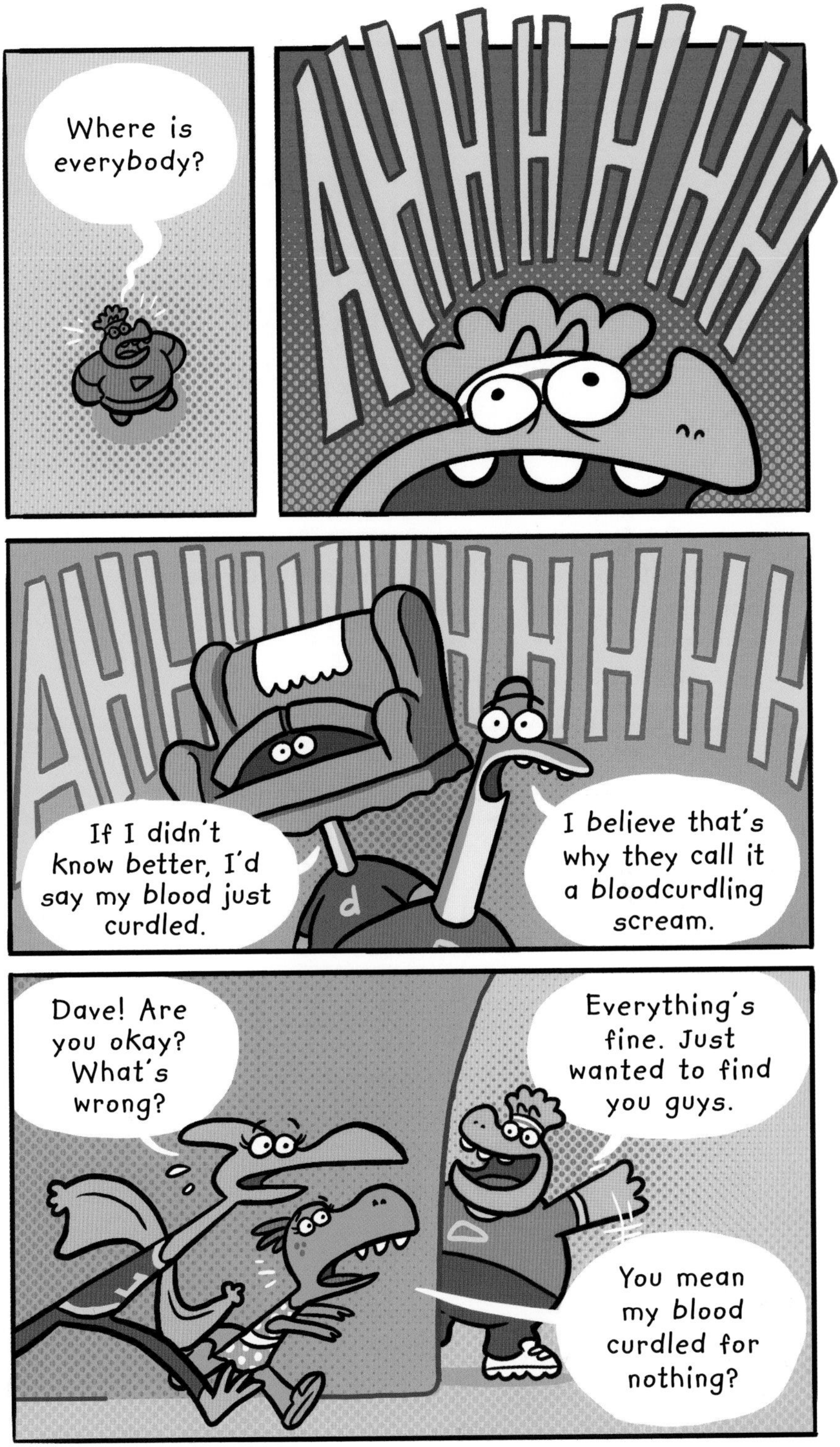
Where is everybody?
AHHHHHHHH
AHHHHHHHHHHHHHH
If I didn't know better, I'd say my blood just curdled.
I believe that's why they call it a bloodcurdling scream.
Dave! Are you okay? What's wrong?
Everything's fine. Just wanted to find you guys.
You mean my blood curdled for nothing?

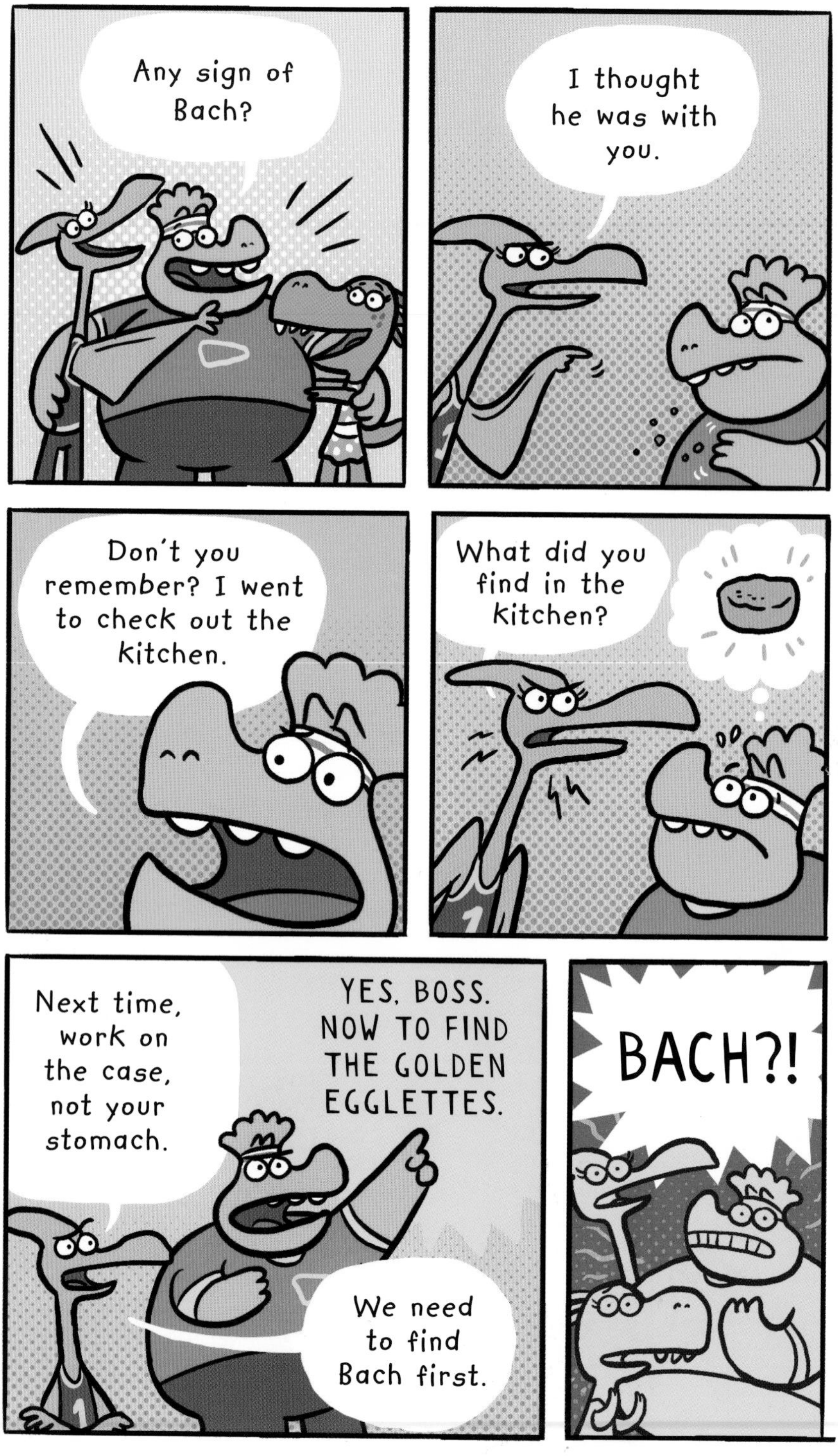
Any sign of Bach?
I thought he was with you.
Don't you remember? I went to check out the kitchen.
What did you find in the kitchen?
Next time, work on the case, not your stomach.
YES, BOSS. NOW TO FIND THE GOLDEN EGGLETTES.
We need to find Bach first.
BACH?!

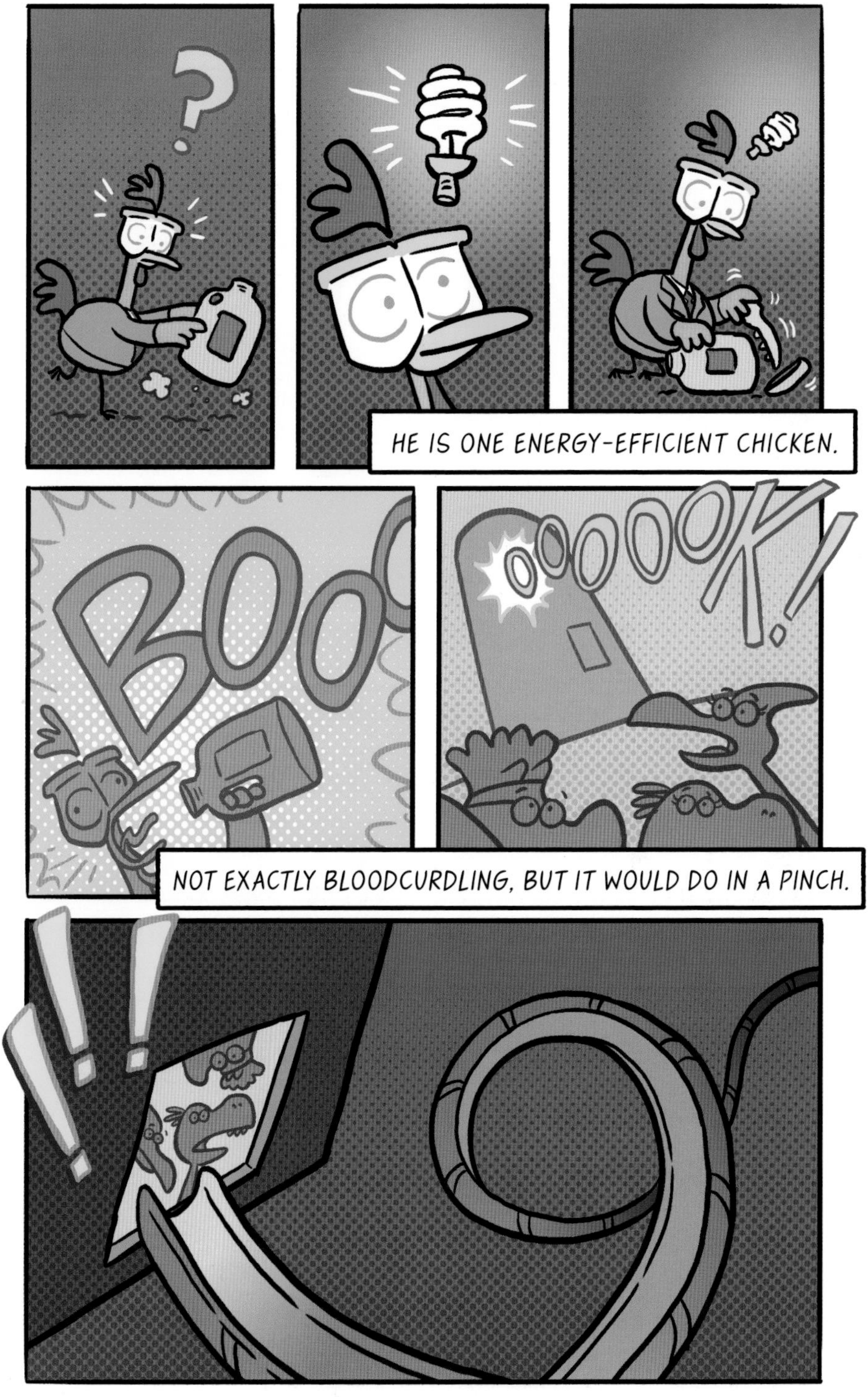
HE IS ONE ENERGY-EFFICIENT CHICKEN.
BOOOOOOOOK!
NOT EXACTLY BLOODCURDLING, BUT IT WOULD DO IN A PINCH.

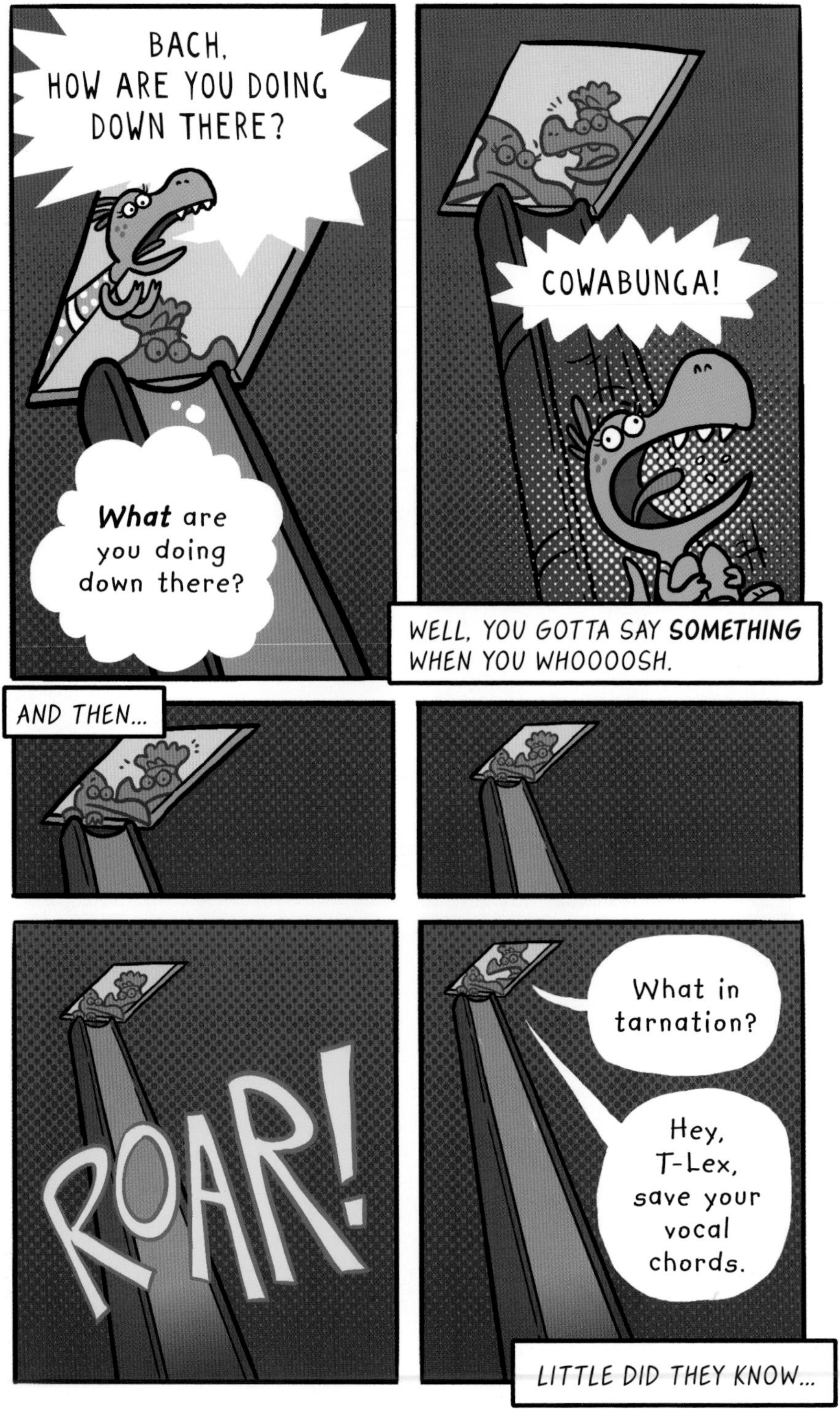
BACH, HOW ARE YOU DOING DOWN THERE?
What are you doing down there?
COWABUNGA!
WELL, YOU GOTTA SAY **SOMETHING** WHEN YOU WHOOOOSH.
AND THEN...
ROAR!
What in tarnation?
Hey, T-Lex, save your vocal chords.
LITTLE DID THEY KNOW...

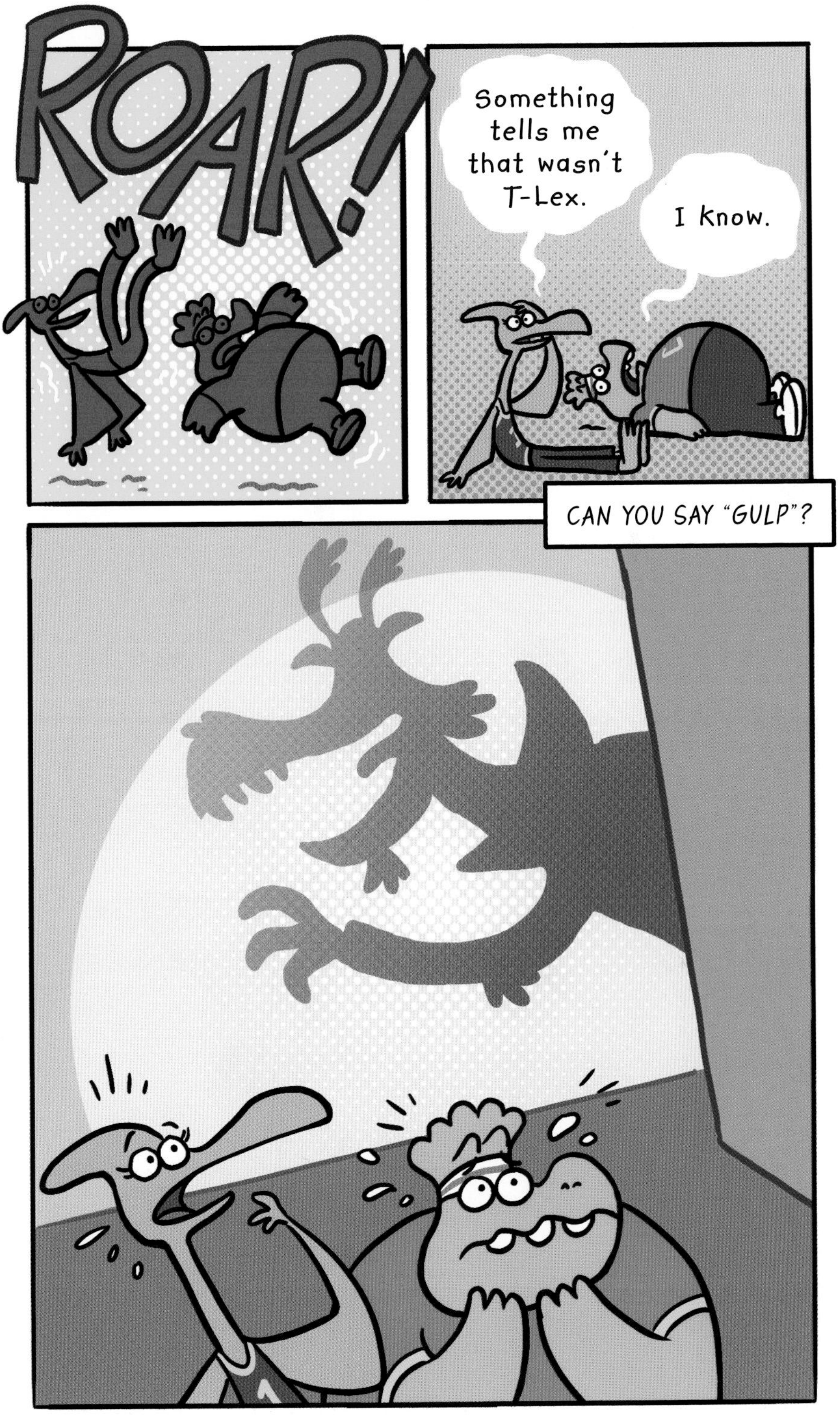
ROAR!
Something tells me that wasn't T-Lex.
I know.
CAN YOU SAY "GULP"?

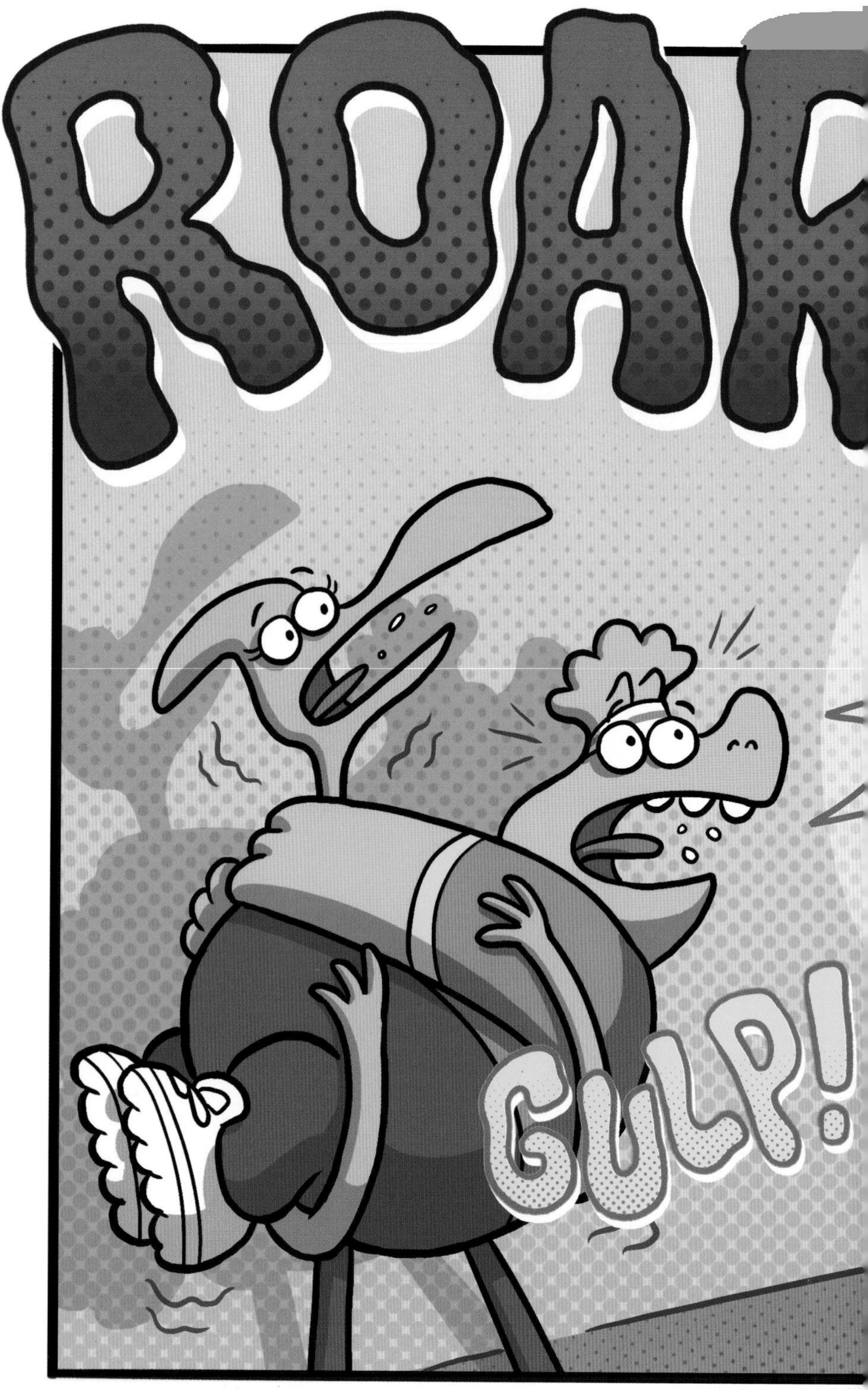
ROAR
GULP!

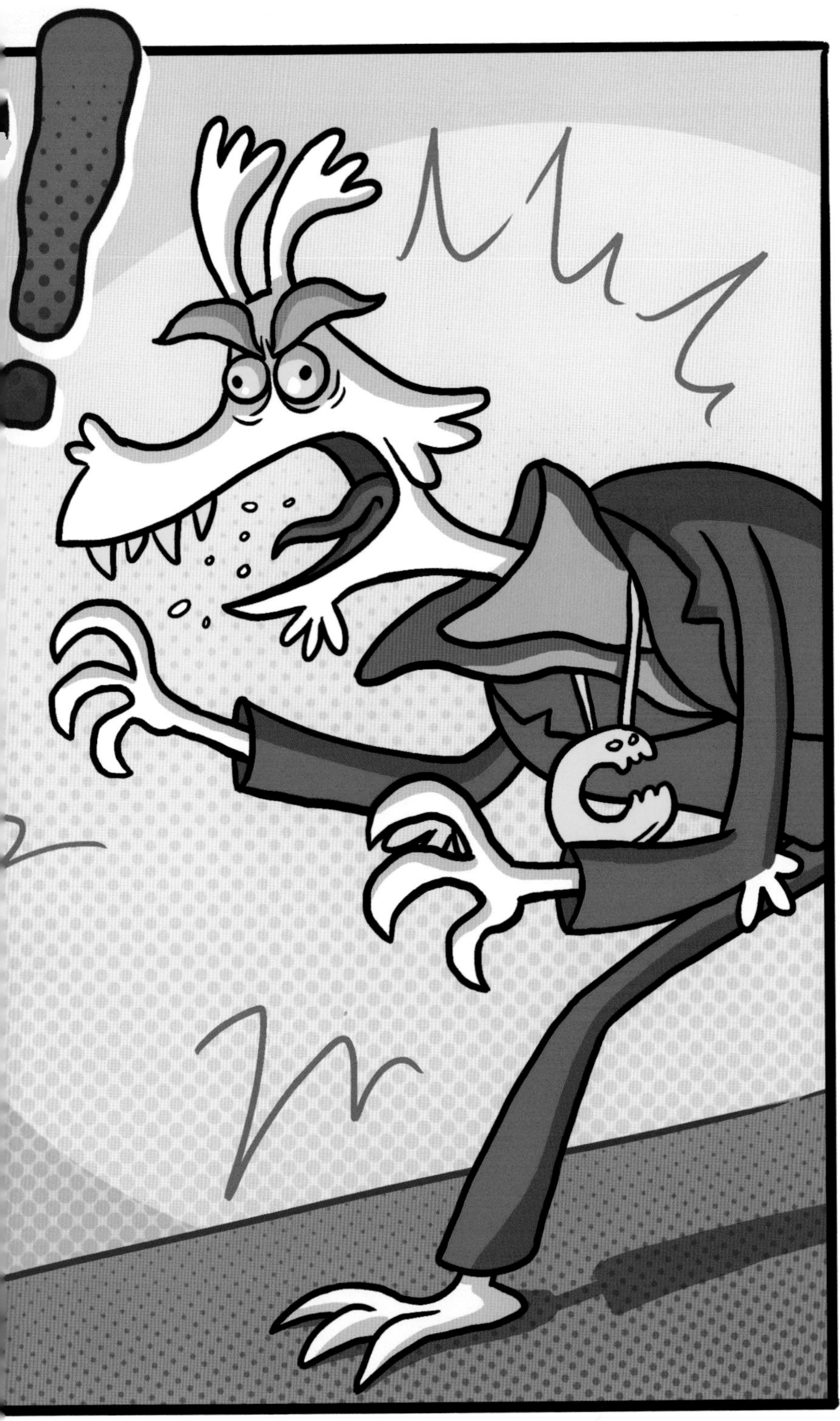

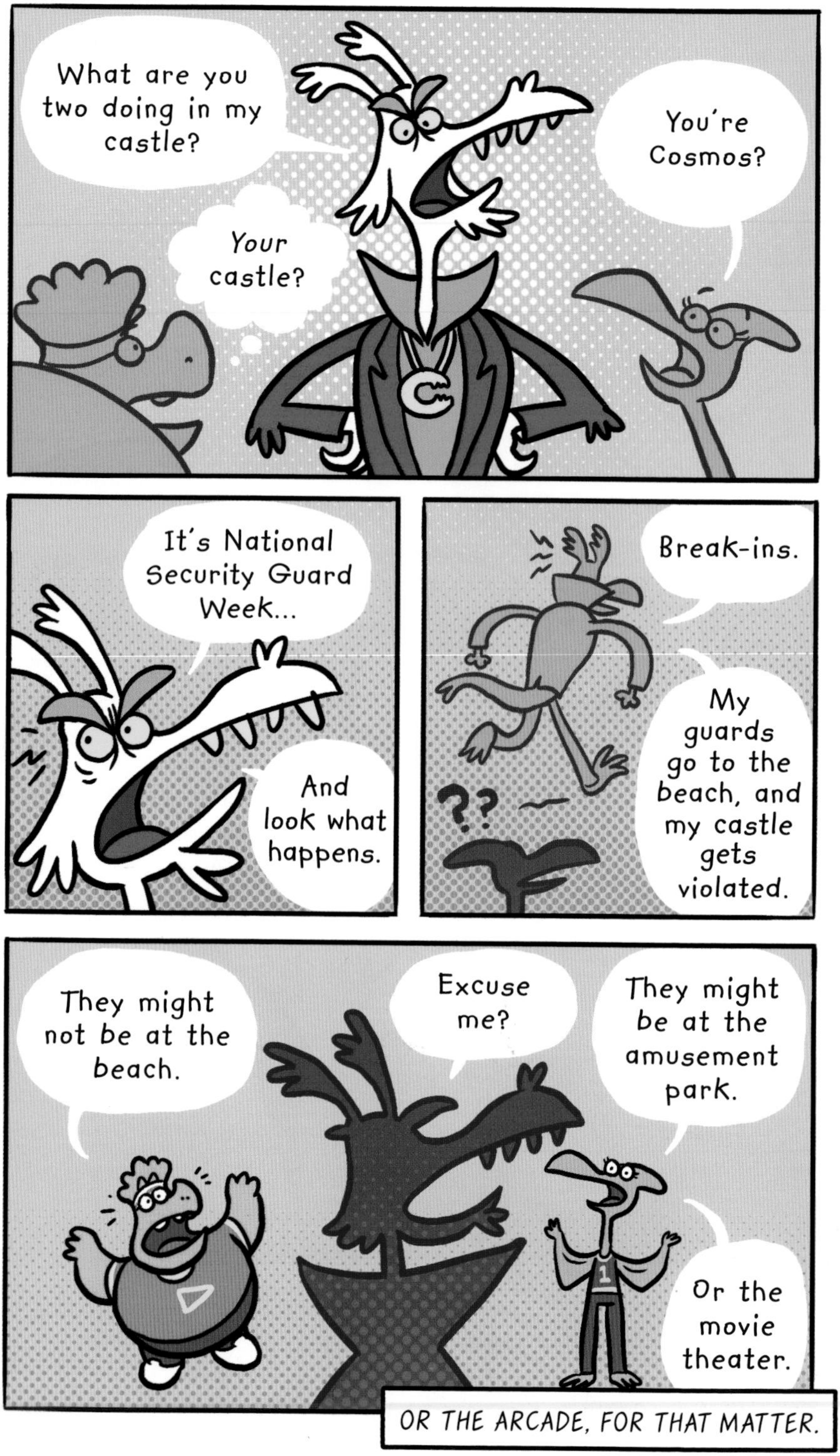
What are you two doing in my castle?
Your castle?
You're Cosmos?
It's National Security Guard Week...
And look what happens.
Break-ins.
My guards go to the beach, and my castle gets violated.
They might not be at the beach.
Excuse me?
They might be at the amusement park.
Or the movie theater.
OR THE ARCADE, FOR THAT MATTER.

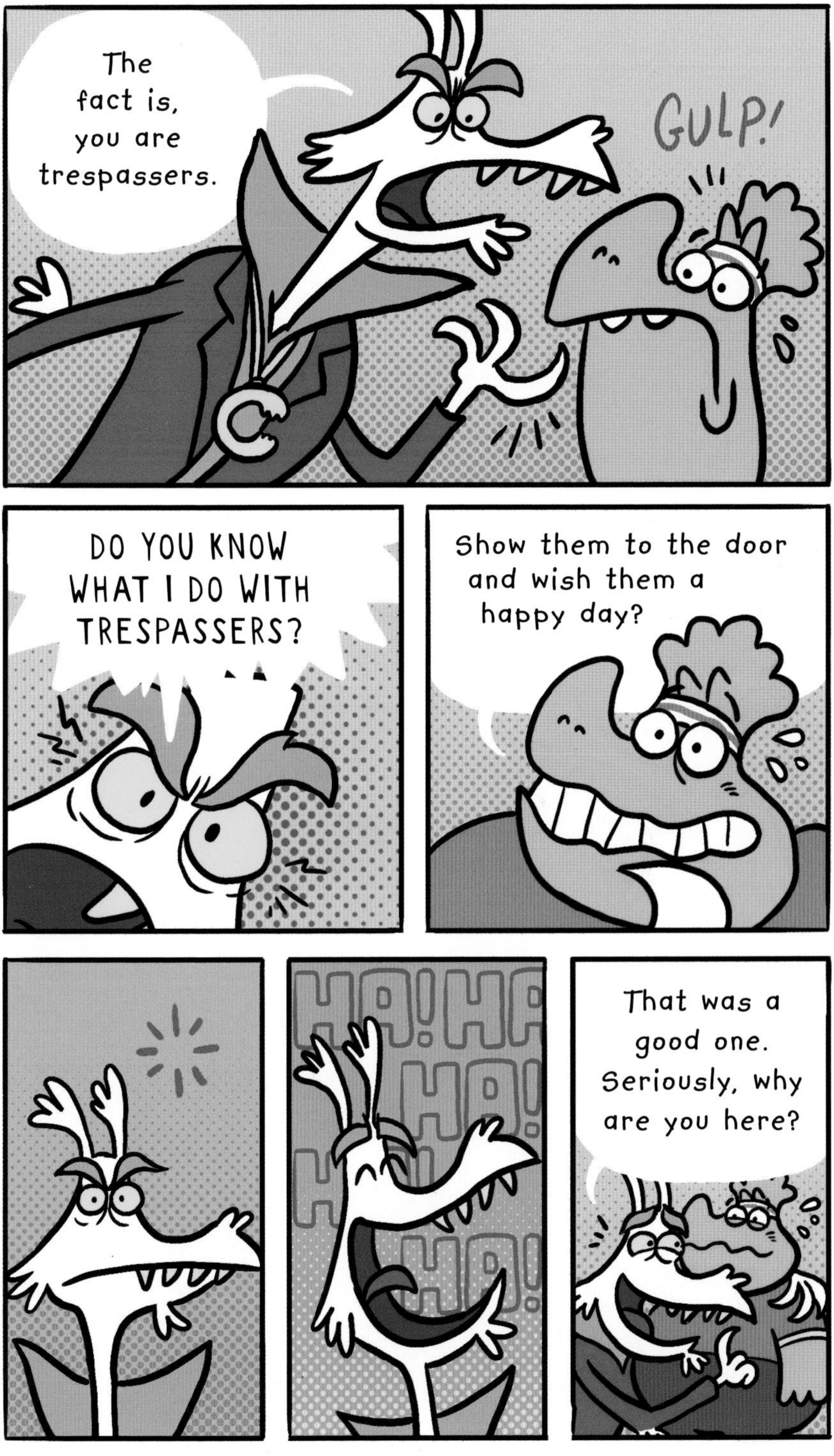

The fact is, you are trespassers.
GULP!
DO YOU KNOW WHAT I DO WITH TRESPASSERS?
Show them to the door and wish them a happy day?
HA! HA
HA!
HA
HA
HO!
That was a good one. Seriously, why are you here?

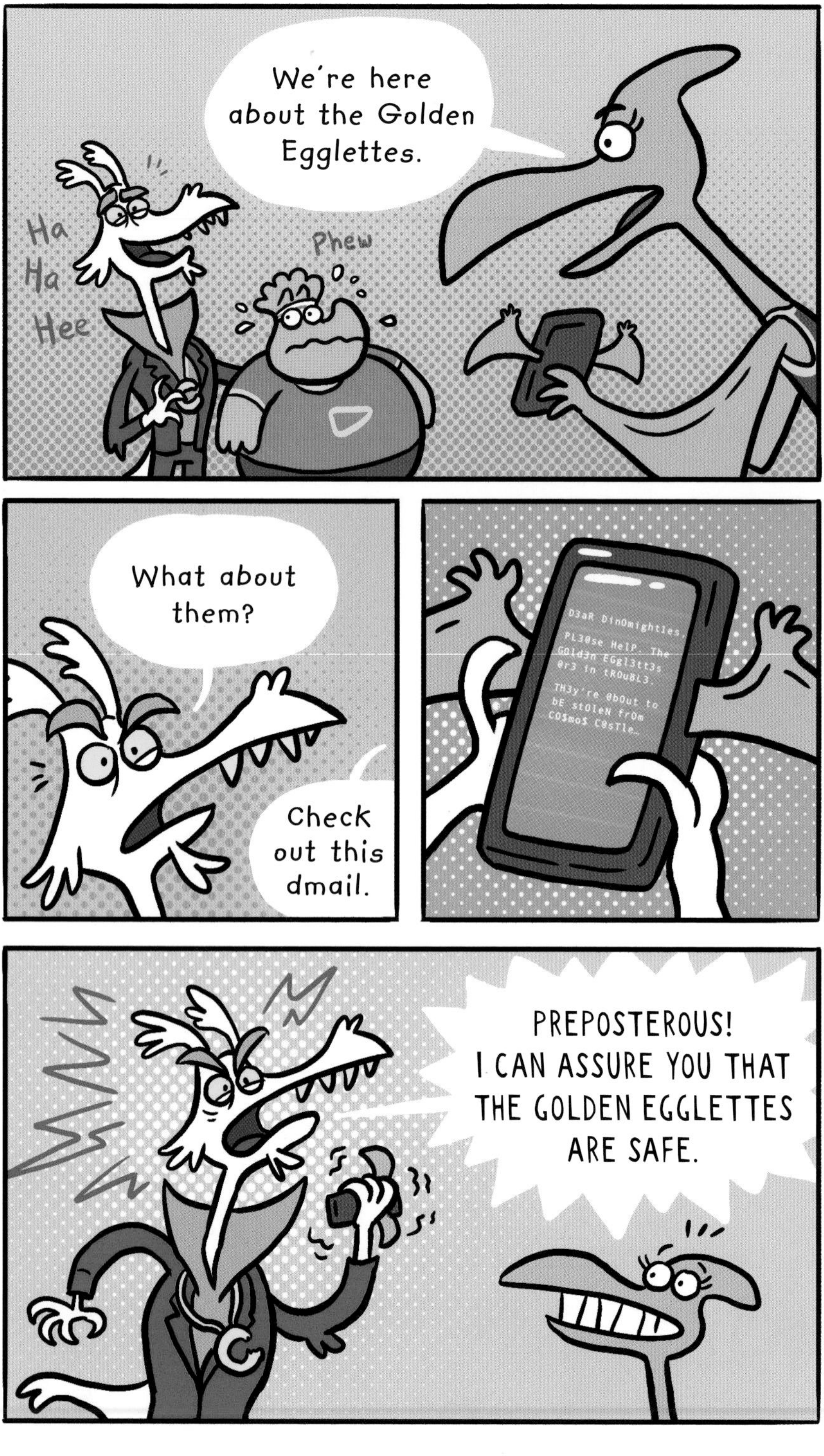
We're here about the Golden Egglettes.
Ha Ha Hee
Phew
What about them?
Check out this dmail.
D3aR DinOmightles,
PL3@se HelP. The GOld3n EGgl3tt3s @r3 in tROuBL3.
TH3y're @bOut to bE stOleN frOm COSmoS C@sTle…
PREPOSTEROUS! I CAN ASSURE YOU THAT THE GOLDEN EGGLETTES ARE SAFE.

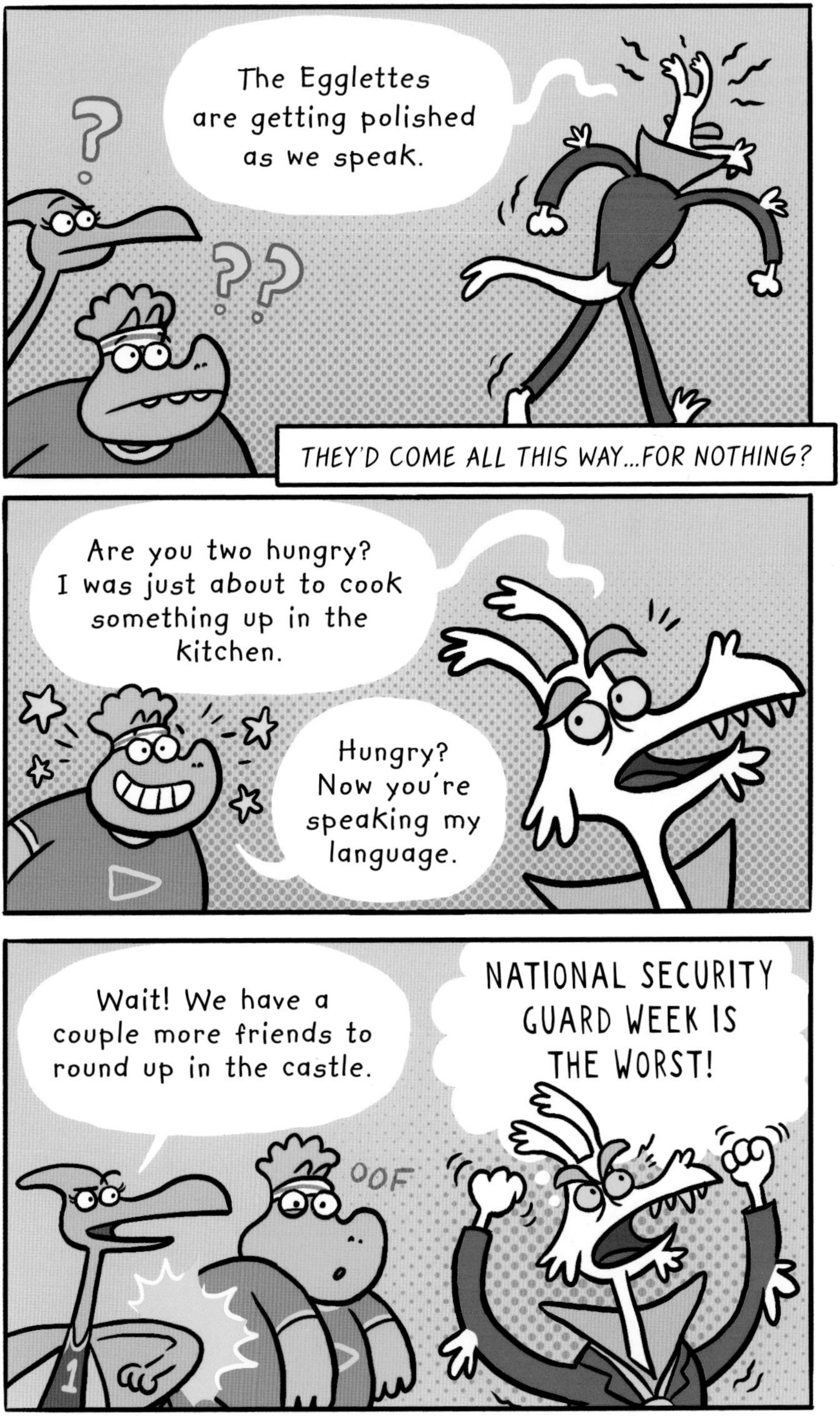

The Egglettes are getting polished as we speak.
THEY'D COME ALL THIS WAY...FOR NOTHING?
Are you two hungry? I was just about to cook something up in the kitchen.
Hungry? Now you're speaking my language.
Wait! We have a couple more friends to round up in the castle.
NATIONAL SECURITY GUARD WEEK IS THE WORST!
OOF

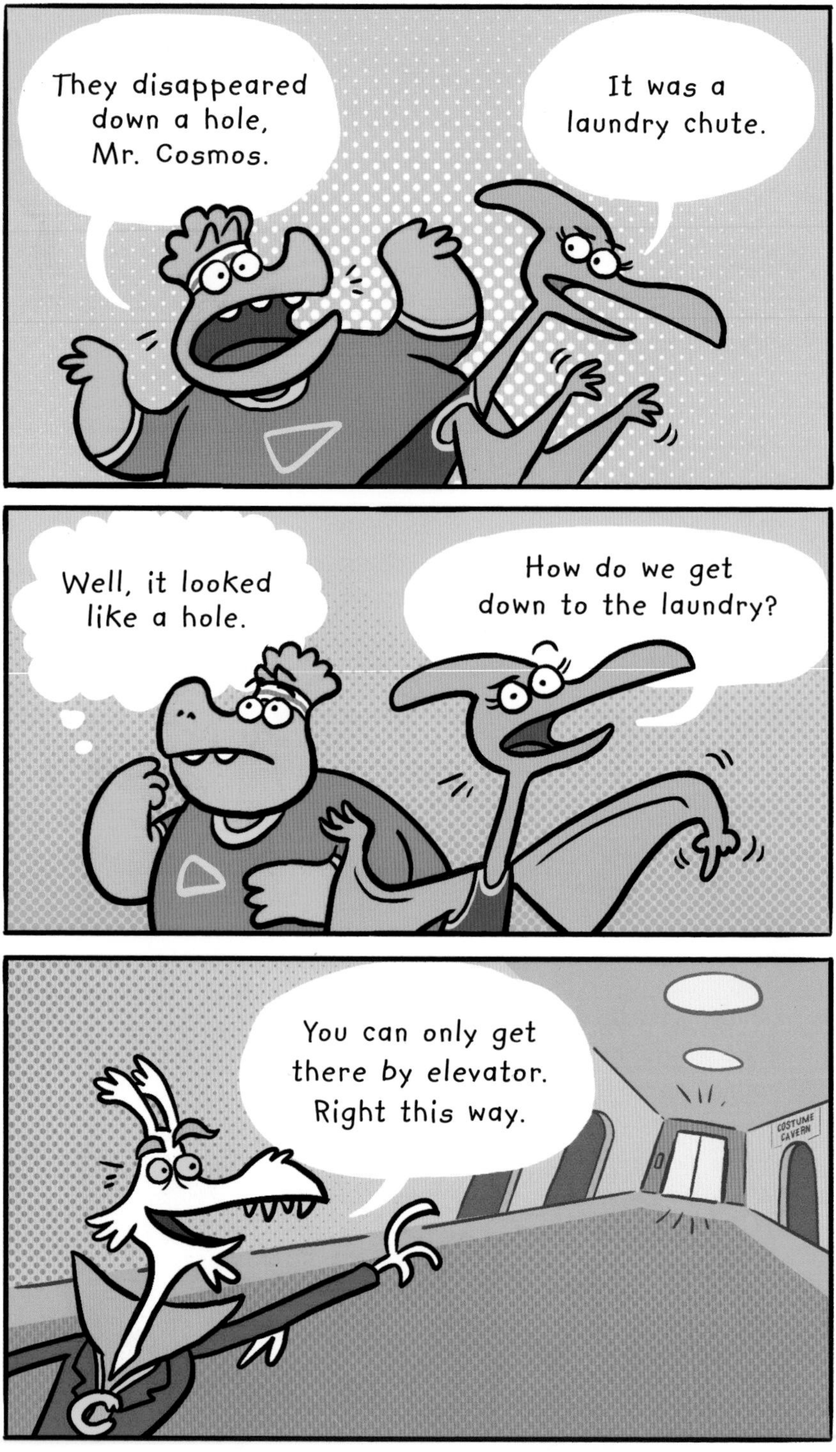
They disappeared down a hole, Mr. Cosmos.
It was a laundry chute.
Well, it looked like a hole.
How do we get down to the laundry?
You can only get there by elevator. Right this way.
COSTUME CAVERN

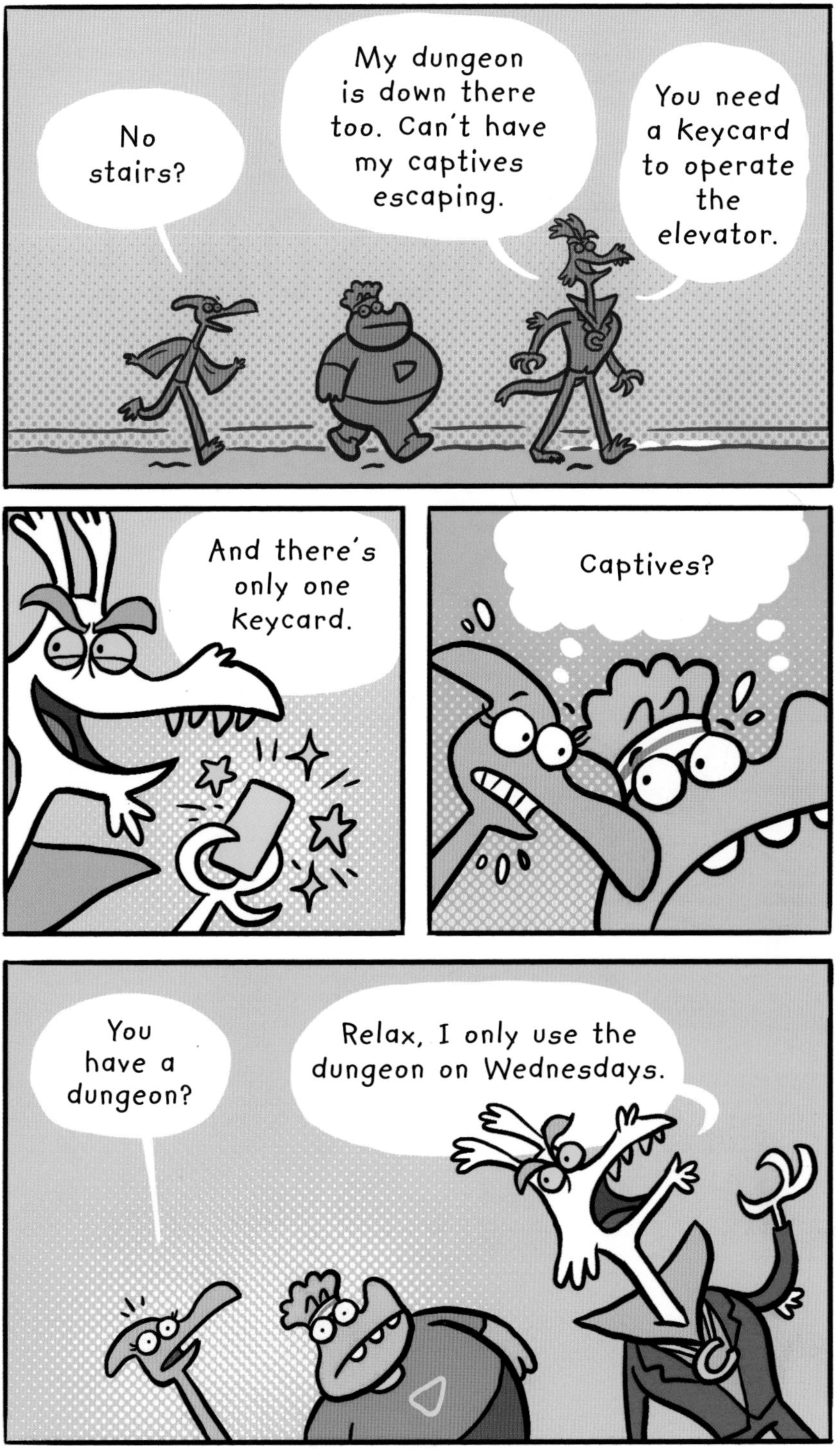
No stairs?
My dungeon is down there too. Can't have my captives escaping.
You need a keycard to operate the elevator.
And there's only one keycard.
Captives?
You have a dungeon?
Relax, I only use the dungeon on Wednesdays.

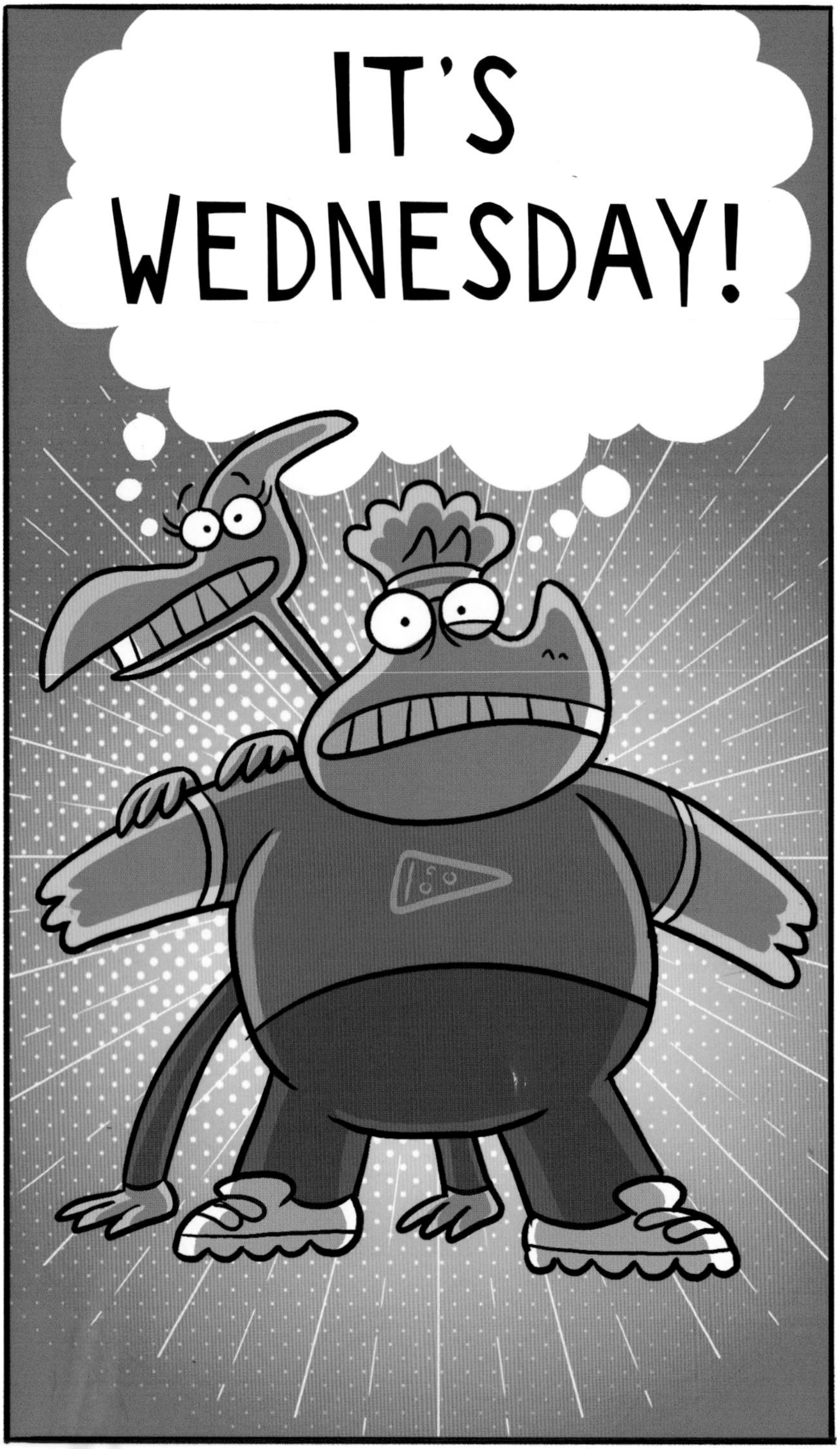
IT'S WEDNESDAY!

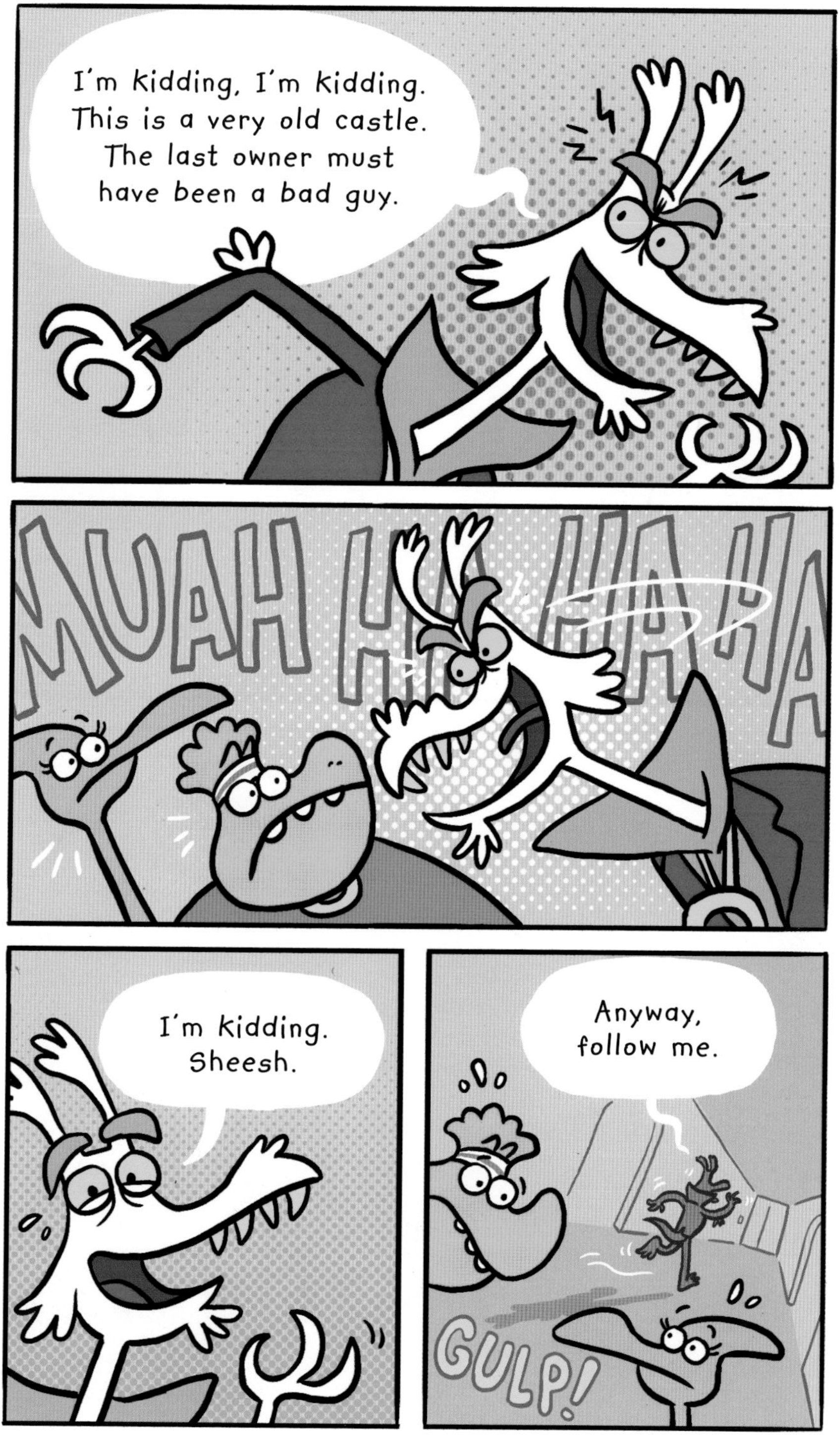
I'm kidding, I'm kidding. This is a very old castle. The last owner must have been a bad guy.
MUAH HA HA HA
I'm kidding. Sheesh.
Anyway, follow me.
GULP!

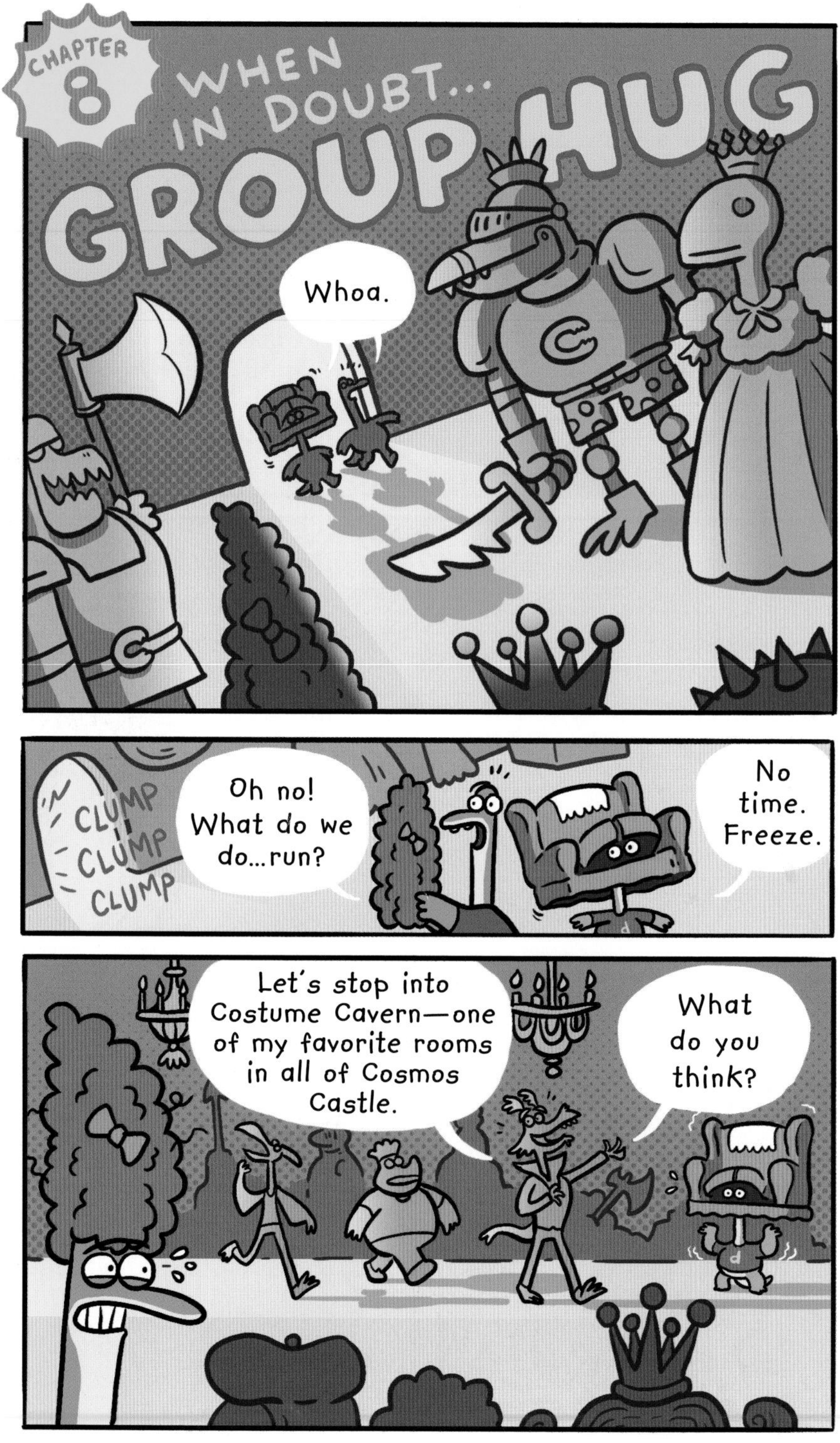
CHAPTER 8
WHEN IN DOUBT...
GROUP HUG
Whoa.
CLUMP CLUMP CLUMP
Oh no! What do we do...run?
No time. Freeze.
Let's stop into Costume Cavern—one of my favorite rooms in all of Cosmos Castle.
What do you think?

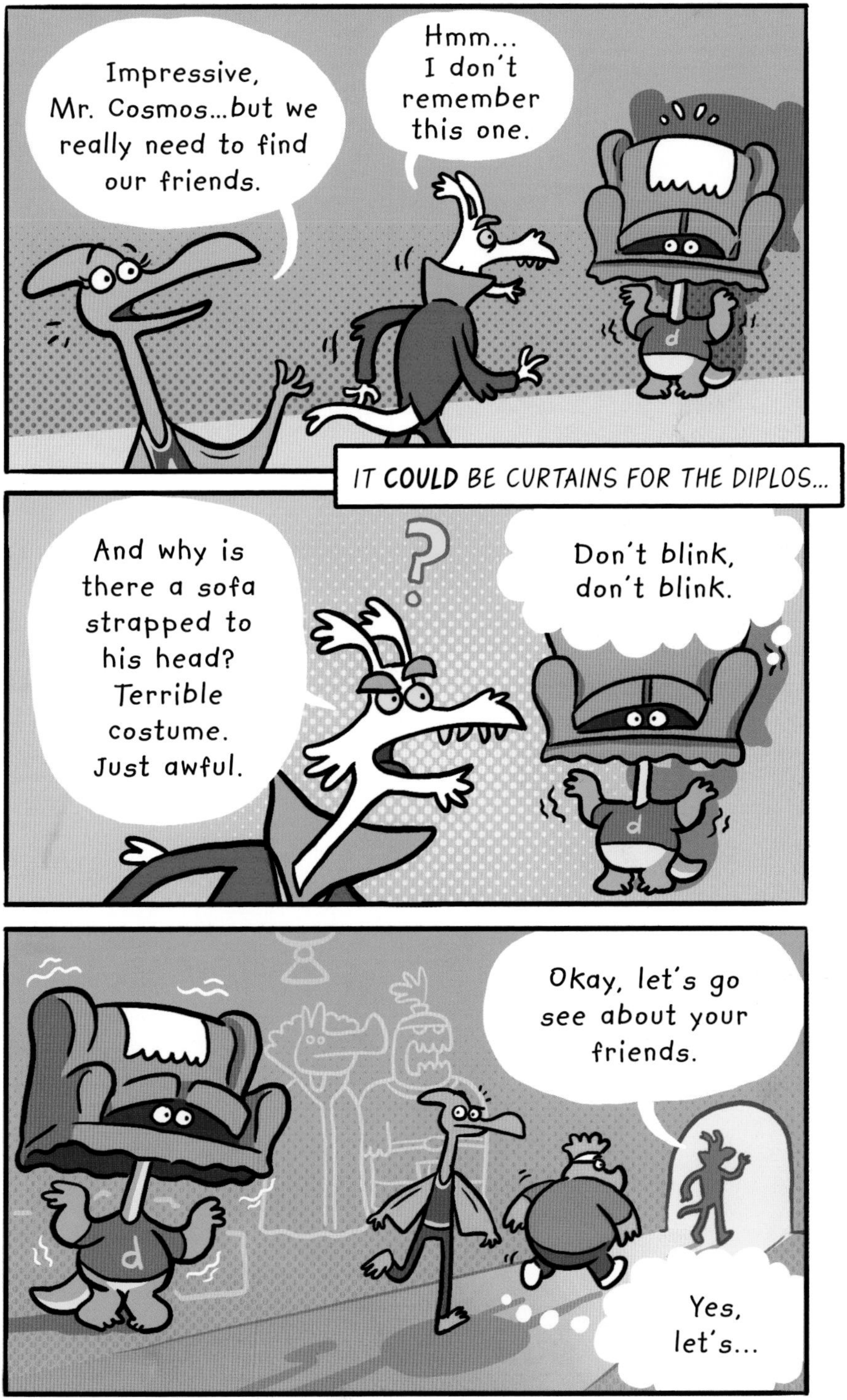
Impressive, Mr. Cosmos...but we really need to find our friends.
Hmm... I don't remember this one.
IT COULD BE CURTAINS FOR THE DIPLOS...
And why is there a sofa strapped to his head? Terrible costume. Just awful.
?
Don't blink, don't blink.
Okay, let's go see about your friends.
Yes, let's...

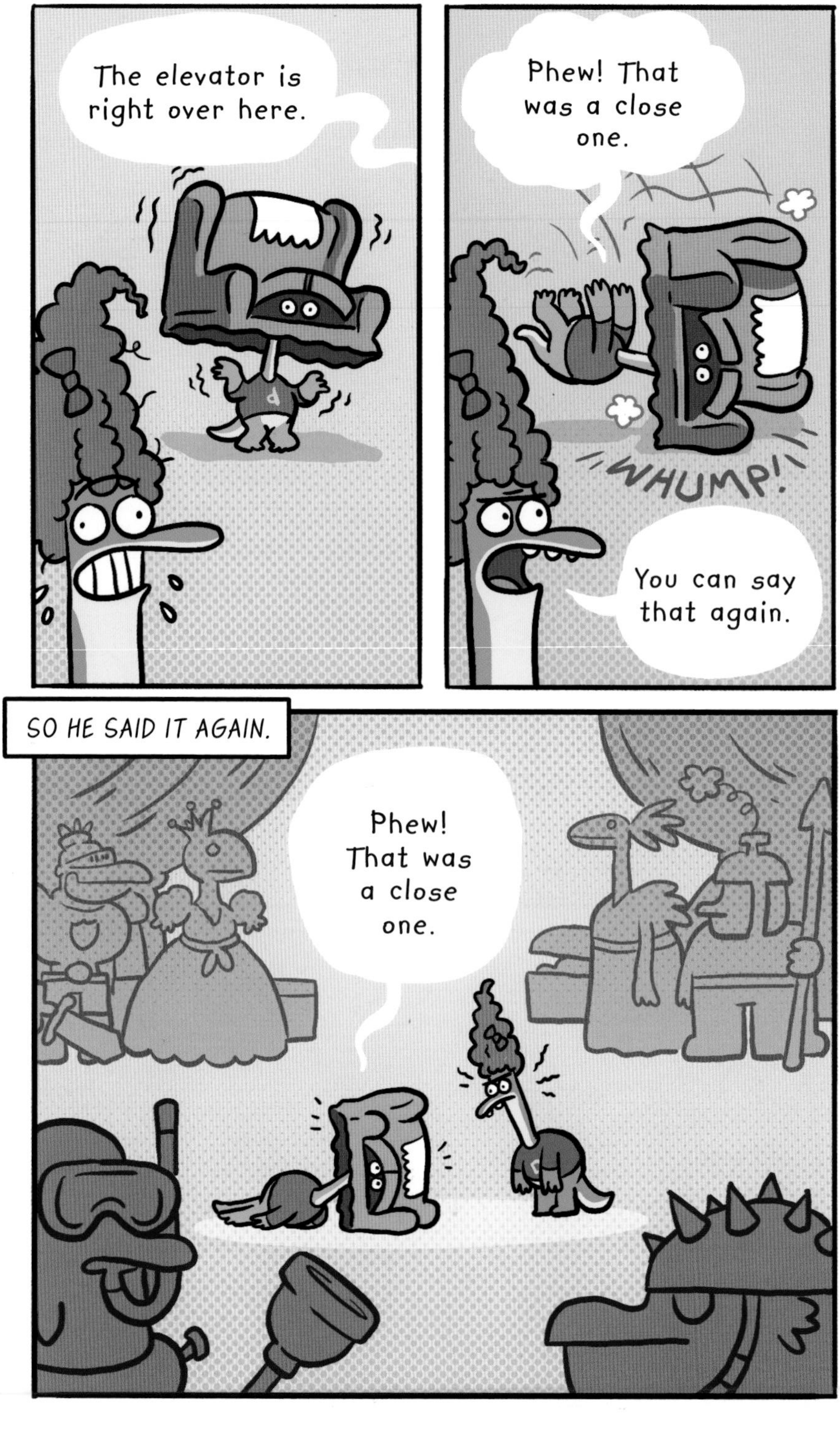
The elevator is right over here.
Phew! That was a close one.
WHUMP!
You can say that again.
SO HE SAID IT AGAIN.
Phew! That was a close one.

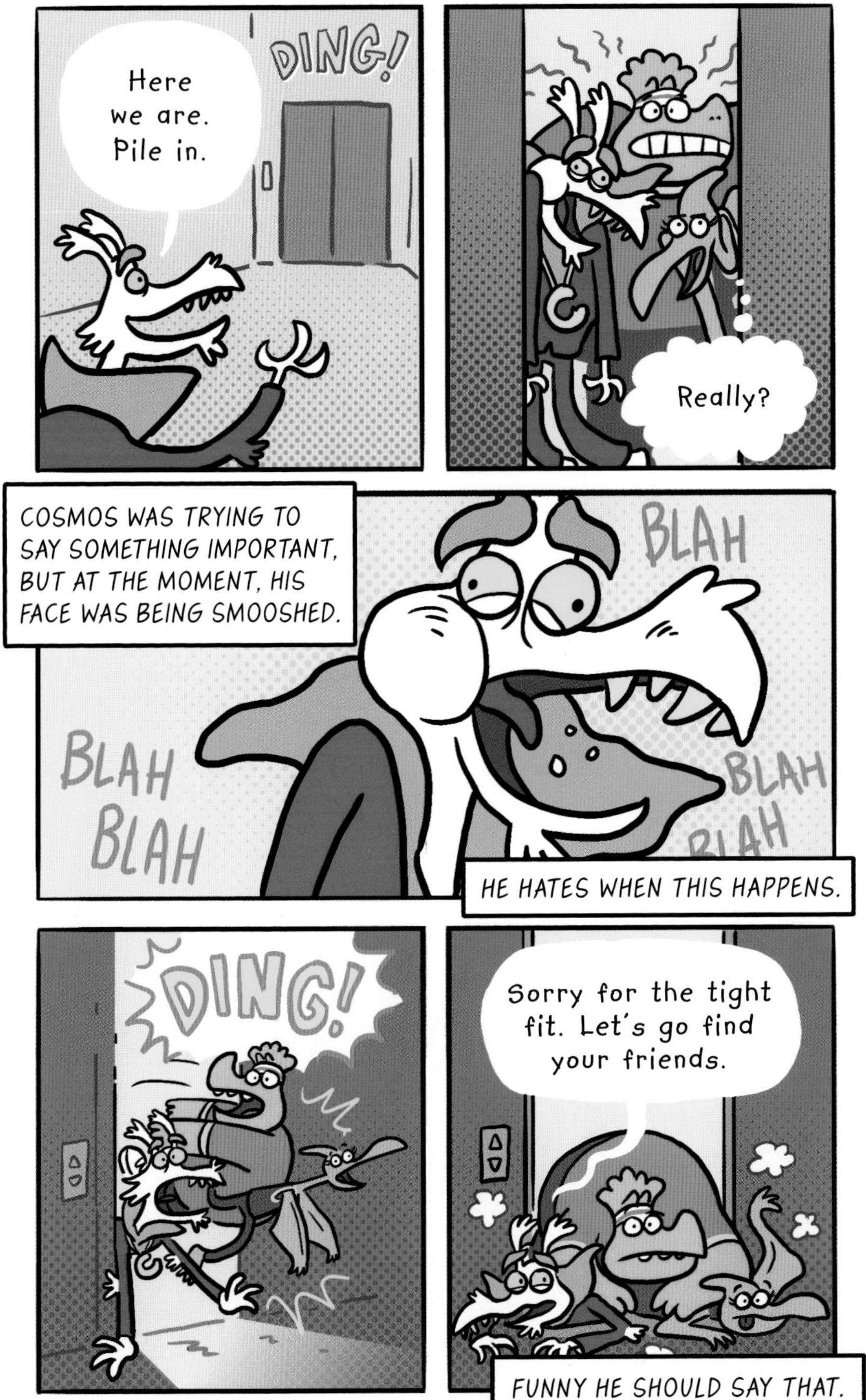
DING!
Here we are. Pile in.
Really?
COSMOS WAS TRYING TO SAY SOMETHING IMPORTANT, BUT AT THE MOMENT, HIS FACE WAS BEING SMOOSHED.
BLAH
BLAH BLAH
BLAH
HE HATES WHEN THIS HAPPENS.
DING!
Sorry for the tight fit. Let's go find your friends.
FUNNY HE SHOULD SAY THAT.

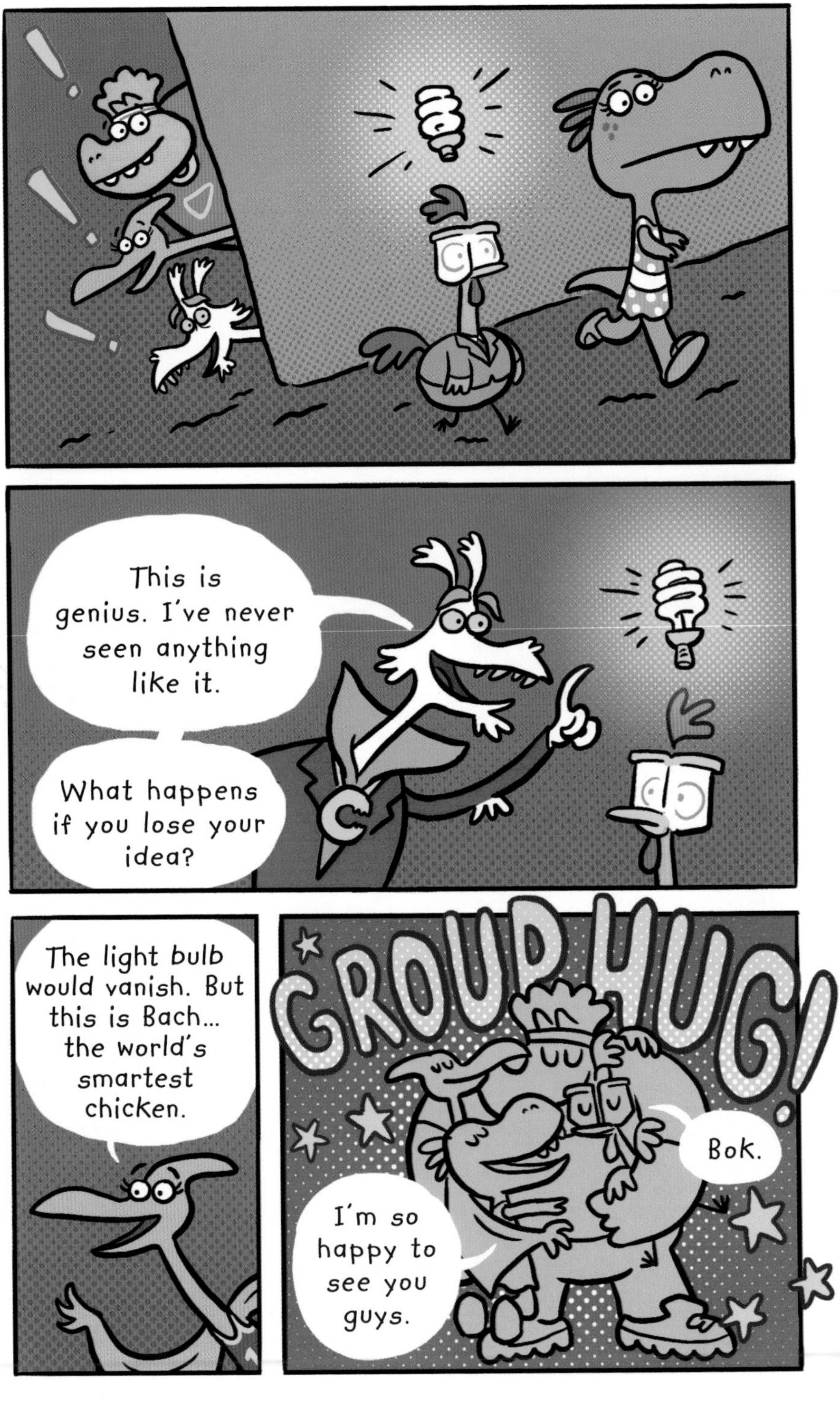
This is genius. I've never seen anything like it.
What happens if you lose your idea?
The light bulb would vanish. But this is Bach... the world's smartest chicken.
GROUP HUG!
Bok.
I'm so happy to see you guys.

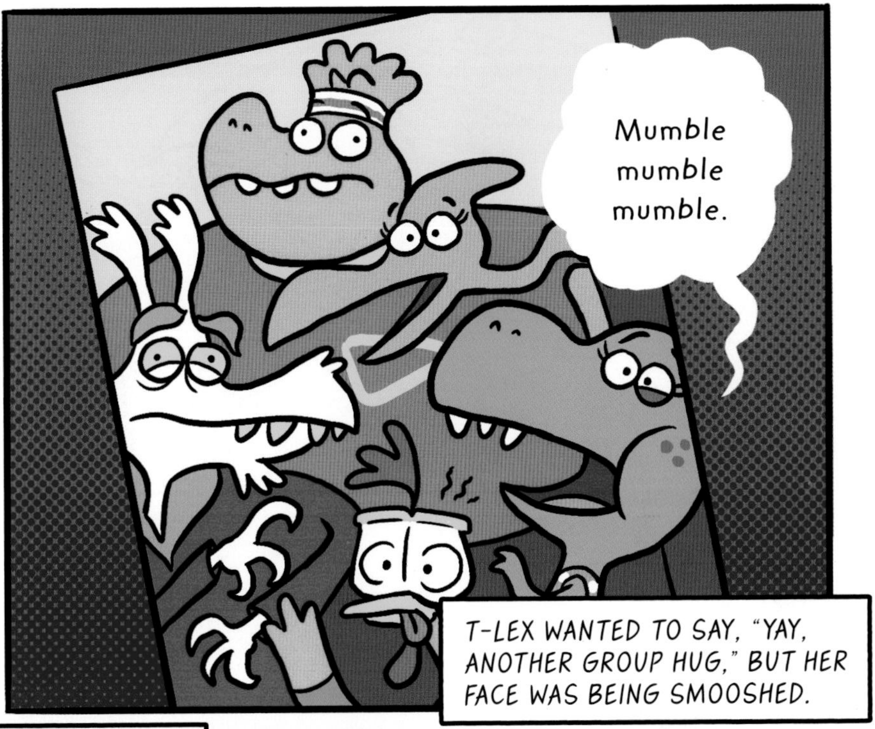
Mumble
mumble
mumble.
T-LEX WANTED TO SAY, "YAY, ANOTHER GROUP HUG," BUT HER FACE WAS BEING SMOOSHED.

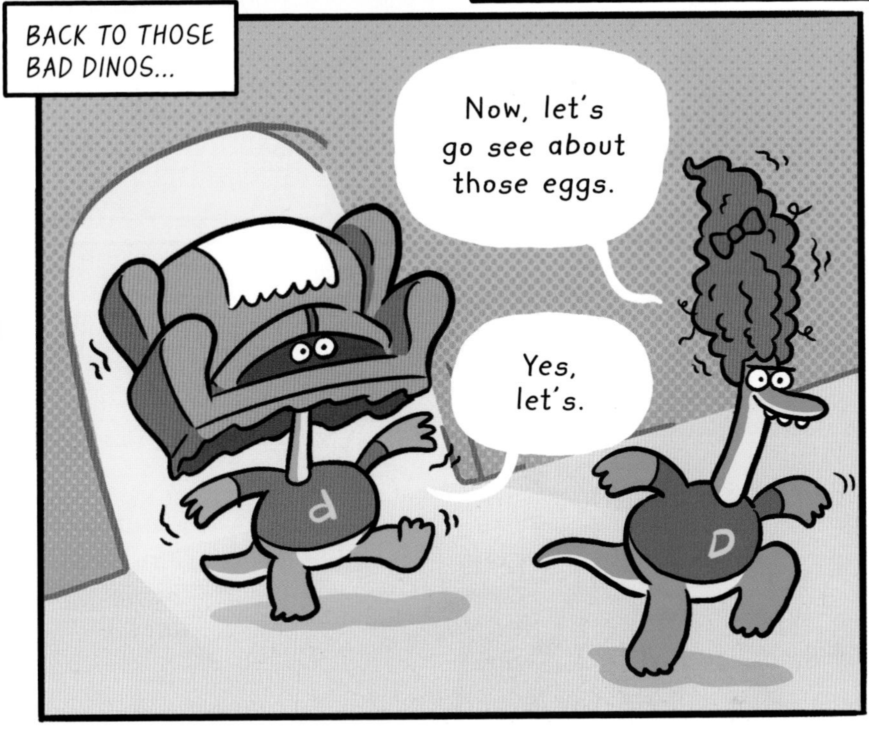
BACK TO THOSE BAD DINOS...
Now, let's go see about those eggs.
Yes, let's.
D

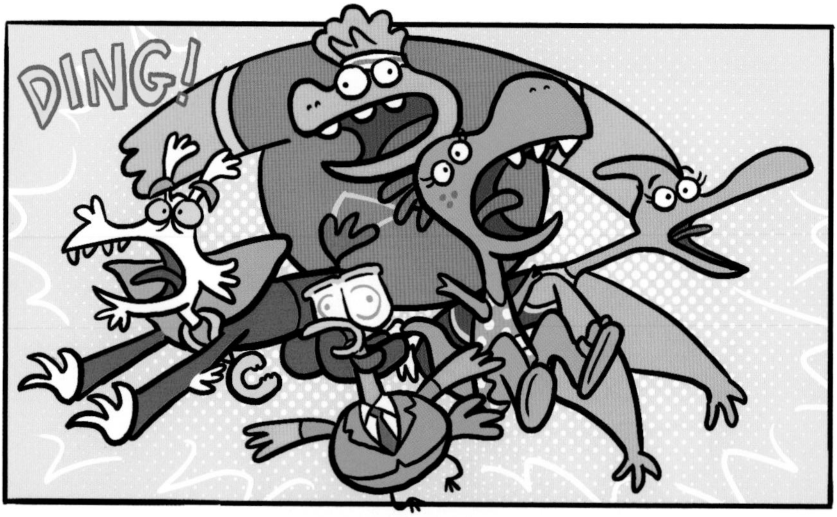
DING!

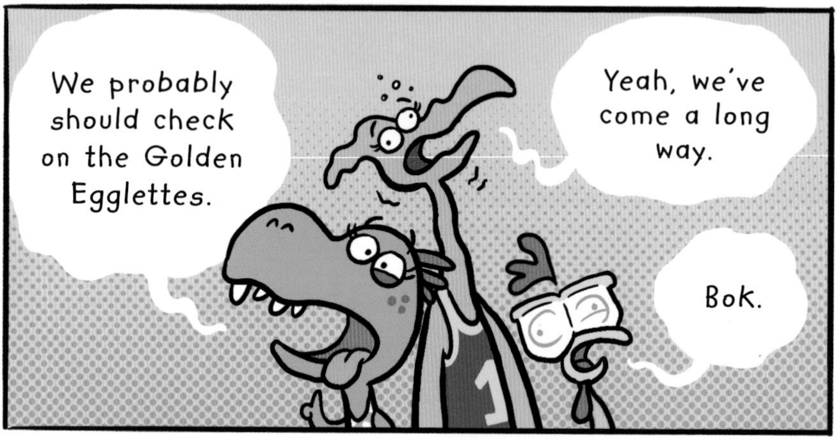
We probably should check on the Golden Egglettes.
Yeah, we've come a long way.
Bok.

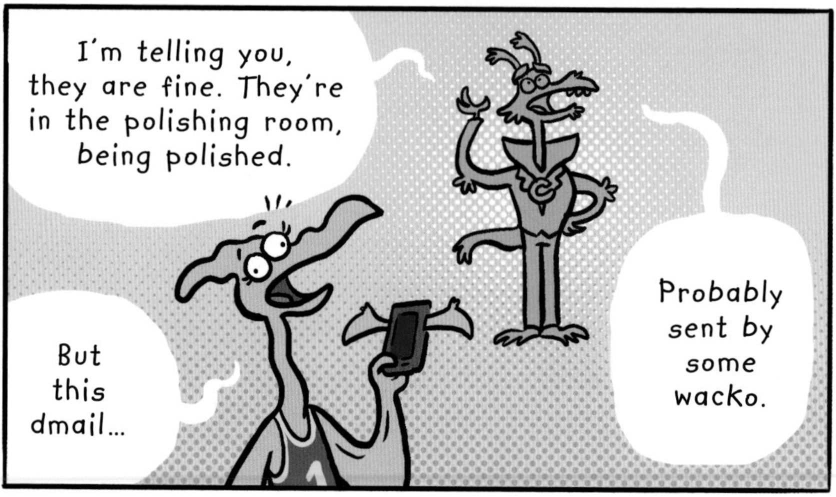
I'm telling you, they are fine. They're in the polishing room, being polished.
But this dmail...
Probably sent by some wacko.

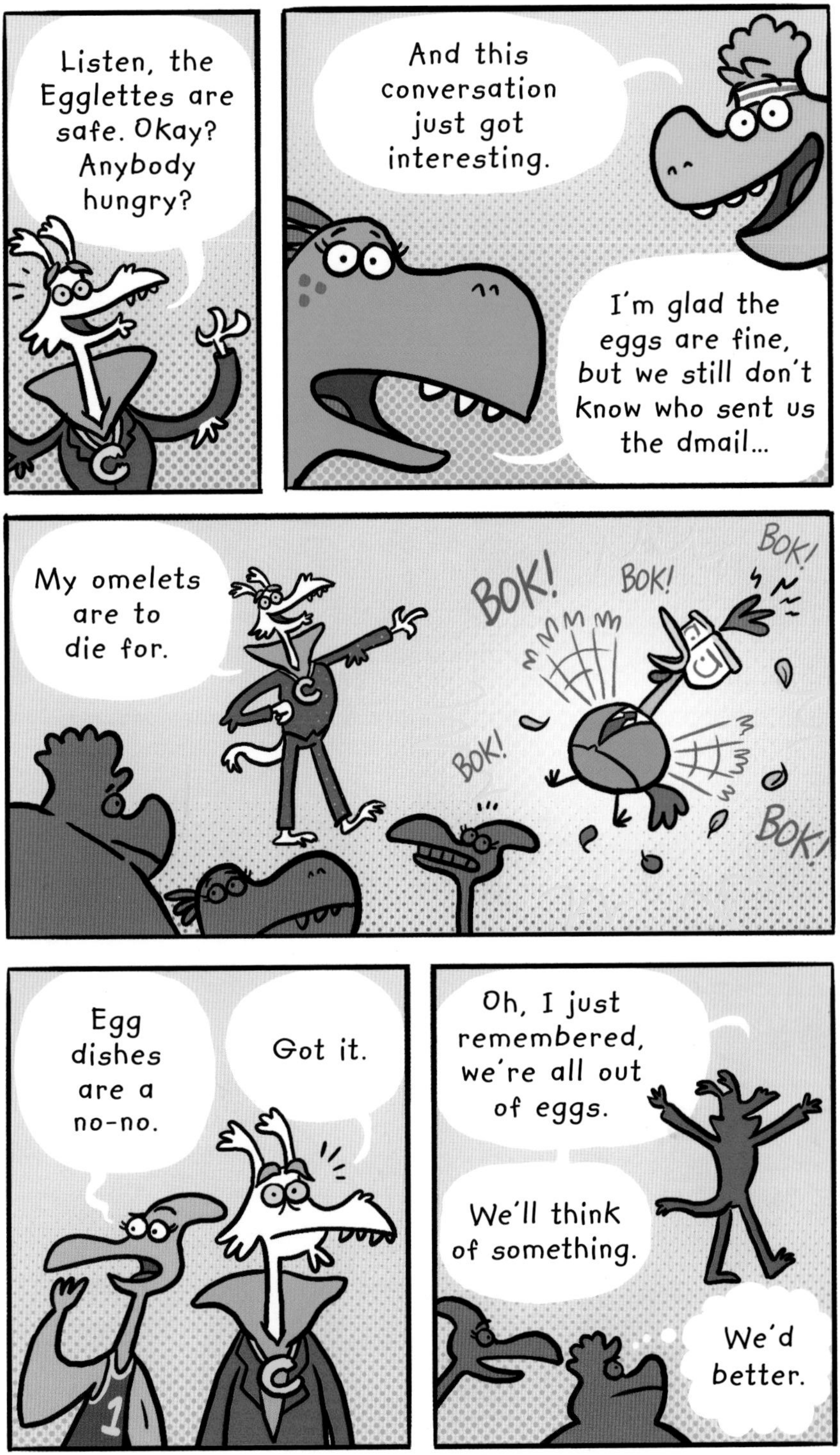

Listen, the Egglettes are safe. Okay? Anybody hungry?
And this conversation just got interesting.
I'm glad the eggs are fine, but we still don't know who sent us the dmail...
My omelets are to die for.
BOK!
BOK!
BOK!
BOK!
BOK!
Egg dishes are a no-no.
Got it.
Oh, I just remembered, we're all out of eggs.
We'll think of something.
We'd better.

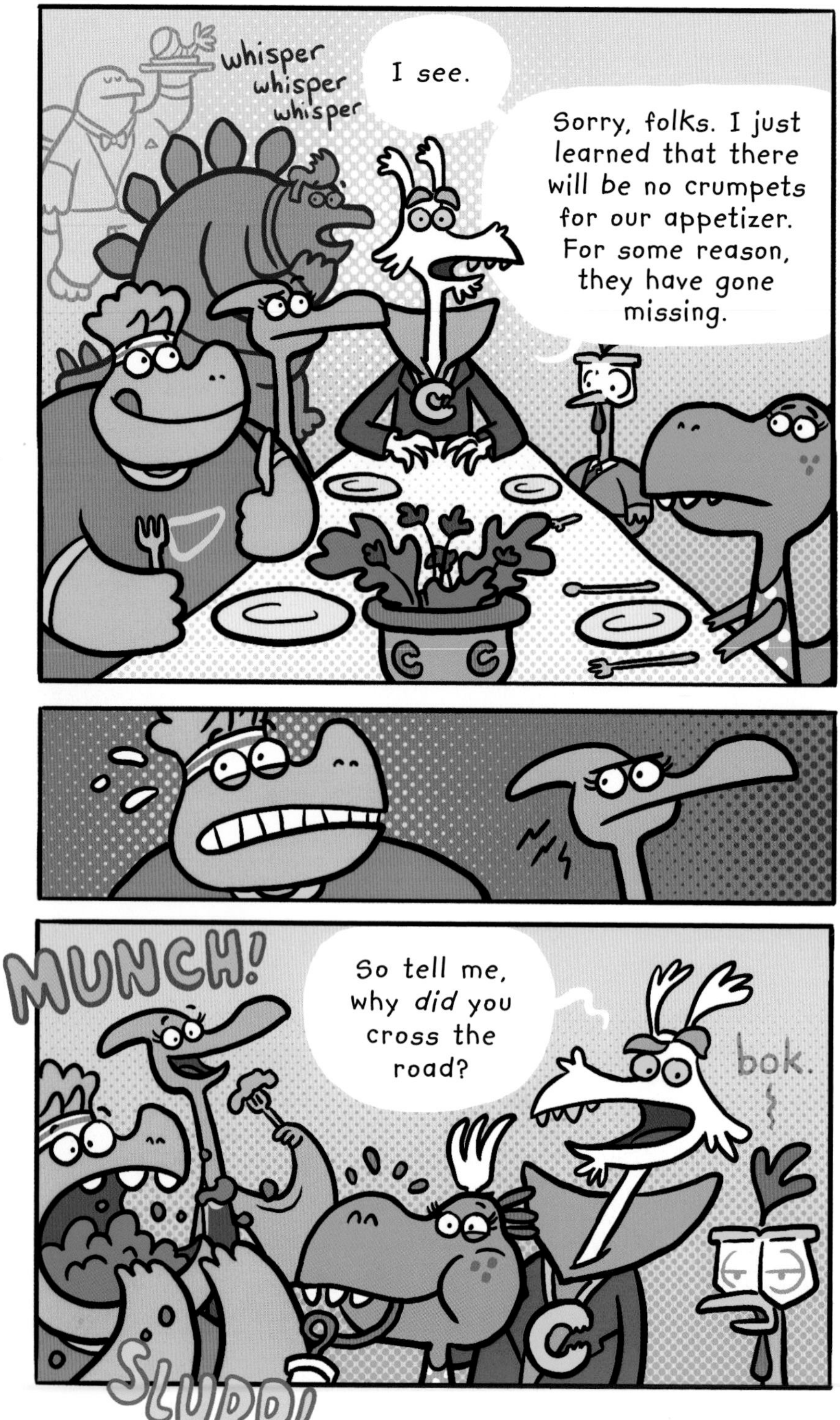
whisper
whisper
whisper
I see.
Sorry, folks. I just learned that there will be no crumpets for our appetizer. For some reason, they have gone missing.
MUNCH!
So tell me, why *did* you cross the road?
bok.
SLURP!

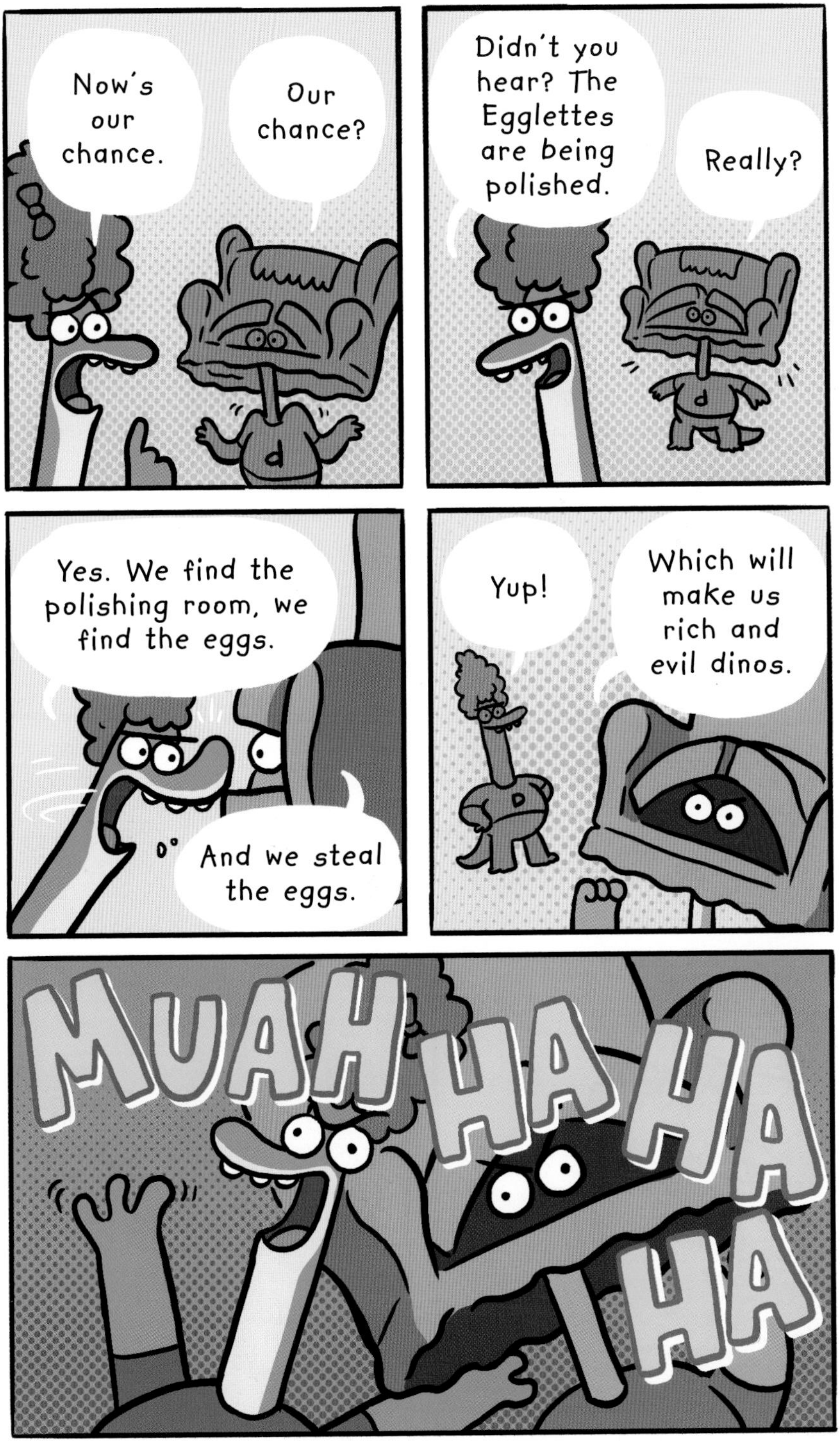
Now's our chance.
Our chance?
Didn't you hear? The Egglettes are being polished.
Really?
Yes. We find the polishing room, we find the eggs.
And we steal the eggs.
Yup!
Which will make us rich and evil dinos.
MUAH HA HA HA HA

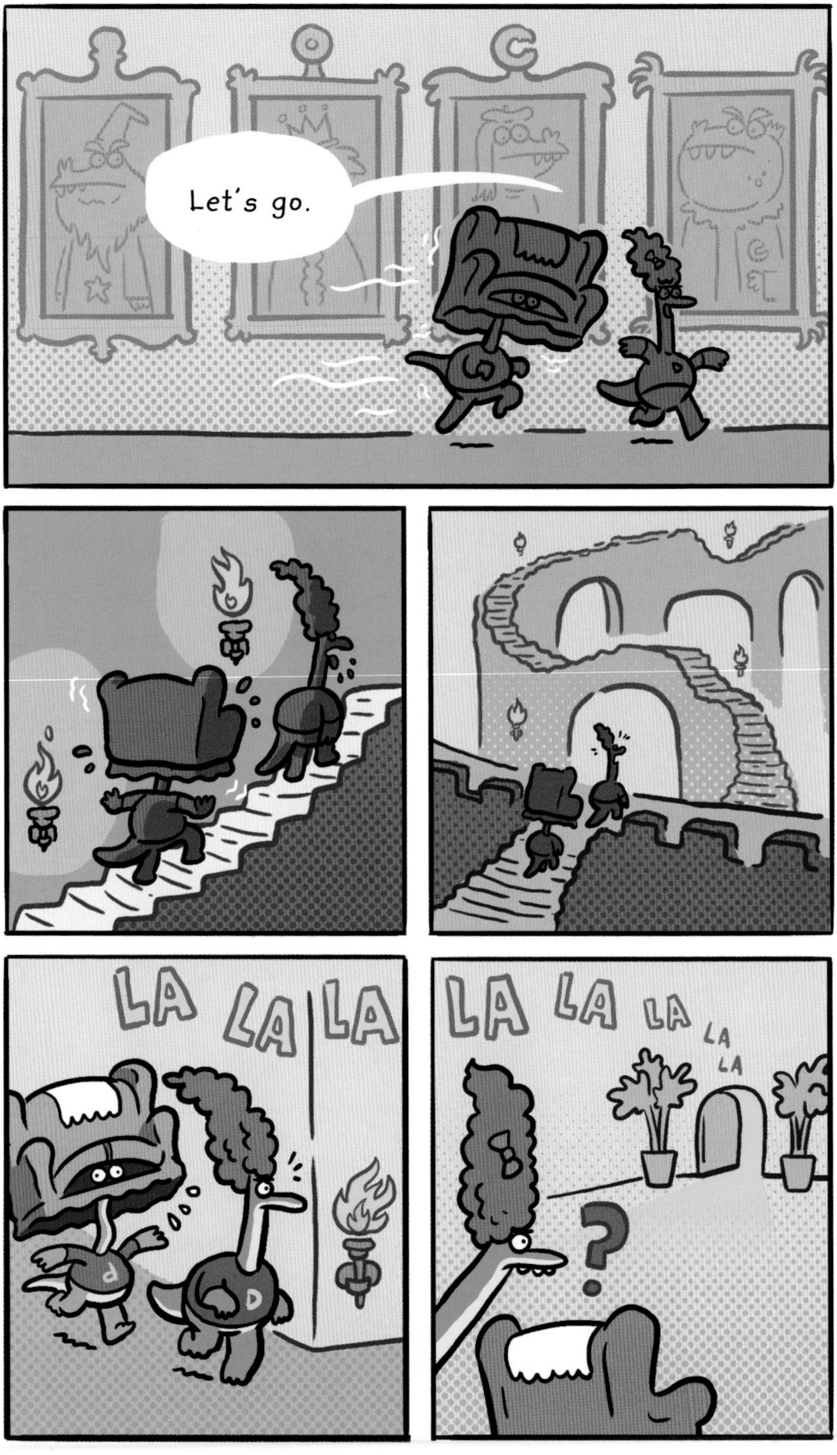
Let's go.
LA LA LA
LA LA LA LA LA
?

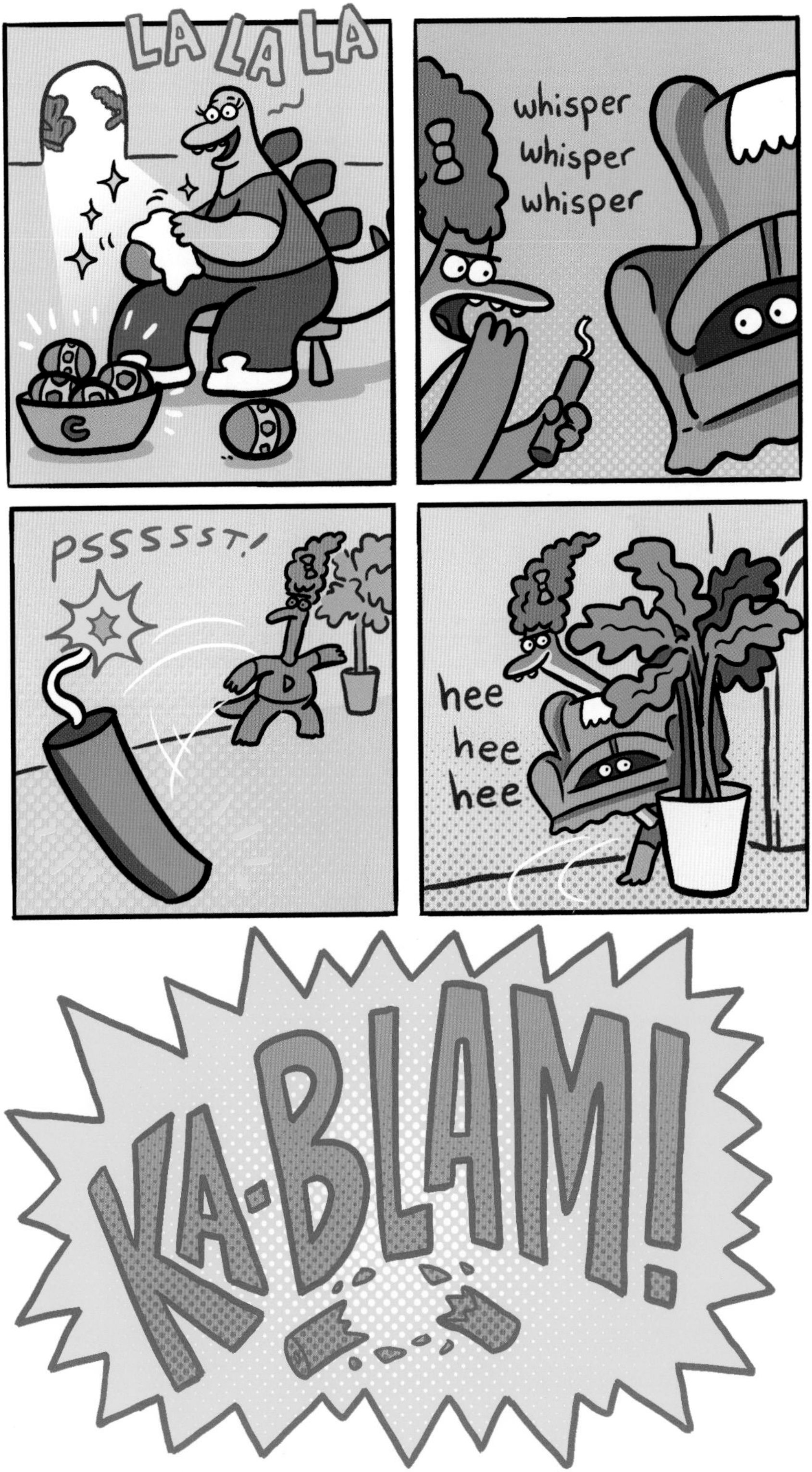
LA LA LA
whisper
whisper
whisper
PSSSSST!
hee
hee
hee
KA-BLAM!

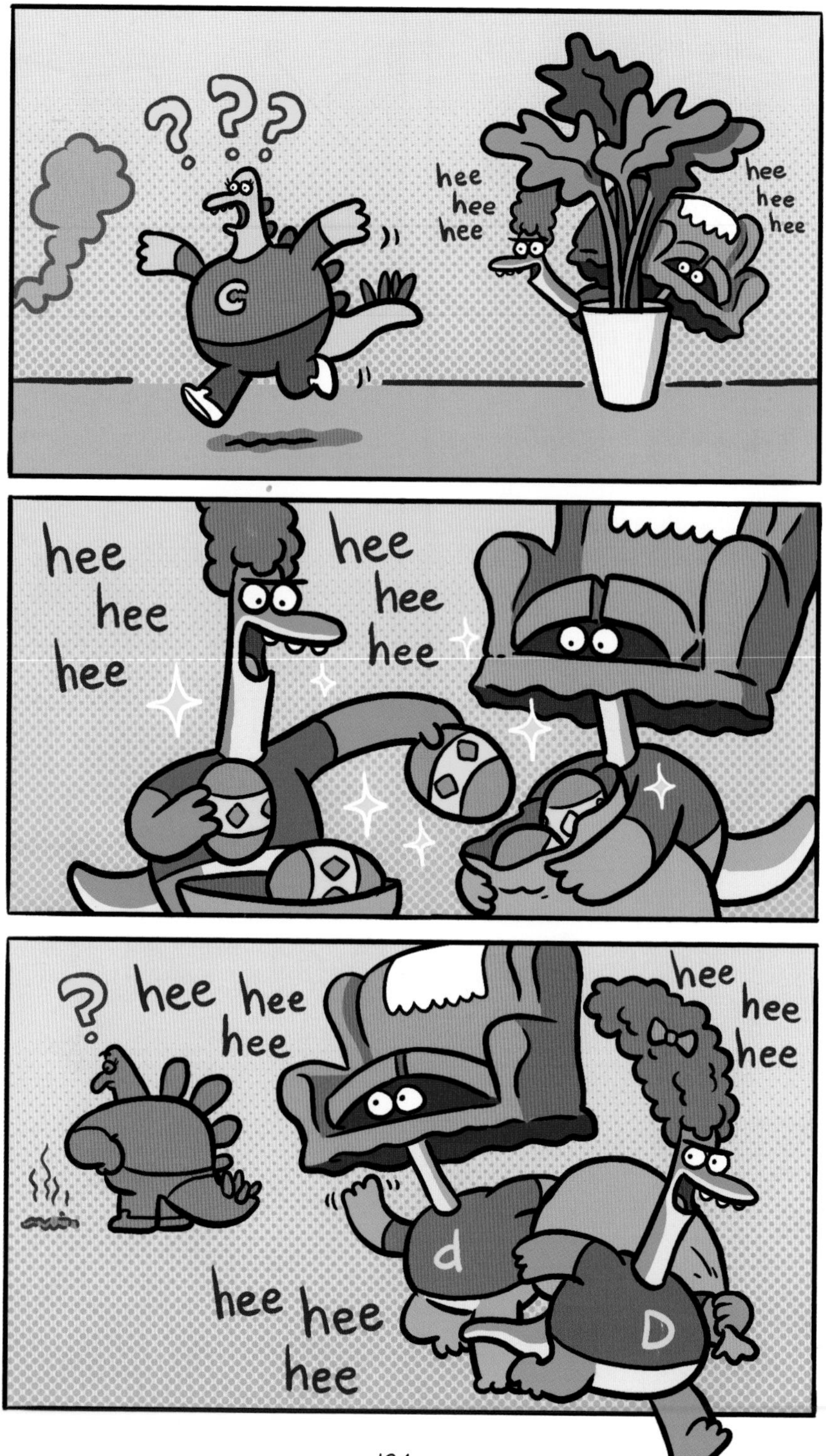
???
hee hee hee
hee hee hee
hee hee hee
hee hee hee
?
hee hee hee
hee hee hee
hee hee hee

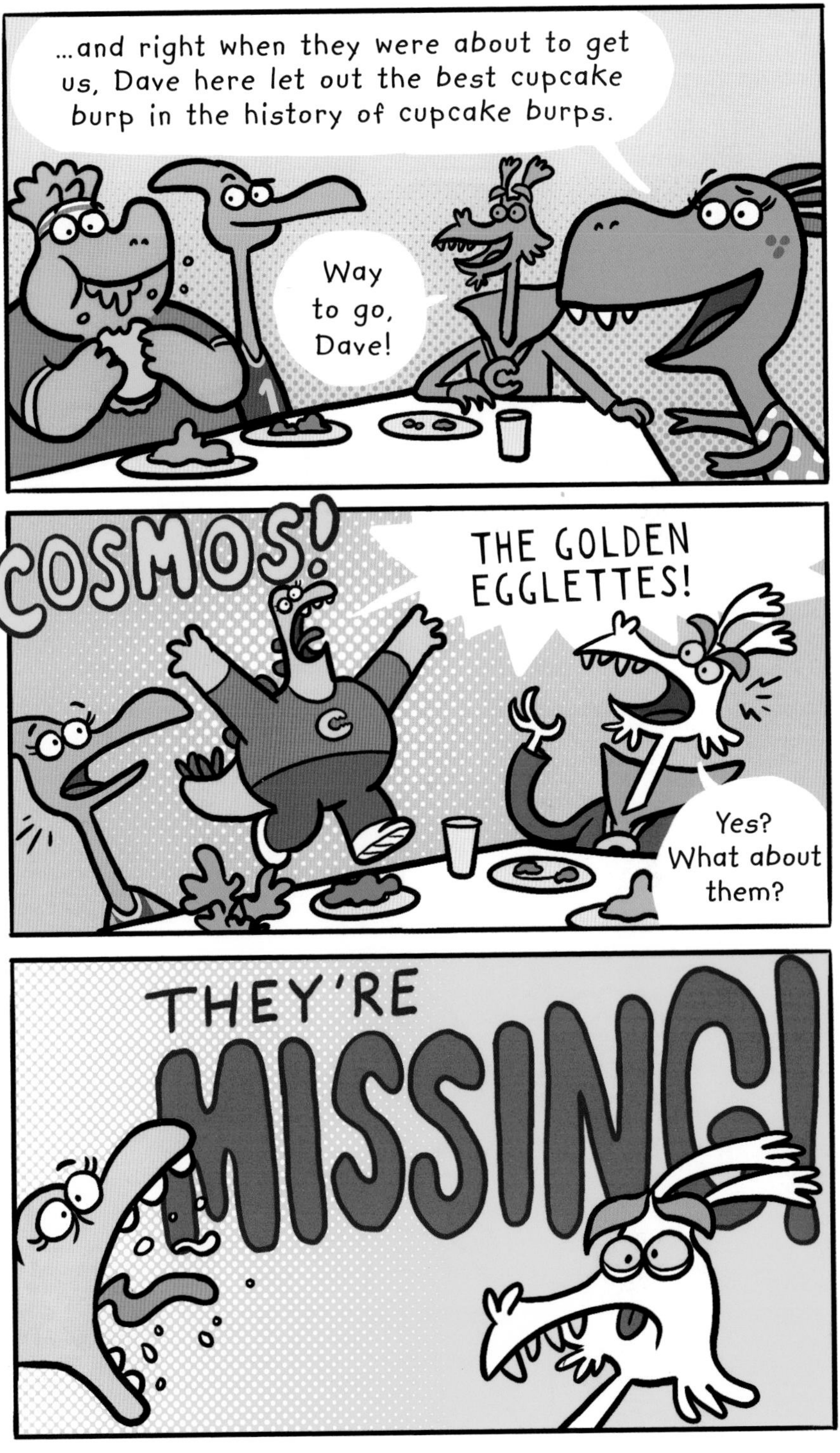
...and right when they were about to get us, Dave here let out the *best* cupcake burp in the history of cupcake burps.
Way to go, Dave!
COSMOS!
THE GOLDEN EGGLETTES!
Yes? What about them?
THEY'RE MISSING!

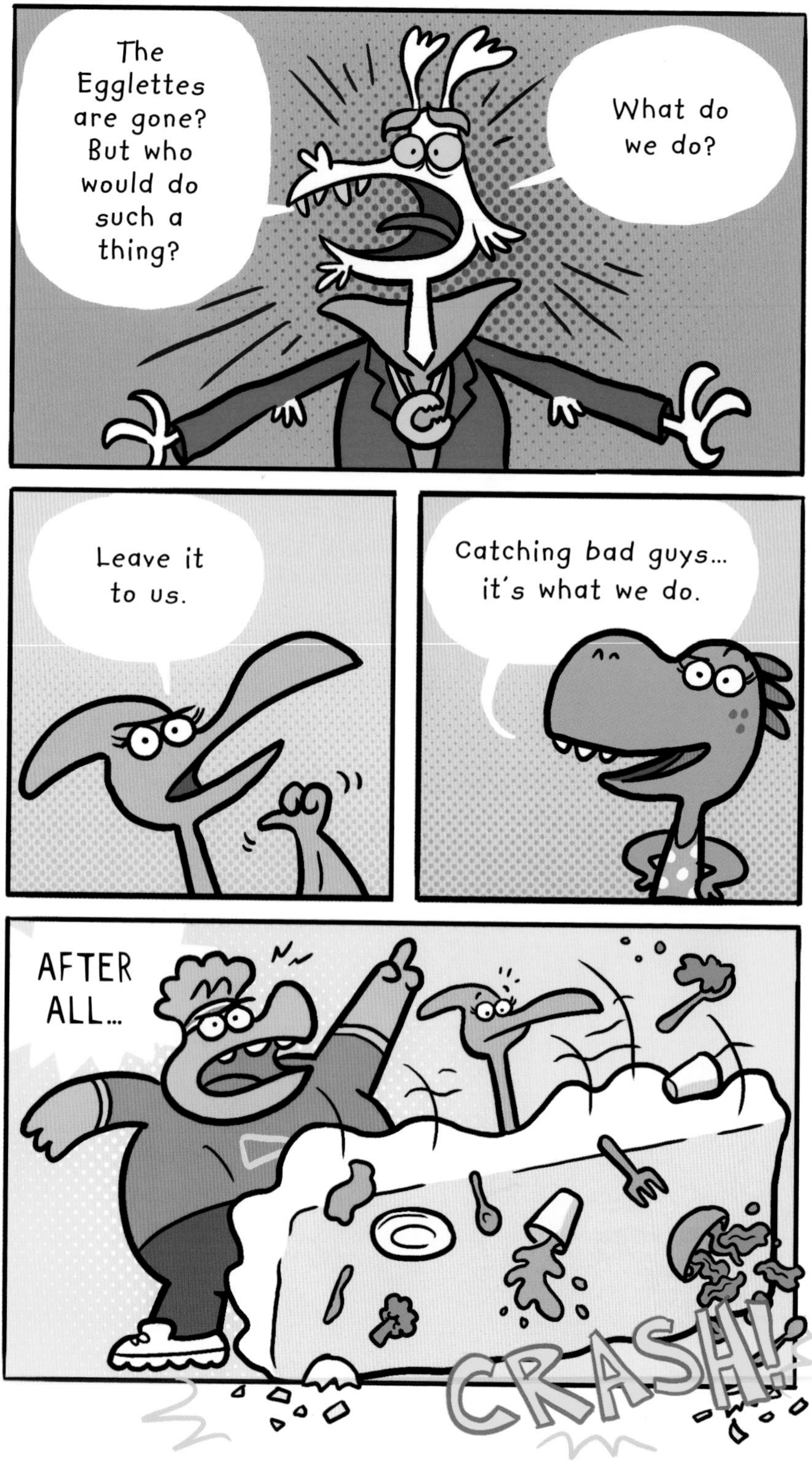
The Egglettes are gone? But who would do such a thing?
What do we do?
Leave it to us.
Catching bad guys... it's what we do.
AFTER ALL...
CRASH!

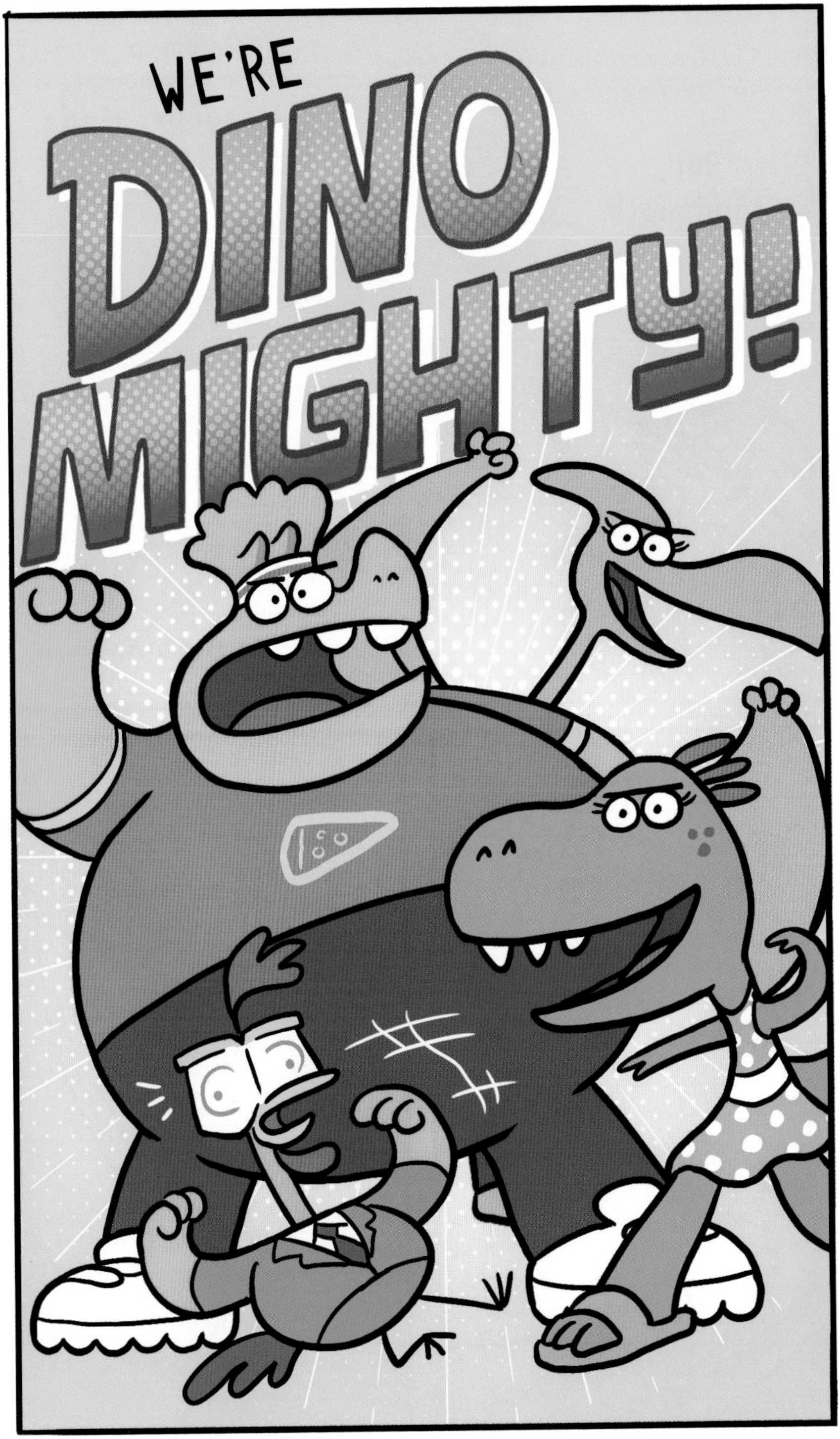
WE'RE
DINO MIGHTY!

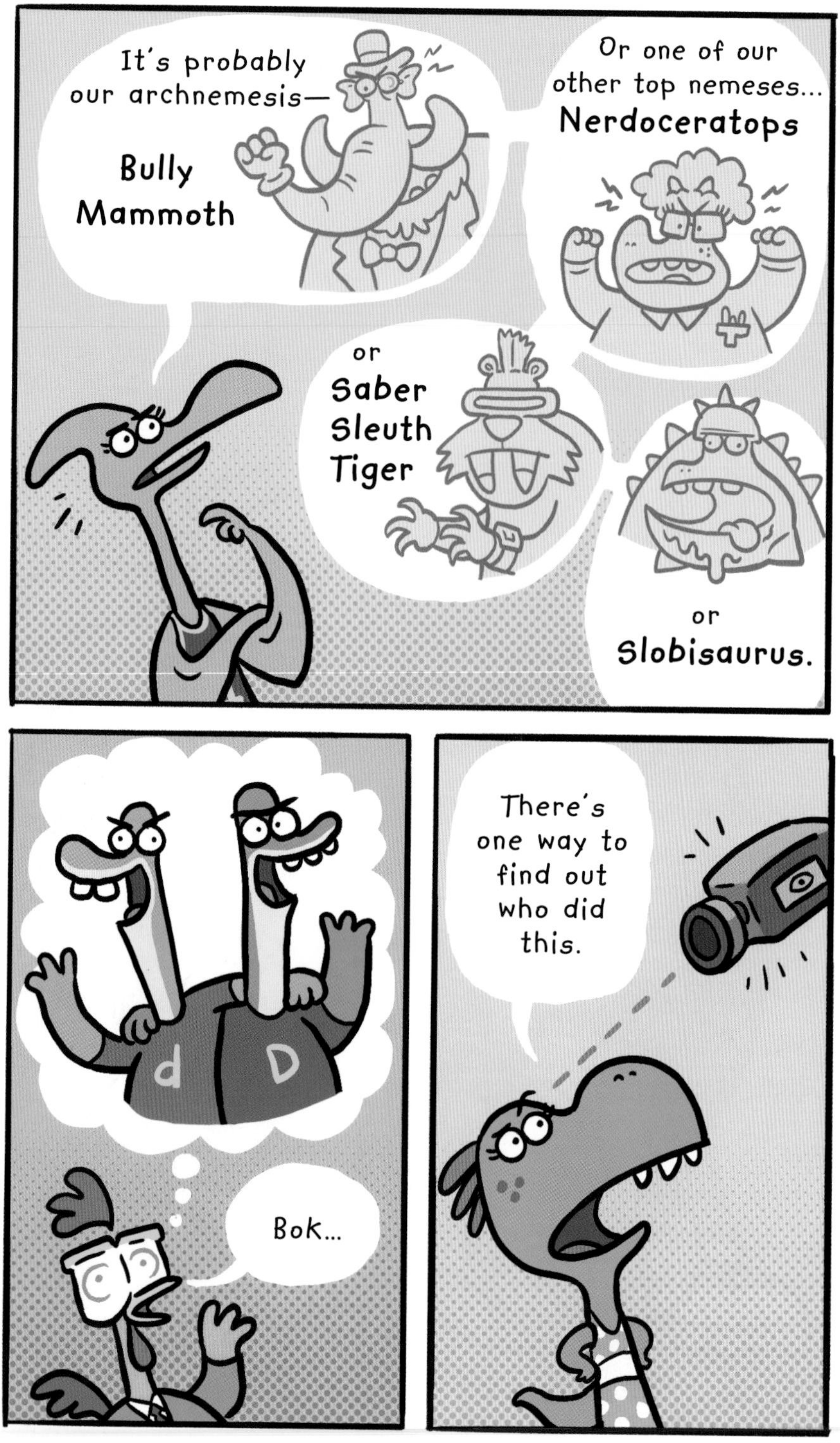
It's probably our archnemesis—
Bully Mammoth
Or one of our other top nemeses...
Nerdoceratops
or
Saber Sleuth Tiger
or
Slobisaurus.
Bok...
There's one way to find out who did this.

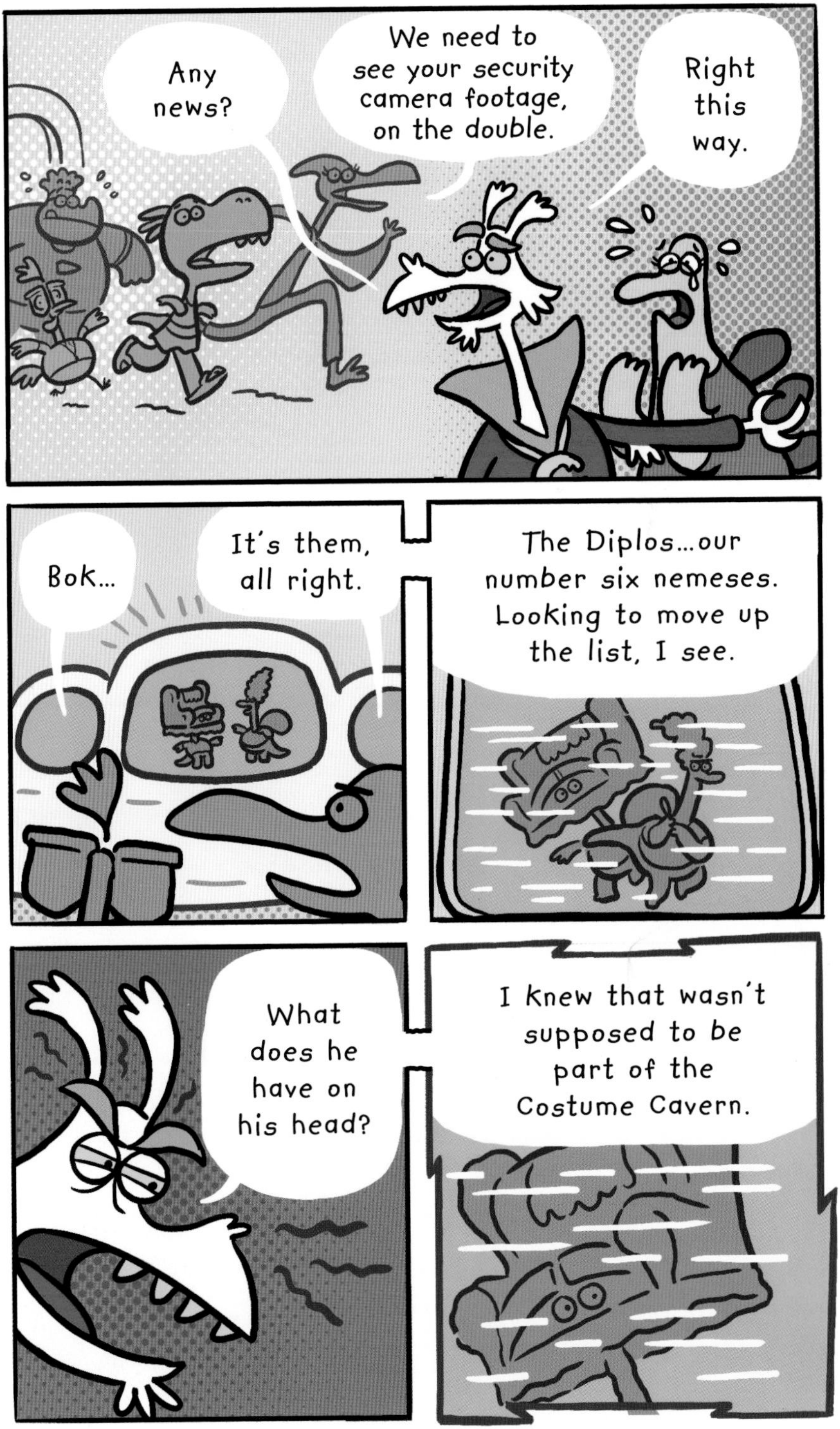
Any news?
We need to see your security camera footage, on the double.
Right this way.
Bok...
It's them, all right.
The Diplos...our number six nemeses. Looking to move up the list, I see.
What does he have on his head?
I knew that wasn't supposed to be part of the Costume Cavern.

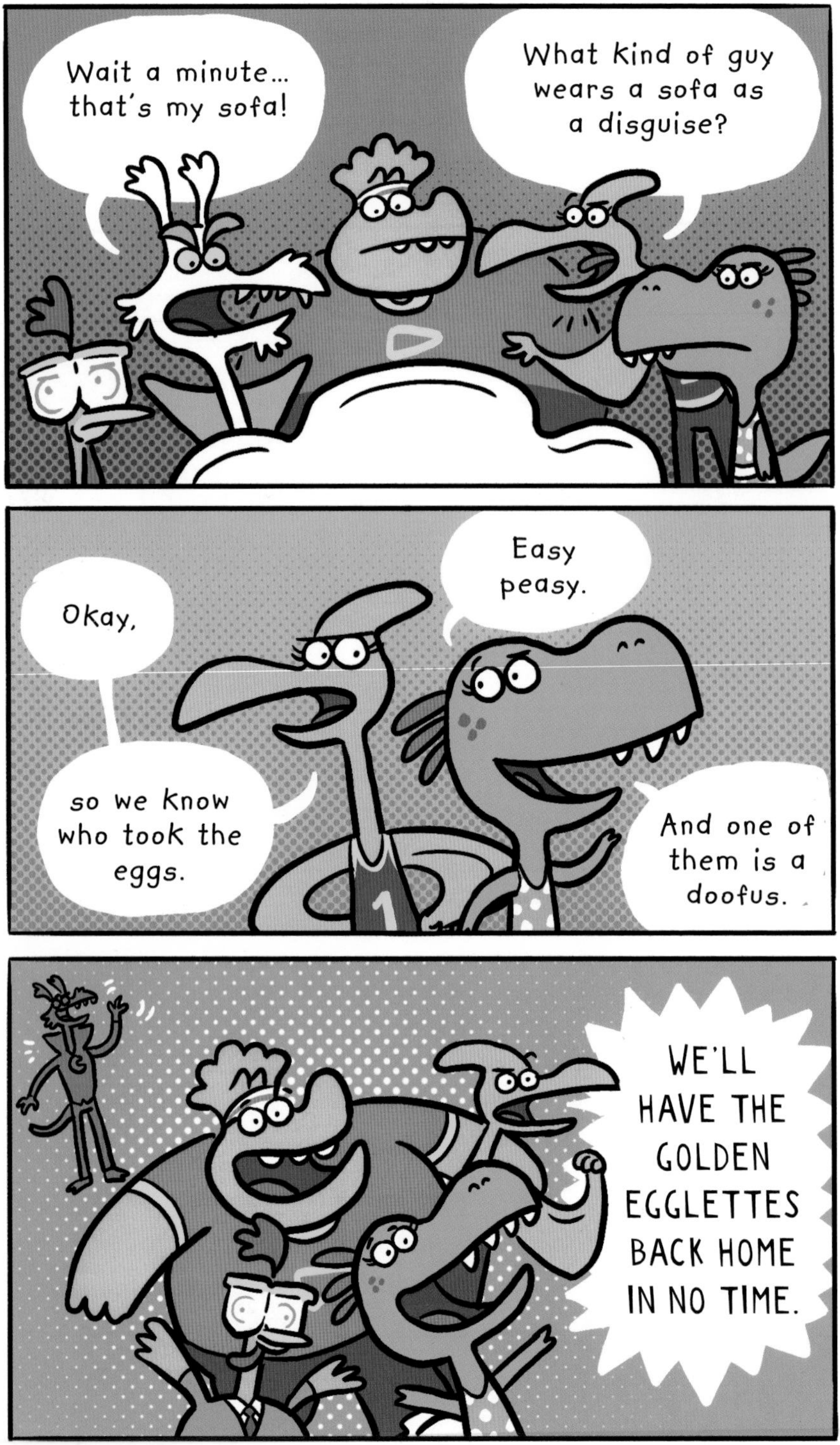
Wait a minute... that's my sofa!
What kind of guy wears a sofa as a disguise?
Okay,
Easy peasy.
so we know who took the eggs.
And one of them is a doofus.
WE'LL HAVE THE GOLDEN EGGLETTES BACK HOME IN NO TIME.

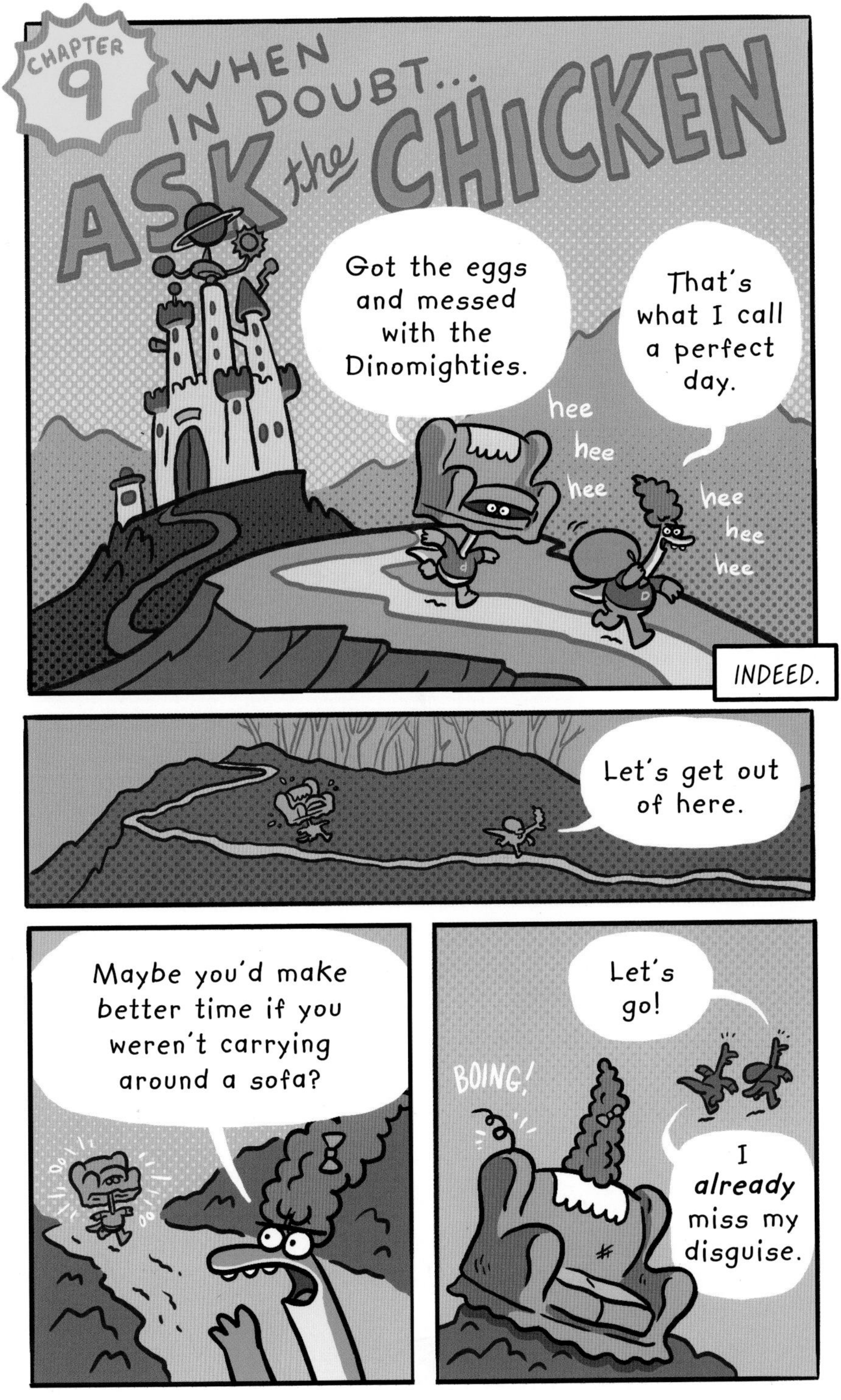
CHAPTER 9
WHEN IN DOUBT...
ASK the CHICKEN
Got the eggs and messed with the Dinomighties.
hee hee hee
That's what I call a perfect day.
hee hee hee
INDEED.
Let's get out of here.
Maybe you'd make better time if you weren't carrying around a sofa?
Let's go!
BOING!
I *already* miss my disguise.

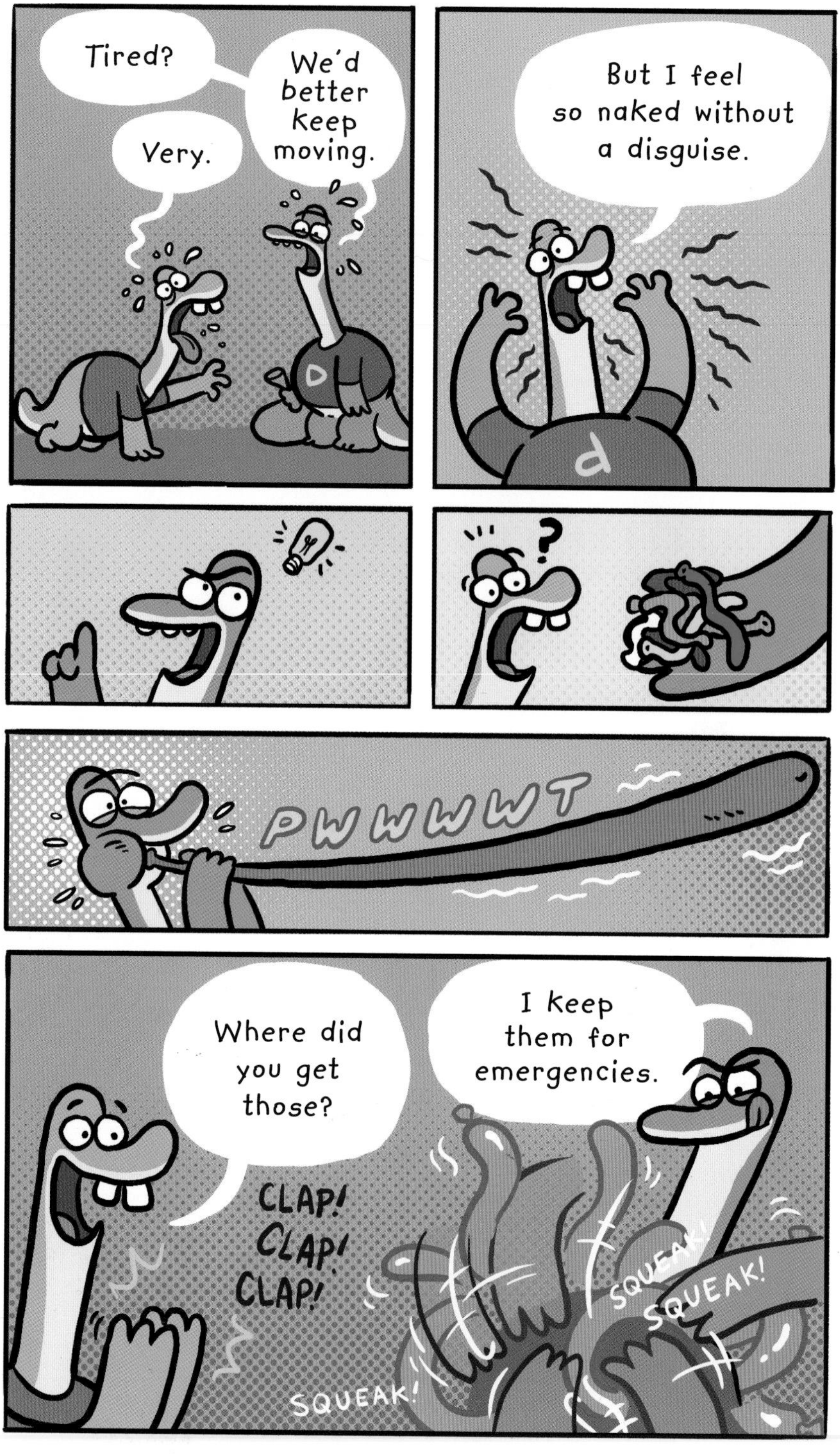
Tired?
Very.
We'd better keep moving.
But I feel so naked without a disguise.
PWWWWT
Where did you get those?
I keep them for emergencies.
CLAP! CLAP! CLAP!
SQUEAK!
SQUEAK!
SQUEAK!

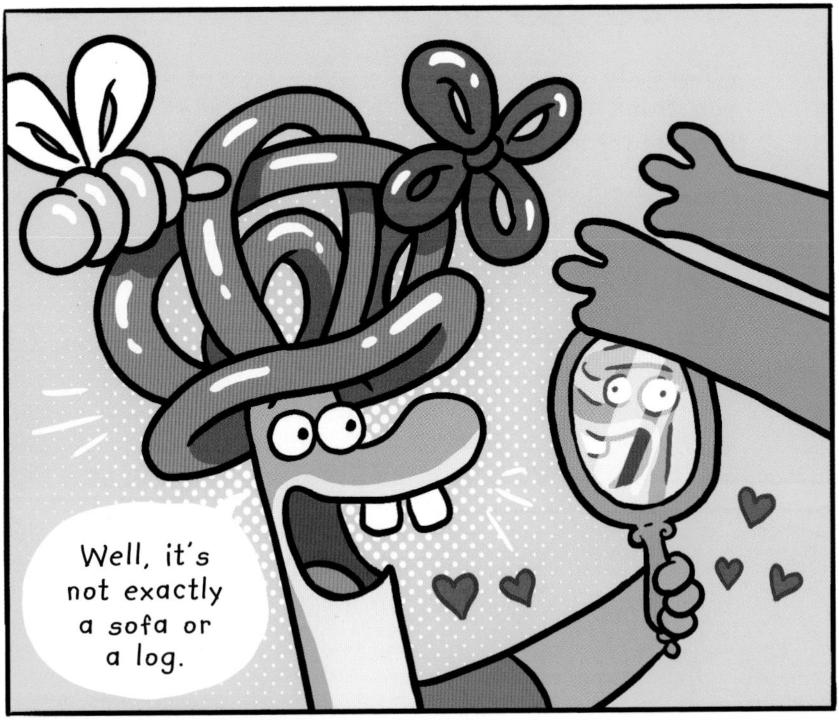
Well, it's not exactly a sofa or a log.

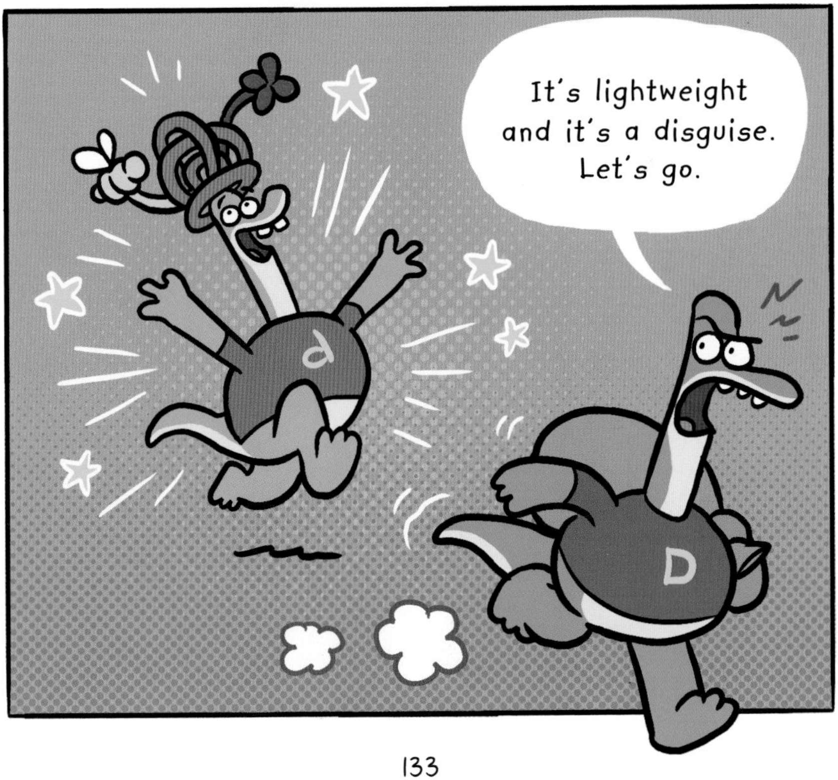
It's lightweight and it's a disguise. Let's go.

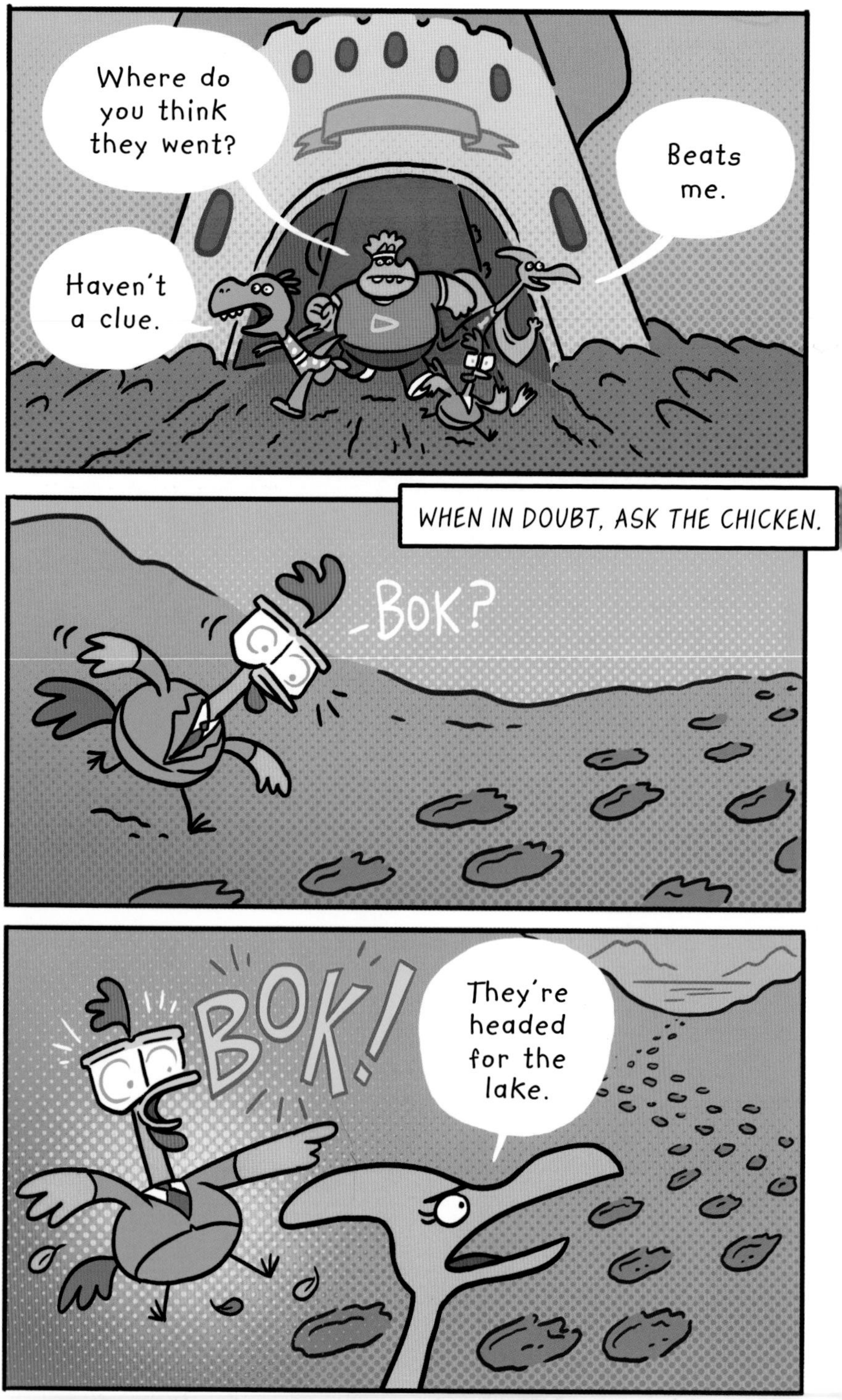
Where do you think they went?
Haven't a clue.
Beats me.
WHEN IN DOUBT, ASK THE CHICKEN.
BOK?
BOK!
They're headed for the lake.

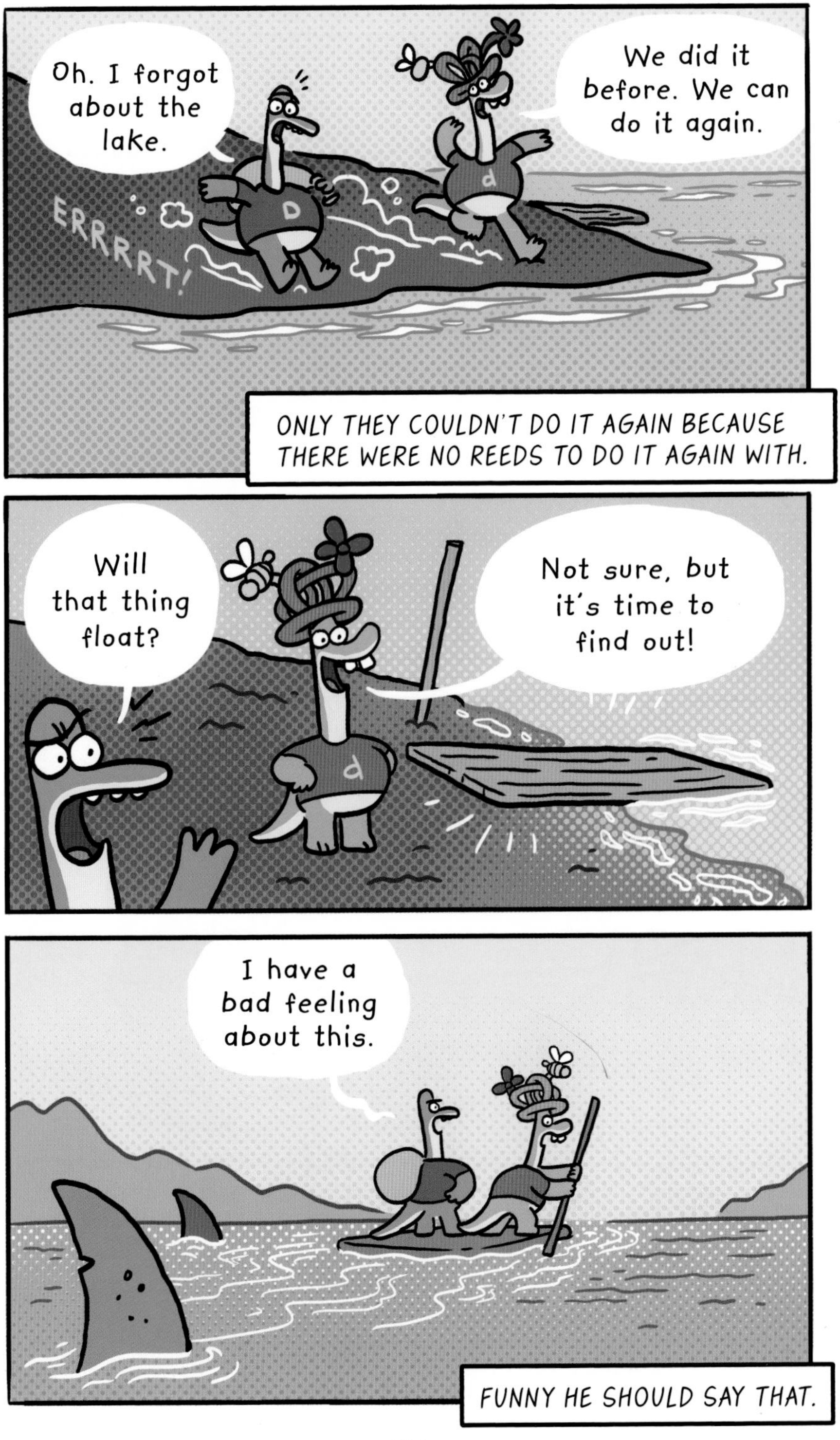
Oh. I forgot about the lake.
ERRRRRT!
We did it before. We can do it again.
ONLY THEY COULDN'T DO IT AGAIN BECAUSE THERE WERE NO REEDS TO DO IT AGAIN WITH.
Will that thing float?
Not sure, but it's time to find out!
I have a bad feeling about this.
FUNNY HE SHOULD SAY THAT.

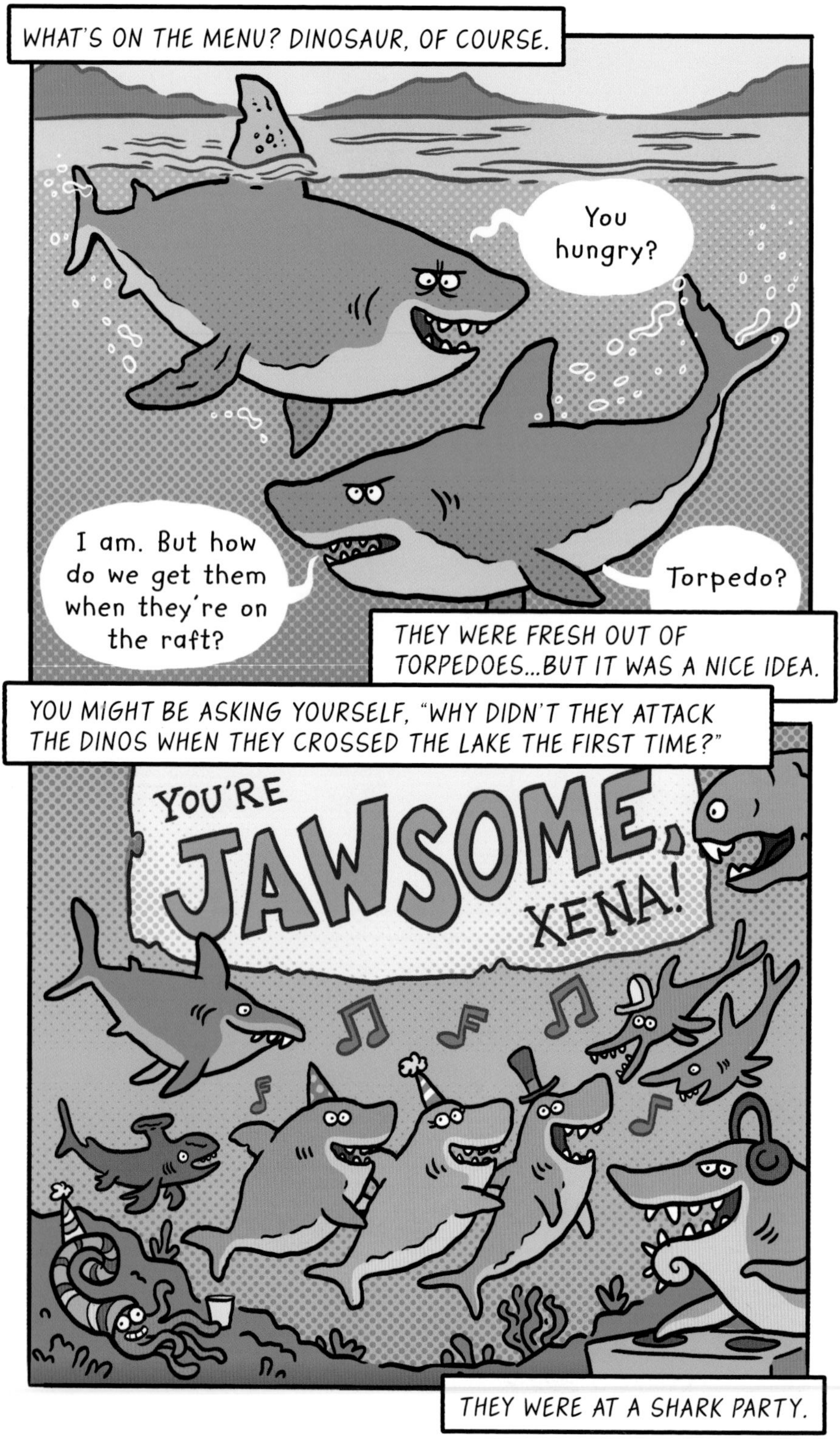
WHAT'S ON THE MENU? DINOSAUR, OF COURSE.
You hungry?
I am. But how do we get them when they're on the raft?
Torpedo?
THEY WERE FRESH OUT OF TORPEDOES...BUT IT WAS A NICE IDEA.
YOU MIGHT BE ASKING YOURSELF, "WHY DIDN'T THEY ATTACK THE DINOS WHEN THEY CROSSED THE LAKE THE FIRST TIME?"
YOU'RE JAWSOME, XENA!
THEY WERE AT A SHARK PARTY.

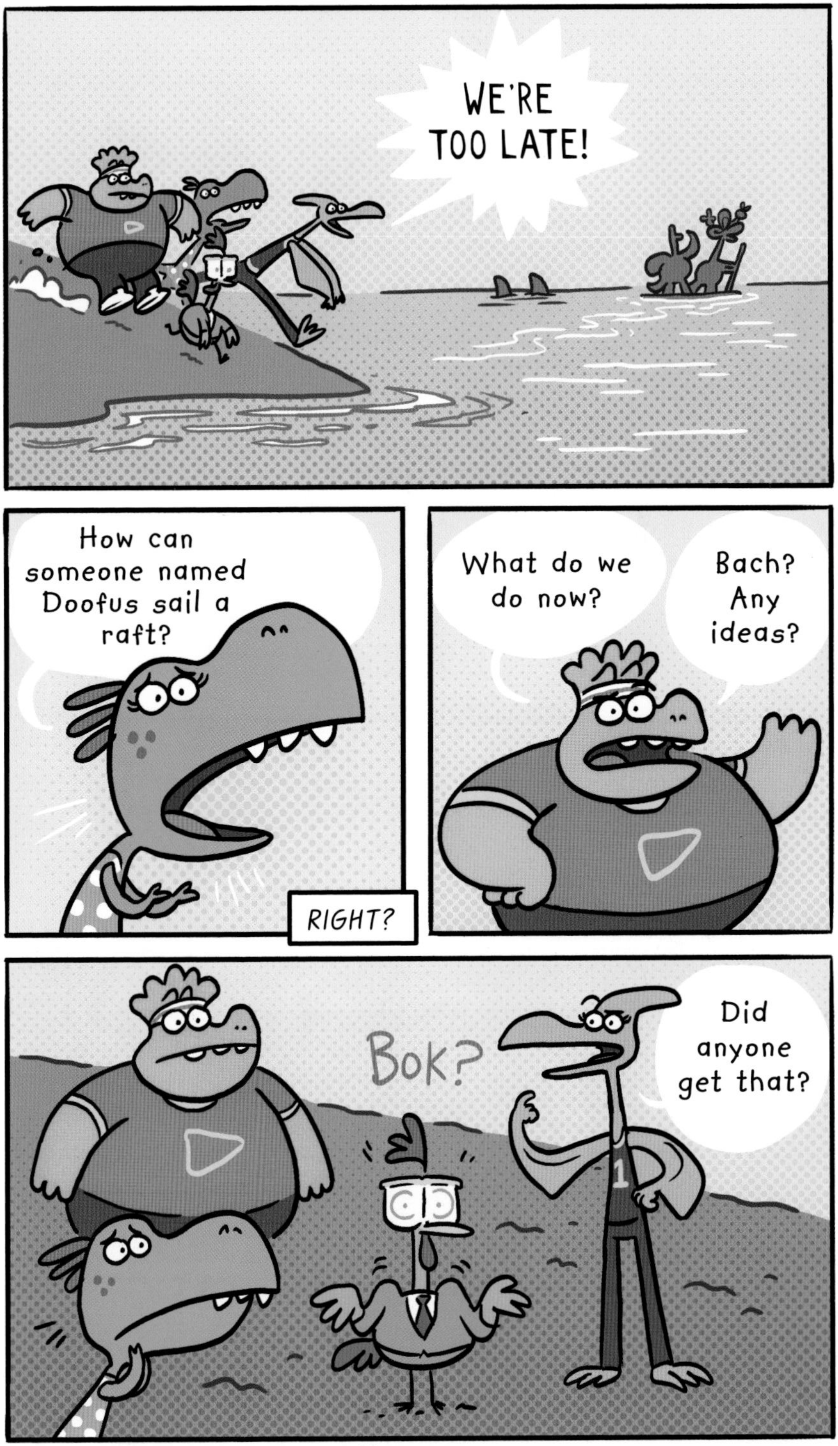
WE'RE TOO LATE!
How can someone named Doofus sail a raft?
RIGHT?
What do we do now?
Bach? Any ideas?
BOK?
Did anyone get that?

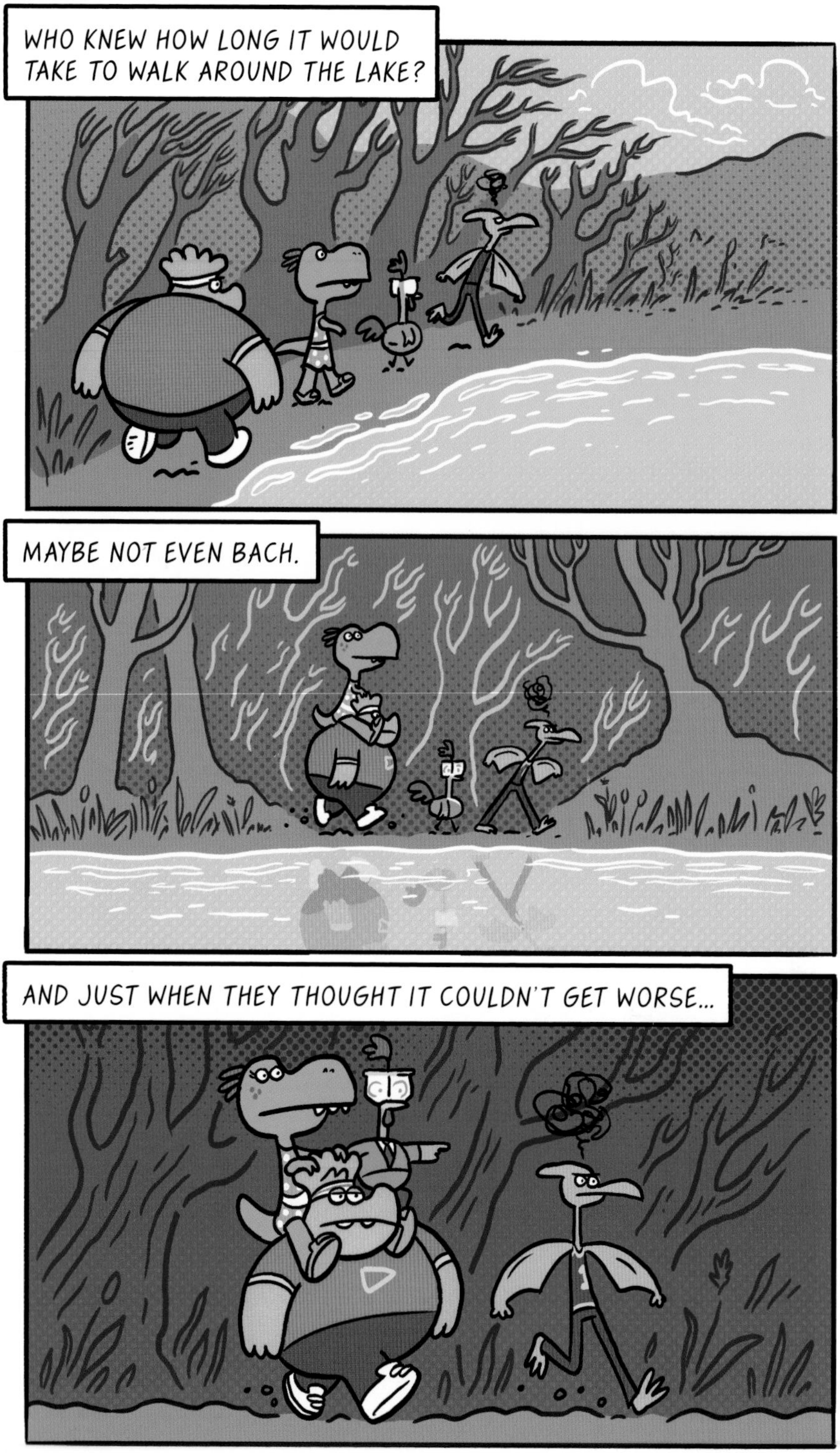
WHO KNEW HOW LONG IT WOULD TAKE TO WALK AROUND THE LAKE?
MAYBE NOT EVEN BACH.
AND JUST WHEN THEY THOUGHT IT COULDN'T GET WORSE...

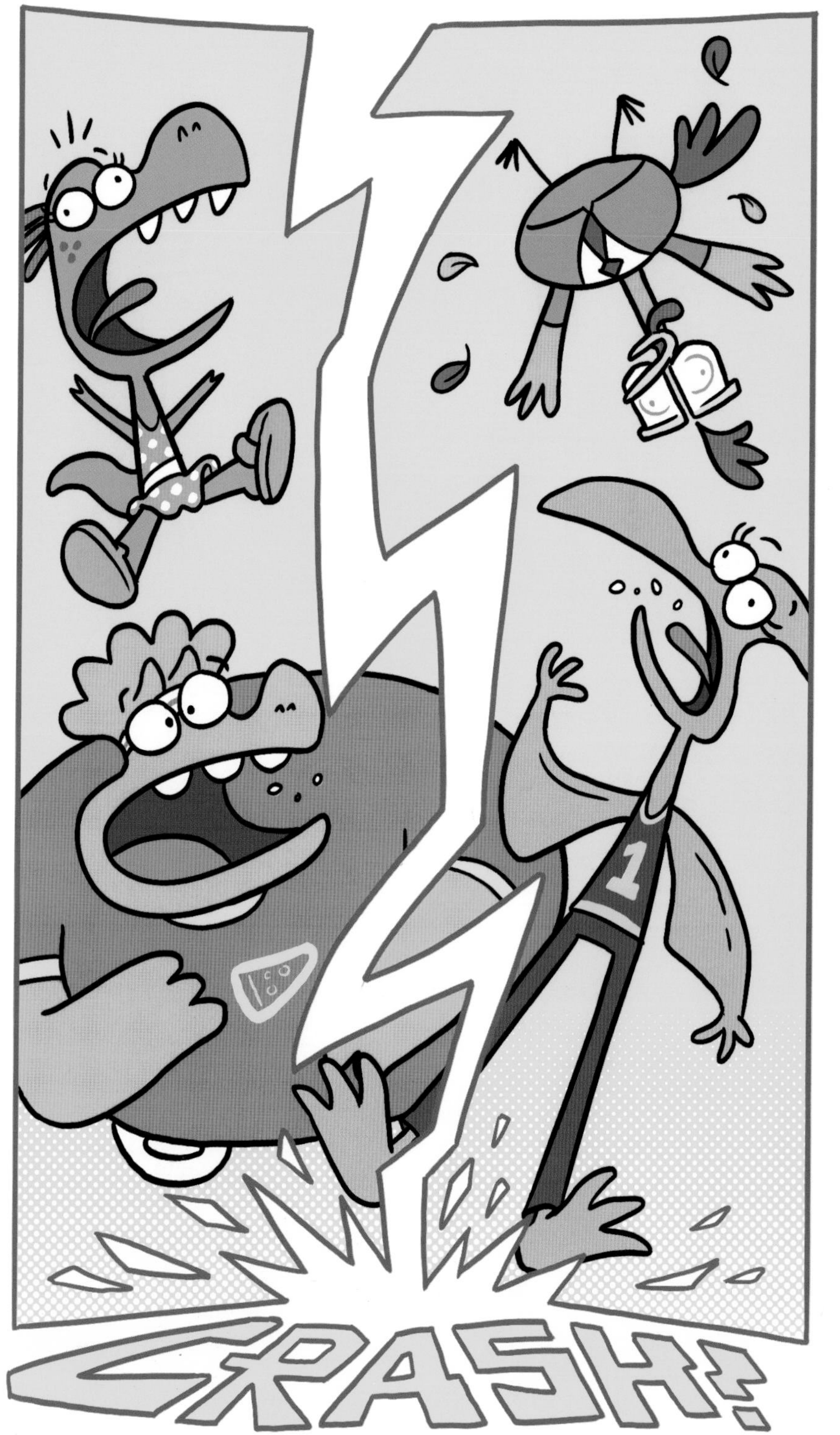
CRASH!

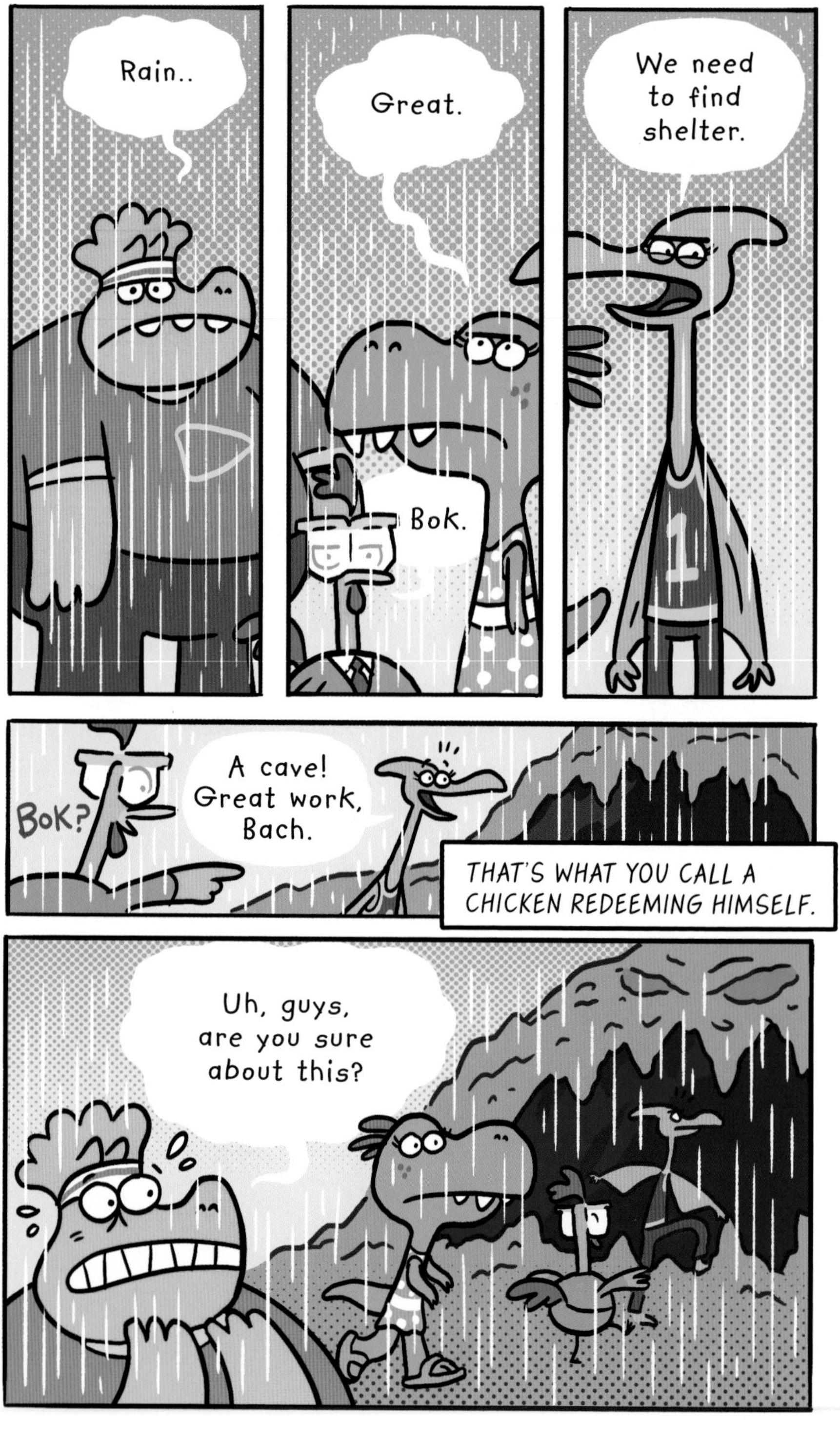
Rain..
Great.
Bok.
We need to find shelter.
BOK?
A cave! Great work, Bach.
THAT'S WHAT YOU CALL A CHICKEN REDEEMING HIMSELF.
Uh, guys, are you sure about this?

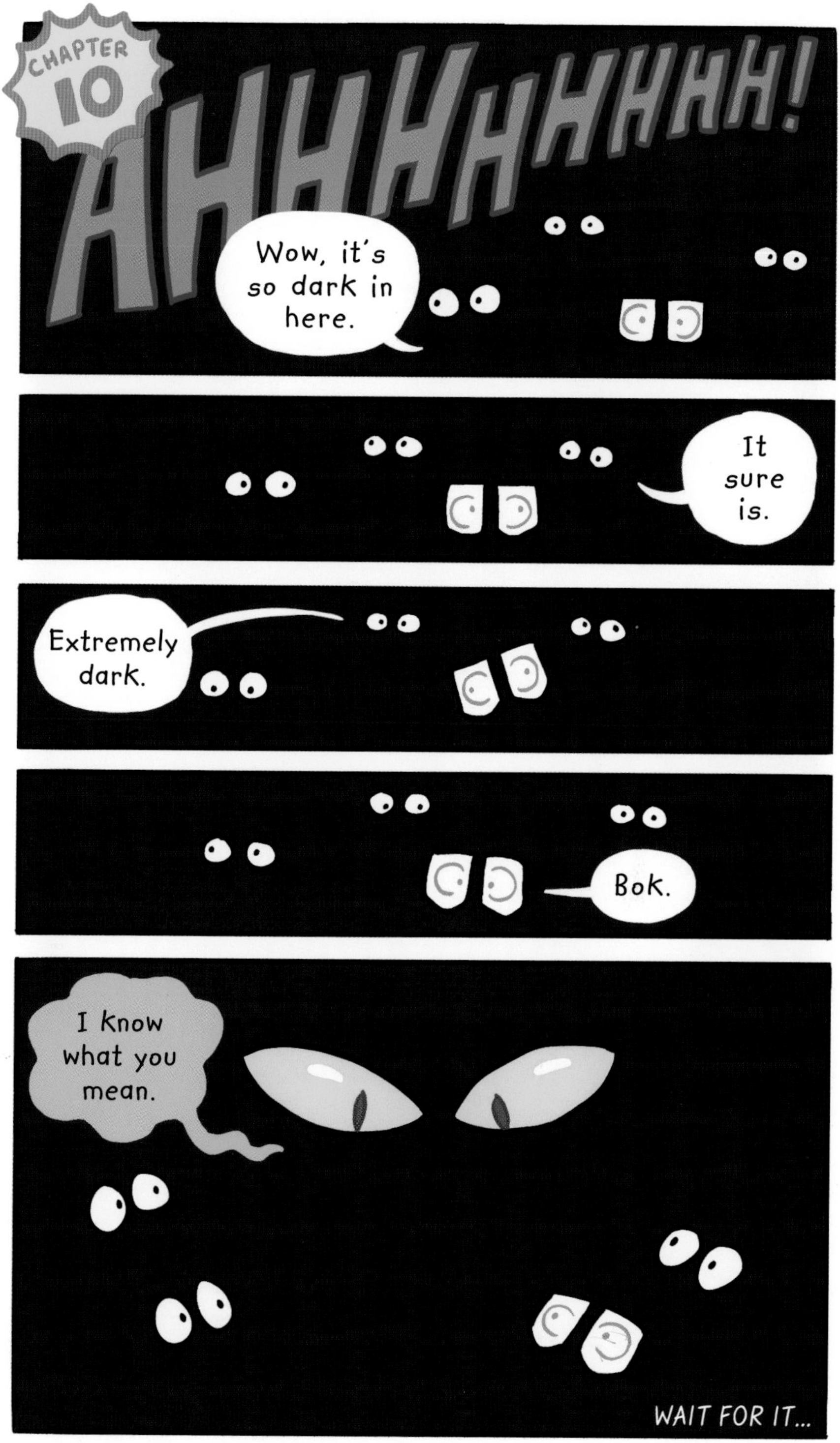
CHAPTER 10
AHHHHHHHHH!
Wow, it's so dark in here.
It sure is.
Extremely dark.
Bok.
I know what you mean.
WAIT FOR IT...

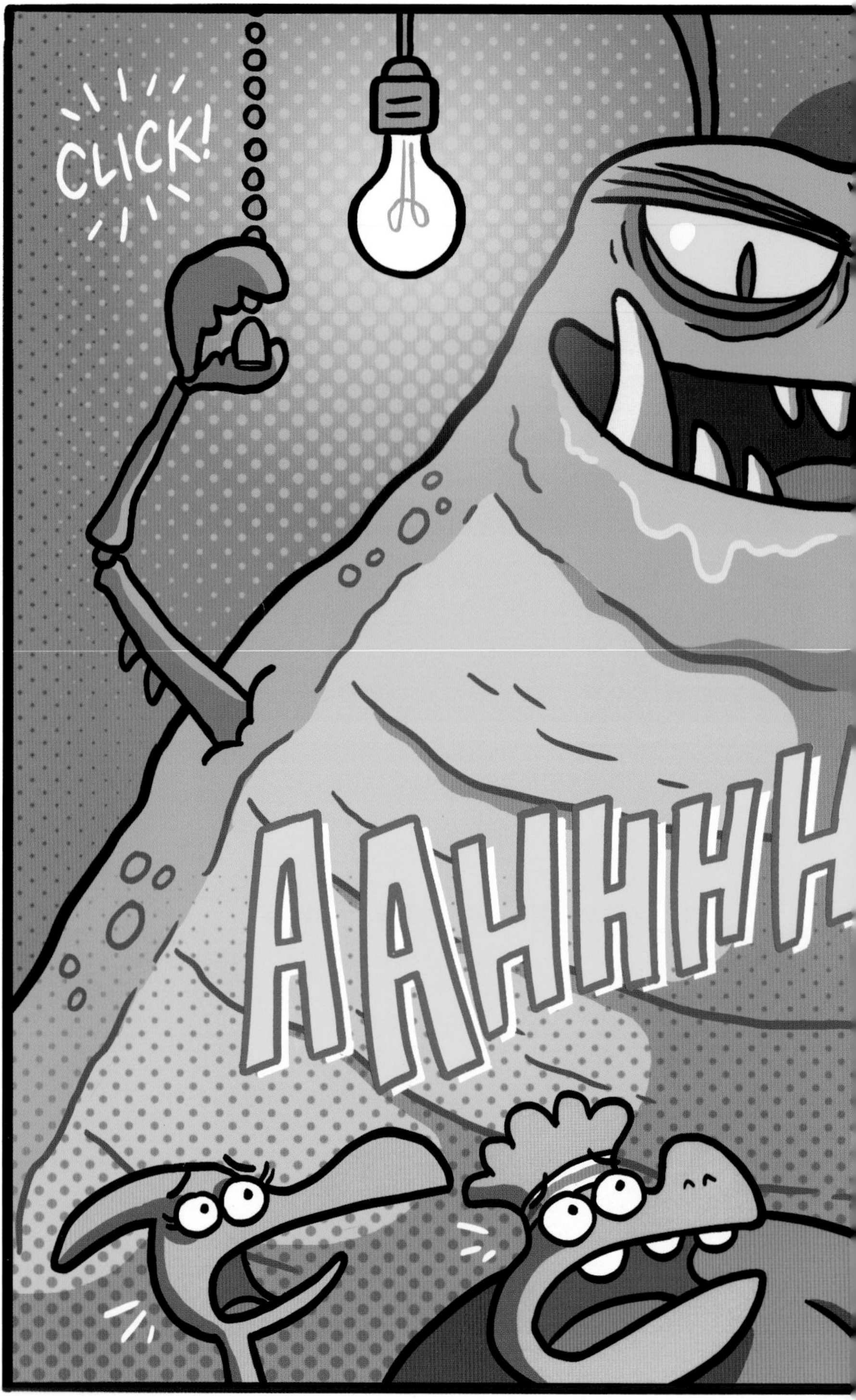
CLICK!
AAHHHH

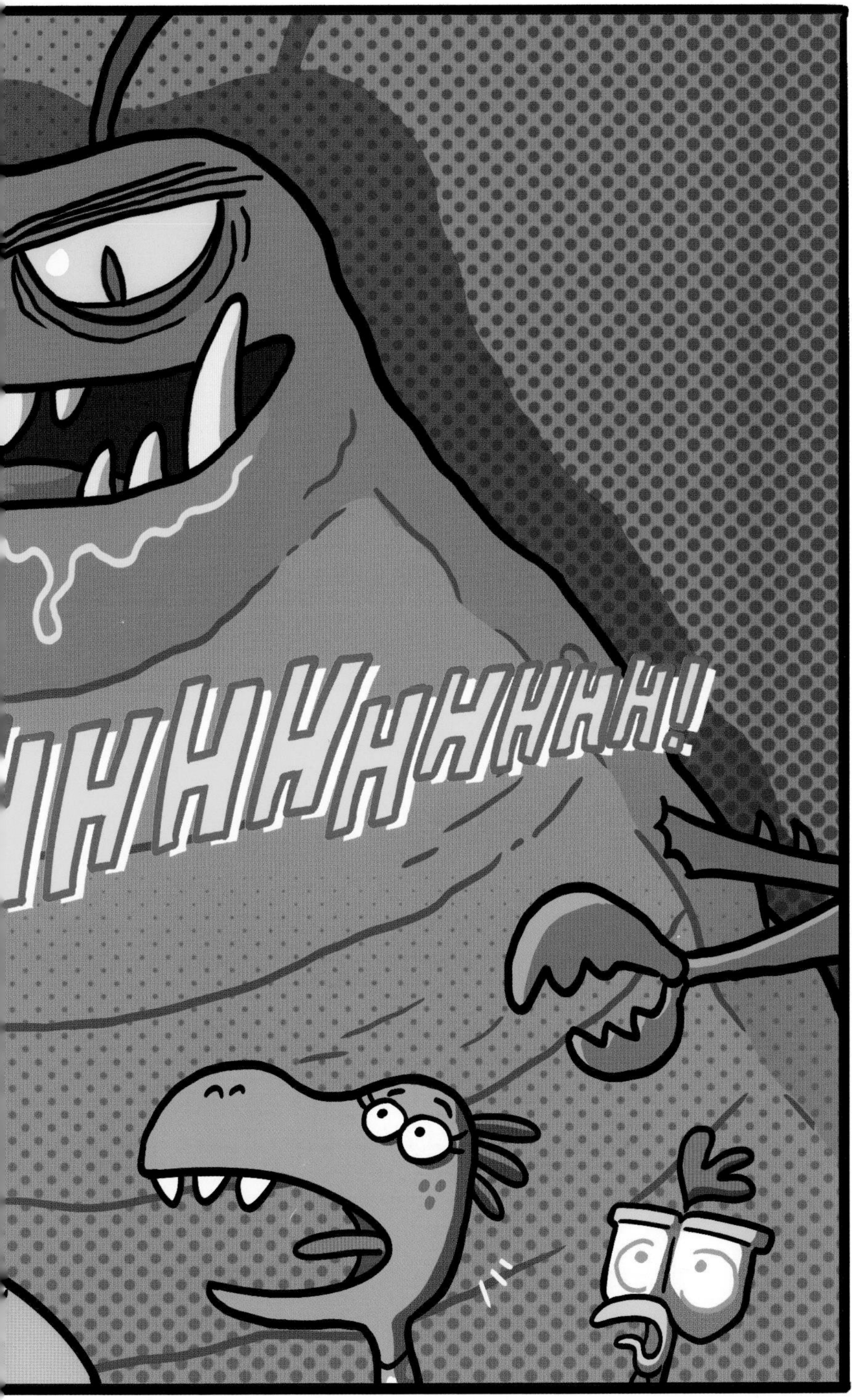
HHHHHHHHHHHH!

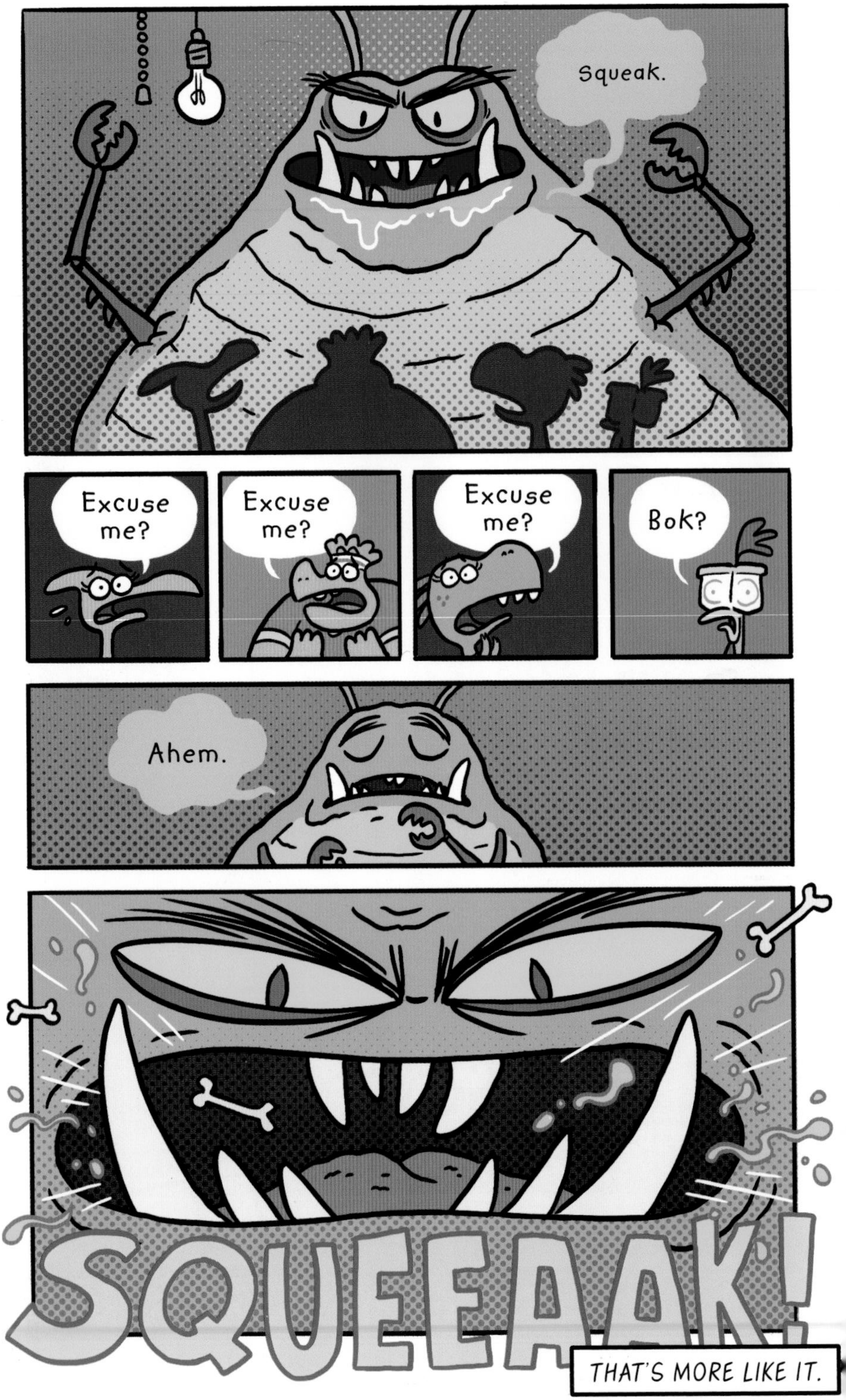
Squeak.
Excuse me?
Excuse me?
Excuse me?
Bok?
Ahem.
SQUEEAAK!
THAT'S MORE LIKE IT.

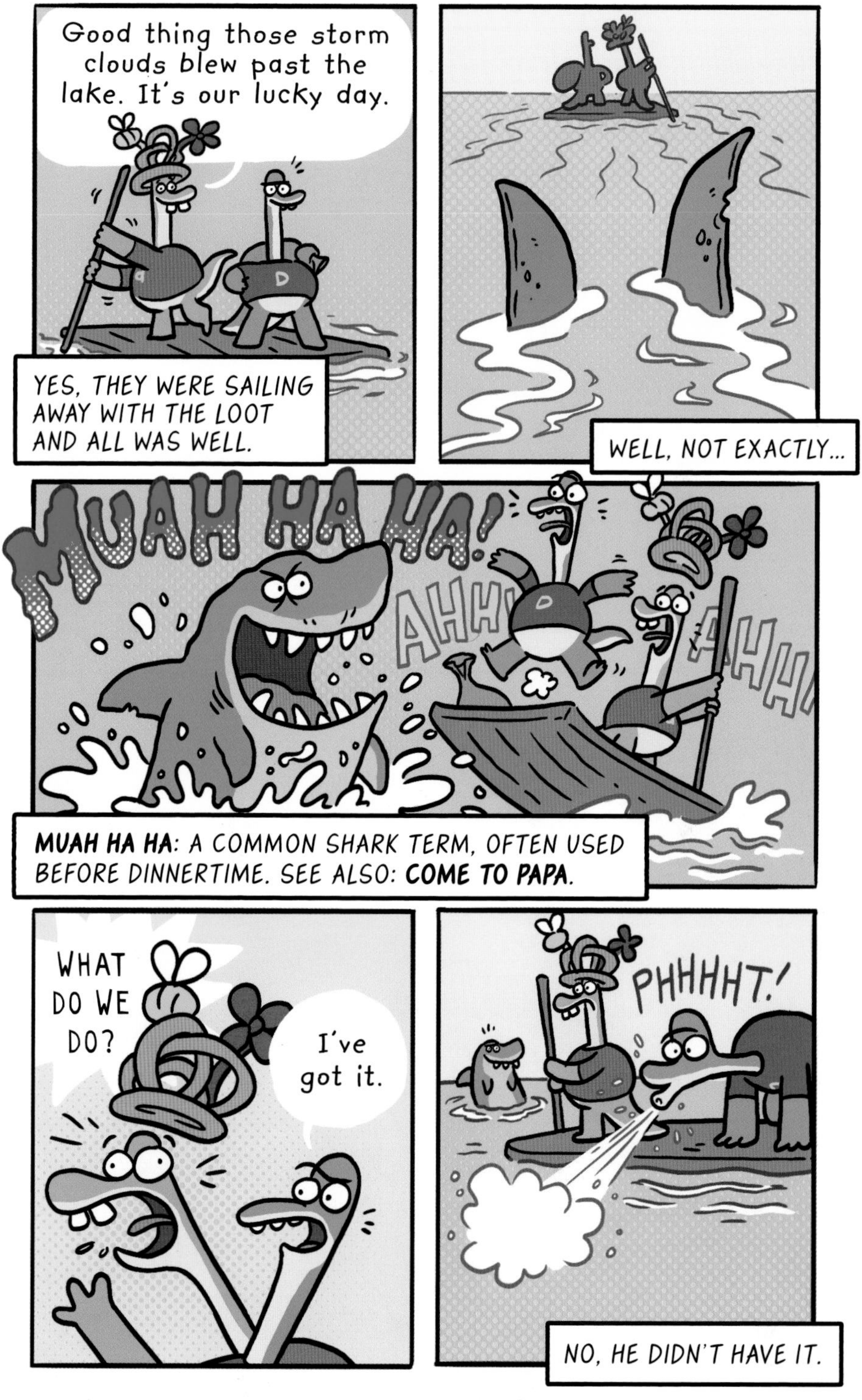

Good thing those storm clouds blew past the lake. It's our lucky day.
YES, THEY WERE SAILING AWAY WITH THE LOOT AND ALL WAS WELL.
WELL, NOT EXACTLY...
MUAH HA HA!
AHH
AHH
MUAH HA HA: A COMMON SHARK TERM, OFTEN USED BEFORE DINNERTIME. SEE ALSO: COME TO PAPA.
WHAT DO WE DO?
I've got it.
PHHHHT!
NO, HE DIDN'T HAVE IT.

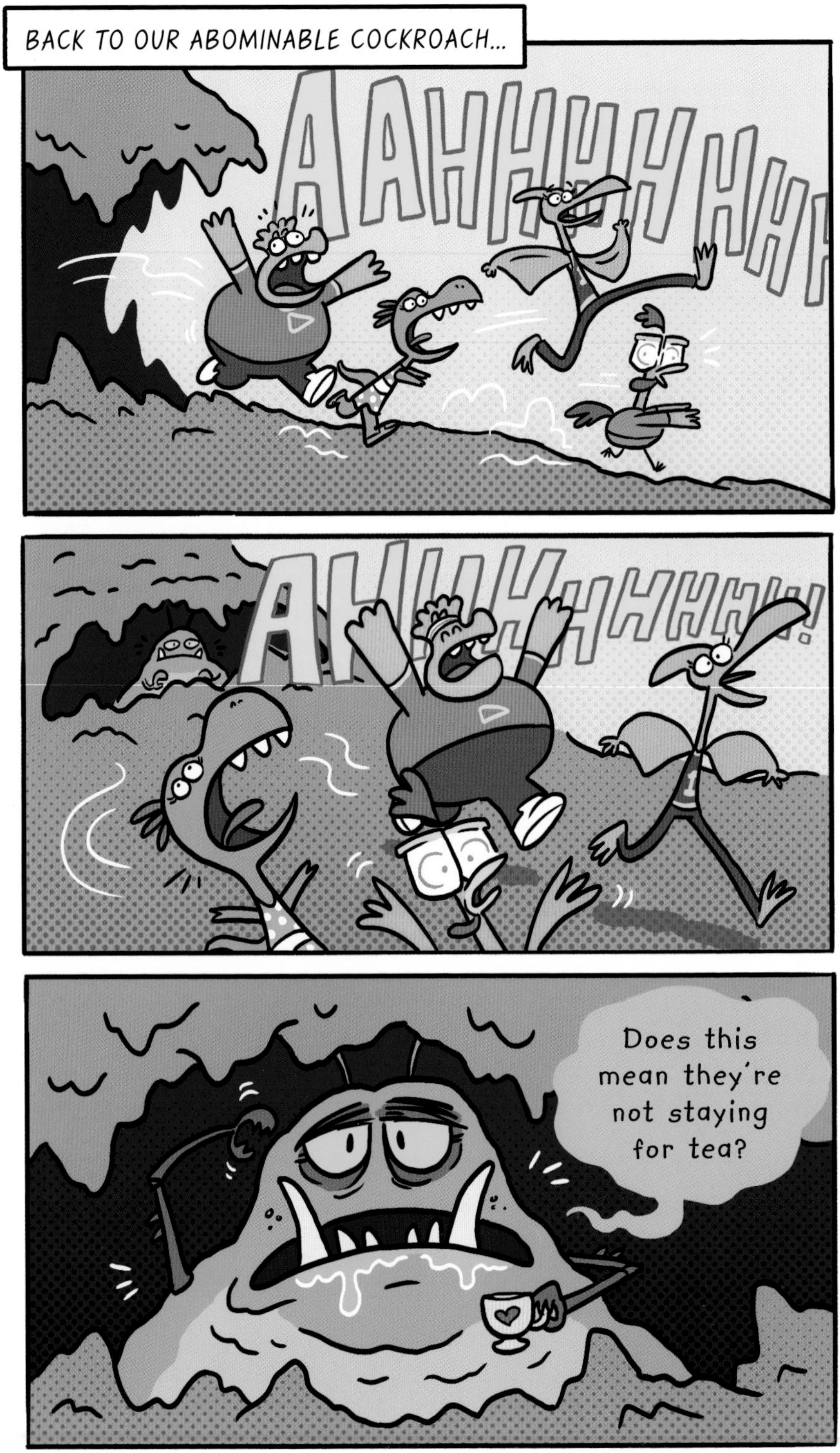
BACK TO OUR ABOMINABLE COCKROACH...
AAHHHHHHHH
AHHHHHHHHH!
Does this mean they're not staying for tea?

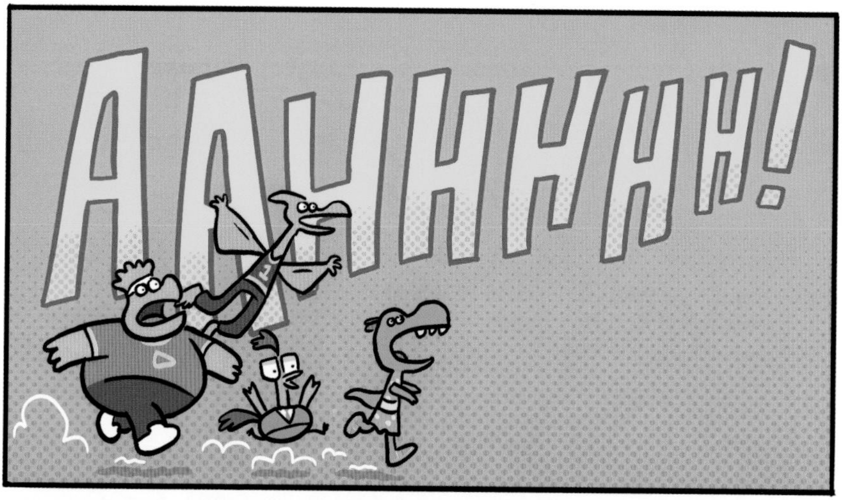
AAHHHHH!

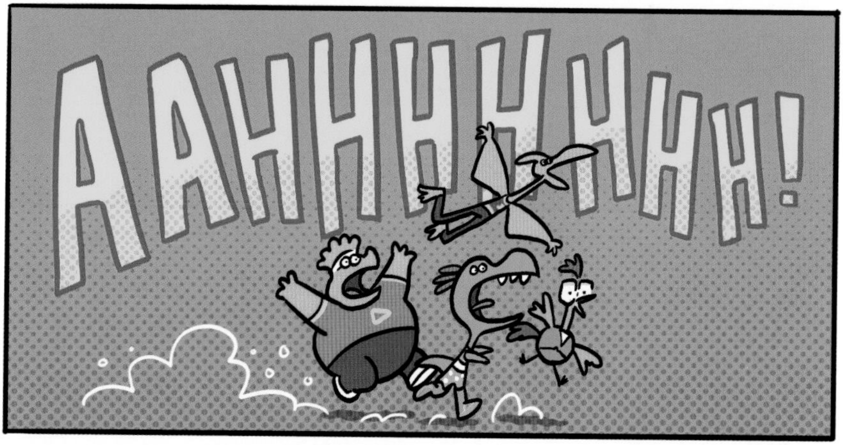
AAHHHHHHH!

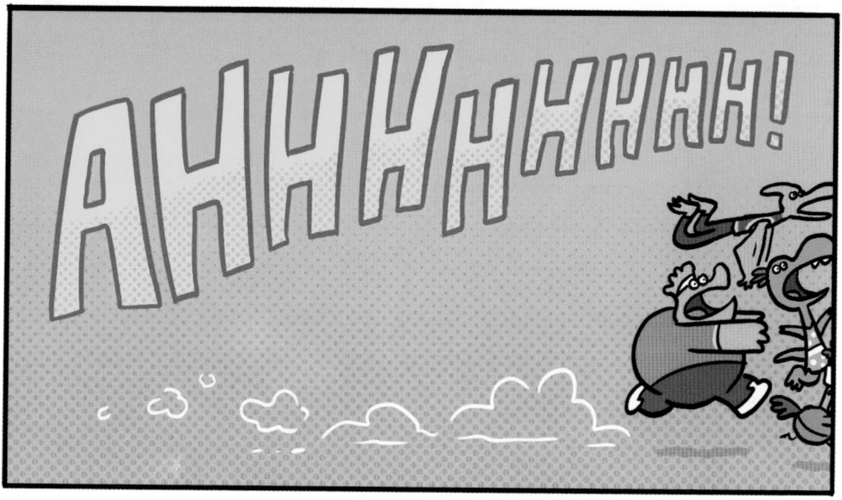
AHHHHHHHH!

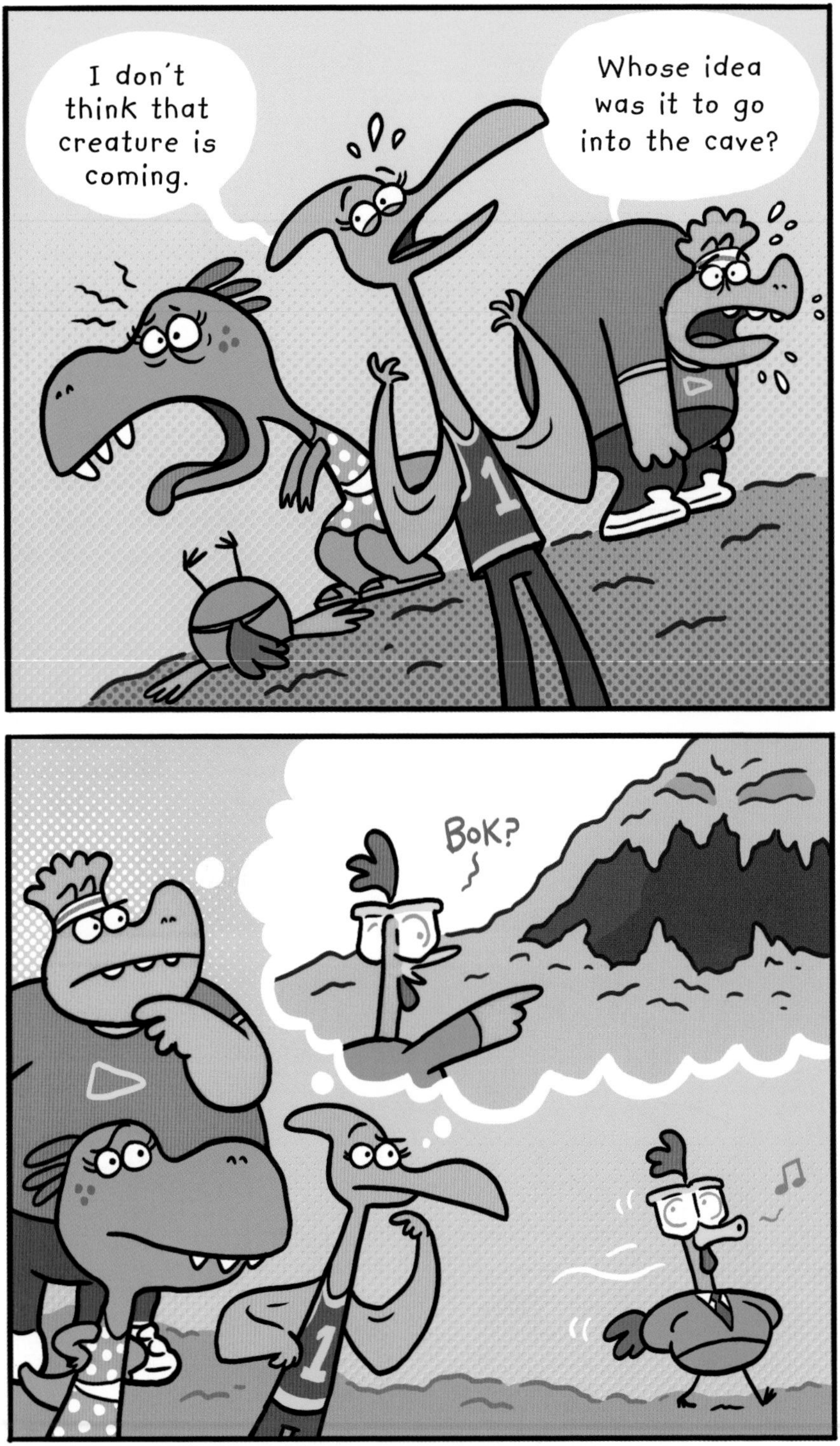
I don't think that creature is coming.
Whose idea was it to go into the cave?
BOK?

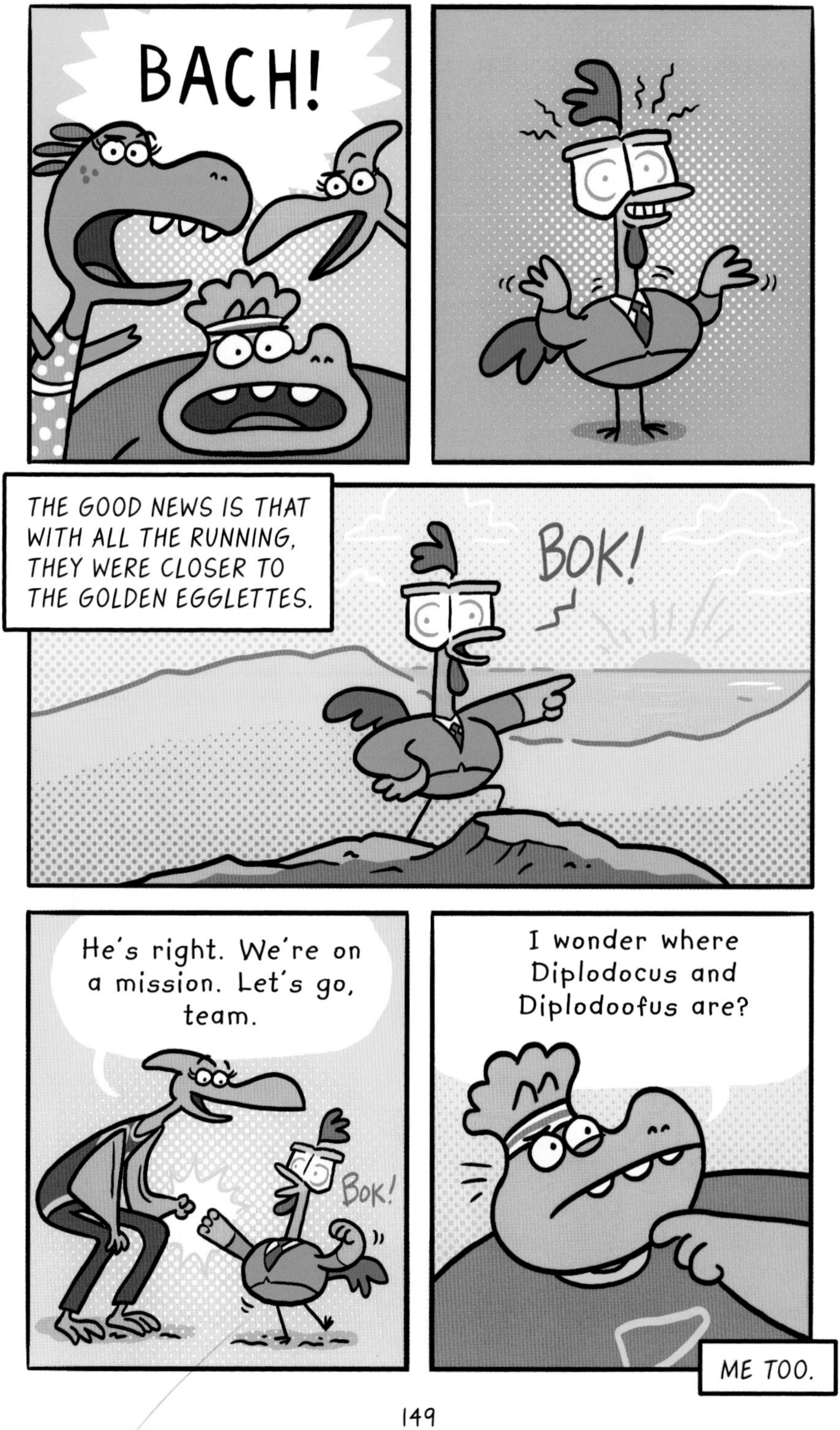
BACH!
THE GOOD NEWS IS THAT WITH ALL THE RUNNING, THEY WERE CLOSER TO THE GOLDEN EGGLETTES.
BOK!
He's right. We're on a mission. Let's go, team.
BOK!
I wonder where Diplodocus and Diplodoofus are?
ME TOO.

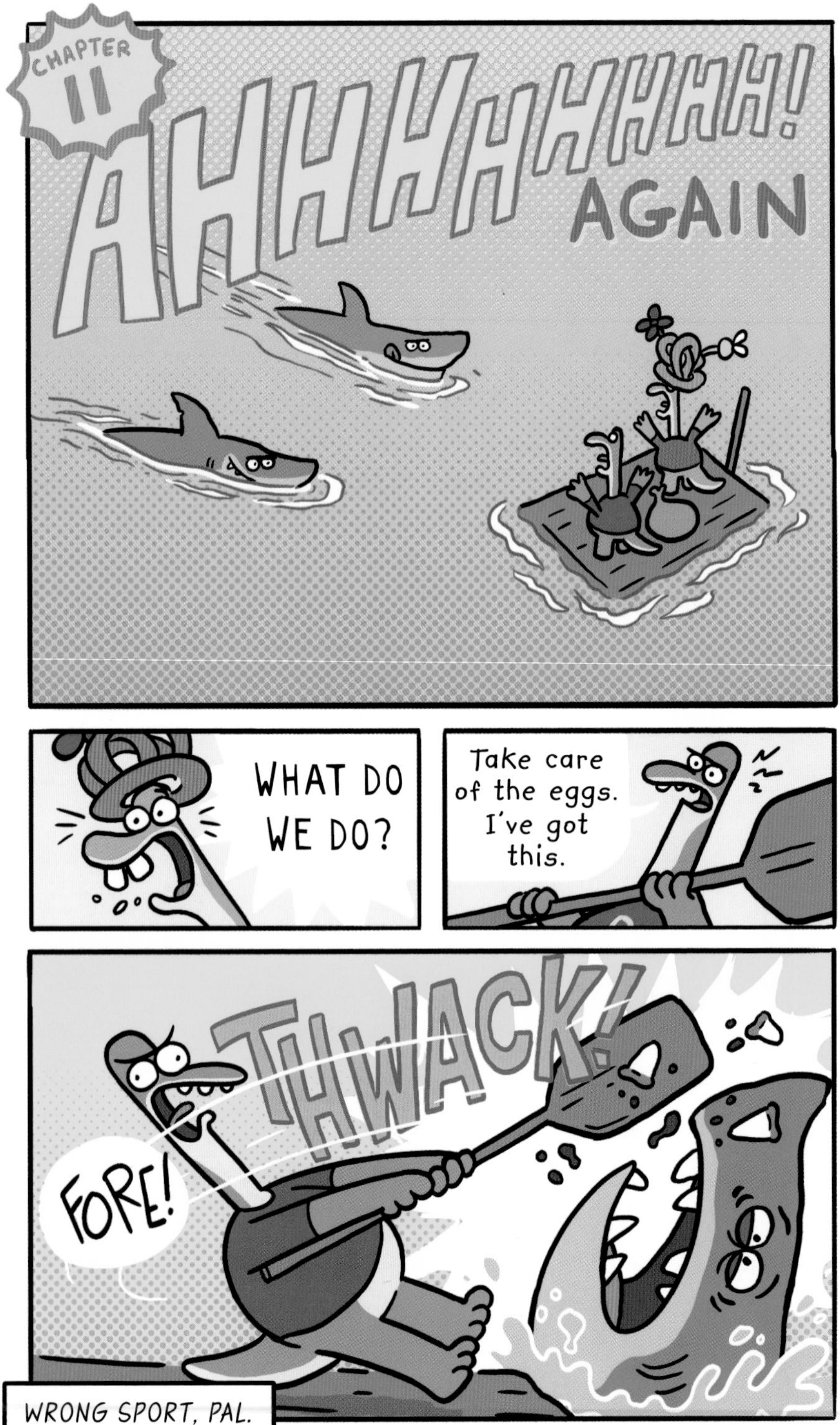
CHAPTER 11
AHHHHHHHHH! AGAIN
WHAT DO WE DO?
Take care of the eggs. I've got this.
THWACK!
FORE!
WRONG SPORT, PAL.

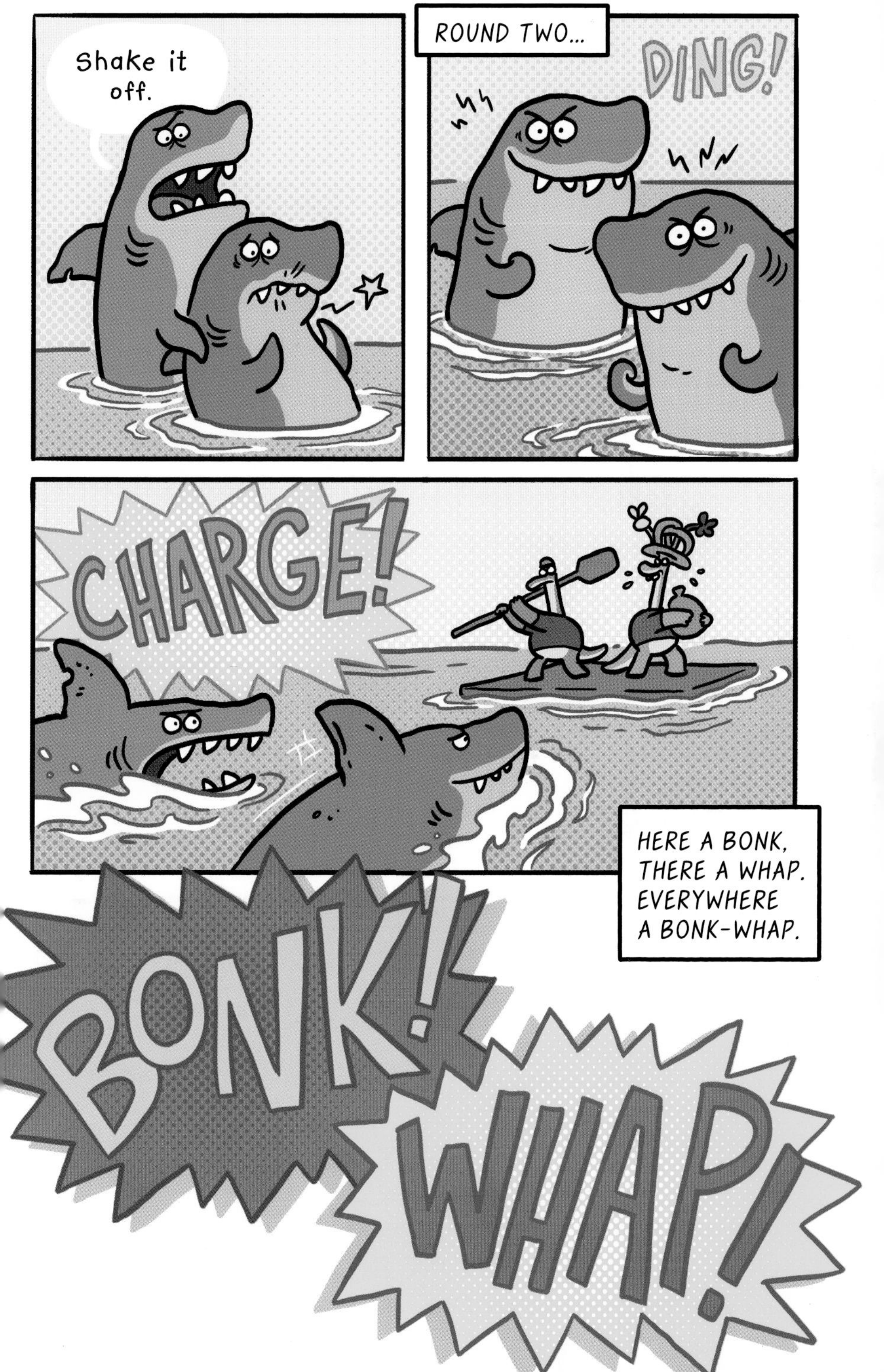
Shake it off.
ROUND TWO...
DING!
CHARGE!
HERE A BONK, THERE A WHAP. EVERYWHERE A BONK-WHAP.
BONK!
WHAP!

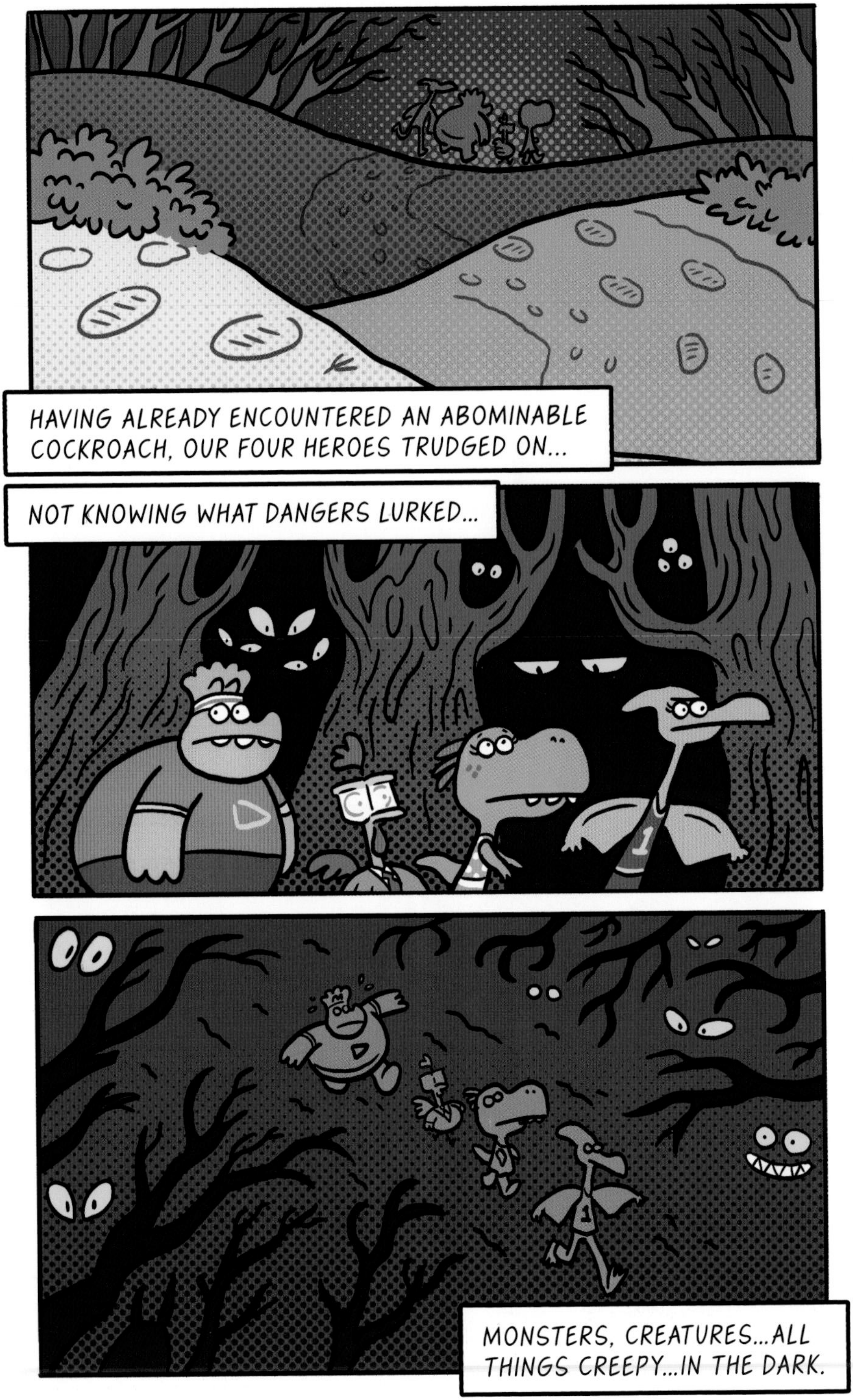
HAVING ALREADY ENCOUNTERED AN ABOMINABLE COCKROACH, OUR FOUR HEROES TRUDGED ON...
NOT KNOWING WHAT DANGERS LURKED...
MONSTERS, CREATURES...ALL THINGS CREEPY...IN THE DARK.

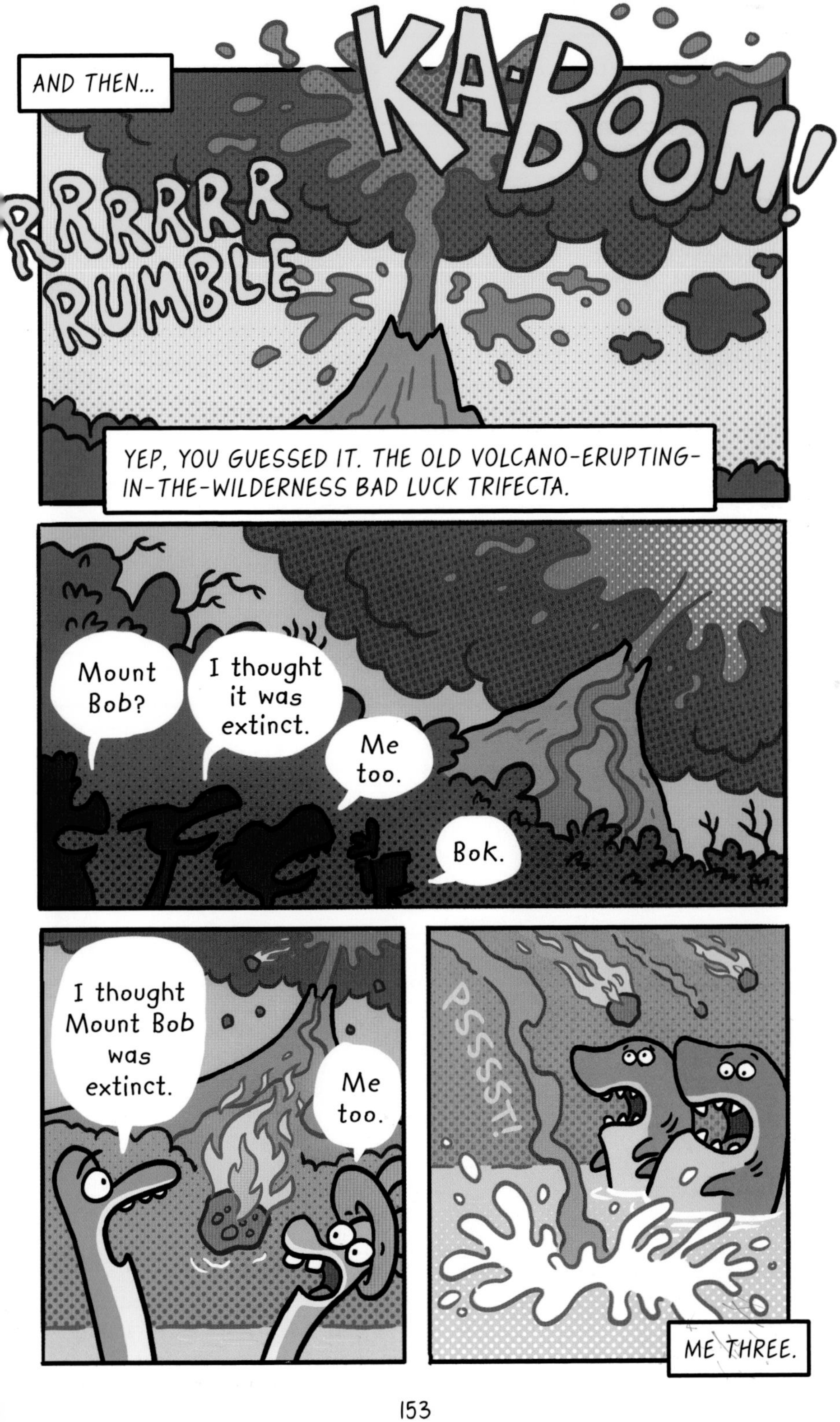
AND THEN...
RRRRRR RUMBLE
KA-BOOOM!
YEP, YOU GUESSED IT. THE OLD VOLCANO-ERUPTING-IN-THE-WILDERNESS BAD LUCK TRIFECTA.
Mount Bob?
I thought it was extinct.
Me too.
Bok.
I thought Mount Bob was extinct.
Me too.
PSSSST!
ME THREE.

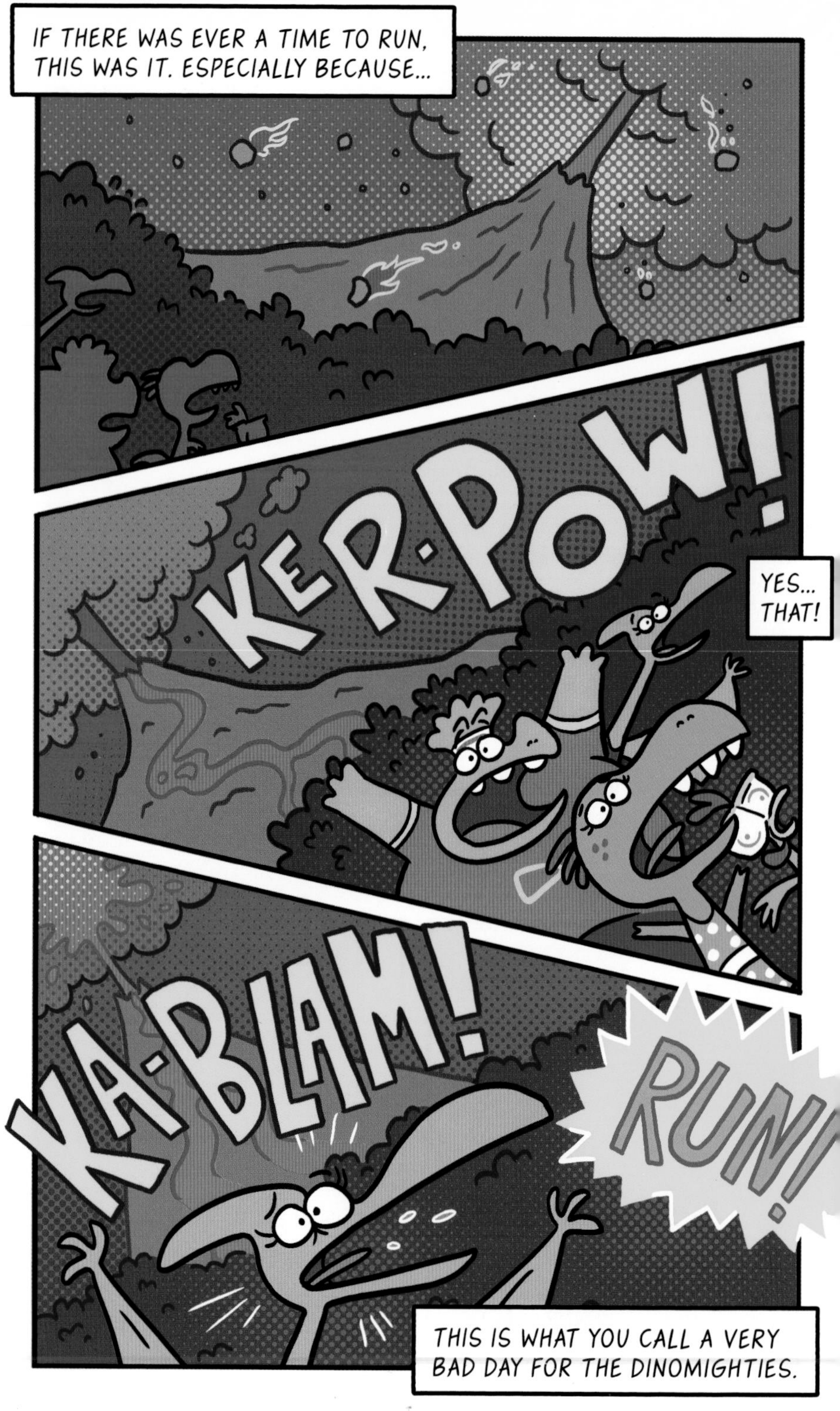
IF THERE WAS EVER A TIME TO RUN, THIS WAS IT. ESPECIALLY BECAUSE...
KER-POW!
YES... THAT!
KA-BLAM!
RUN!
THIS IS WHAT YOU CALL A VERY BAD DAY FOR THE DINOMIGHTIES.

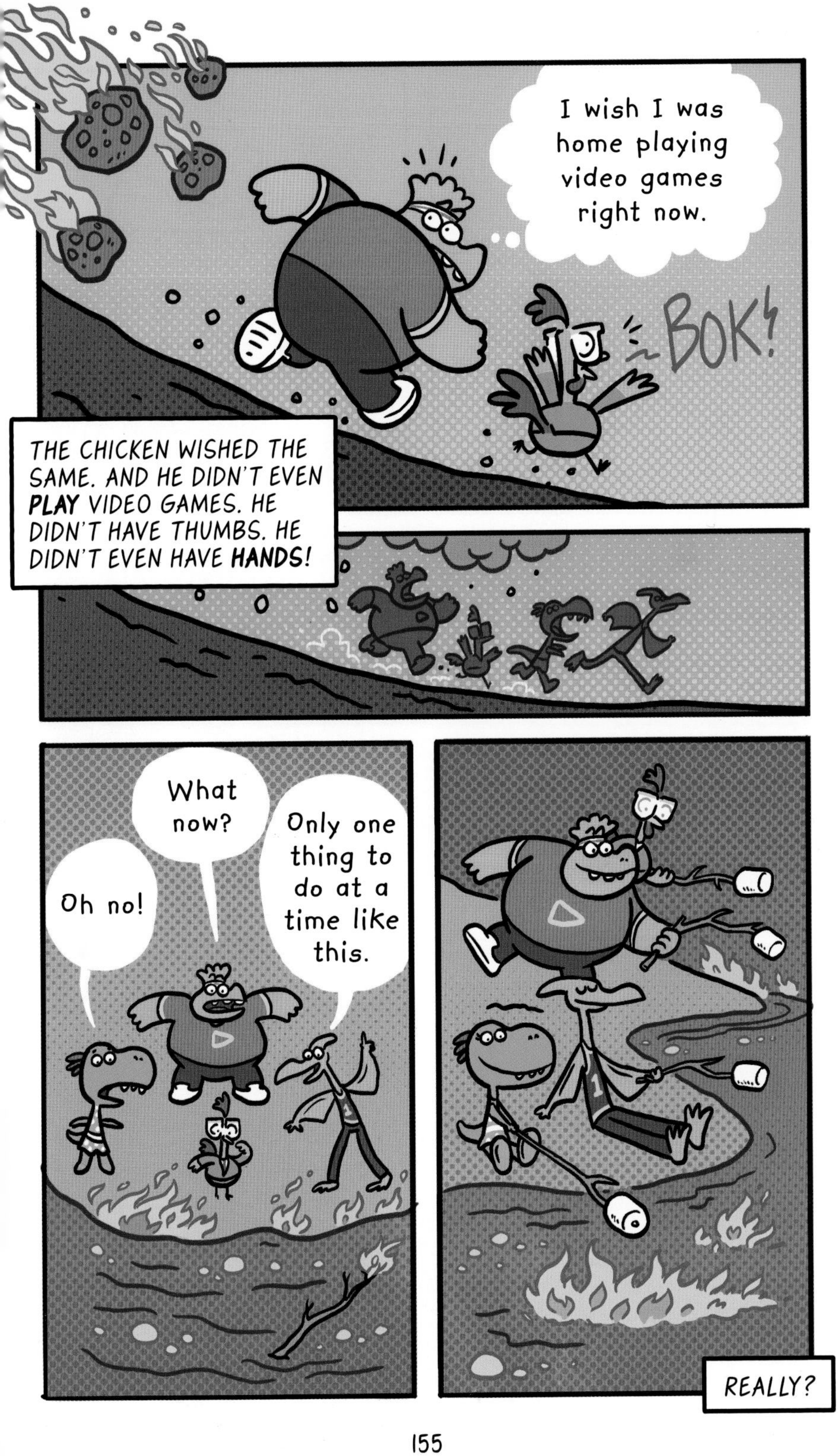
I wish I was home playing video games right now.
BOK!
THE CHICKEN WISHED THE SAME. AND HE DIDN'T EVEN **PLAY** VIDEO GAMES. HE DIDN'T HAVE THUMBS. HE DIDN'T EVEN HAVE **HANDS**!
Oh no!
What now?
Only one thing to do at a time like this.
REALLY?

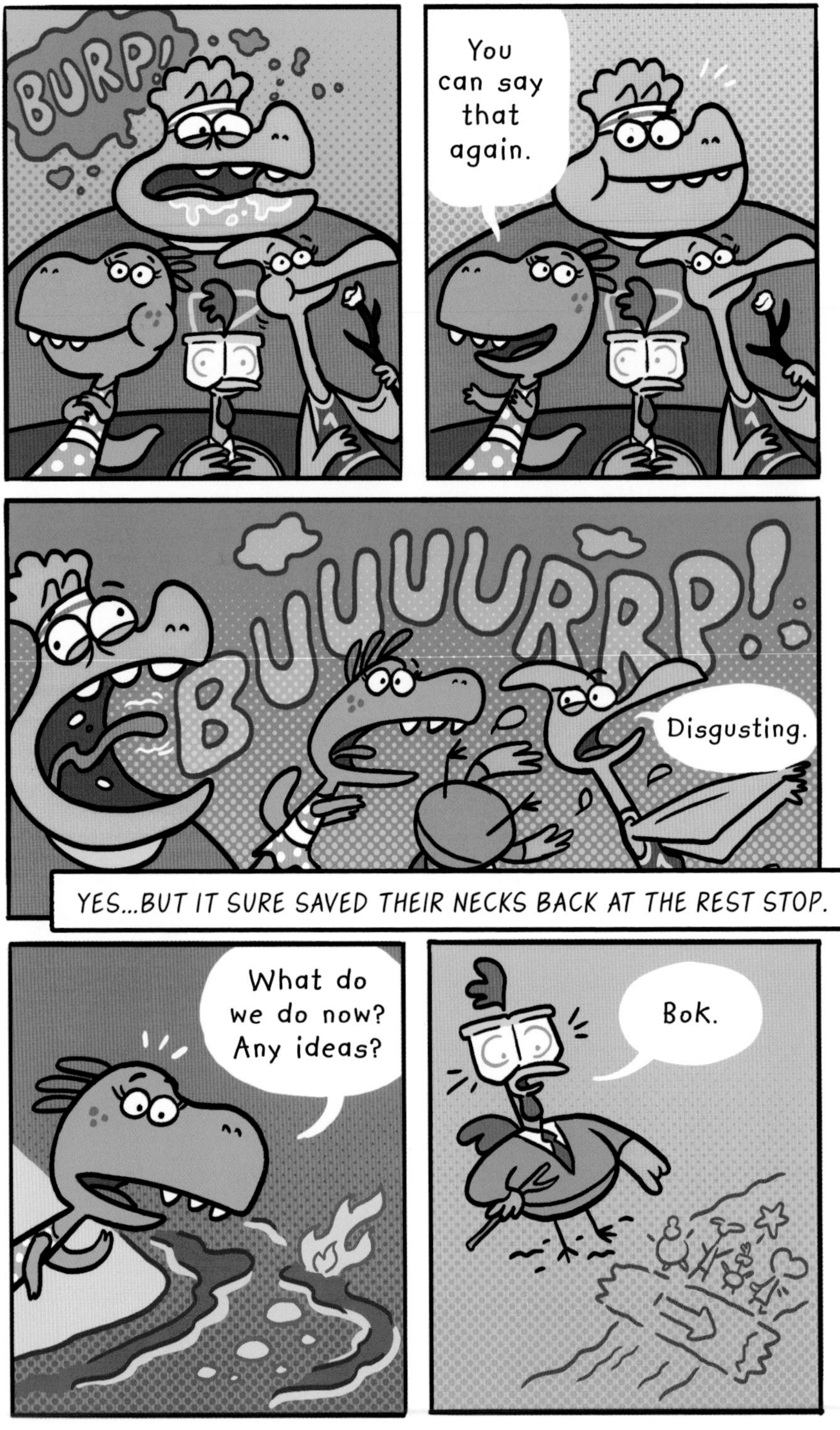
BURP!
You can say that again.
BUUUURRP!
Disgusting.
YES...BUT IT SURE SAVED THEIR NECKS BACK AT THE REST STOP.
What do we do now? Any ideas?
Bok.

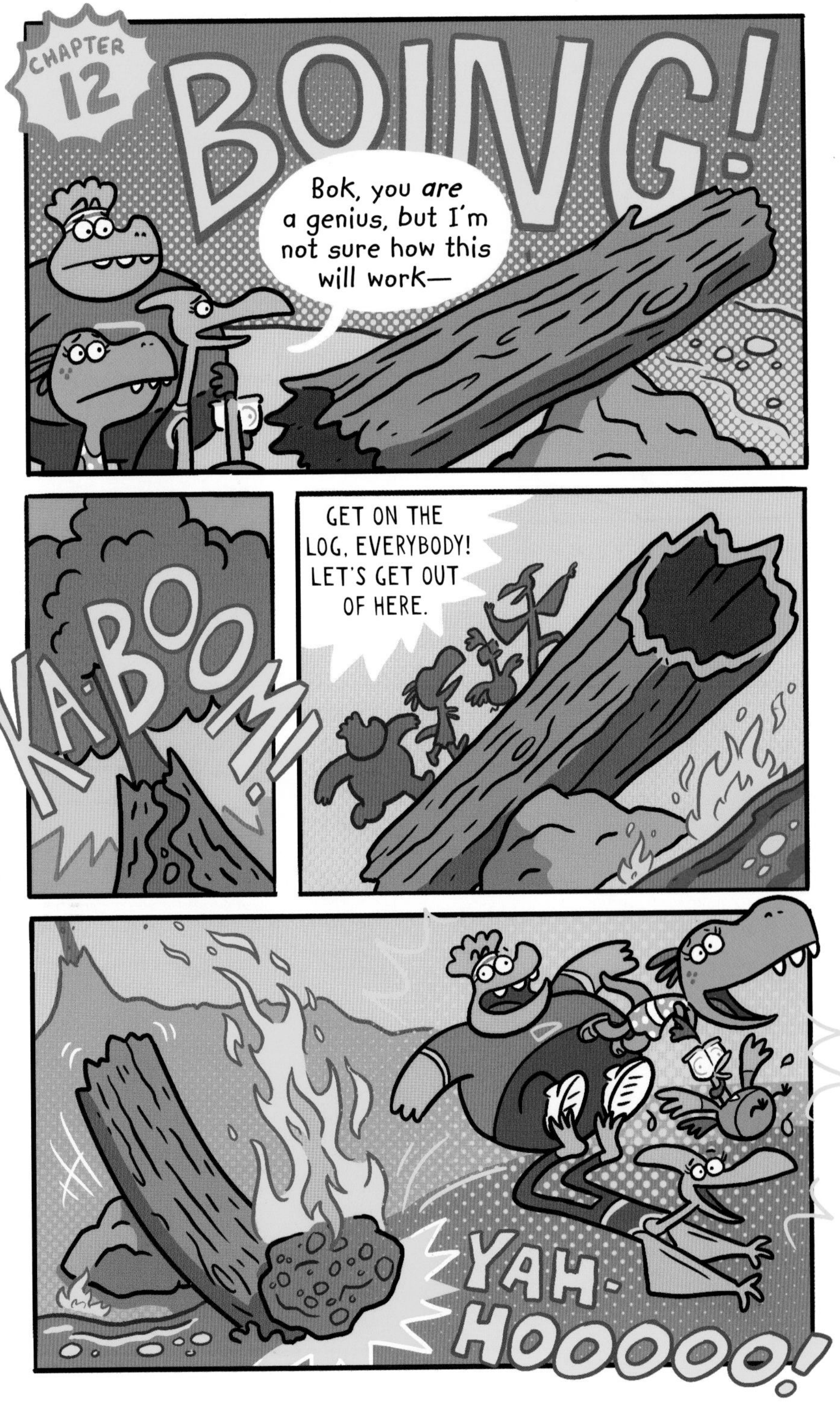
CHAPTER 12
BOING!
Bok, you *are* a genius, but I'm not sure how this will work—
KA-BOOM!
GET ON THE LOG, EVERYBODY! LET'S GET OUT OF HERE.
YAH-HOOOOOO!

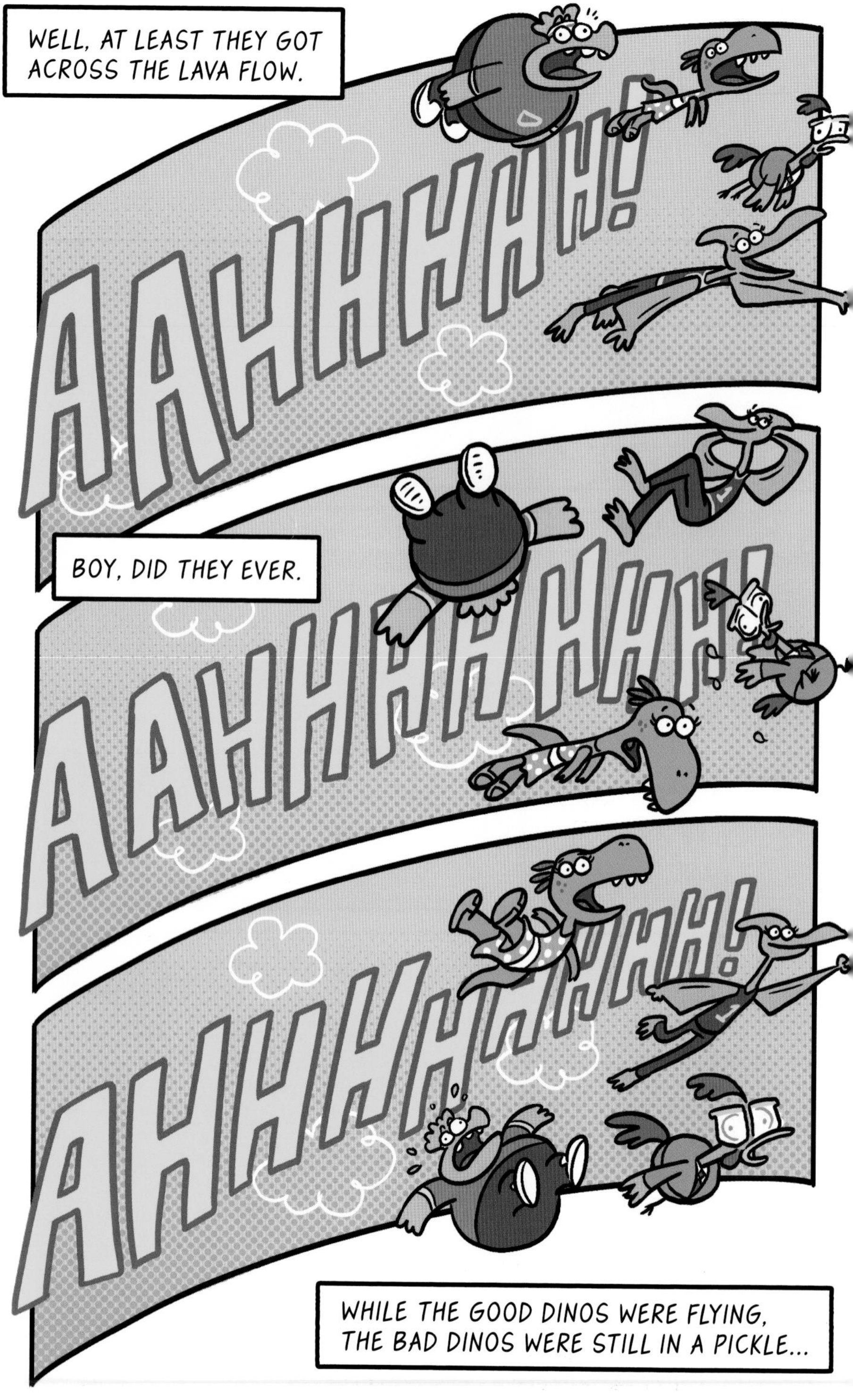

WELL, AT LEAST THEY GOT ACROSS THE LAVA FLOW.
AAHHHHHH!
BOY, DID THEY EVER.
AAHHHHHHHH!
AHHHHHHHHH!
WHILE THE GOOD DINOS WERE FLYING, THE BAD DINOS WERE STILL IN A PICKLE...

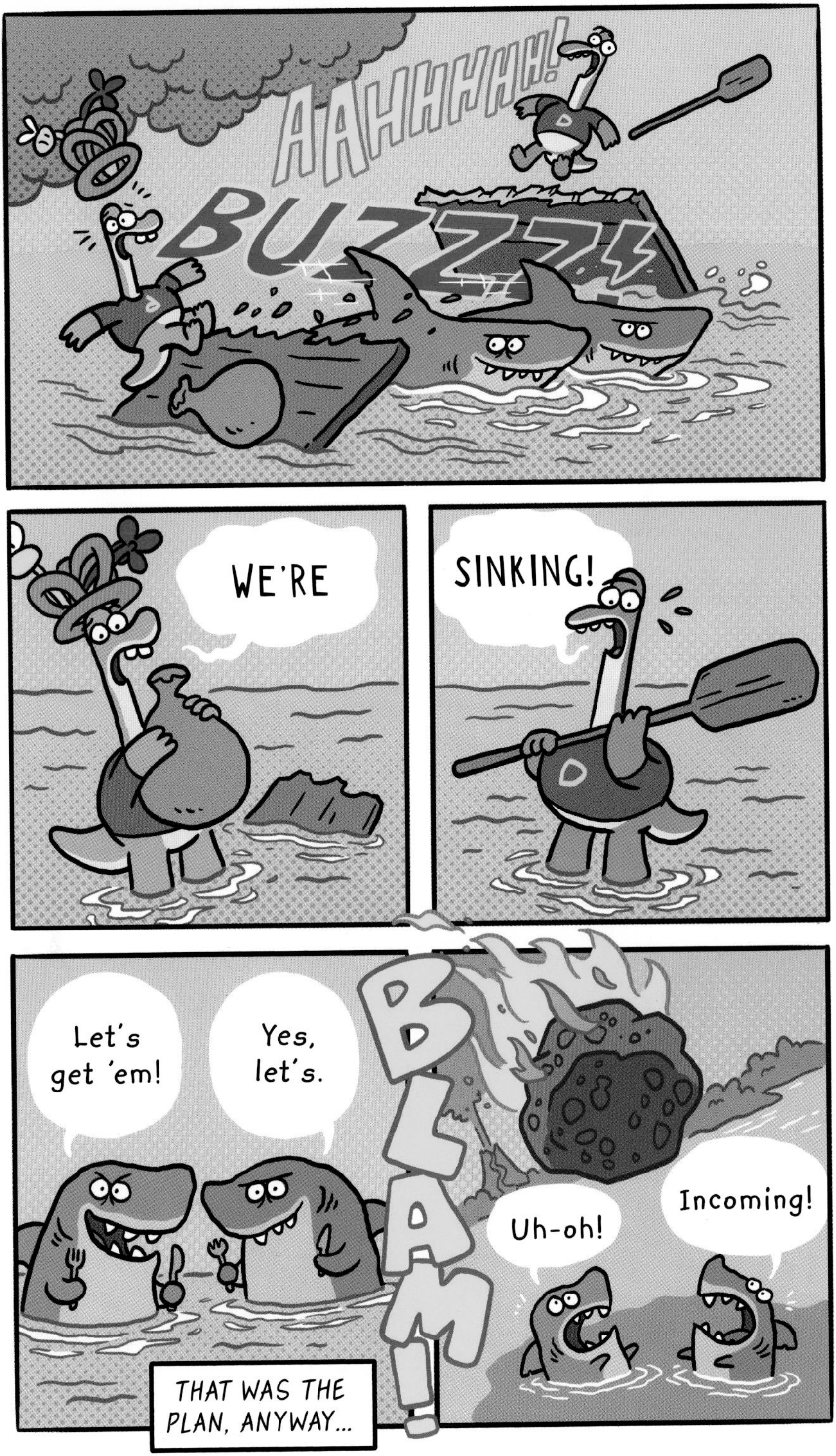
AAHHHHHH!
BUZZZ!
WE'RE
SINKING!
Let's get 'em!
Yes, let's.
BLAM
Uh-oh!
Incoming!
THAT WAS THE PLAN, ANYWAY...

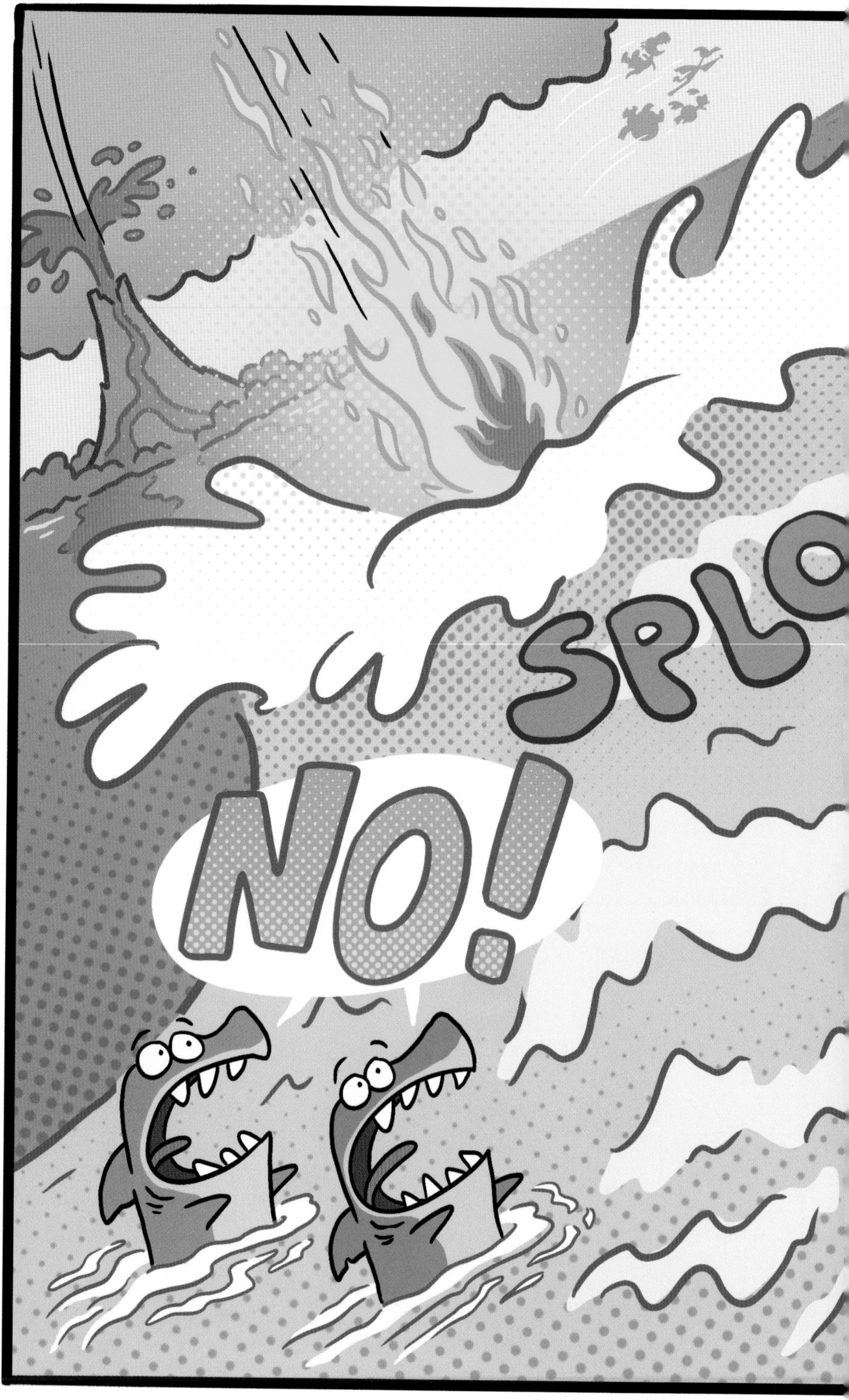
SPLO
NO!

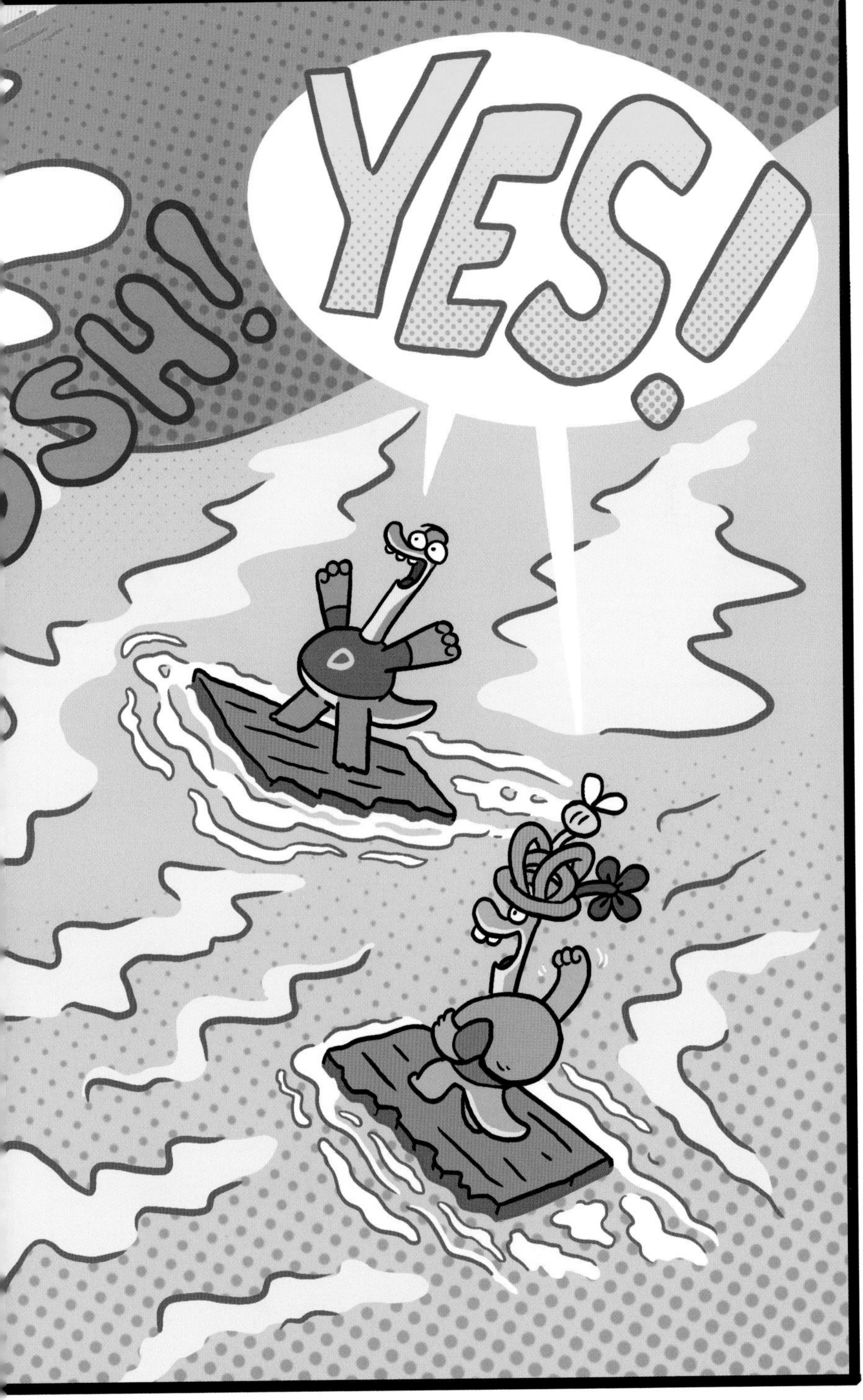
SH!!
YES!

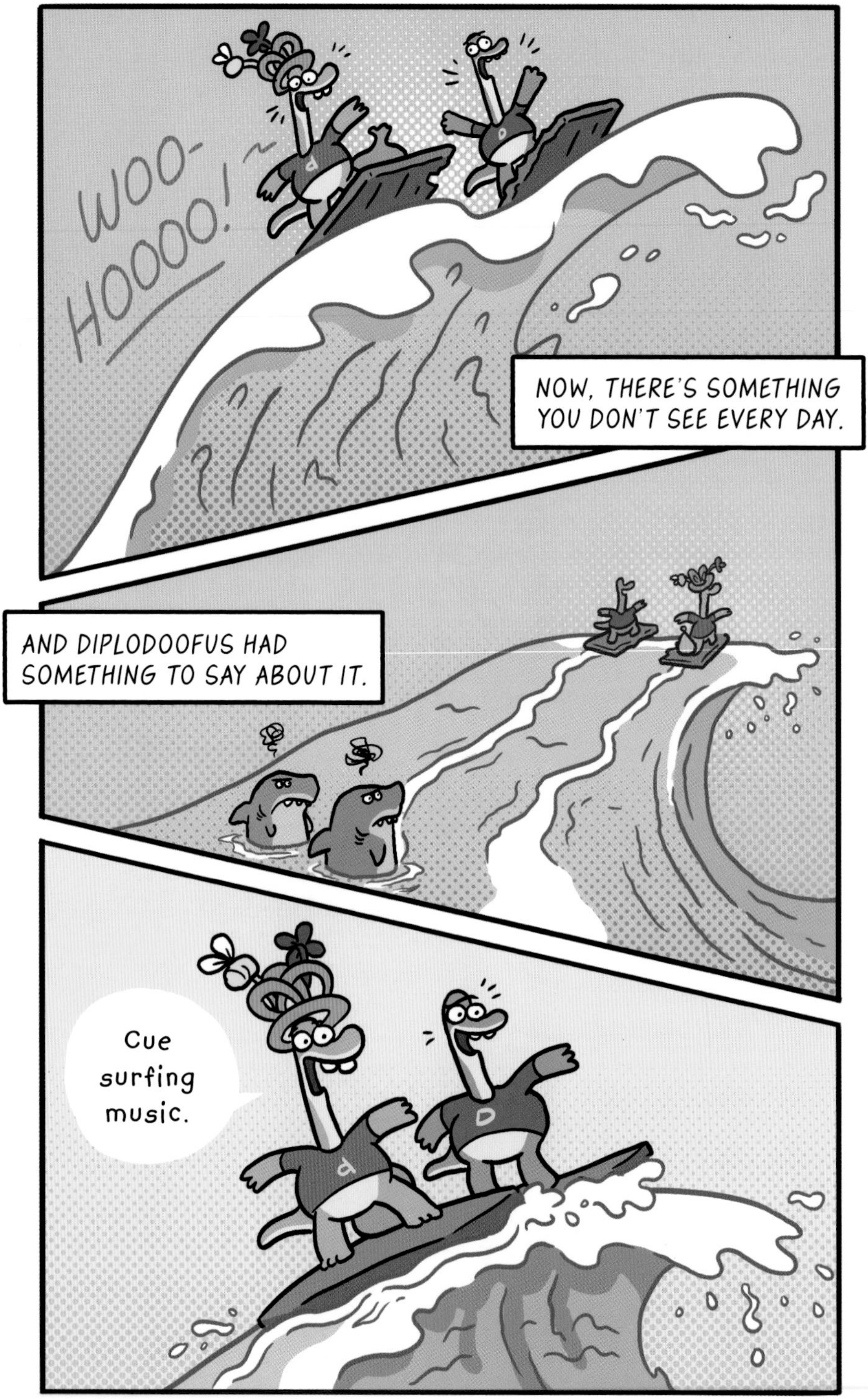
WOO-HOOOO!
NOW, THERE'S SOMETHING YOU DON'T SEE EVERY DAY.
AND DIPLODOOFUS HAD SOMETHING TO SAY ABOUT IT.
Cue surfing music.

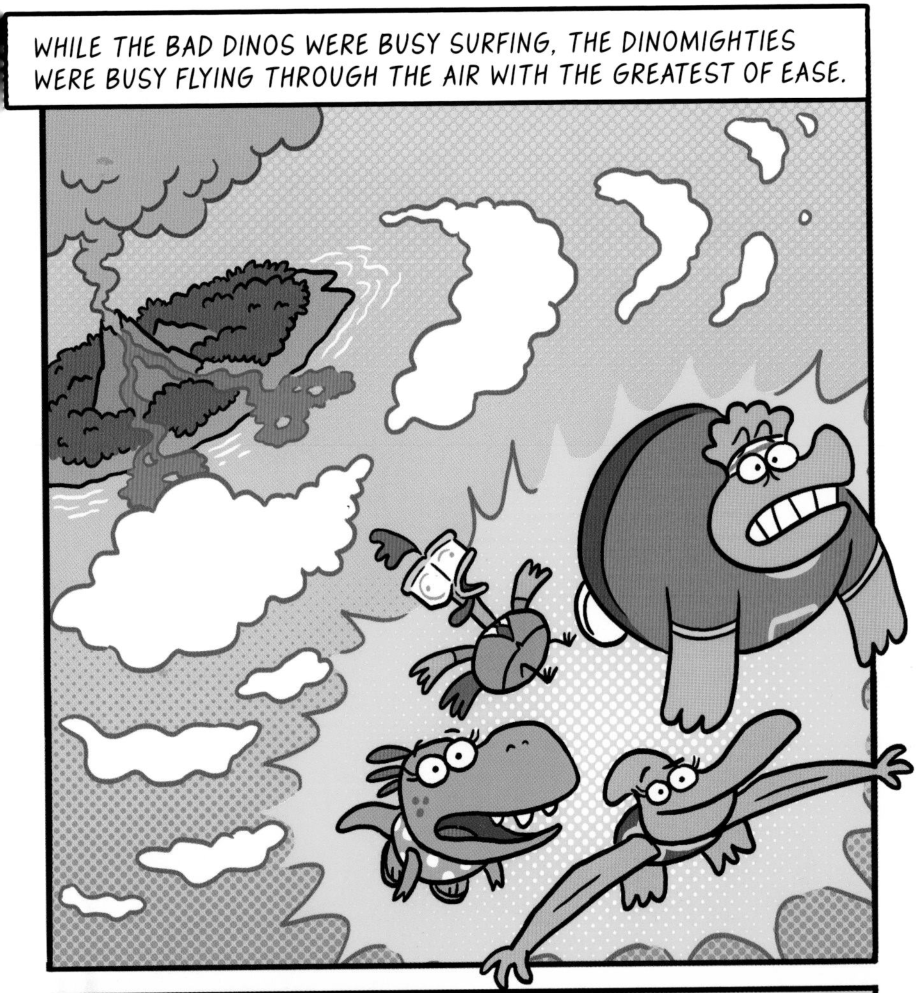
WHILE THE BAD DINOS WERE BUSY SURFING, THE DINOMIGHTIES WERE BUSY FLYING THROUGH THE AIR WITH THE GREATEST OF EASE.

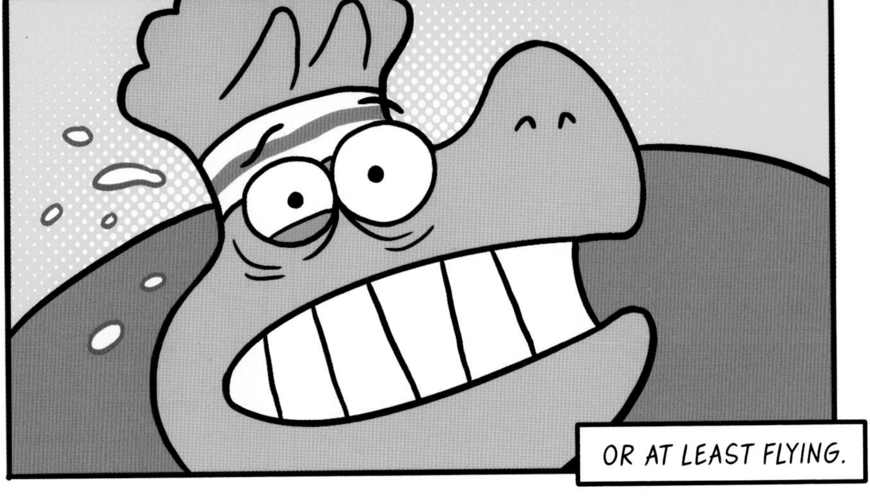
OR AT LEAST FLYING.

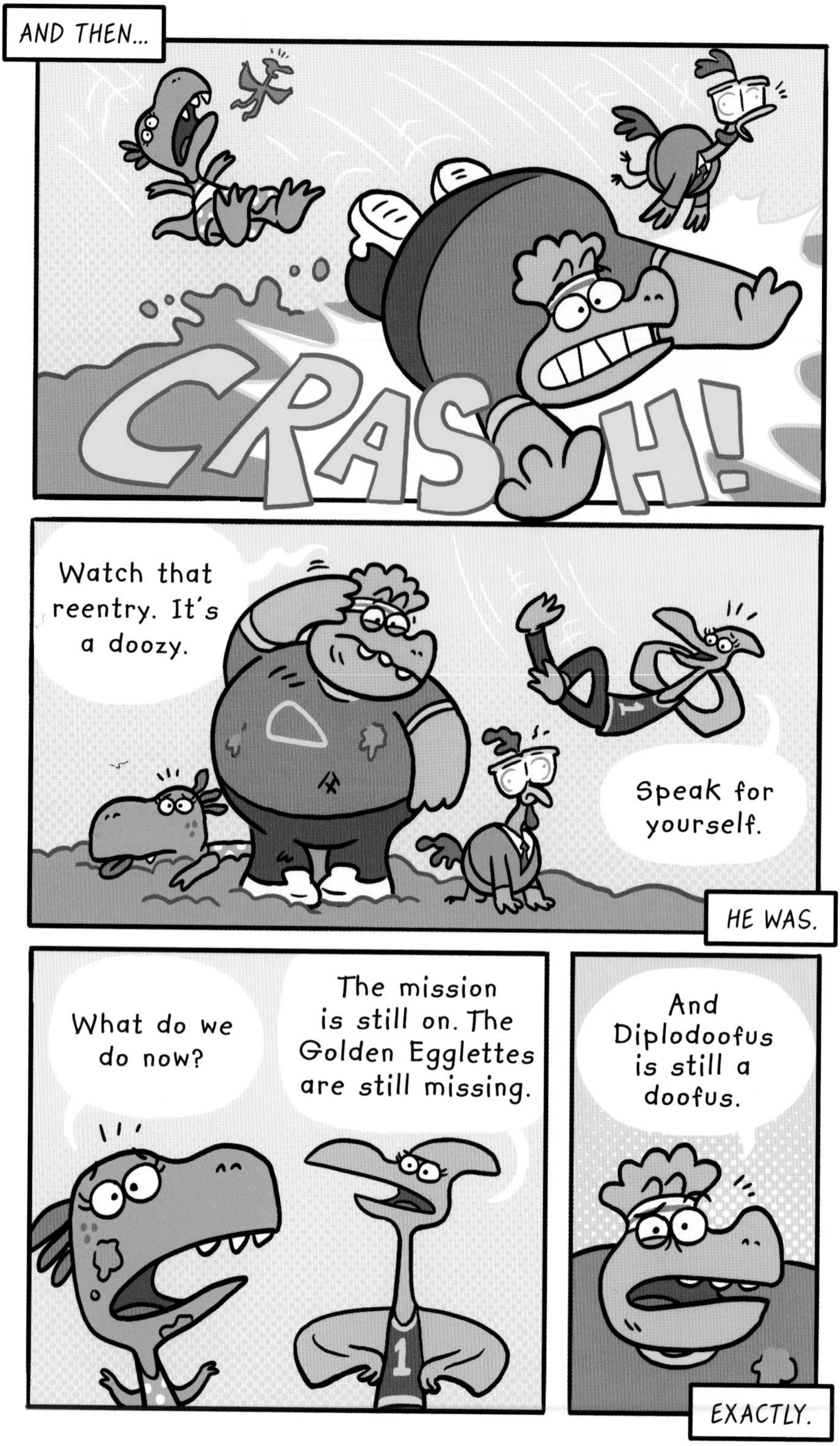
AND THEN...
CRASH!
Watch that reentry. It's a doozy.
Speak for yourself.
HE WAS.
What do we do now?
The mission is still on. The Golden Egglettes are still missing.
And Diplodoofus is still a doofus.
EXACTLY.

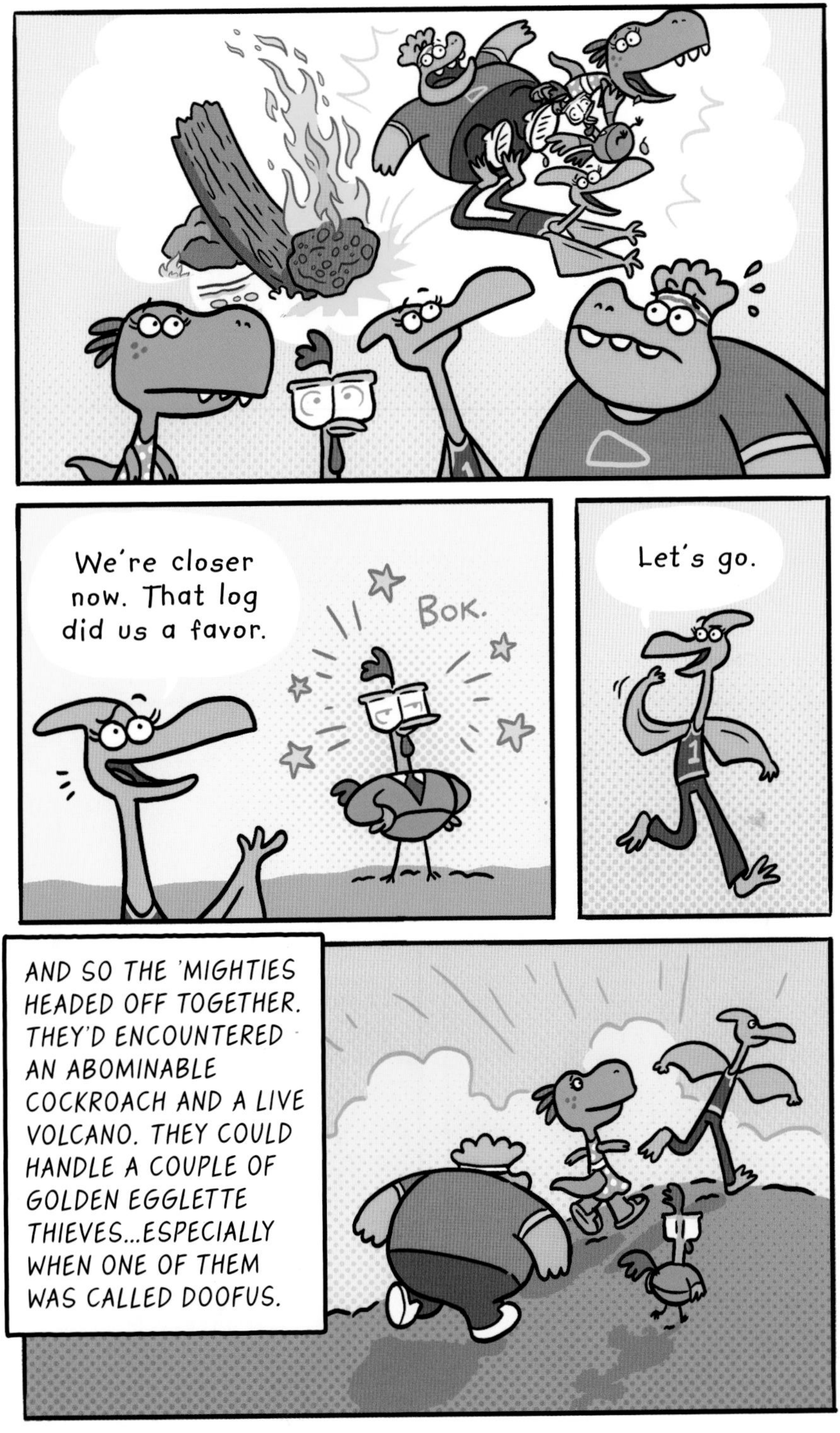
We're closer now. That log did us a favor.
BOK.
Let's go.
AND SO THE 'MIGHTIES HEADED OFF TOGETHER. THEY'D ENCOUNTERED AN ABOMINABLE COCKROACH AND A LIVE VOLCANO. THEY COULD HANDLE A COUPLE OF GOLDEN EGGLETTE THIEVES...ESPECIALLY WHEN ONE OF THEM WAS CALLED DOOFUS.

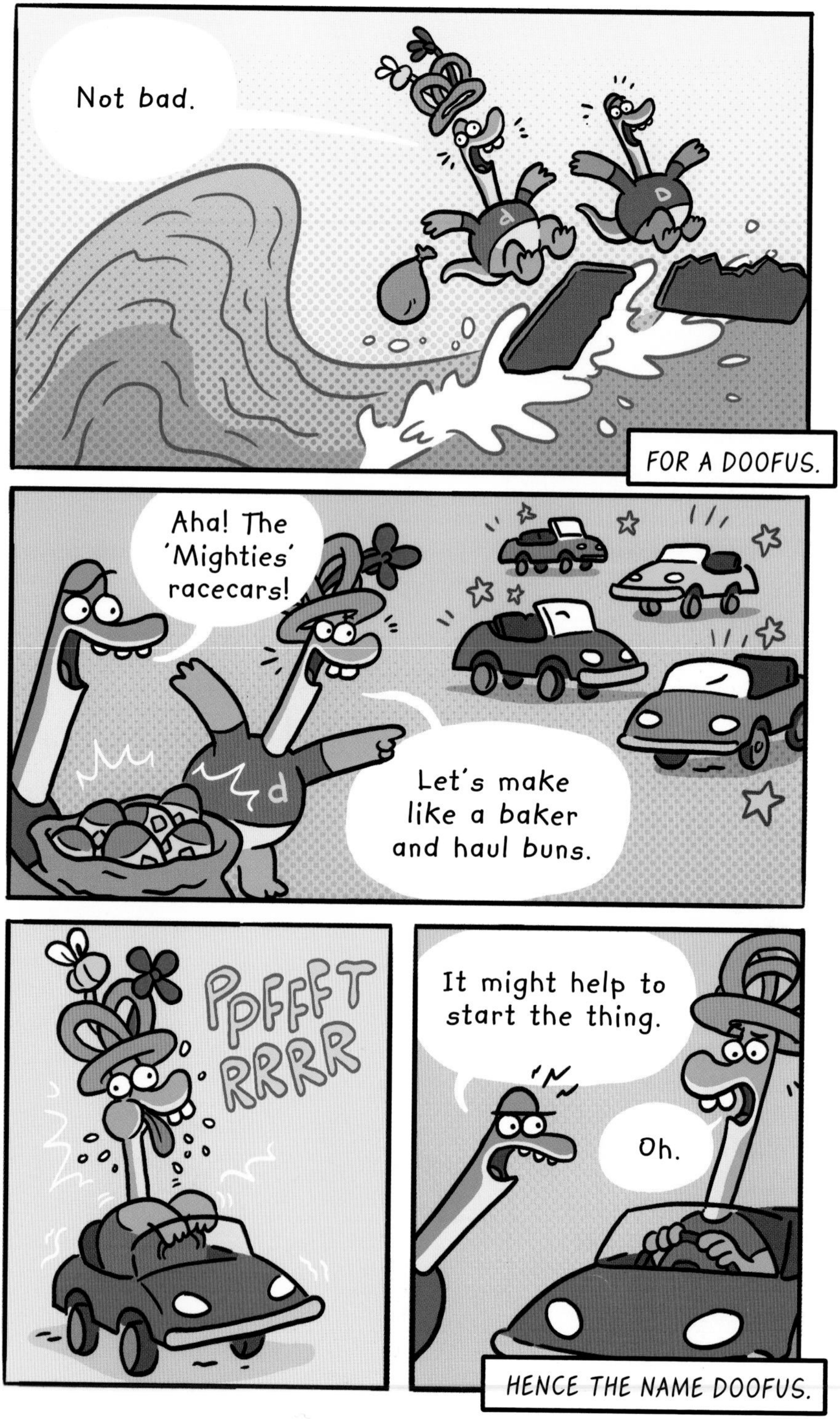

Not bad.
FOR A DOOFUS.
Aha! The 'Mighties' racecars!
Let's make like a baker and haul buns.
PpFFFT RRRR
It might help to start the thing.
Oh.
HENCE THE NAME DOOFUS.

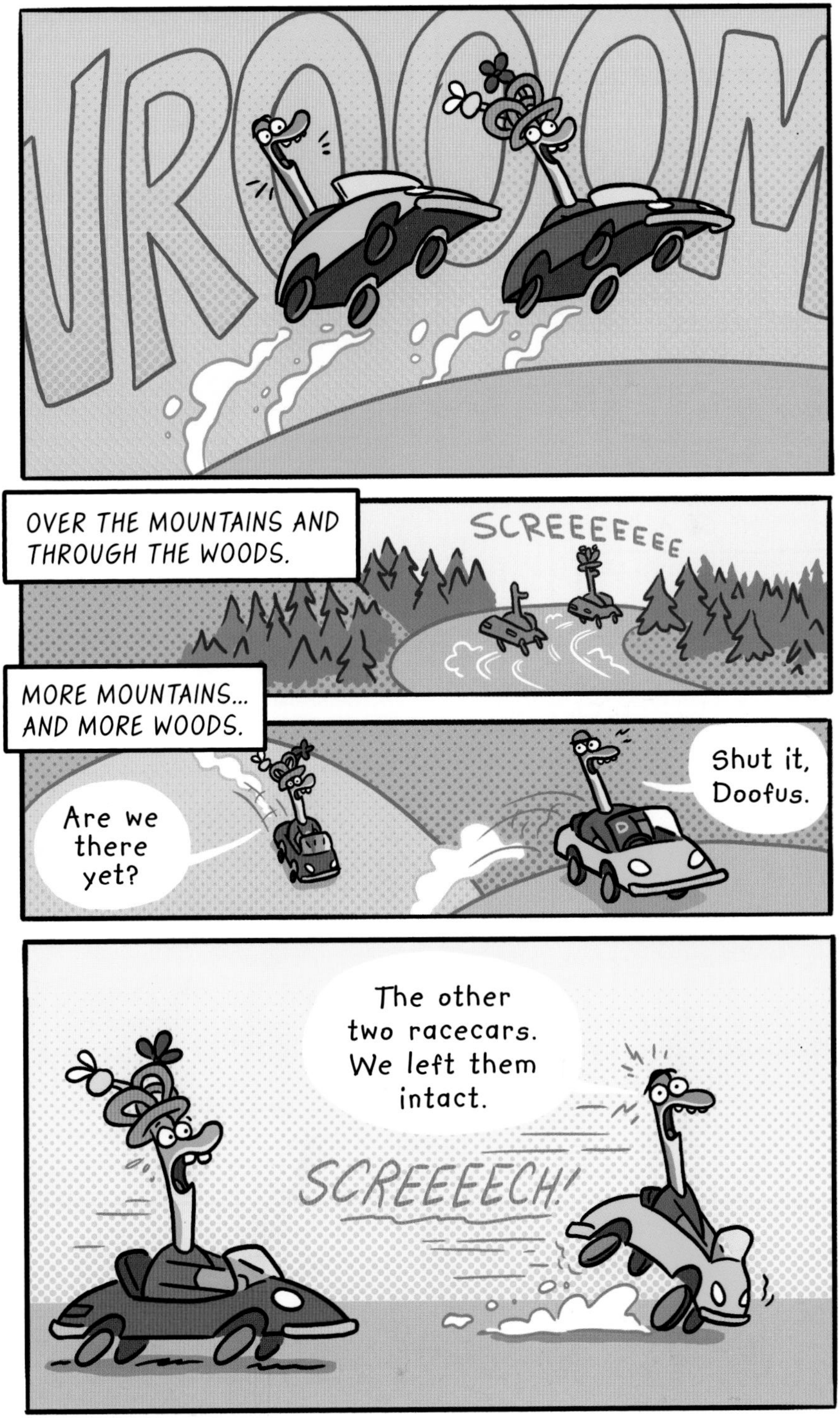
VROOOM
OVER THE MOUNTAINS AND THROUGH THE WOODS.
SCREEEEEEEE
MORE MOUNTAINS... AND MORE WOODS.
Are we there yet?
Shut it, Doofus.
The other two racecars. We left them intact.
SCREEEECH!

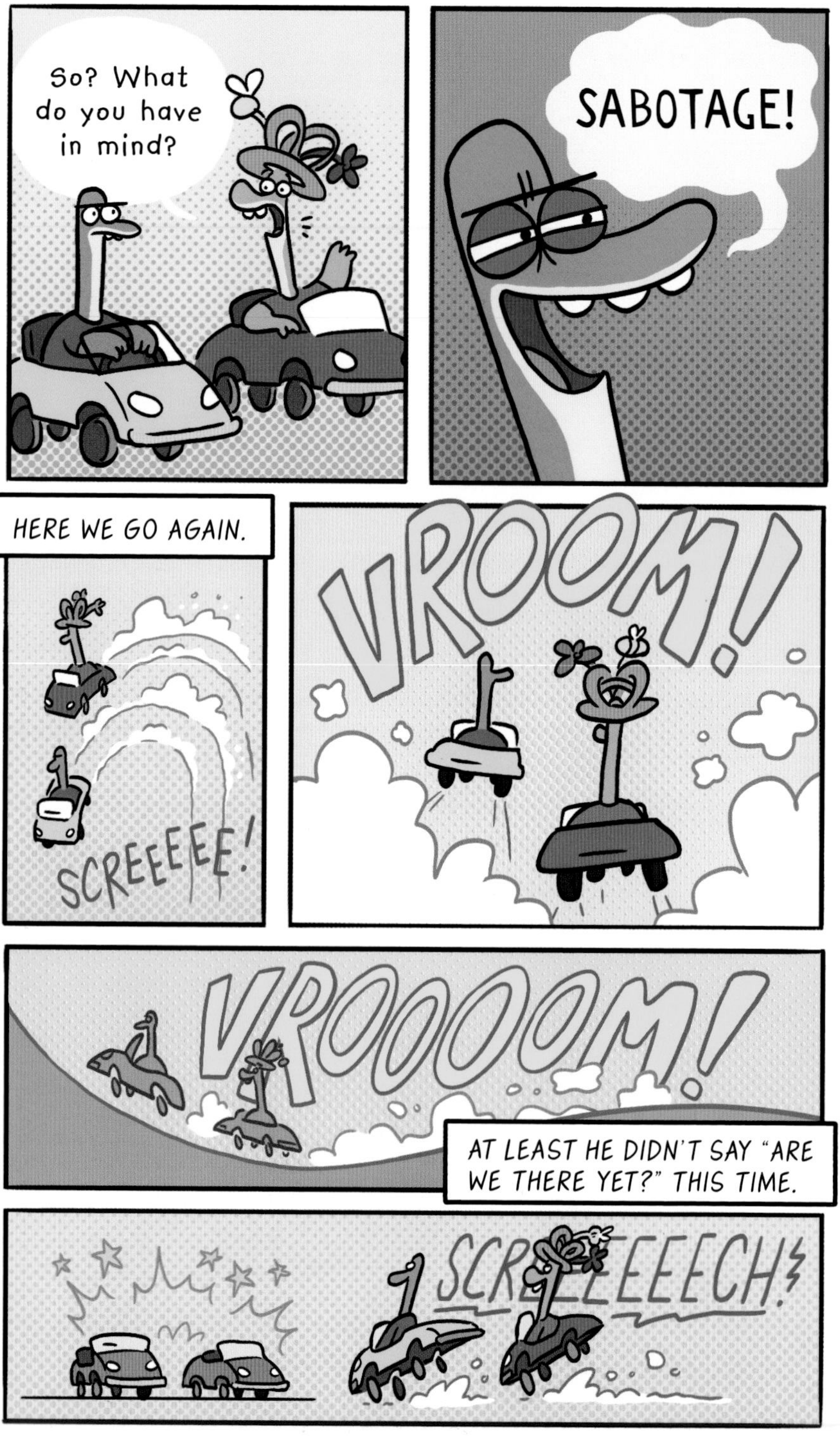
So? What do you have in mind?
SABOTAGE!
HERE WE GO AGAIN.
SCREEEEEE!
VROOM!
VROOOOM!
AT LEAST HE DIDN'T SAY "ARE WE THERE YET?" THIS TIME.
SCREEEEECH!

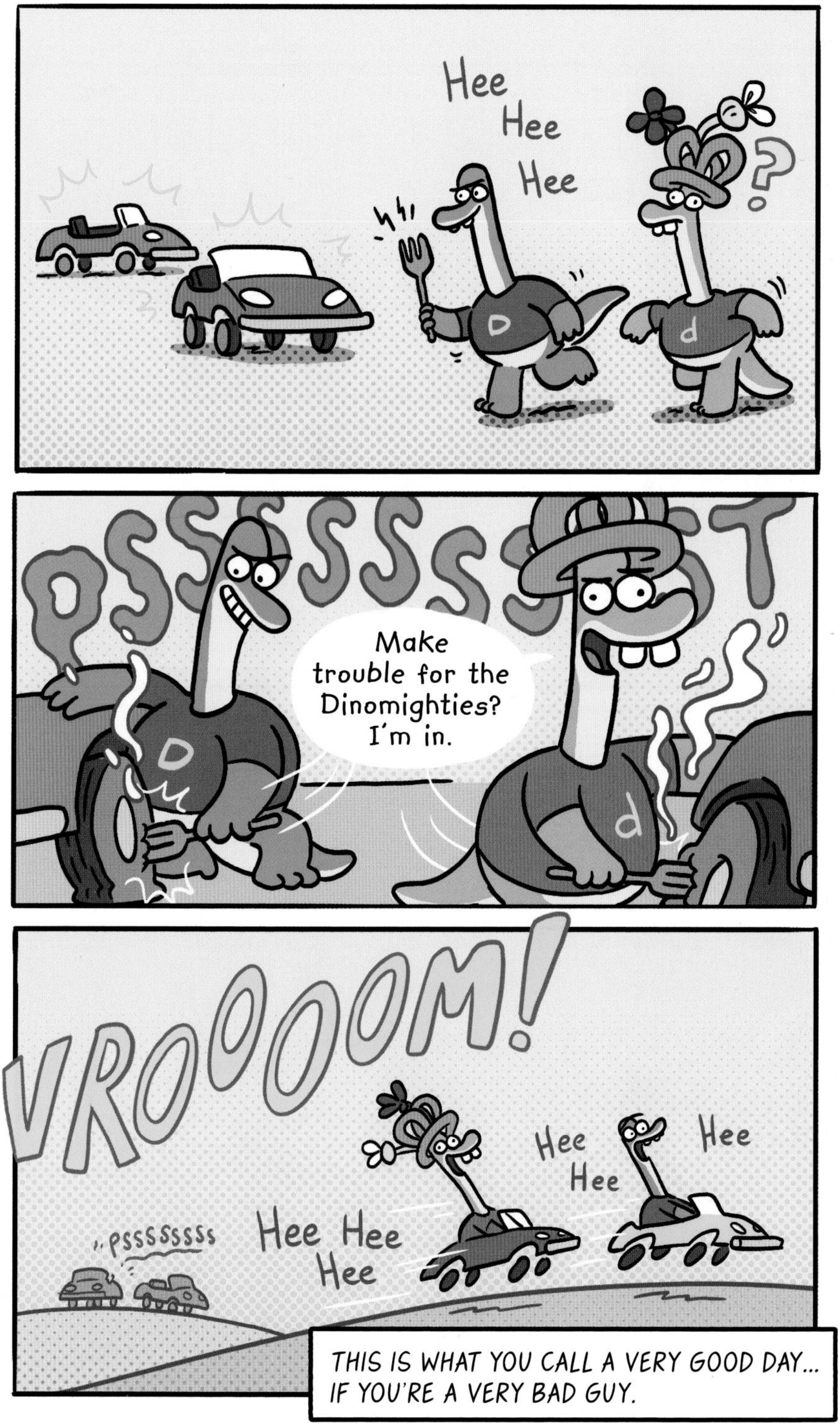
Hee
Hee
Hee
?
PSSSSSSST
Make trouble for the Dinomighties? I'm in.
VROOOOM!
Hee Hee
Hee
Hee Hee
Hee
..pssssssss
Hee Hee
Hee
THIS IS WHAT YOU CALL A VERY GOOD DAY...
IF YOU'RE A VERY BAD GUY.

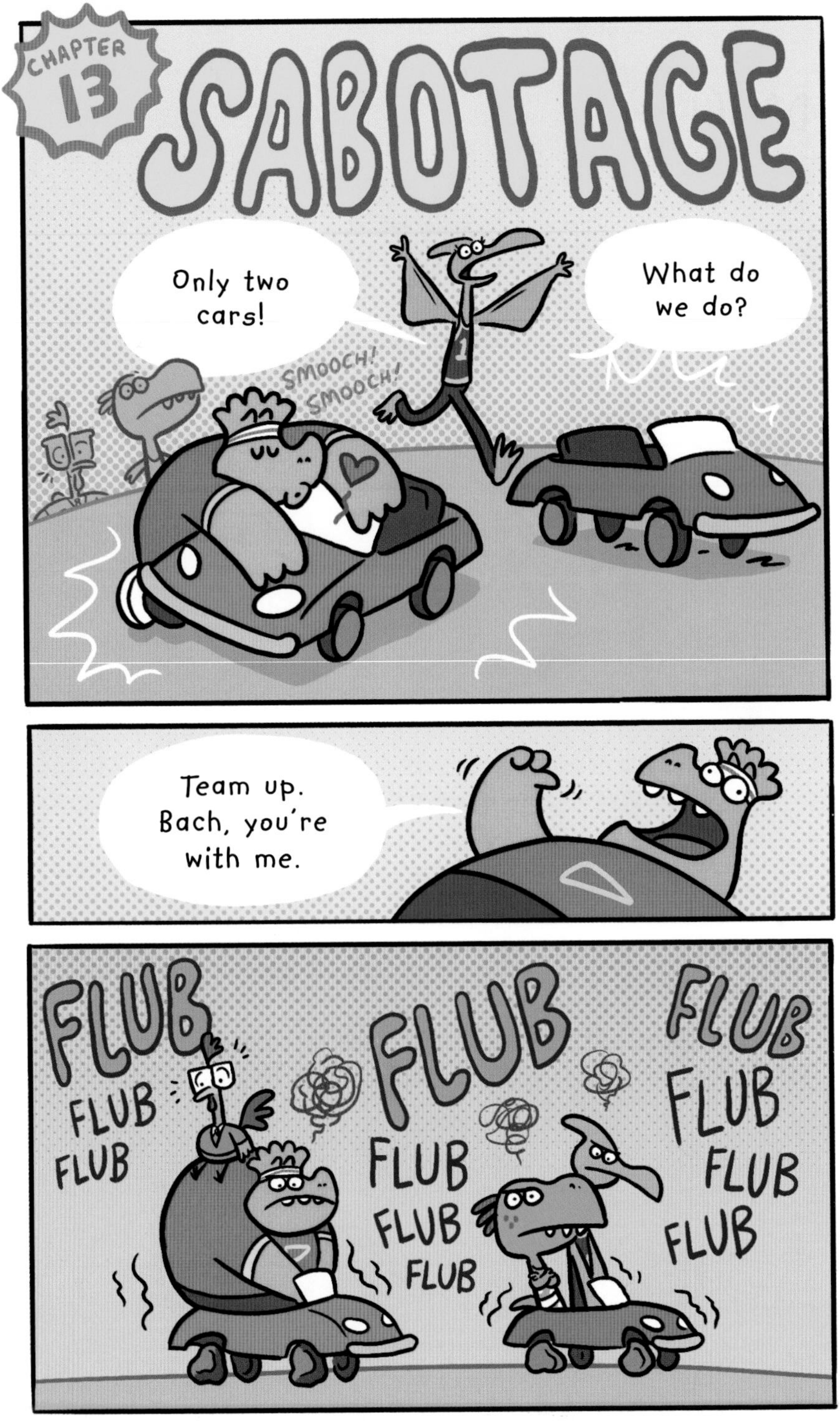
CHAPTER 13
SABOTAGE
Only two cars!
SMOOCH! SMOOCH!
What do we do?
Team up. Bach, you're with me.
FLUB FLUB FLUB
FLUB FLUB FLUB FLUB
FLUB FLUB FLUB FLUB FLUB

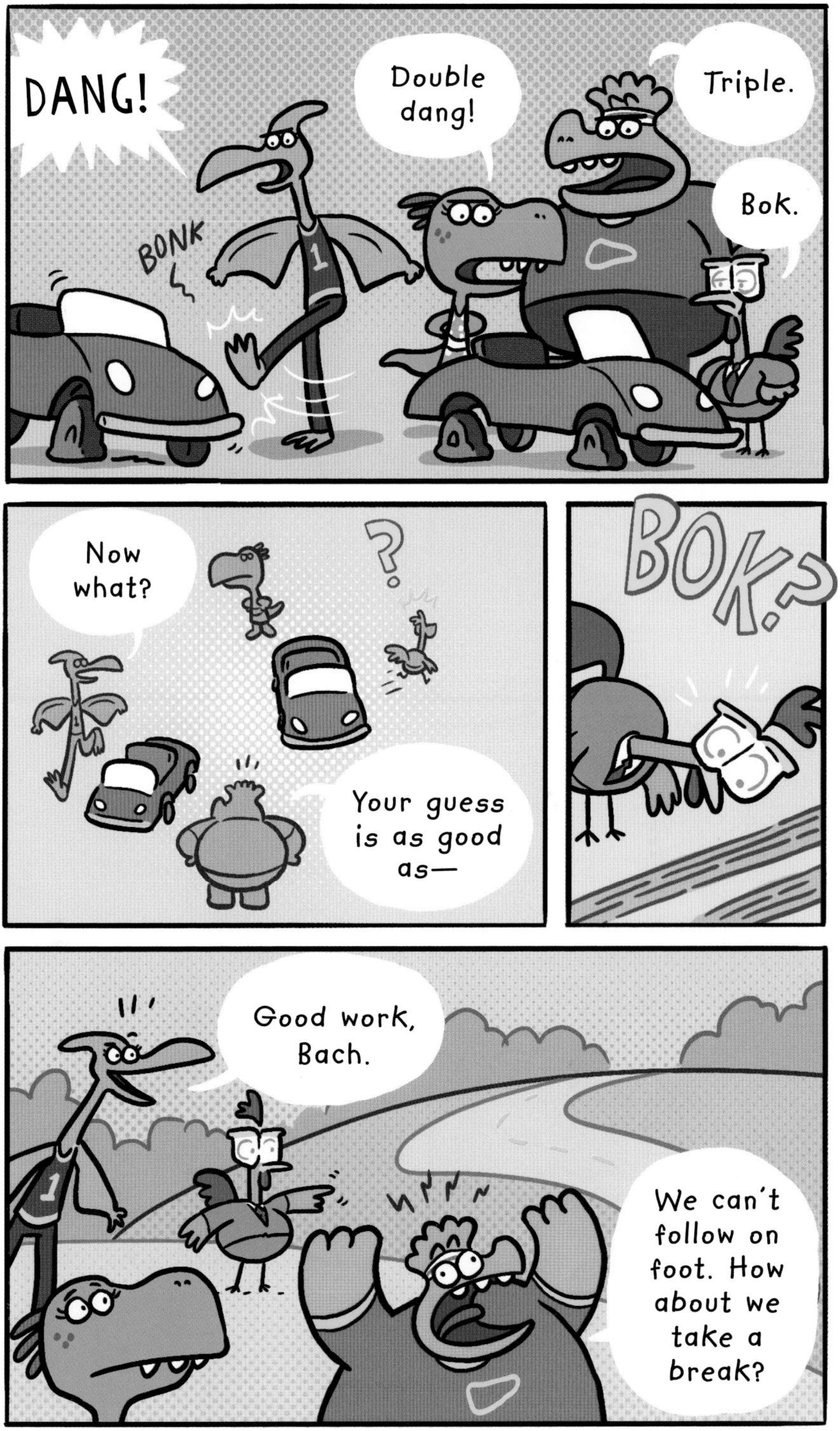
DANG!
Double dang!
Triple.
Bok.
BONK
Now what?
?
Your guess is as good as—
BOK?
Good work, Bach.
We can't follow on foot. How about we take a break?

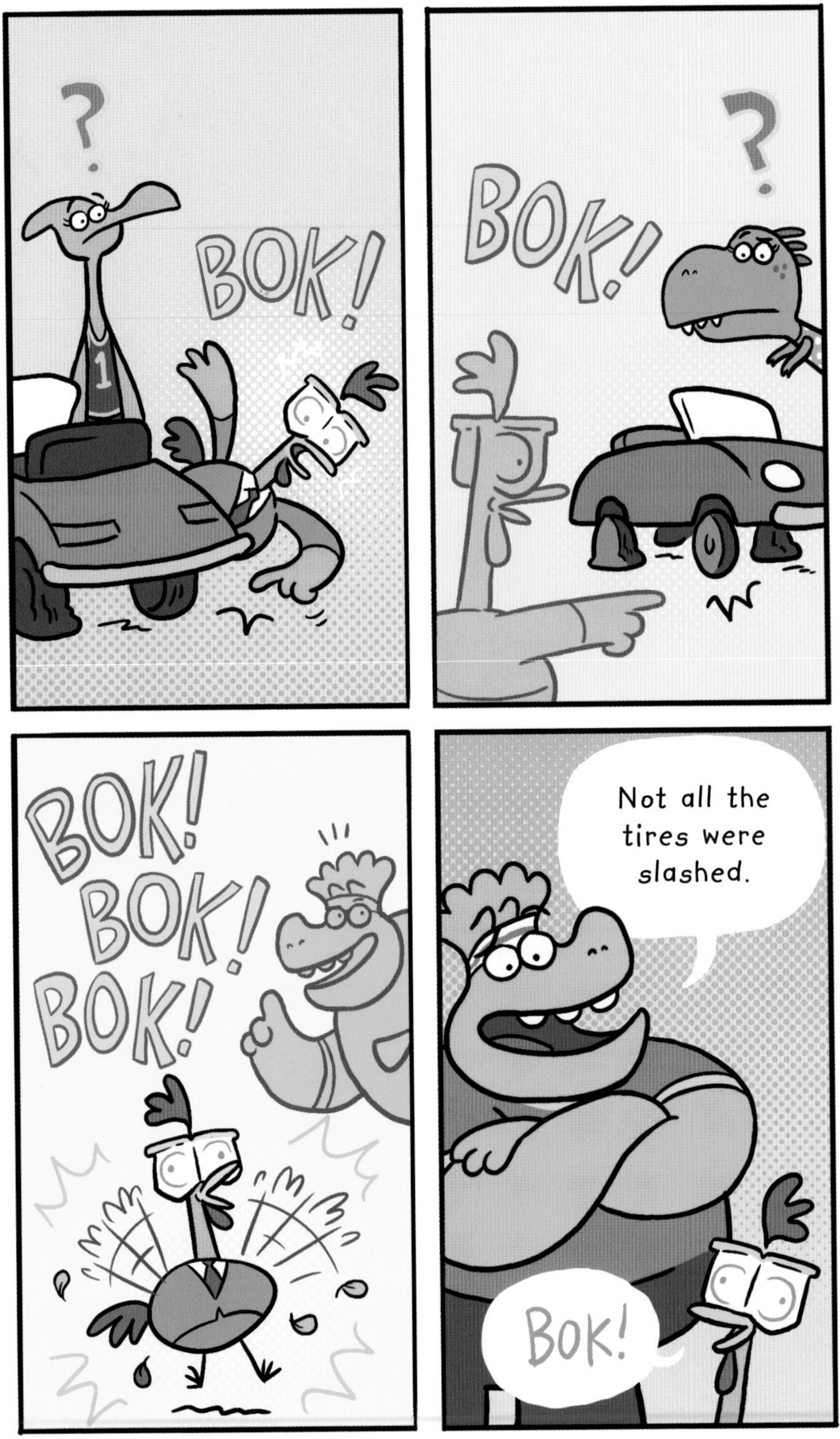
?
BOK!
?
BOK!
BOK!
BOK!
BOK!
Not all the tires were slashed.
BOK!

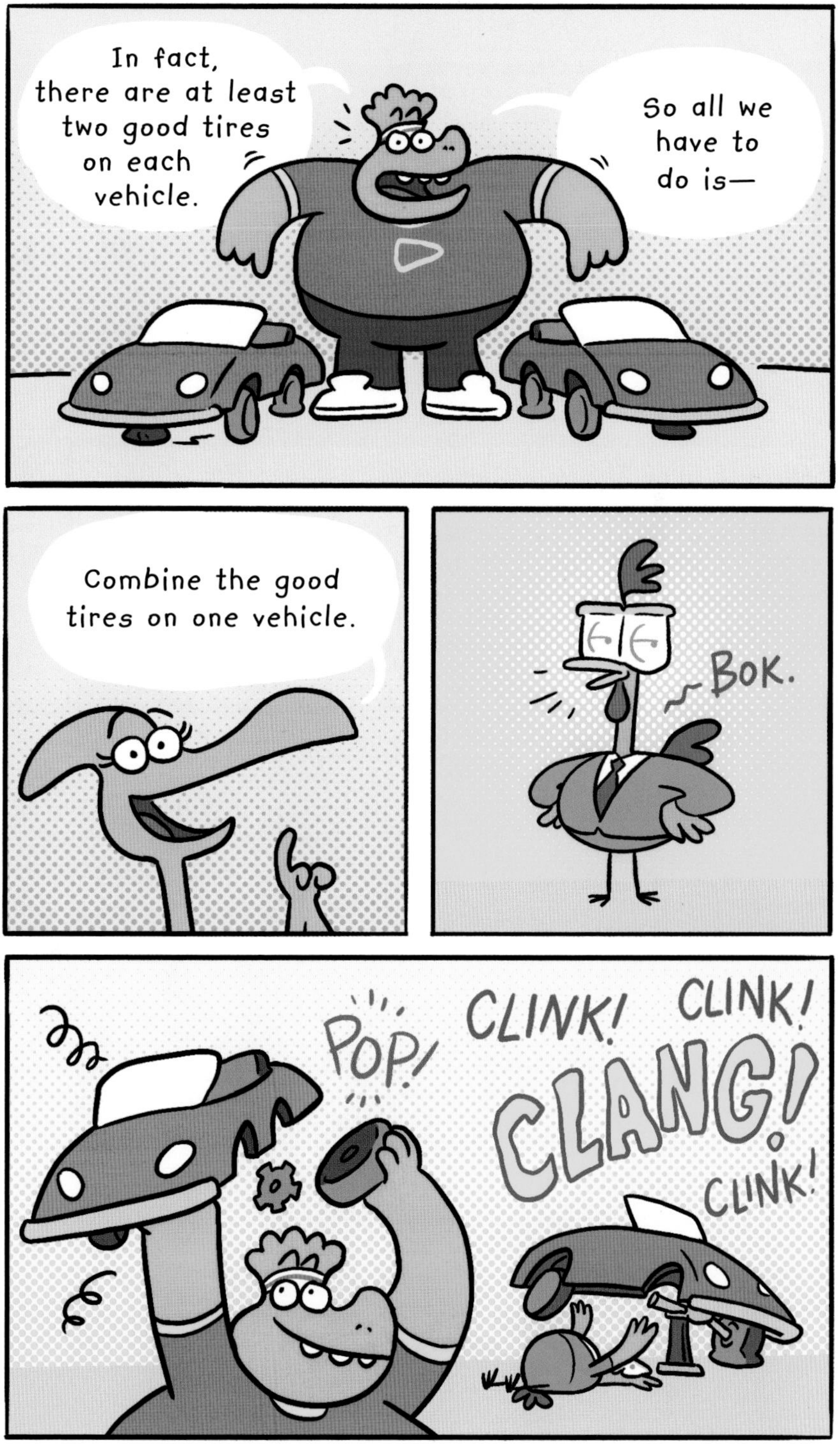
In fact, there are at least two good tires on each vehicle.
So all we have to do is—
Combine the good tires on one vehicle.
BOK.
POP!
CLINK!
CLINK!
CLANG!
CLINK!

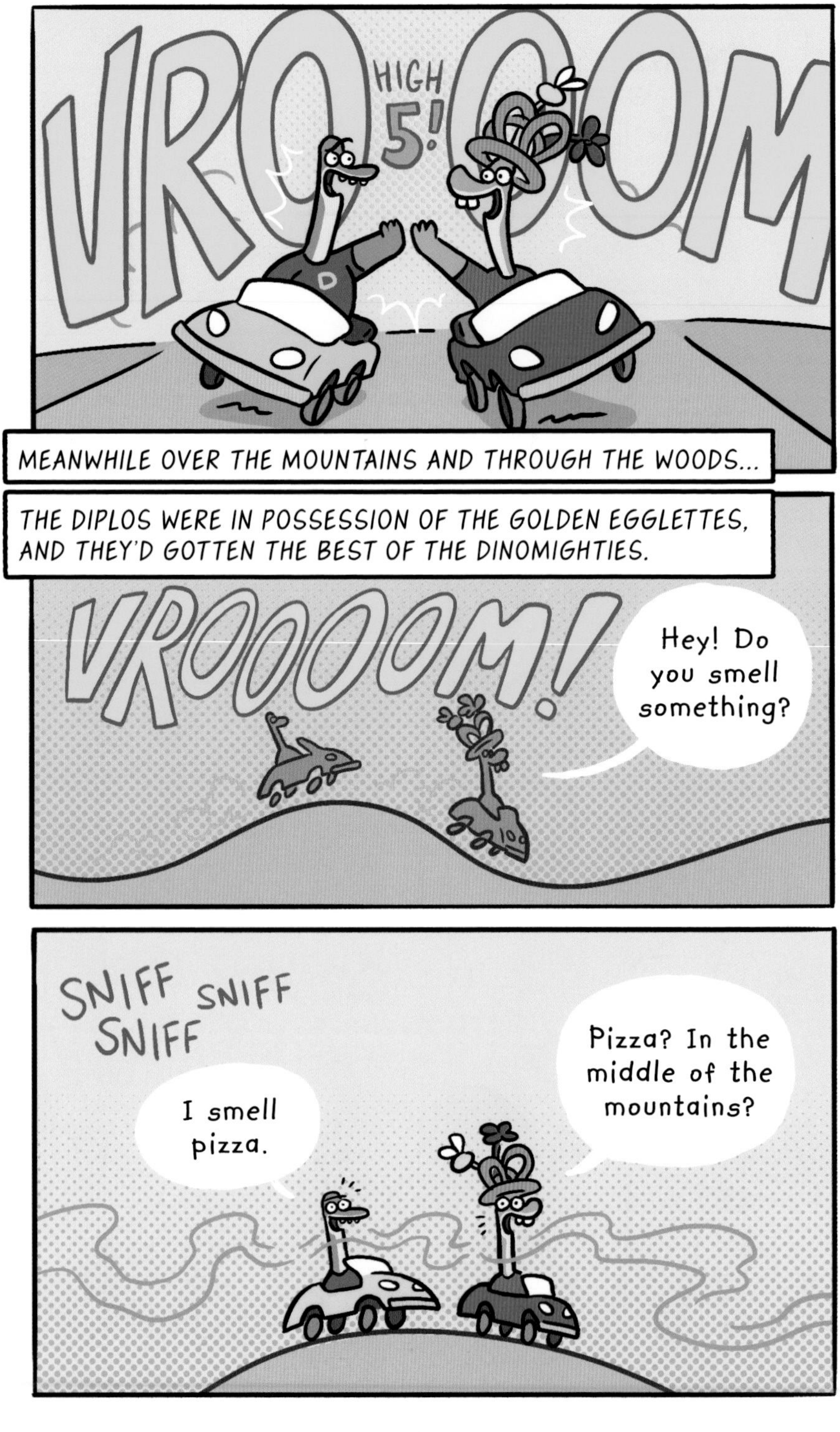
VROOOM
HIGH 5!
MEANWHILE OVER THE MOUNTAINS AND THROUGH THE WOODS...
THE DIPLOS WERE IN POSSESSION OF THE GOLDEN EGGLETTES, AND THEY'D GOTTEN THE BEST OF THE DINOMIGHTIES.
VROOOOM!
Hey! Do you smell something?
SNIFF SNIFF SNIFF
I smell pizza.
Pizza? In the middle of the mountains?

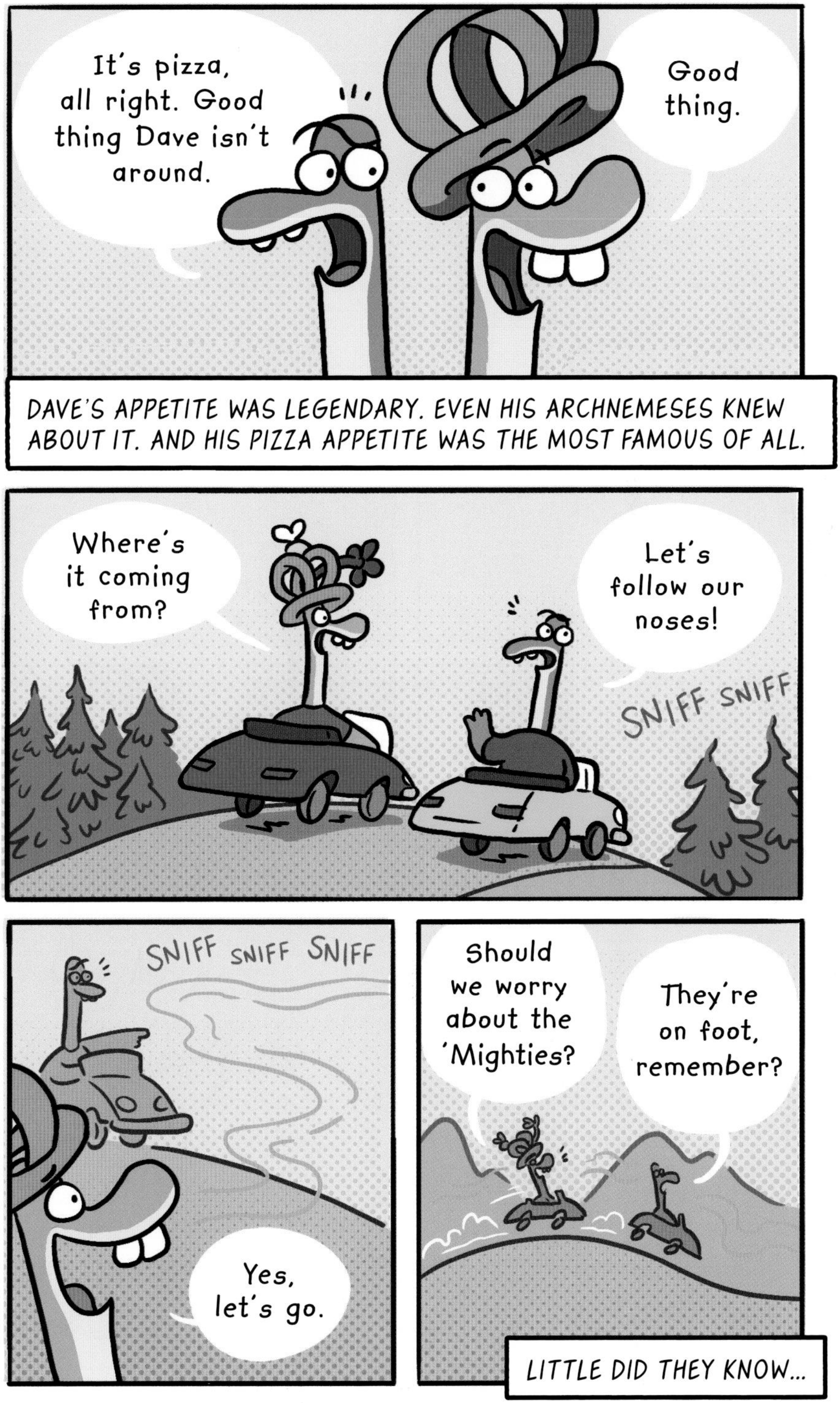
It's pizza, all right. Good thing Dave isn't around.
Good thing.
DAVE'S APPETITE WAS LEGENDARY. EVEN HIS ARCHNEMESES KNEW ABOUT IT. AND HIS PIZZA APPETITE WAS THE MOST FAMOUS OF ALL.
Where's it coming from?
Let's follow our noses!
SNIFF SNIFF
SNIFF SNIFF SNIFF
Yes, let's go.
Should we worry about the 'Mighties?
They're on foot, remember?
LITTLE DID THEY KNOW...

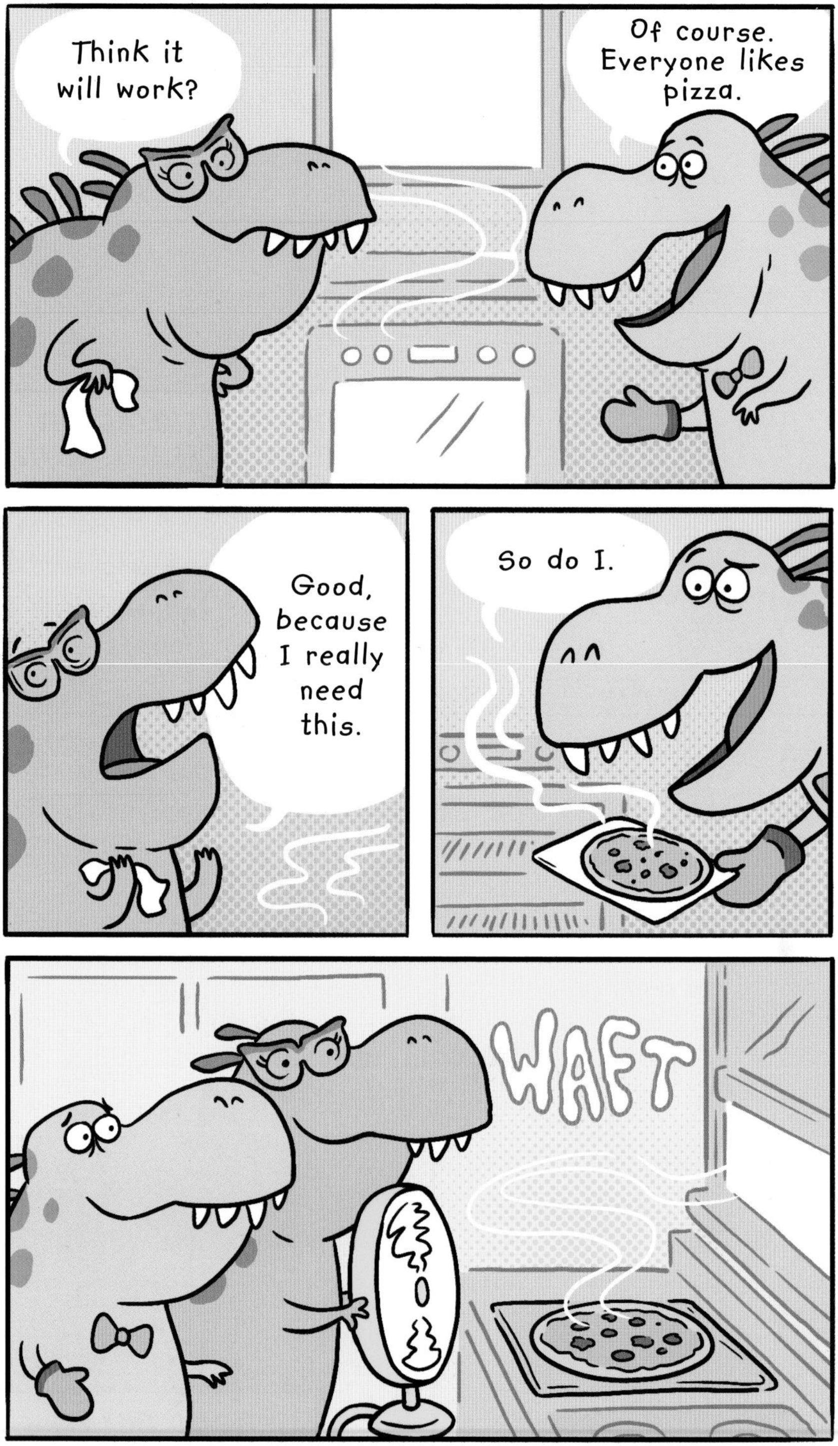

Think it will work?
Of course. Everyone likes pizza.
Good, because I really need this.
So do I.
WAFT

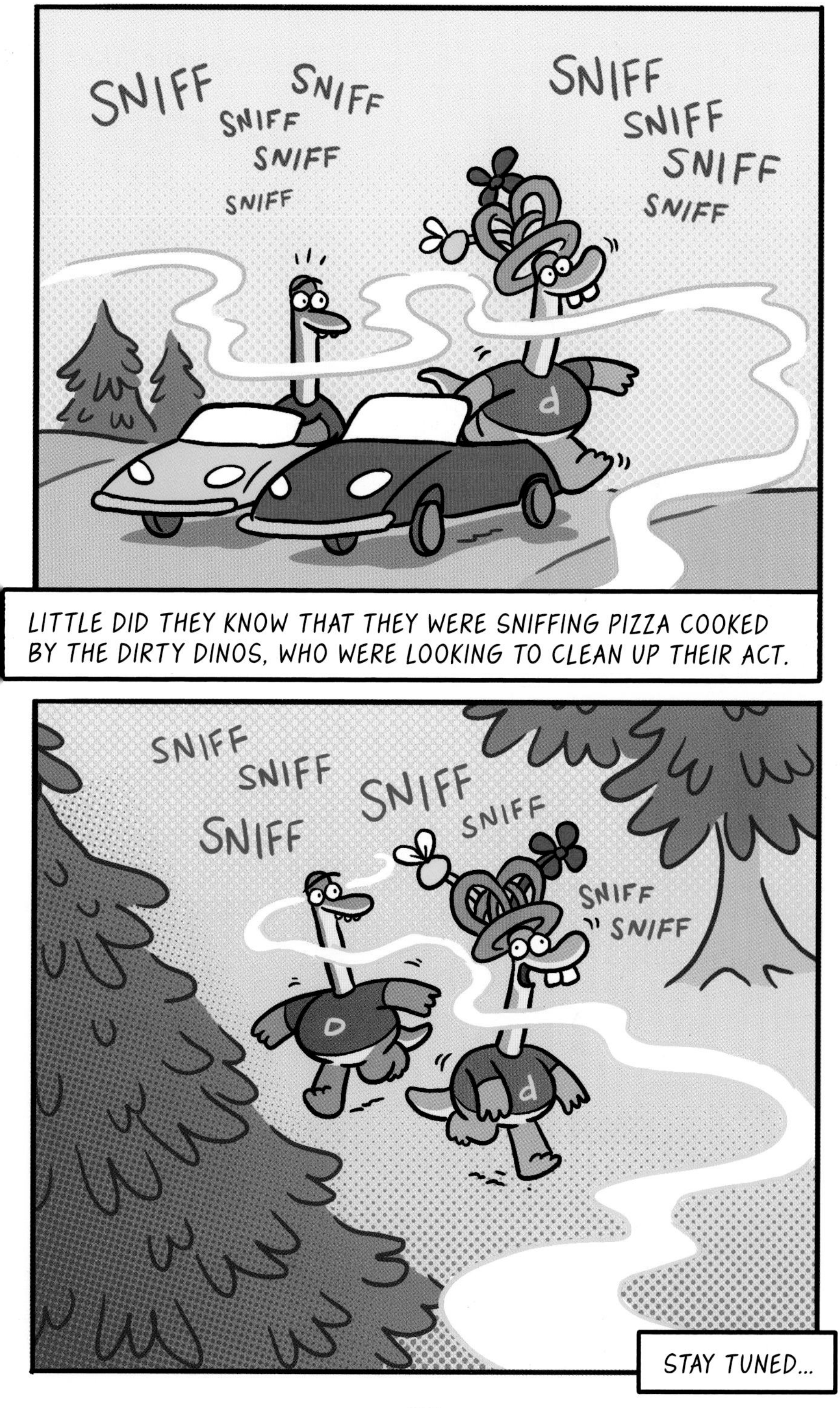
SNIFF
SNIFF
SNIFF
SNIFF
SNIFF
SNIFF
SNIFF
SNIFF
SNIFF
LITTLE DID THEY KNOW THAT THEY WERE SNIFFING PIZZA COOKED BY THE DIRTY DINOS, WHO WERE LOOKING TO CLEAN UP THEIR ACT.
SNIFF
SNIFF
SNIFF
SNIFF
SNIFF
SNIFF
SNIFF
STAY TUNED...

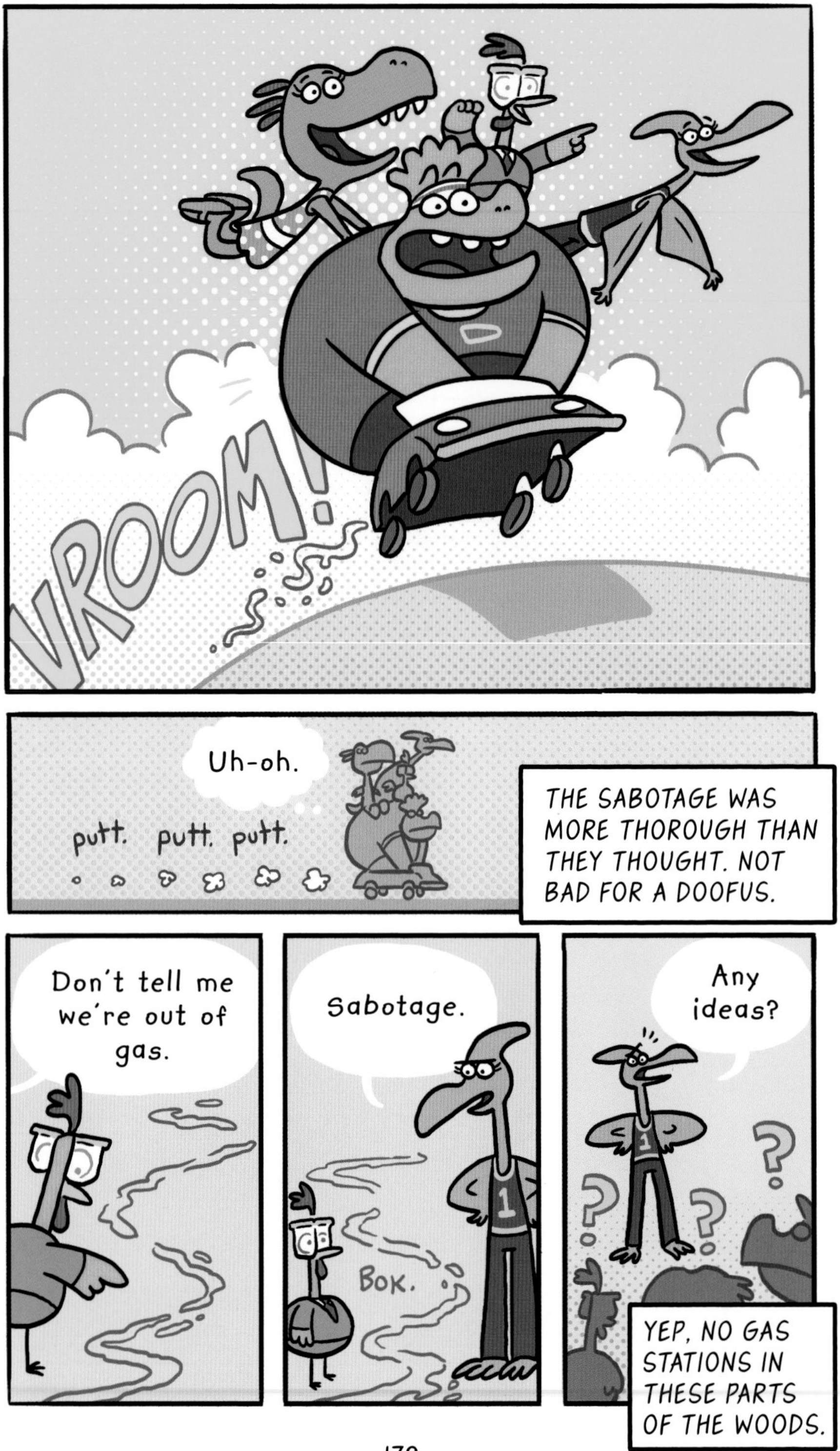
VROOM!
Uh-oh.
putt. putt. putt.
THE SABOTAGE WAS MORE THOROUGH THAN THEY THOUGHT. NOT BAD FOR A DOOFUS.
Don't tell me we're out of gas.
Sabotage.
BOK.
Any ideas?
YEP, NO GAS STATIONS IN THESE PARTS OF THE WOODS.

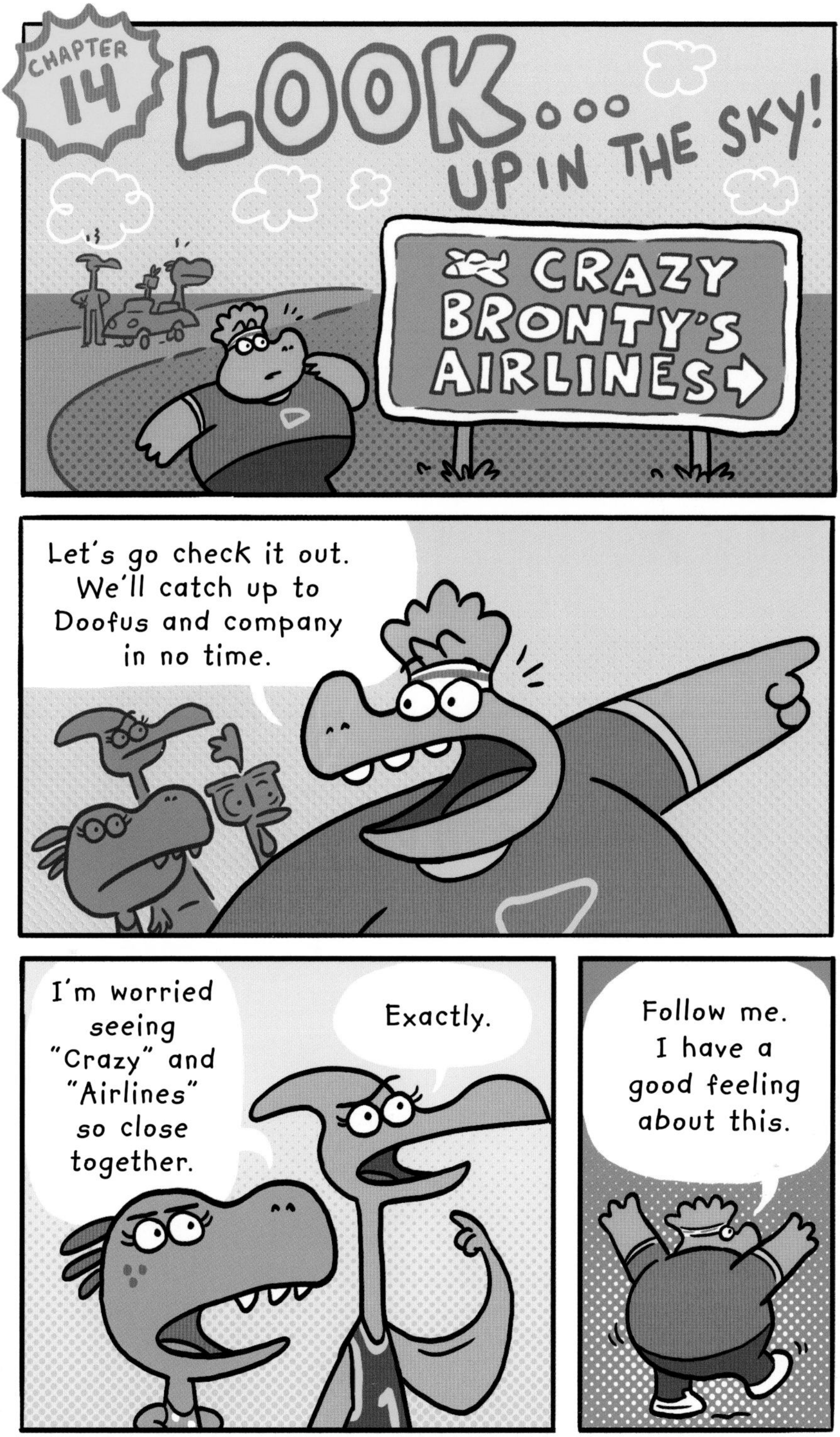
CHAPTER 14
LOOK... UP IN THE SKY!
CRAZY BRONTY'S AIRLINES
Let's go check it out. We'll catch up to Doofus and company in no time.
I'm worried seeing "Crazy" and "Airlines" so close together.
Exactly.
Follow me. I have a good feeling about this.

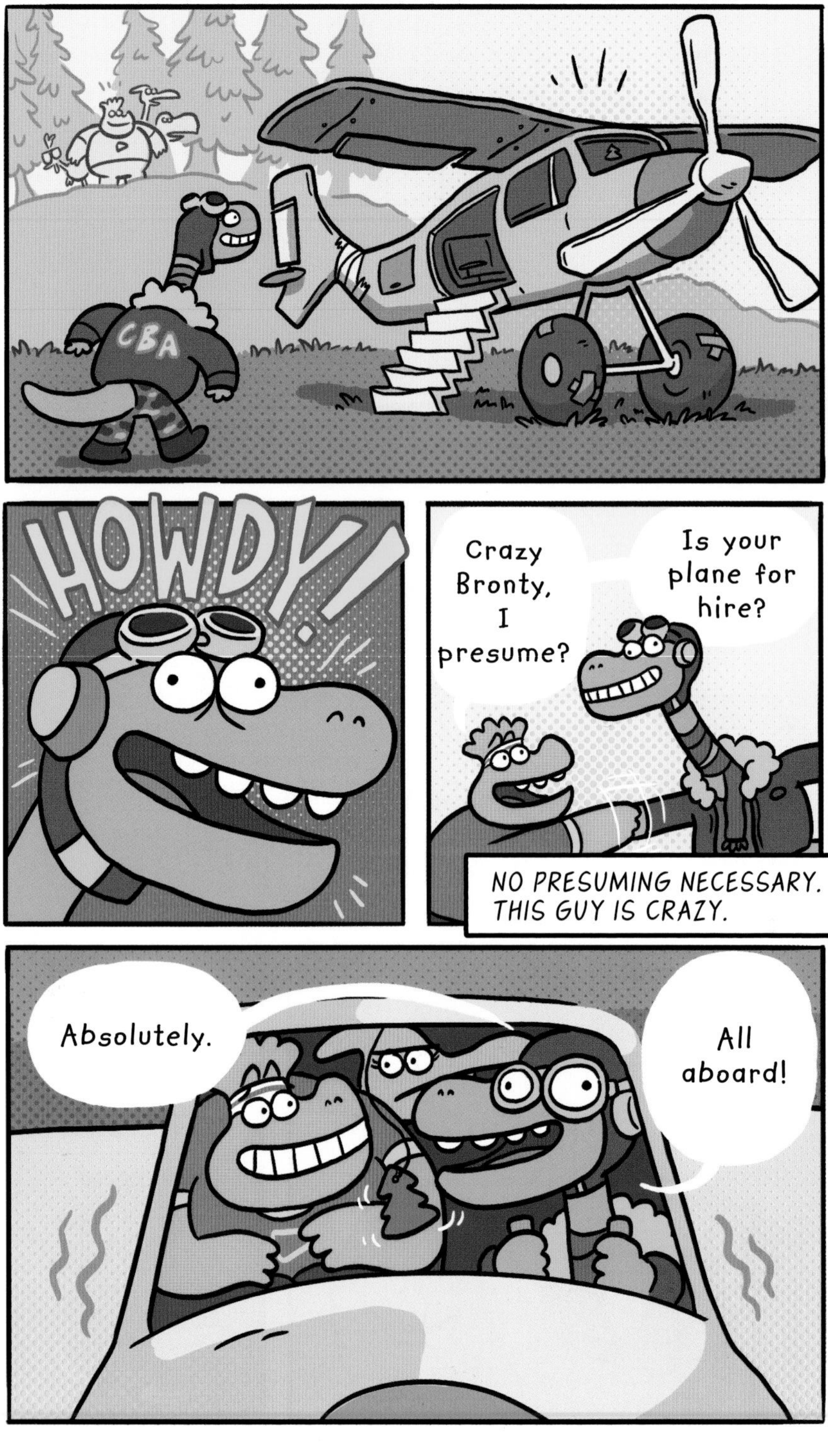
HOWDY!
Crazy Bronty, I presume?
Is your plane for hire?
NO PRESUMING NECESSARY. THIS GUY IS CRAZY.
Absolutely.
All aboard!

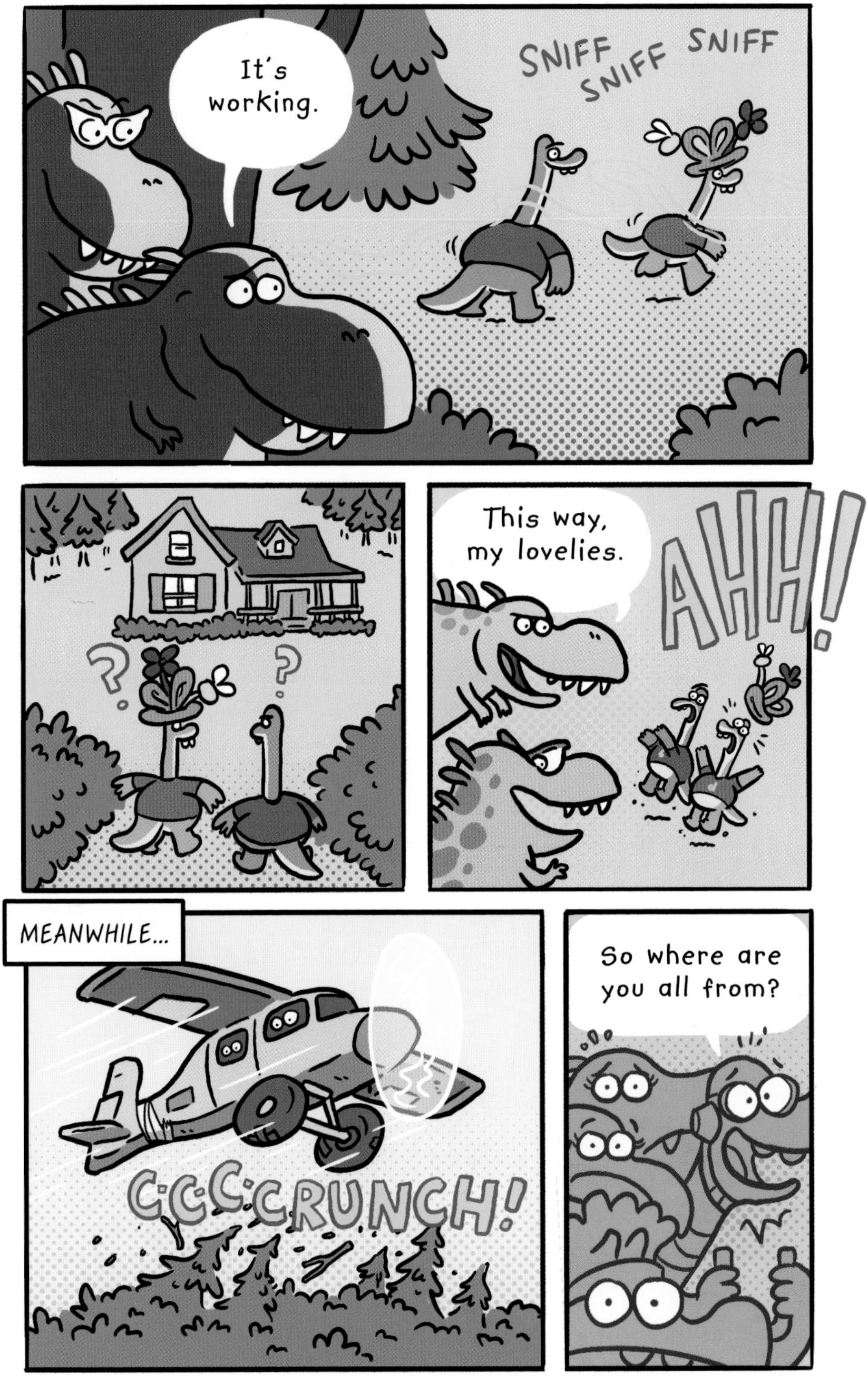
It's working.
SNIFF SNIFF SNIFF
This way, my lovelies.
AHH!!
MEANWHILE...
C-C-C-CRUNCH!
So where are you all from?

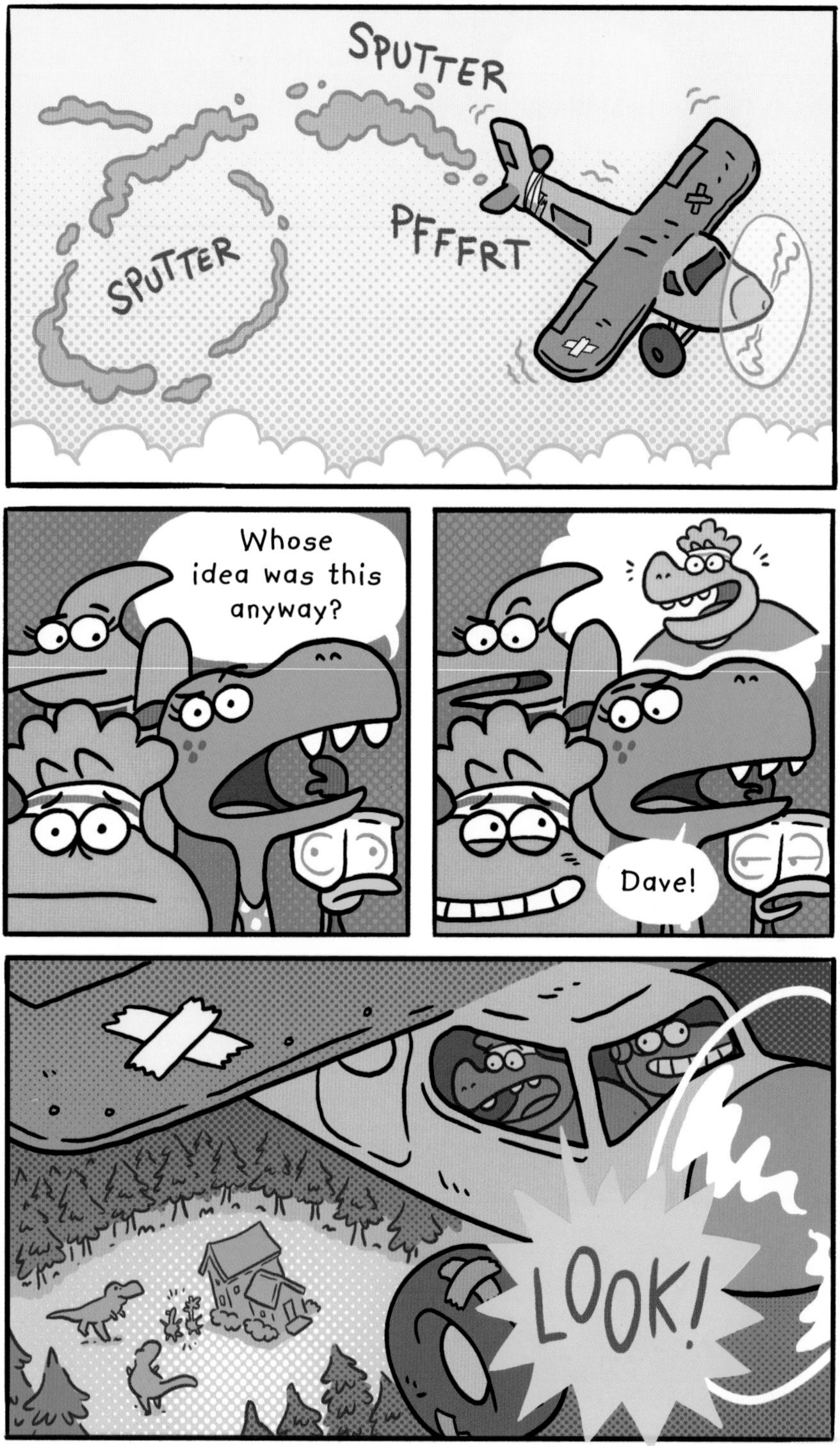
SPUTTER
SPUTTER
PFFFRT
Whose idea was this anyway?
Dave!
LOOK!

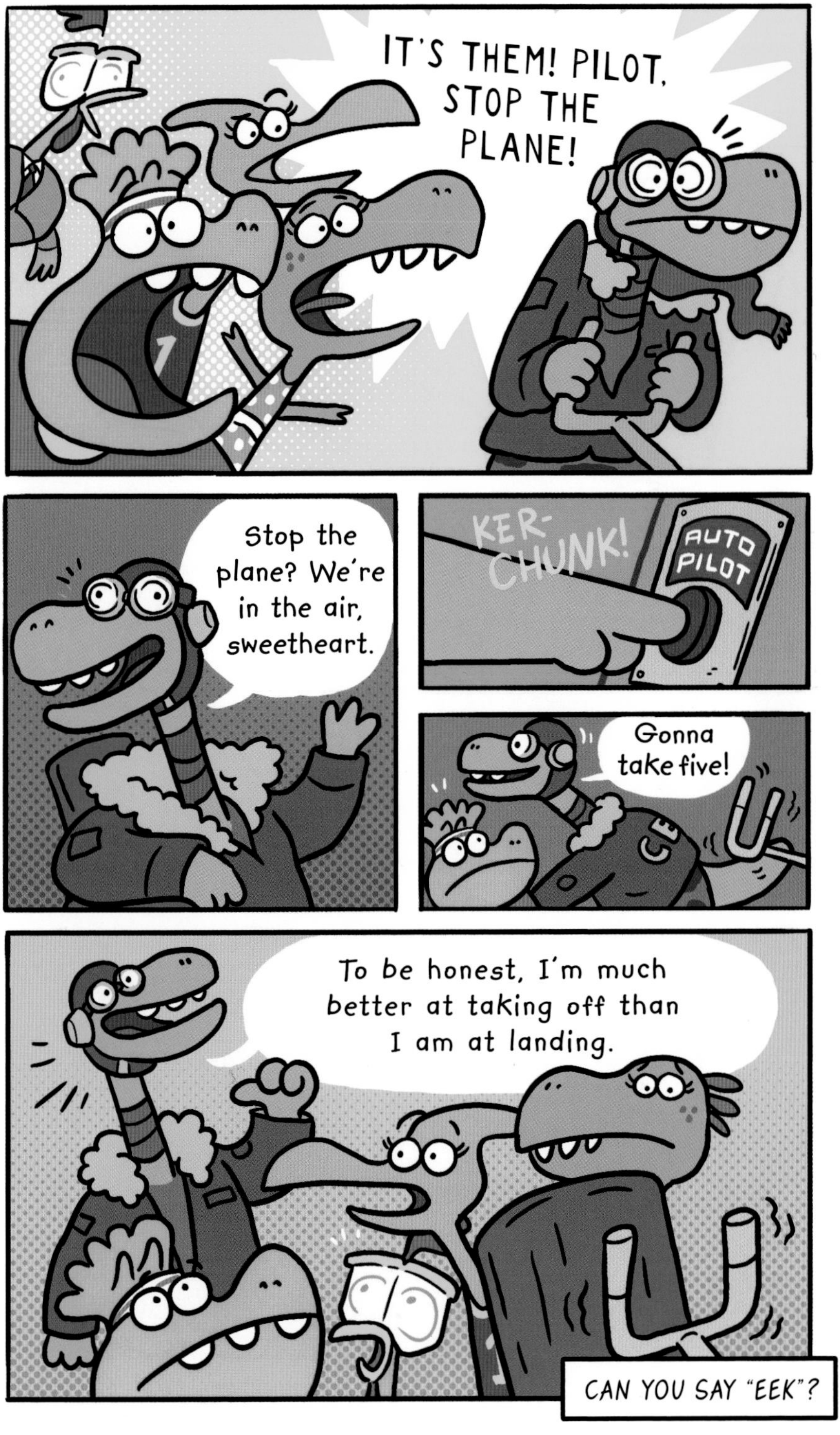
IT'S THEM! PILOT, STOP THE PLANE!
Stop the plane? We're in the air, sweetheart.
KER-CHUNK!
AUTO PILOT
Gonna take five!
To be honest, I'm much better at taking off than I am at landing.
CAN YOU SAY "EEK"?

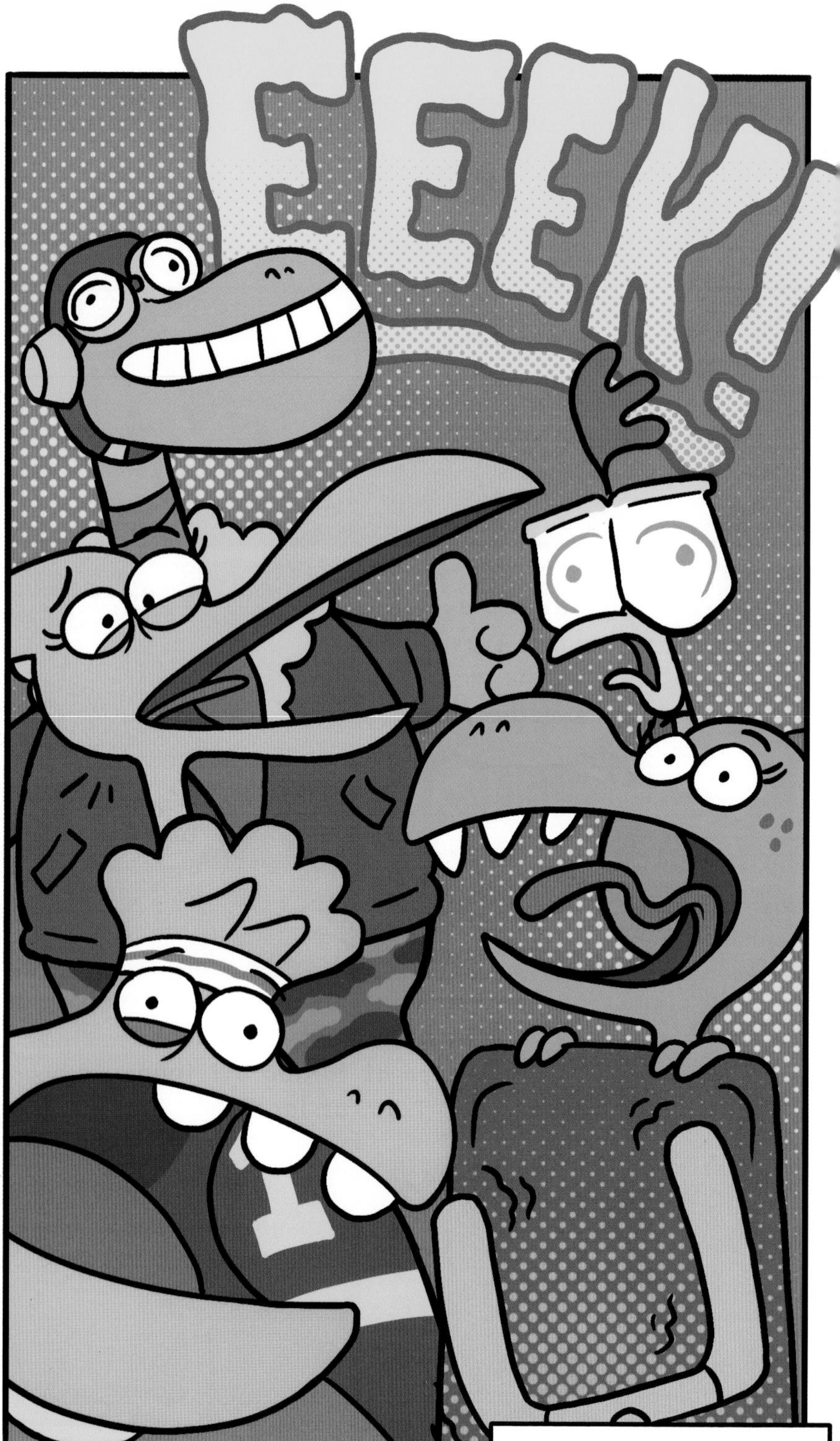
EEEK!!
I'LL TAKE THAT AS A YES.

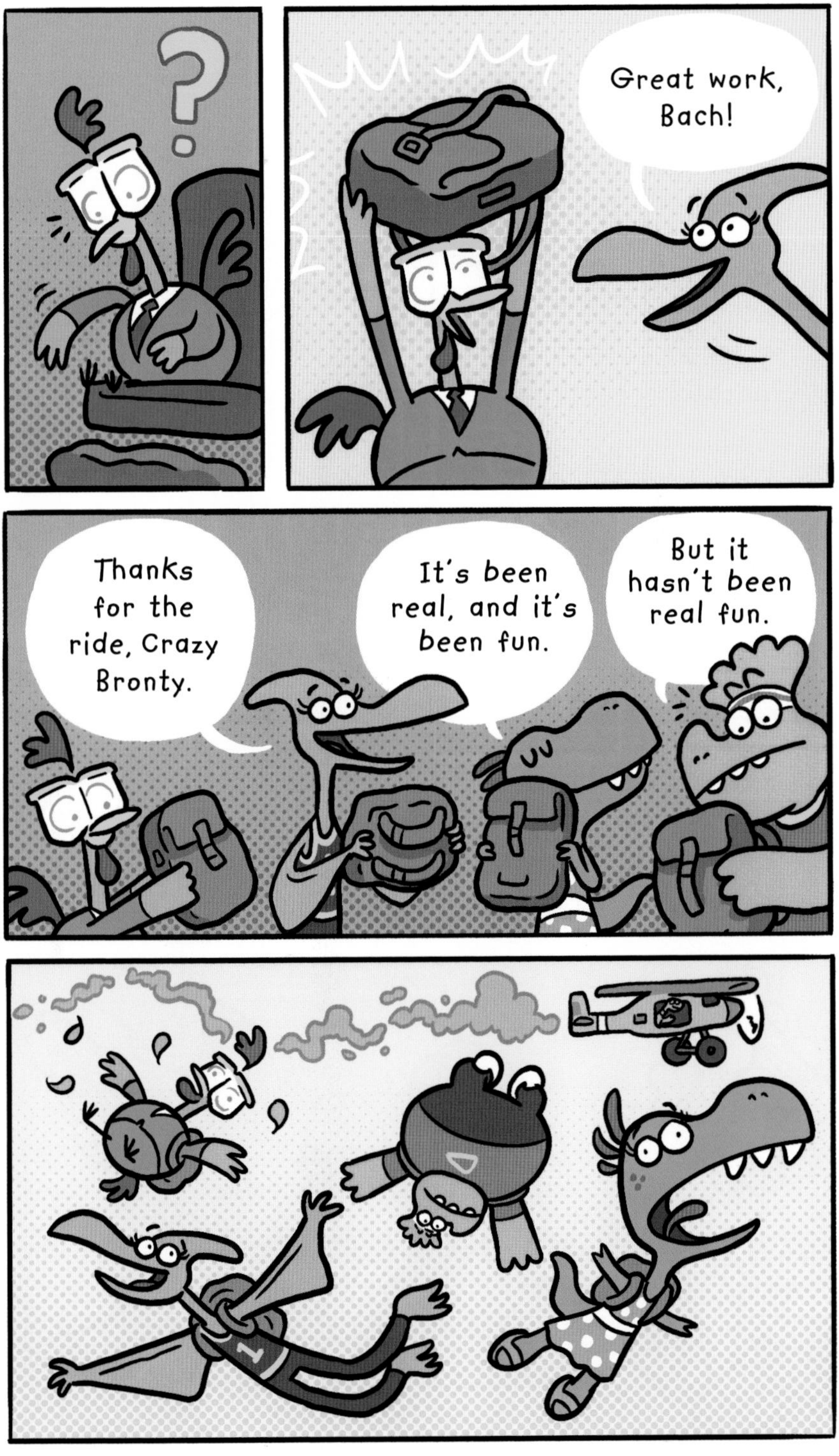
Great work, Bach!
Thanks for the ride, Crazy Bronty.
It's been real, and it's been fun.
But it hasn't been real fun.

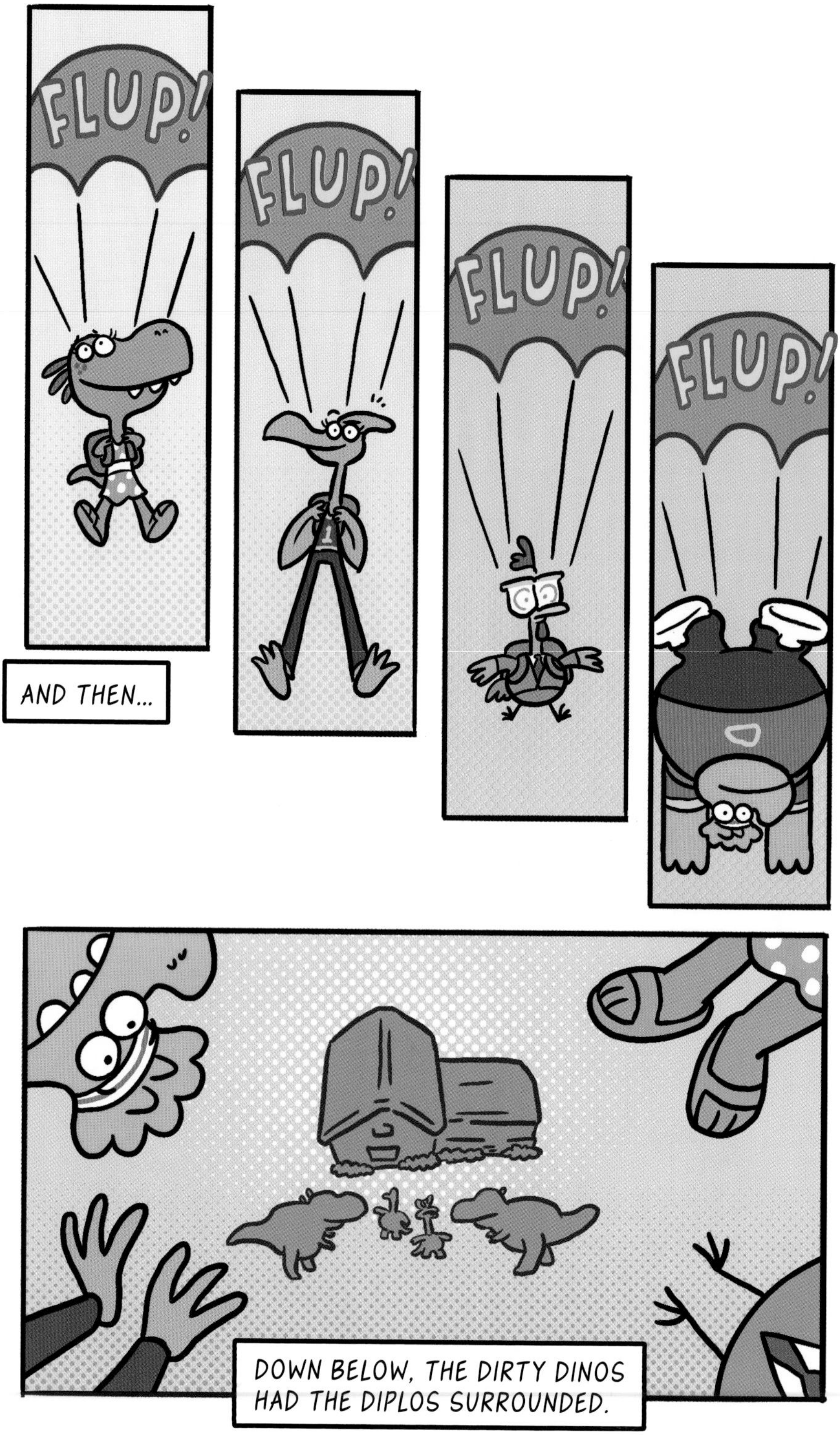
FLUP!
FLUP!
FLUP!
FLUP!
AND THEN...
DOWN BELOW, THE DIRTY DINOS HAD THE DIPLOS SURROUNDED.

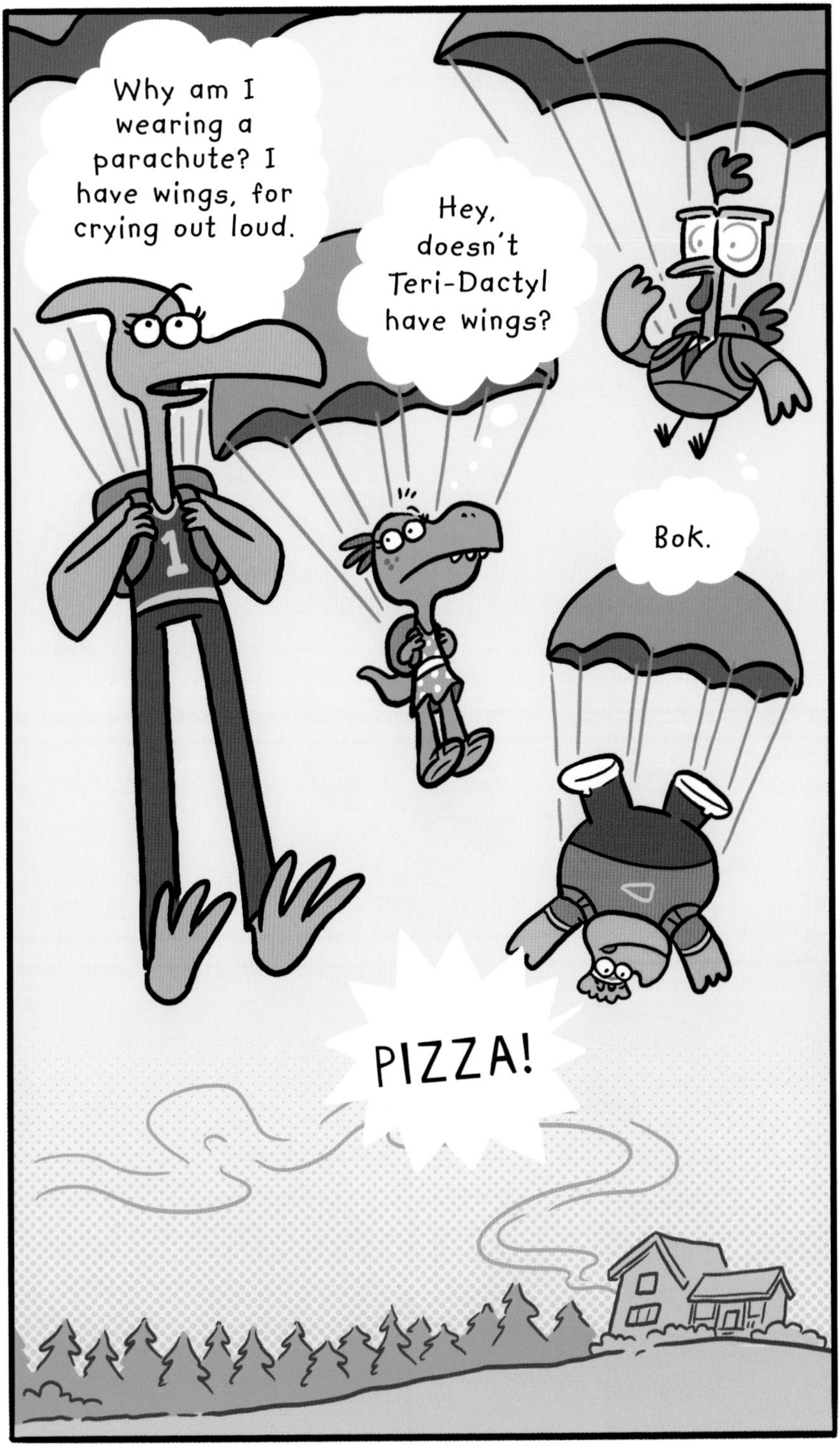
Why am I wearing a parachute? I have wings, for crying out loud.
Hey, doesn't Teri-Dactyl have wings?
Bok.
PIZZA!

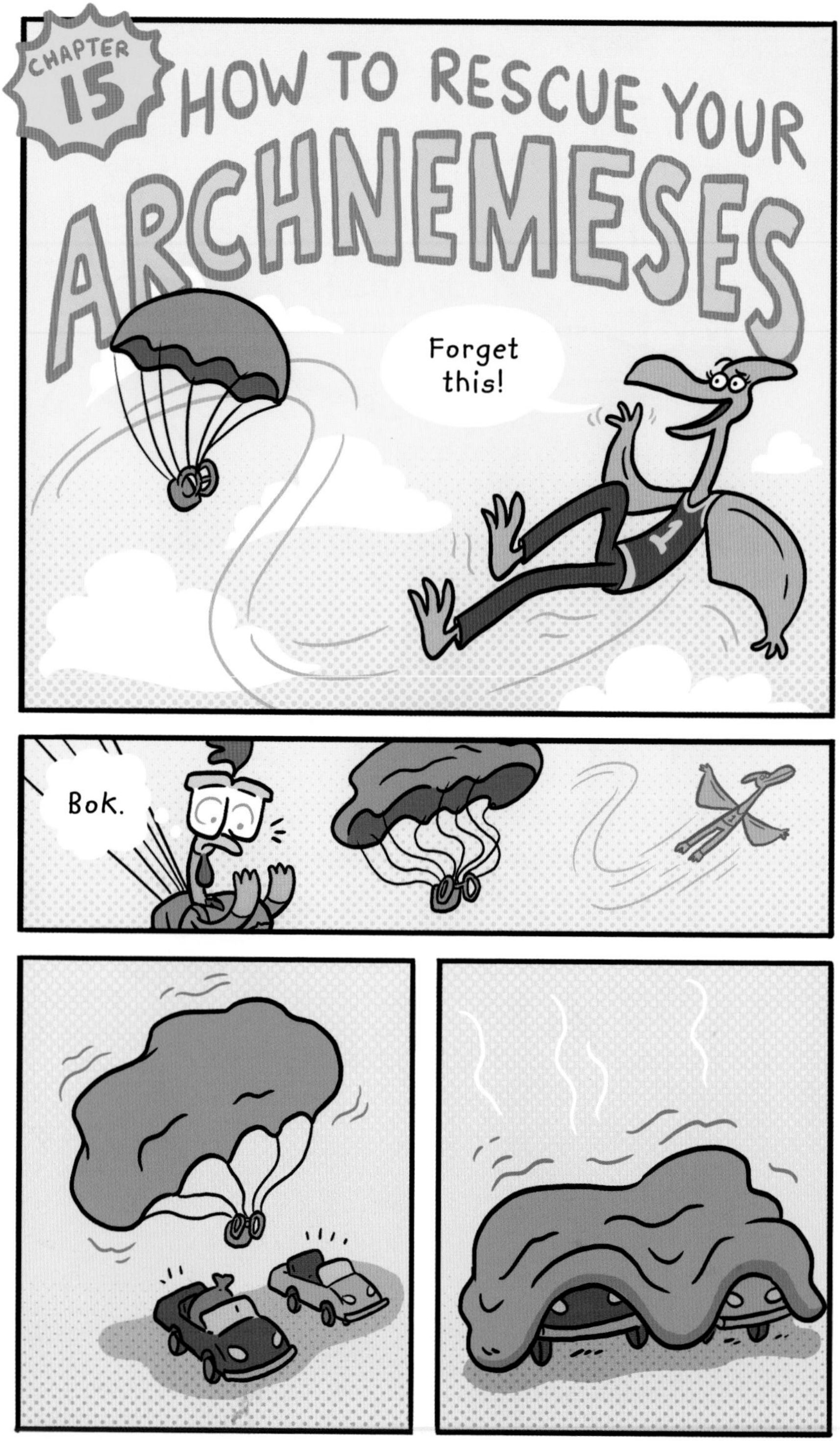
CHAPTER 15
HOW TO RESCUE YOUR ARCHNEMESES
Forget this!
Bok.

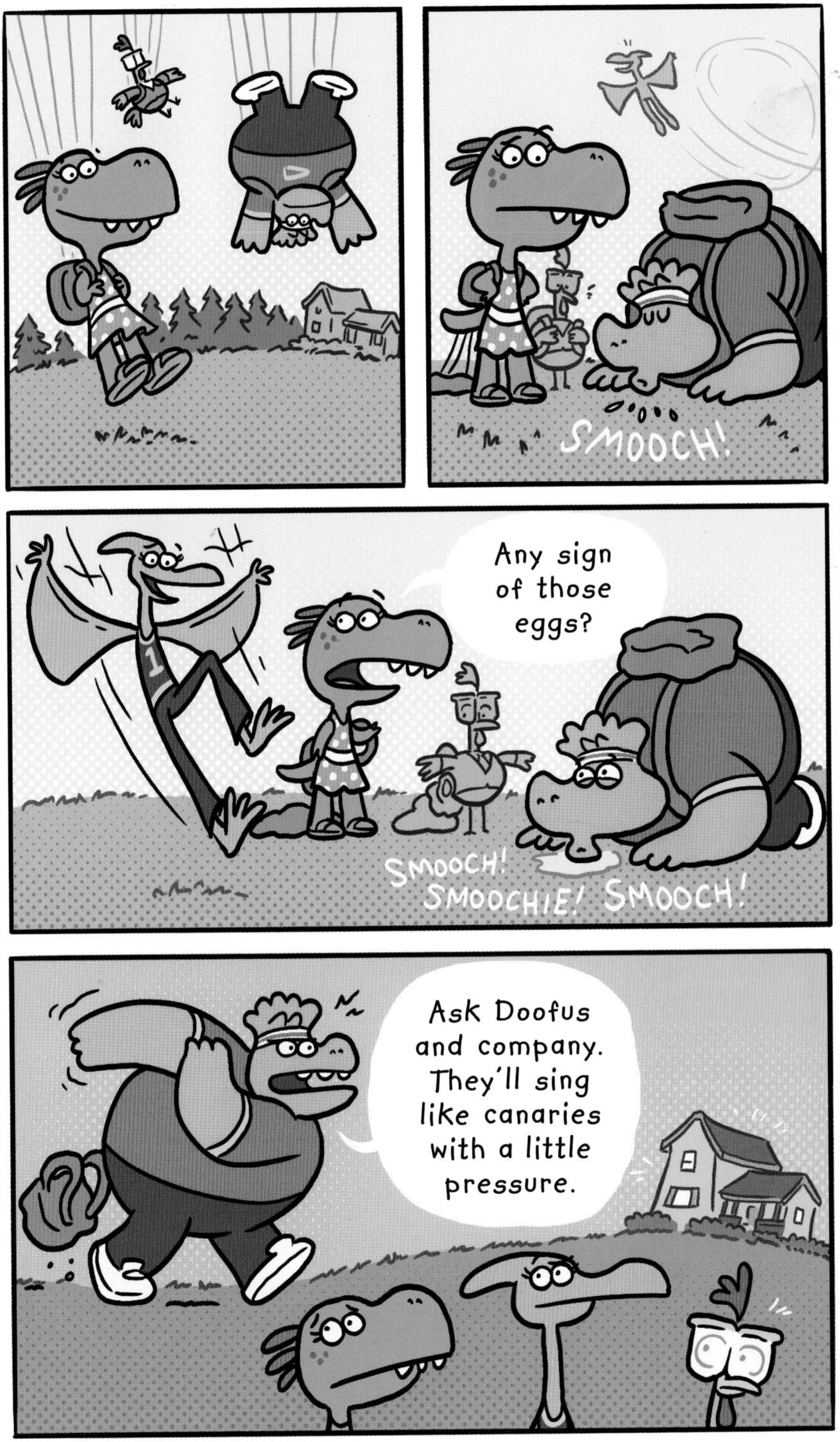
SMOOCH!
Any sign of those eggs?
SMOOCH!
SMOOCHIE! SMOOCH!
Ask Doofus and company. They'll sing like canaries with a little pressure.

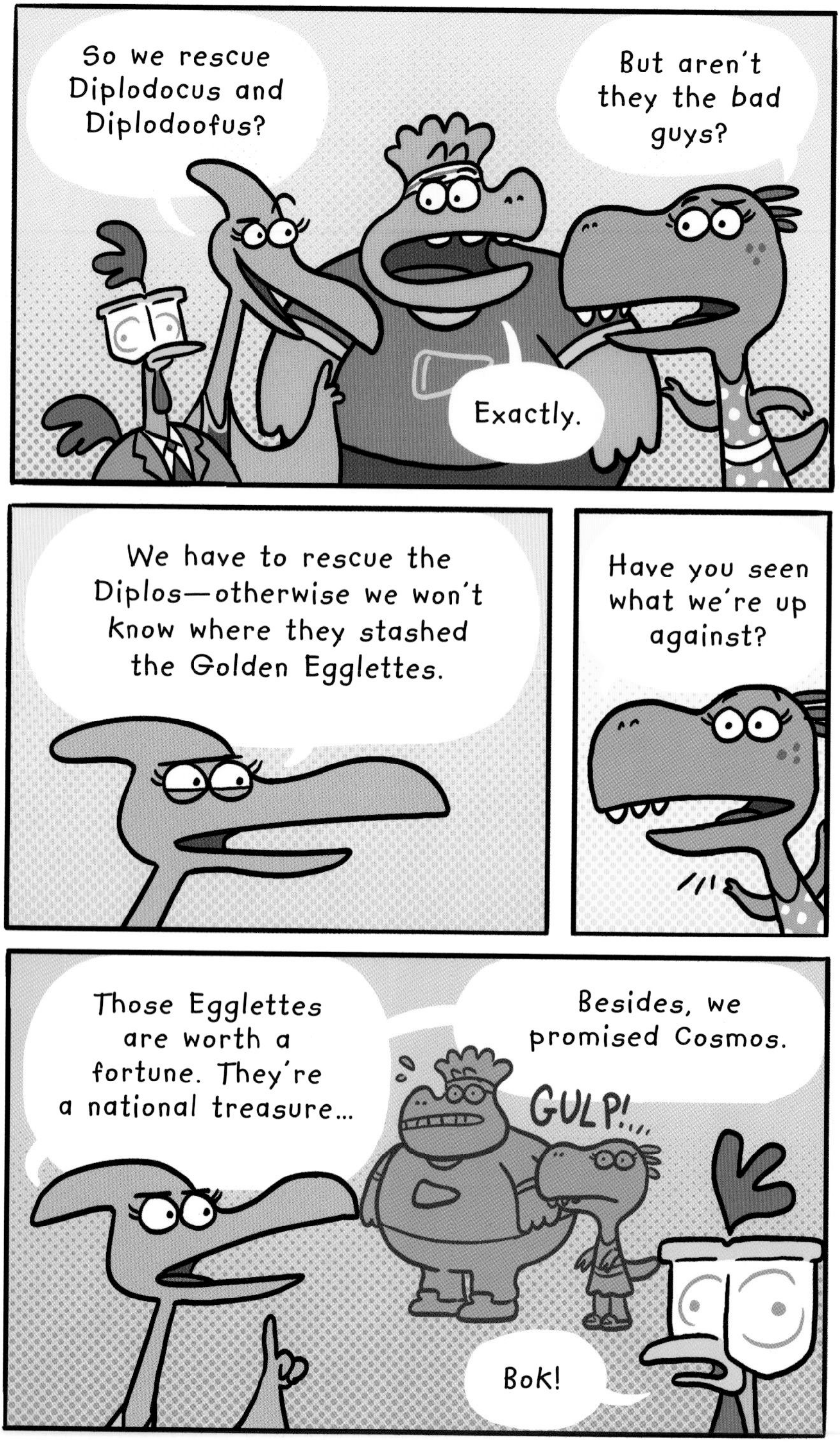
So we rescue Diplodocus and Diplodoofus?
But aren't they the bad guys?
Exactly.
We have to rescue the Diplos—otherwise we won't know where they stashed the Golden Egglettes.
Have you seen what we're up against?
Those Egglettes are worth a fortune. They're a national treasure...
Besides, we promised Cosmos.
GULP!
Bok!

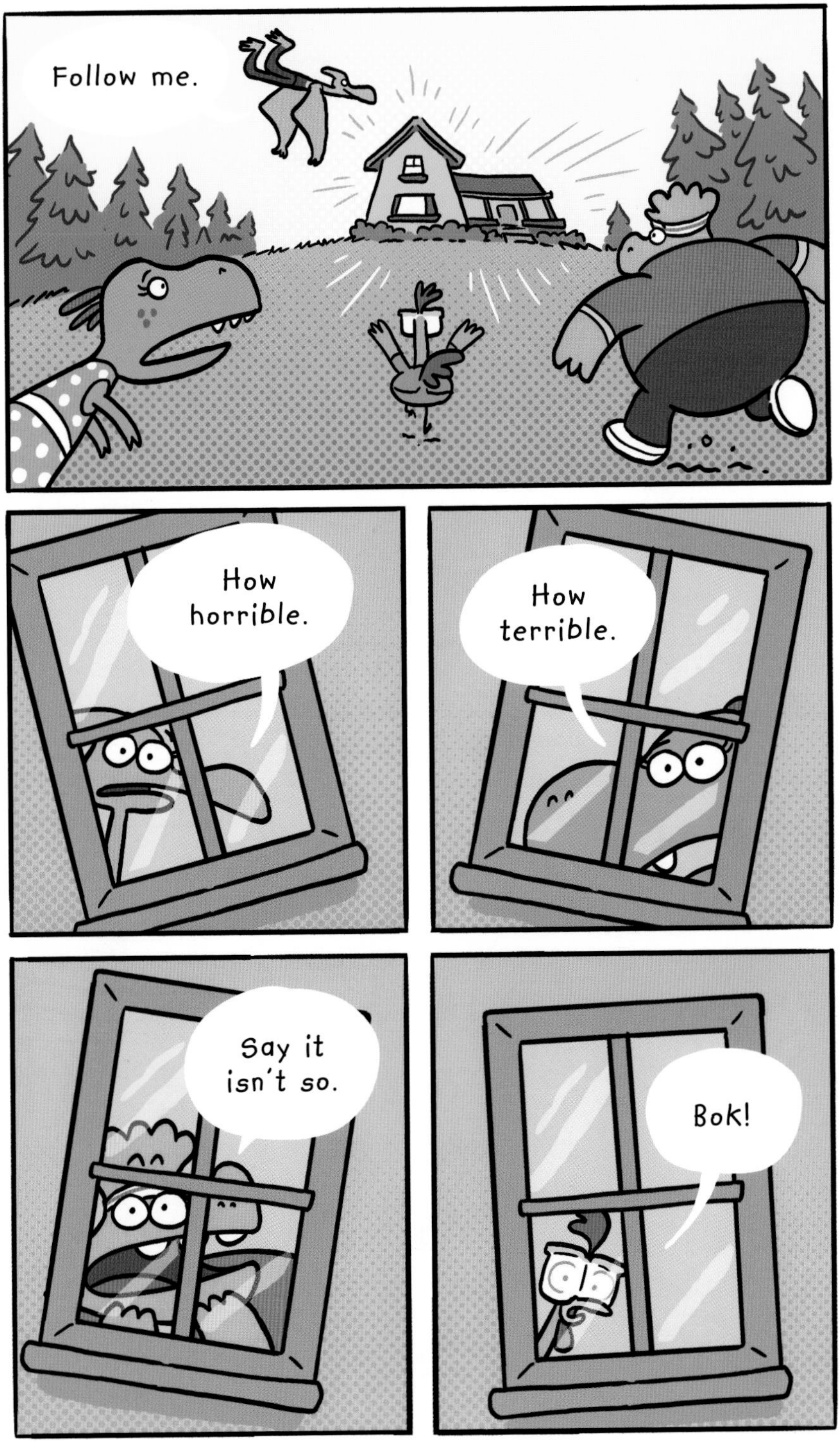
Follow me.
How horrible.
How terrible.
Say it isn't so.
Bok!

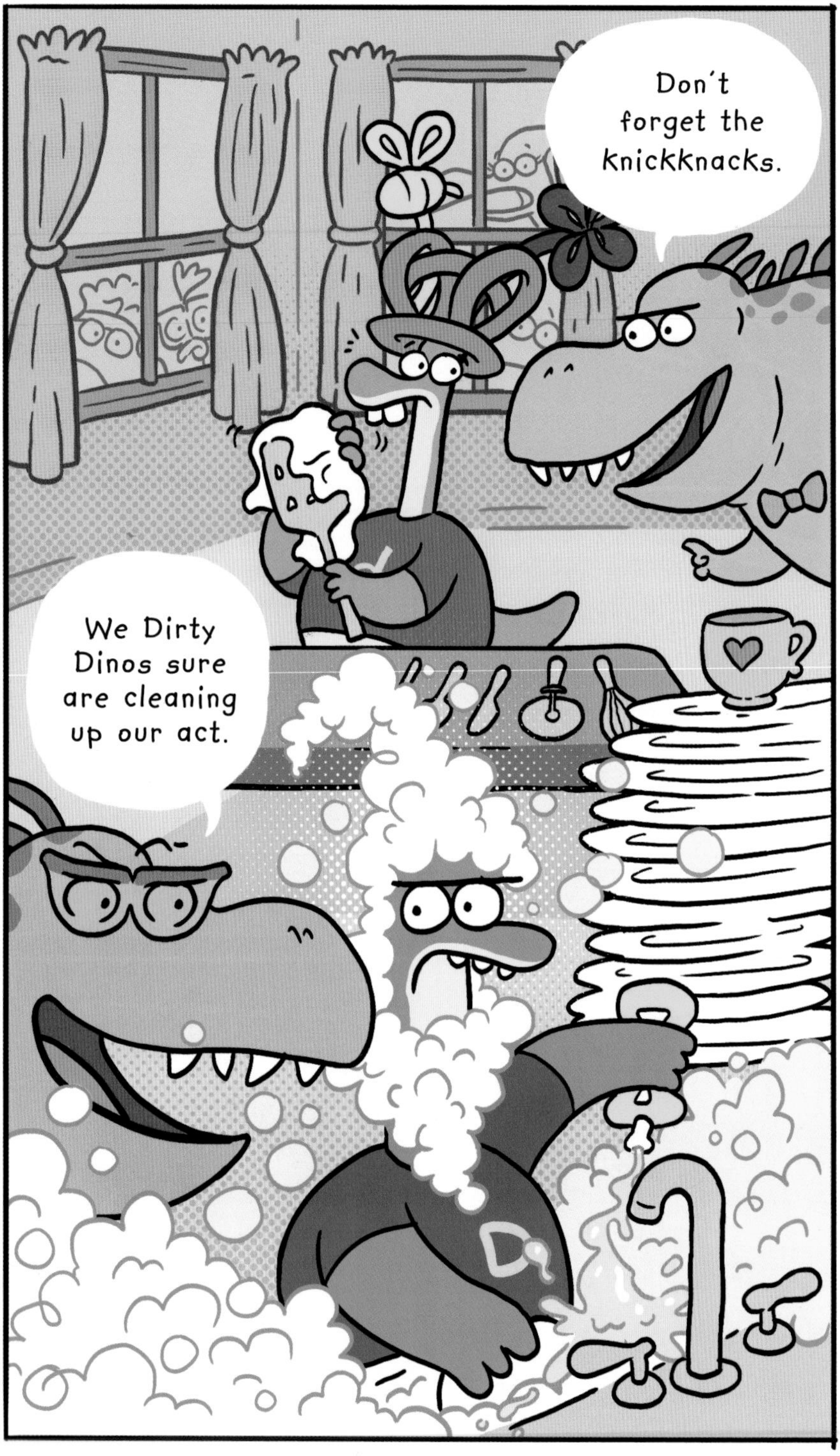
Don't forget the knickknacks.
We Dirty Dinos sure are cleaning up our act.

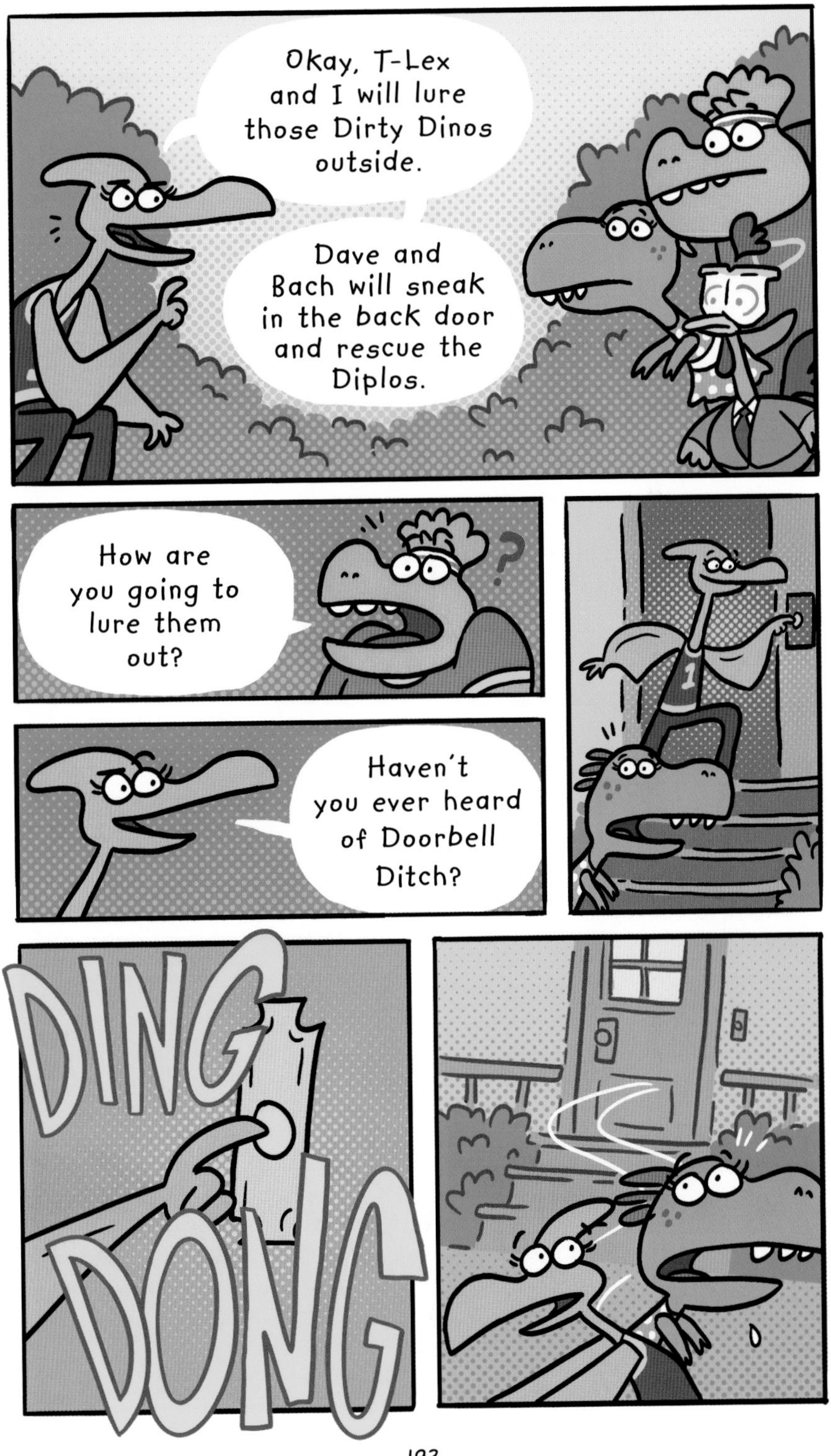
Okay, T-Lex and I will lure those Dirty Dinos outside.
Dave and Bach will sneak in the back door and rescue the Diplos.
How are you going to lure them out?
?
Haven't you ever heard of Doorbell Ditch?
DING DONG

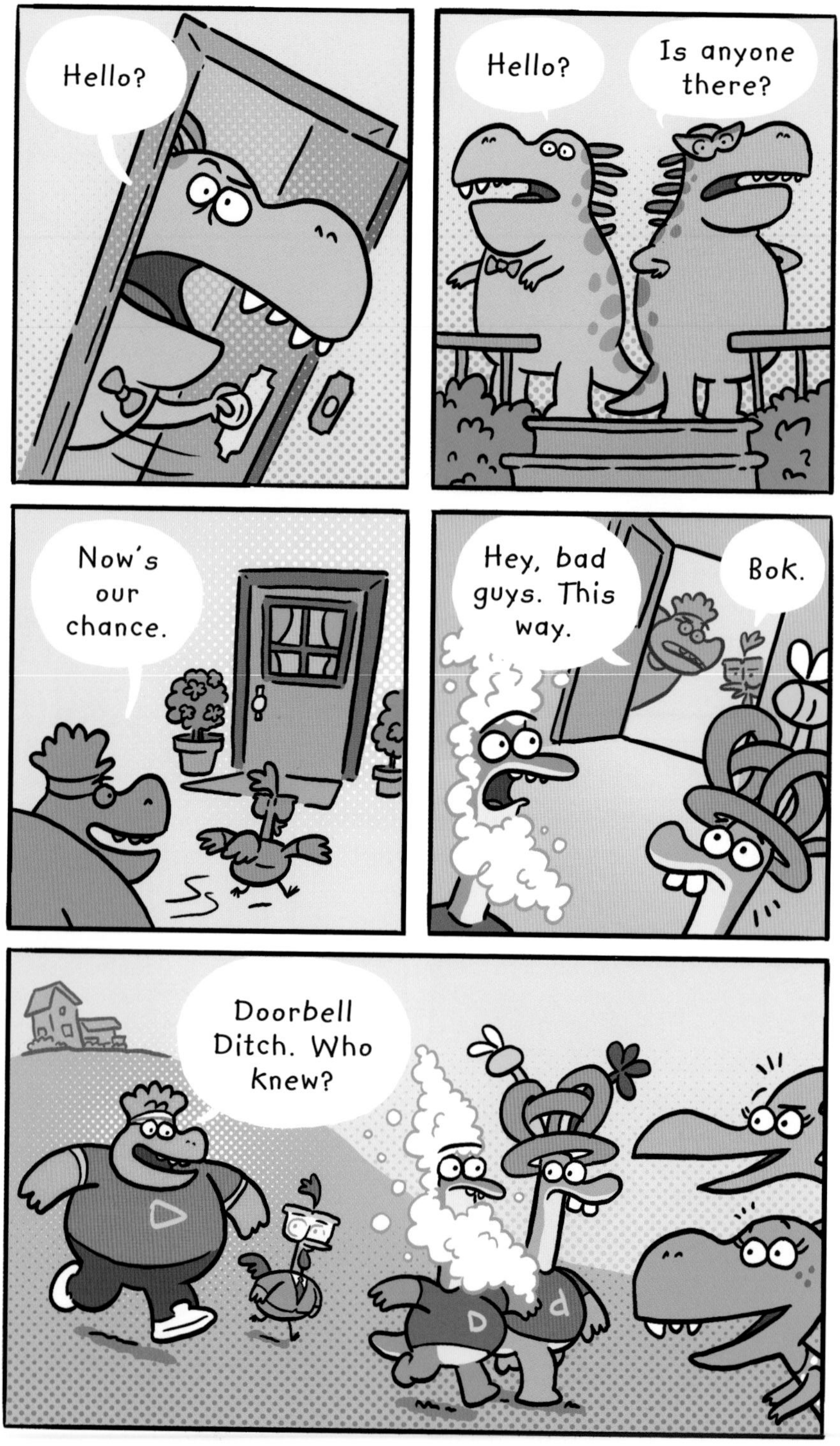
Hello?
Hello?
Is anyone there?
Now's our chance.
Hey, bad guys. This way.
Bok.
Doorbell Ditch. Who knew?

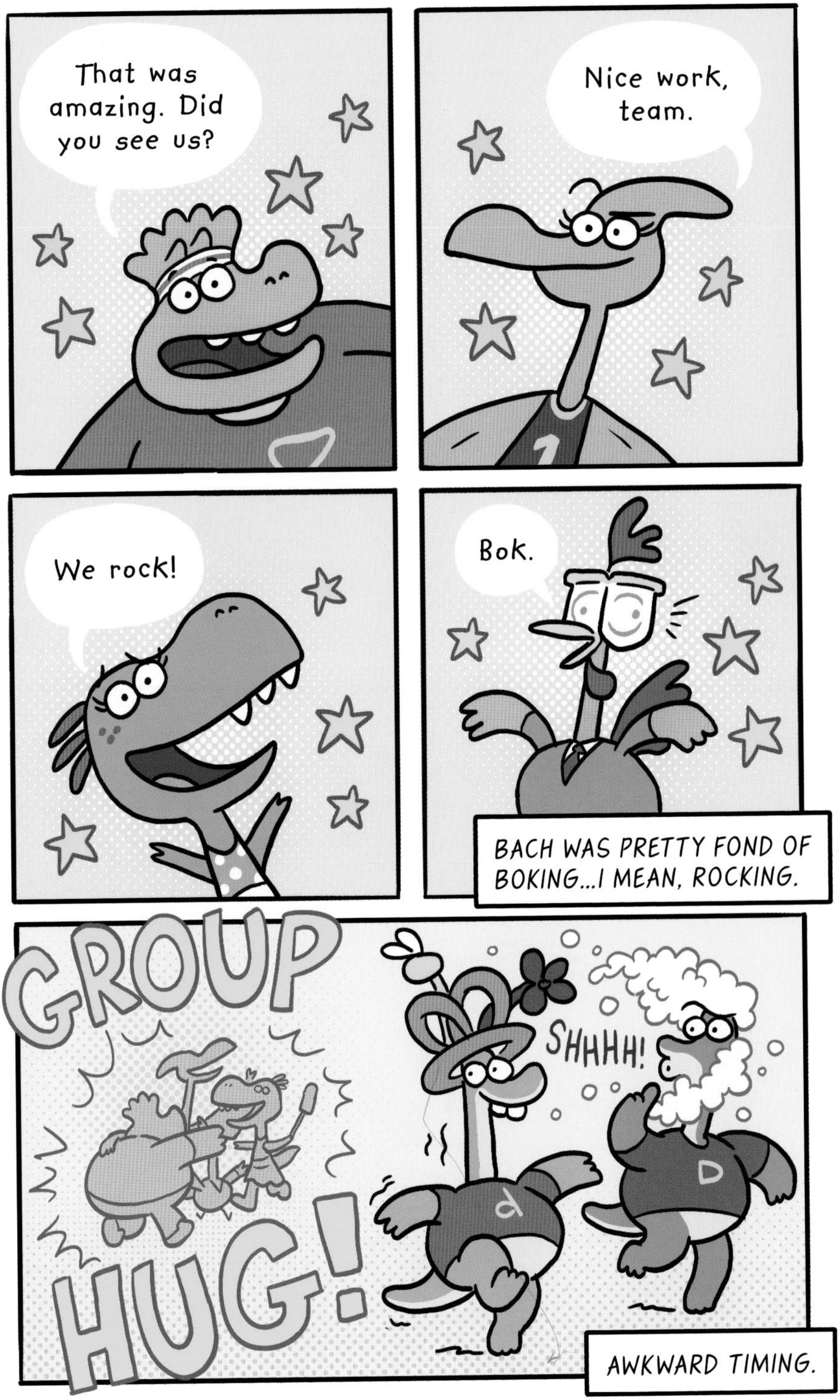
That was amazing. Did you see us?
Nice work, team.
We rock!
Bok.
BACH WAS PRETTY FOND OF BOKING...I MEAN, ROCKING.
GROUP HUG!
SHHHH!
AWKWARD TIMING.

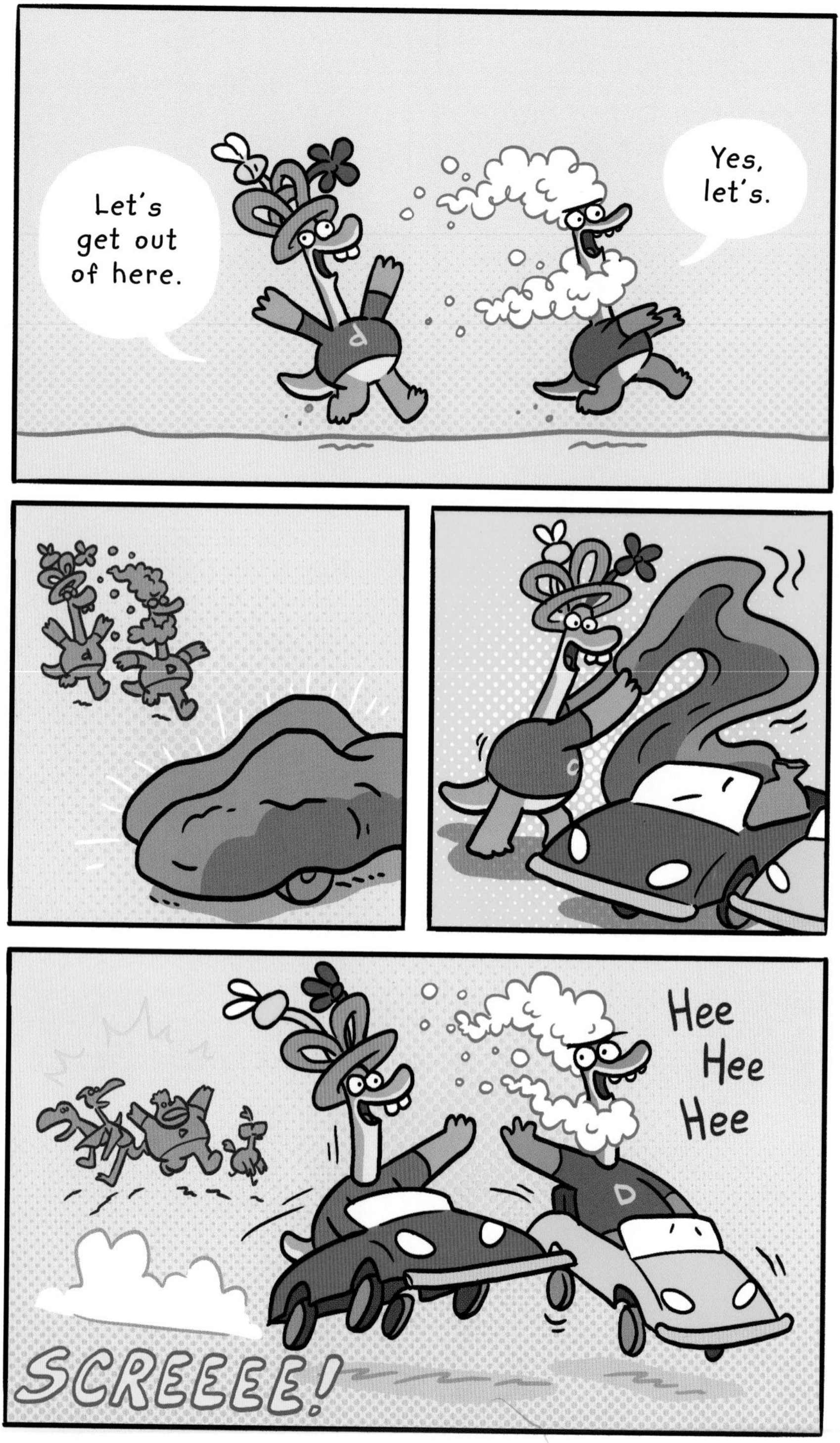
Let's get out of here.
Yes, let's.
Hee Hee Hee
SCREEEE!

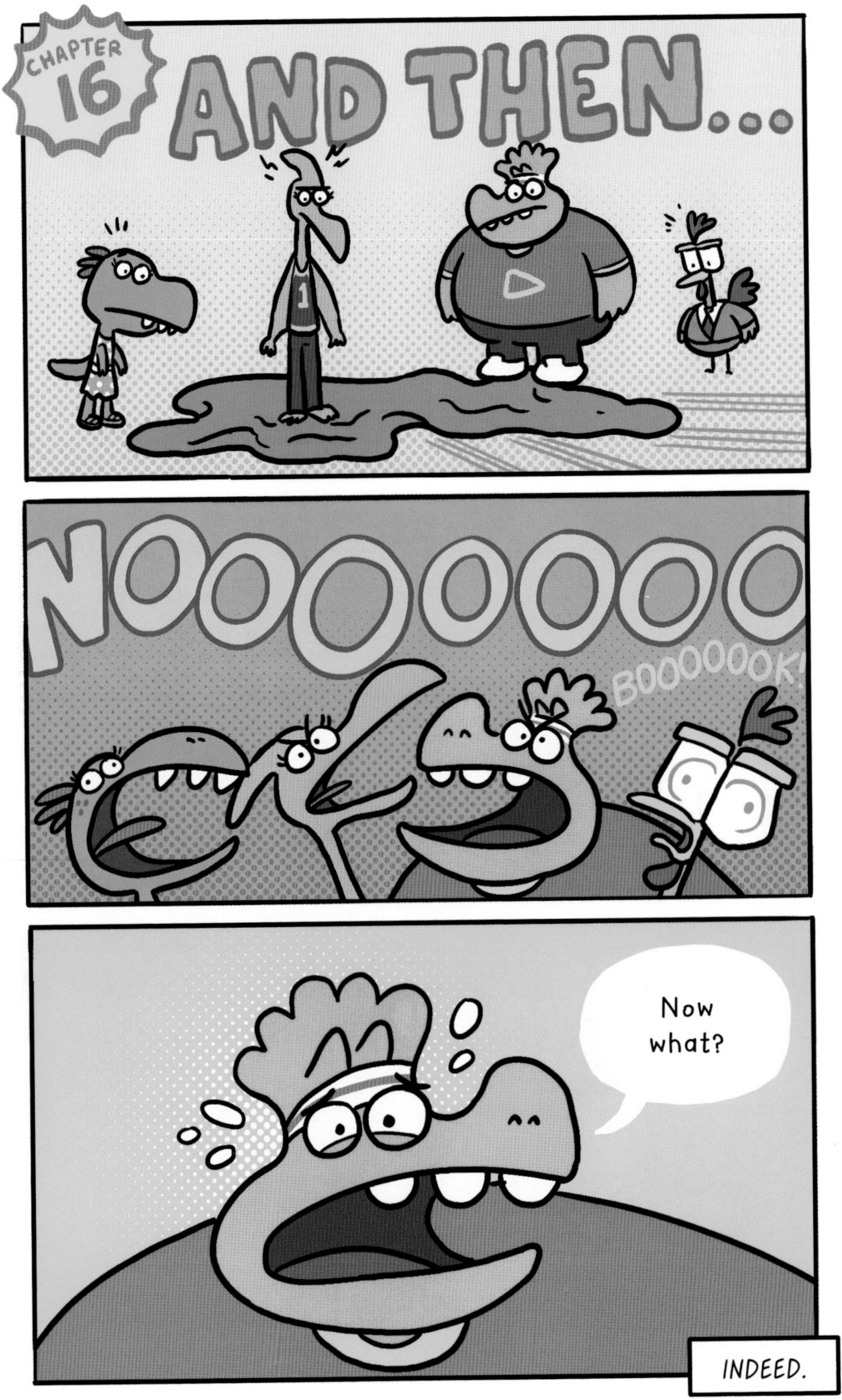
CHAPTER 16
AND THEN...
NOOOOOOO
BOOOOOOK!
Now what?
INDEED.

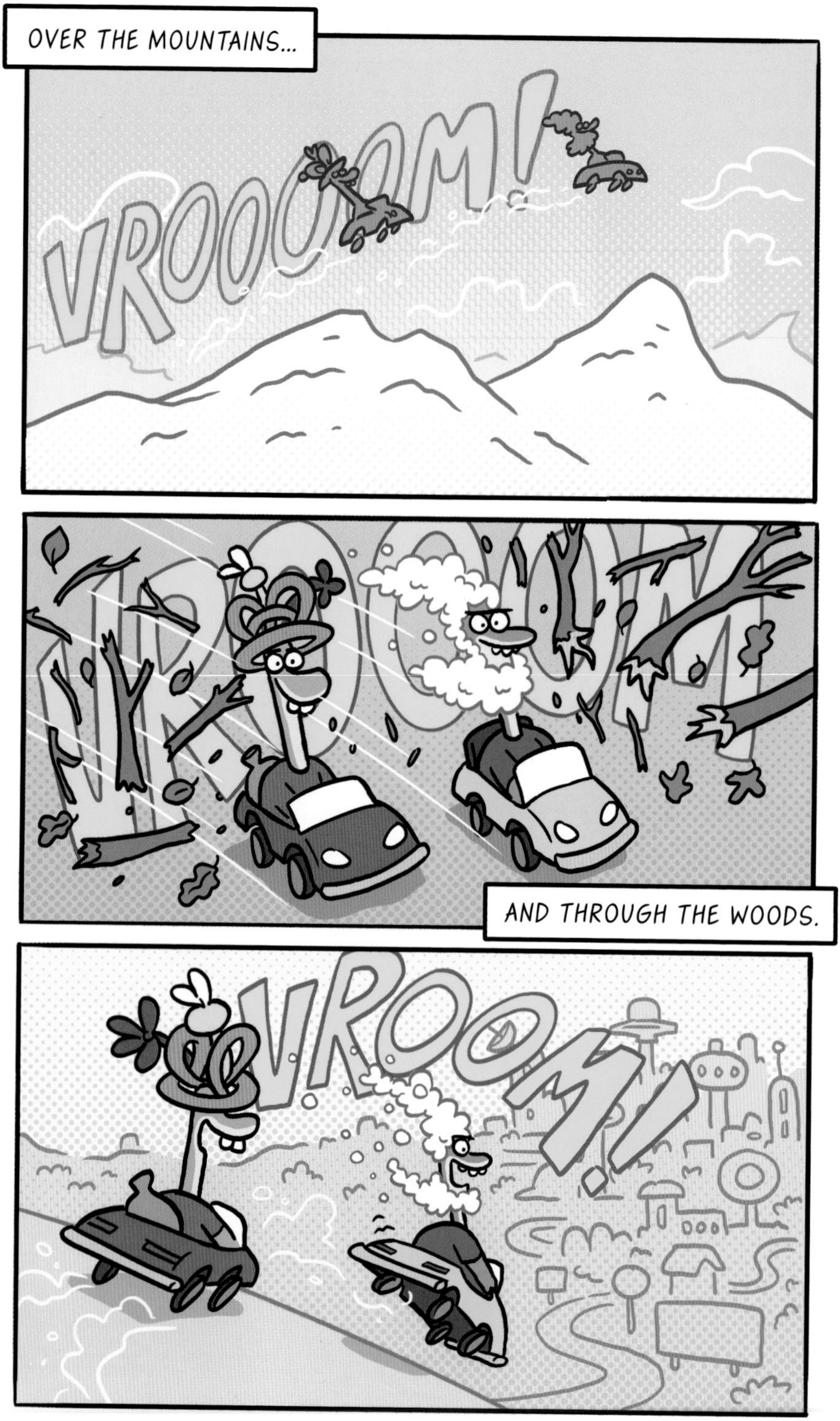
OVER THE MOUNTAINS...
VROOOOM!
AND THROUGH THE WOODS.
VROOM!!

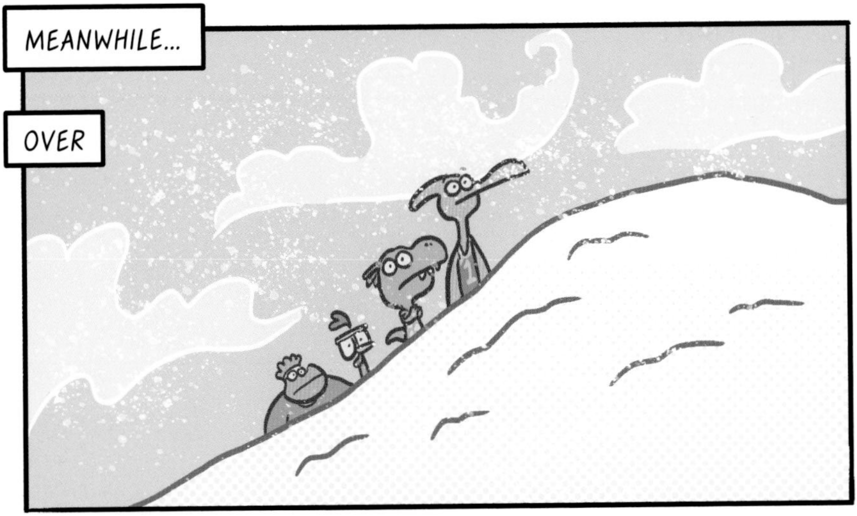
MEANWHILE...
OVER

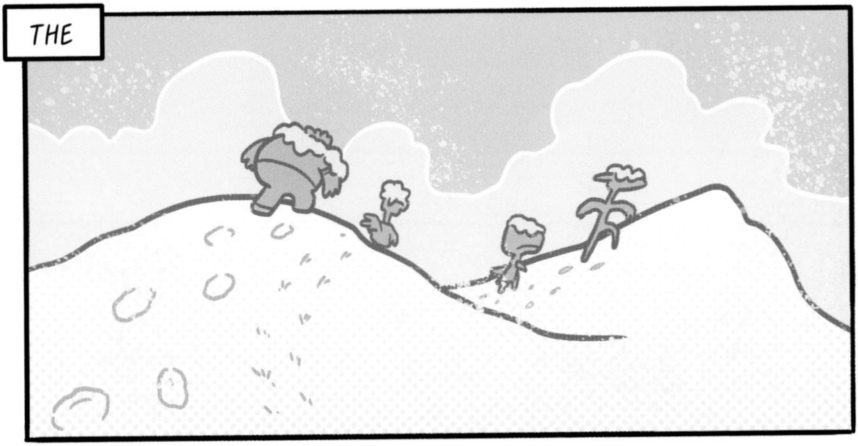
THE

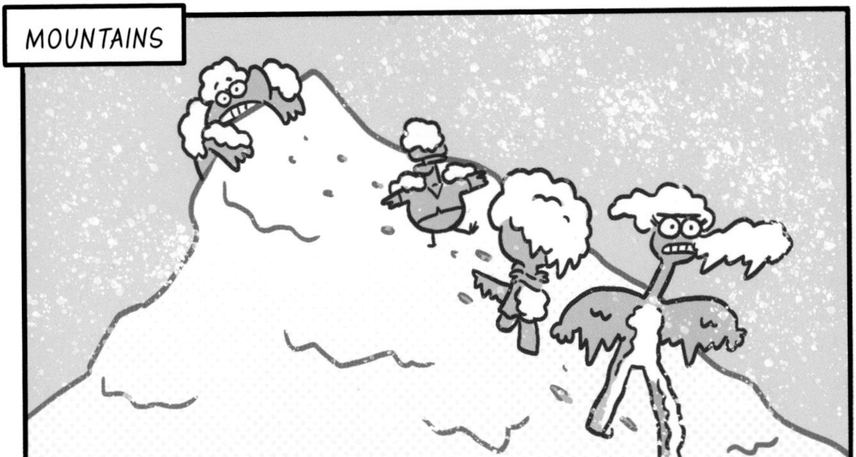
MOUNTAINS

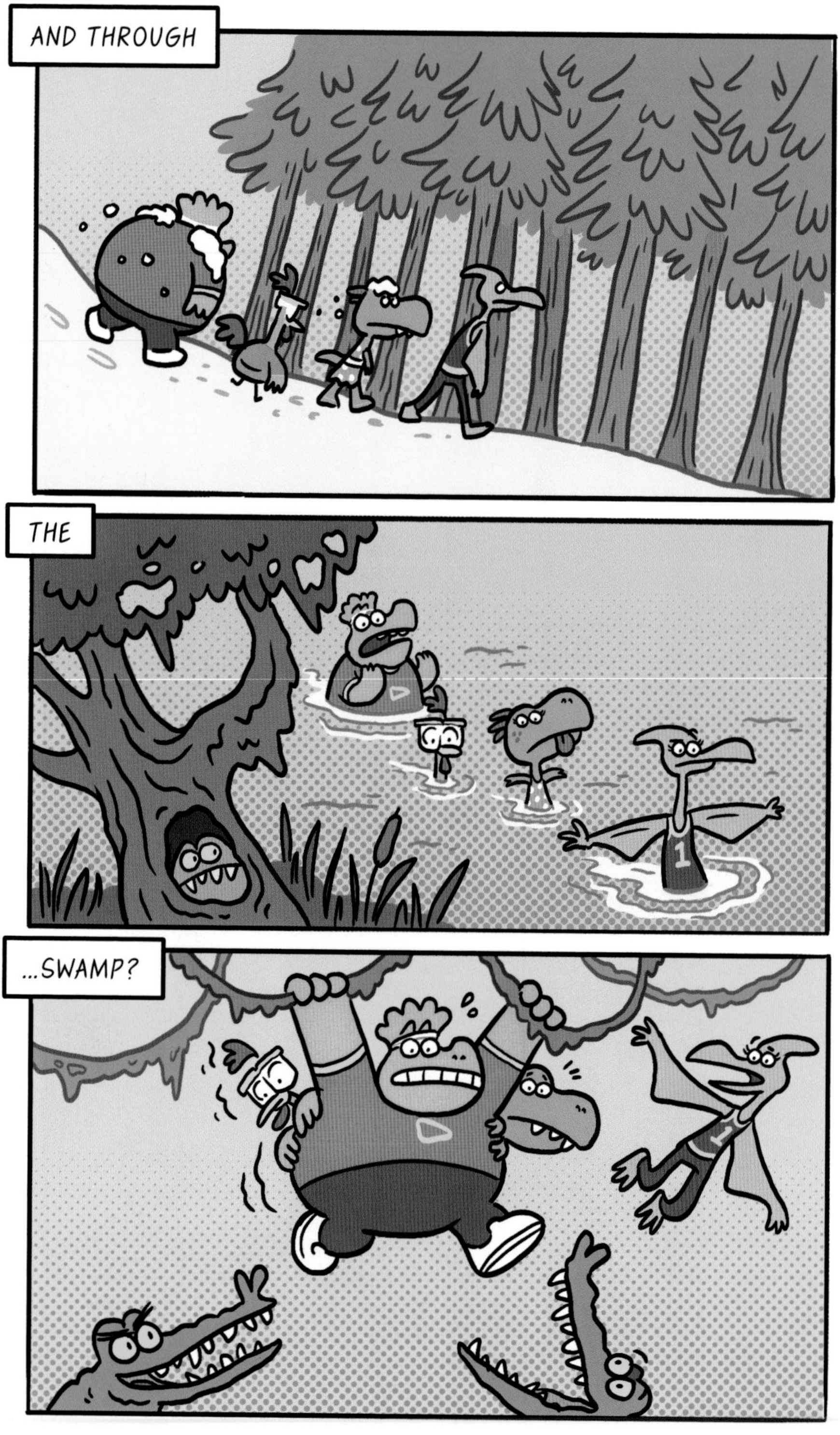
AND THROUGH
THE
...SWAMP?

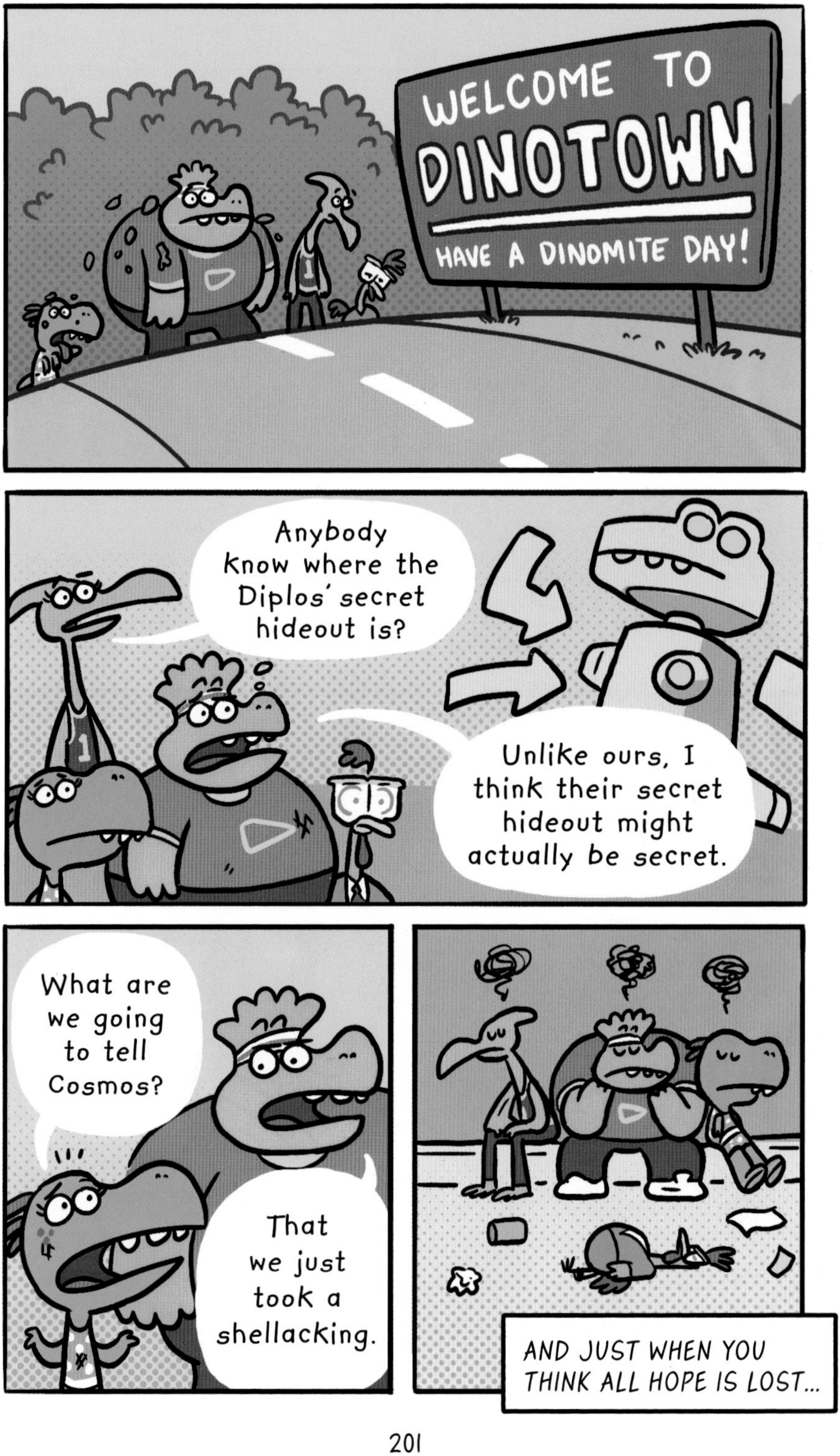
WELCOME TO
DINOTOWN
HAVE A DINOMITE DAY!
Anybody know where the Diplos' secret hideout is?
Unlike ours, I think their secret hideout might actually be secret.
What are we going to tell Cosmos?
That we just took a shellacking.
AND JUST WHEN YOU THINK ALL HOPE IS LOST...

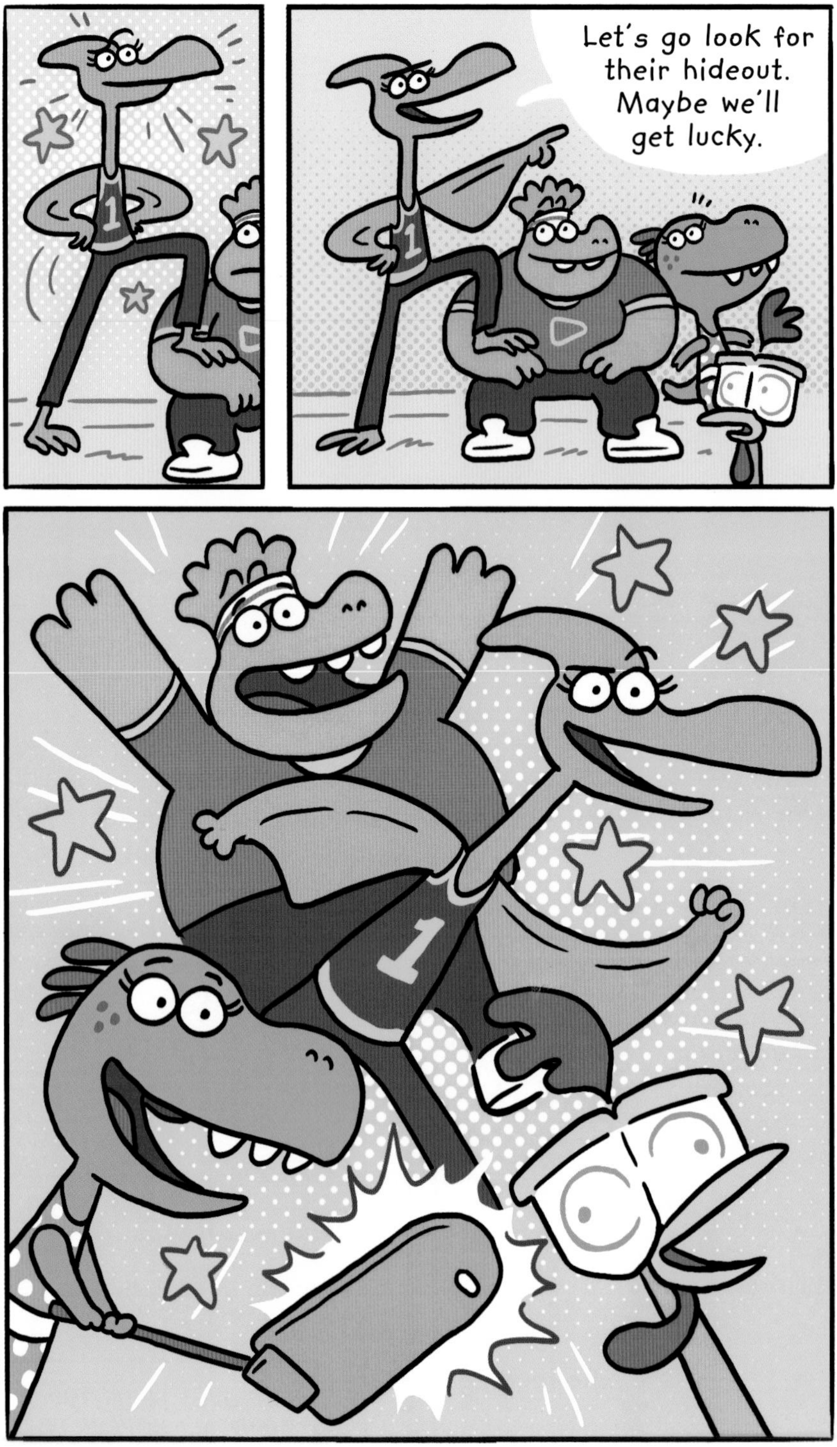
Let's go look for their hideout. Maybe we'll get lucky.

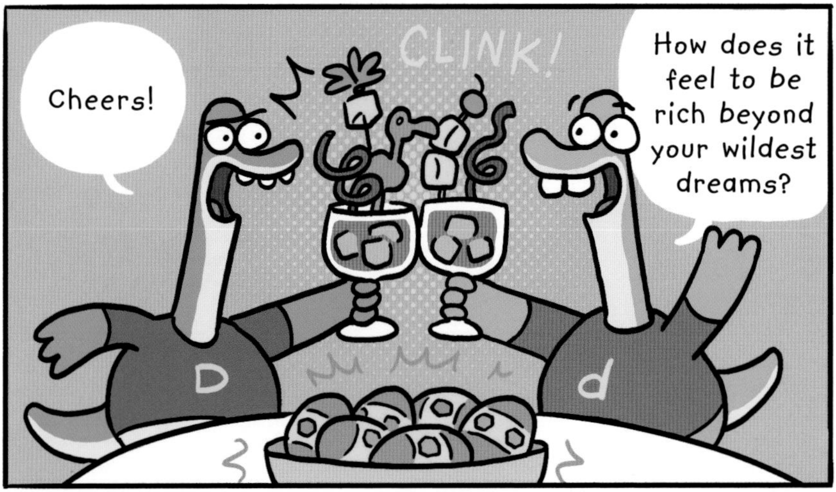
Cheers!
CLINK!
How does it feel to be rich beyond your wildest dreams?
D
d

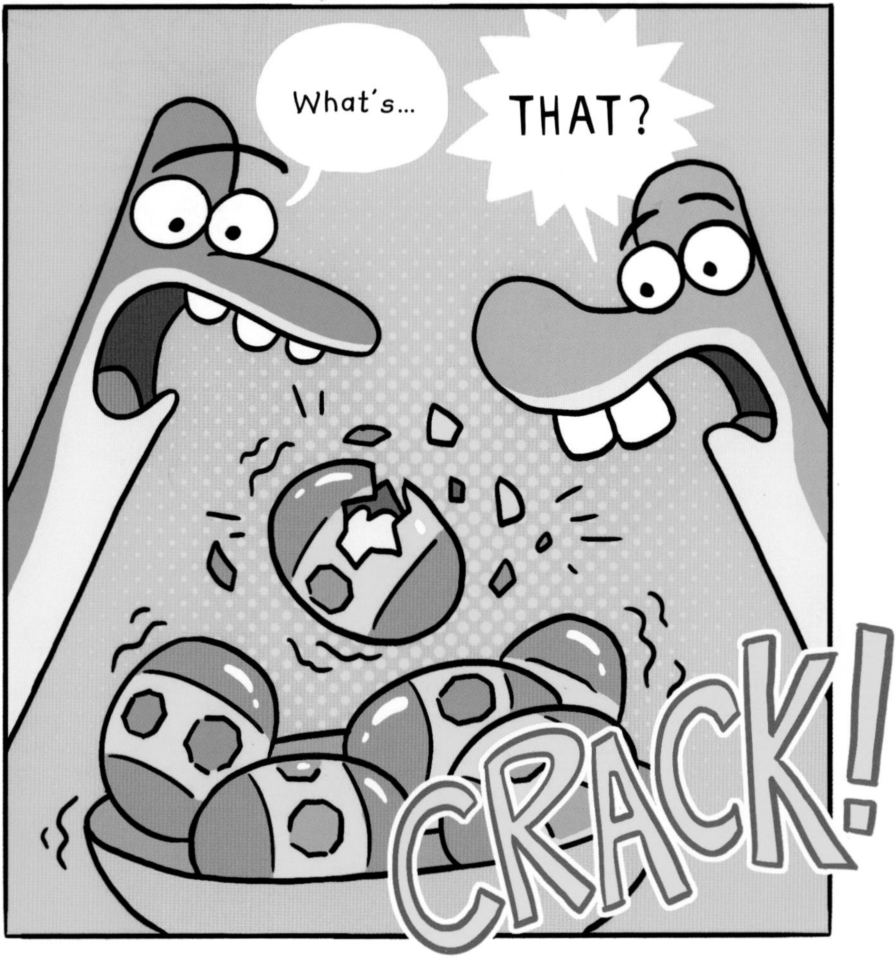
What's...
THAT?
CRACK!

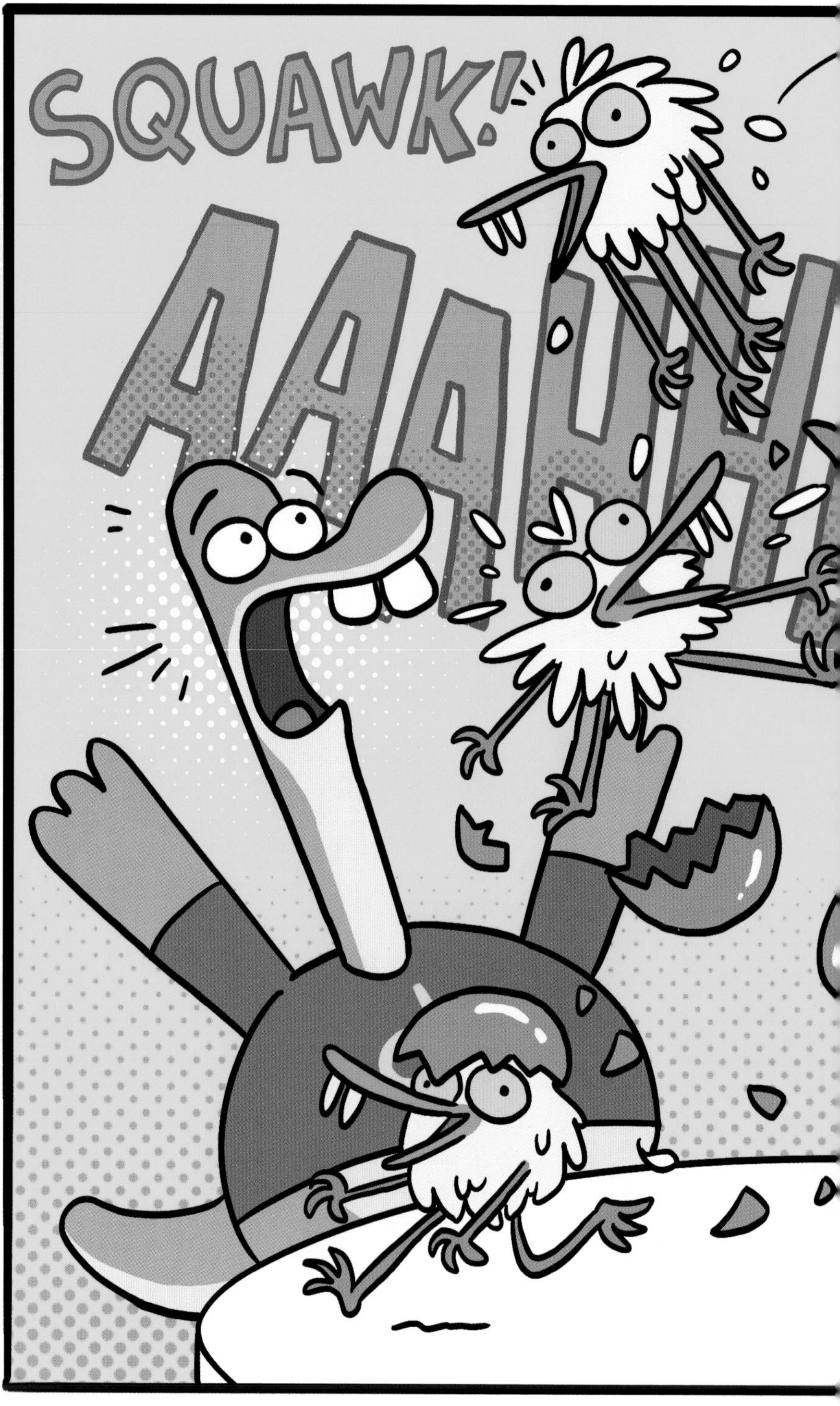
SQUAWK!

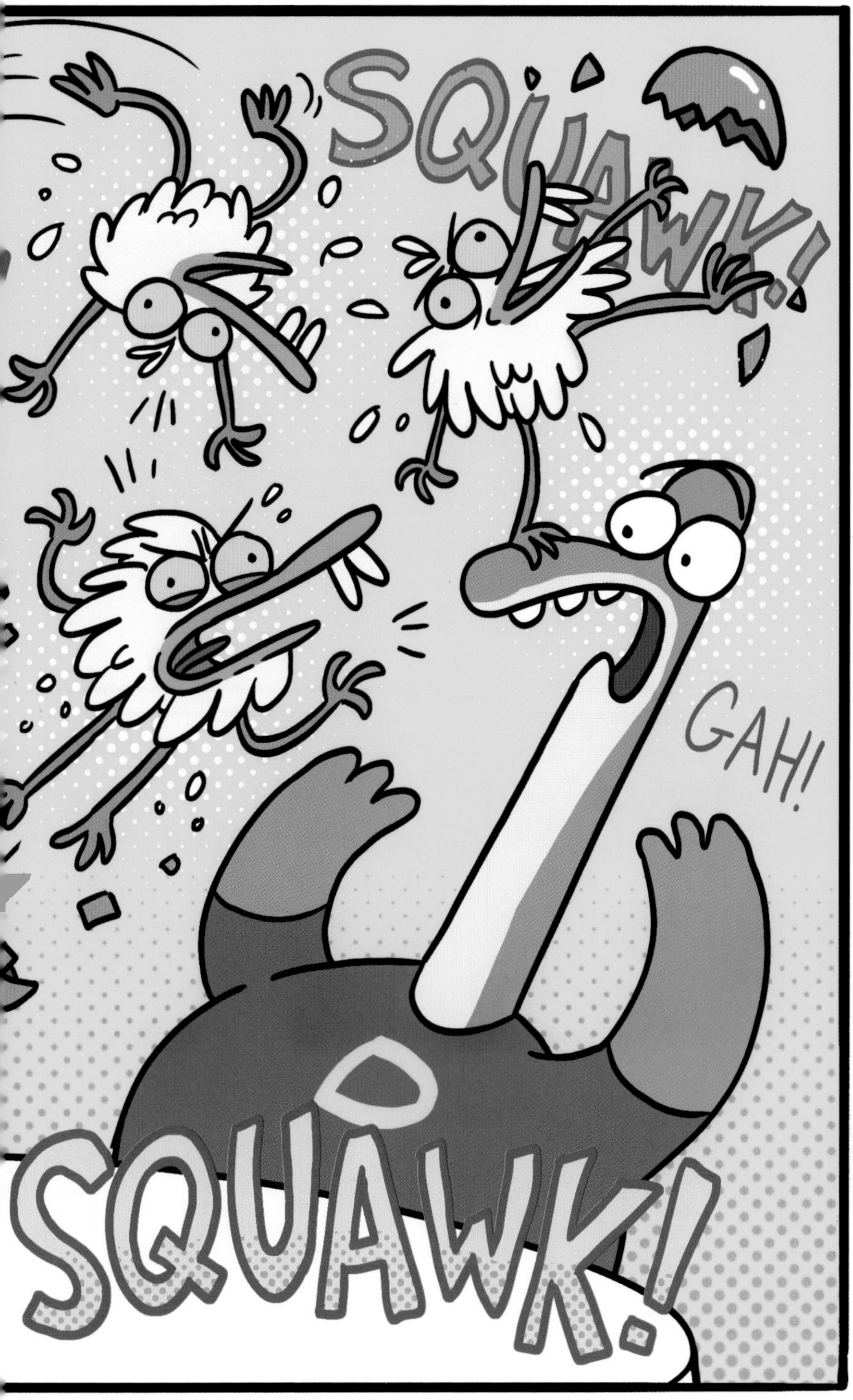
SQUAWK!
GAH!
SQUAWK!

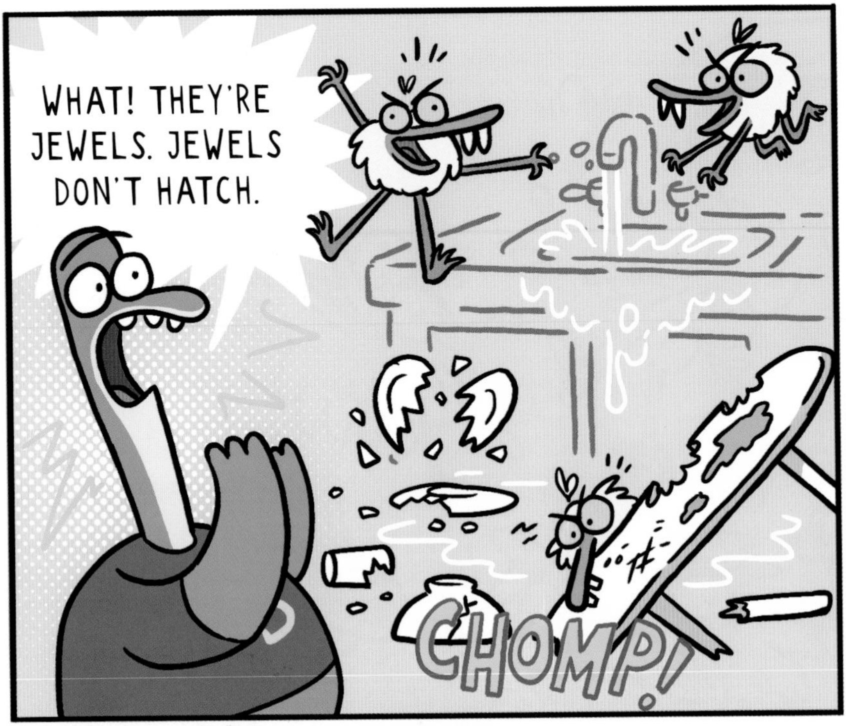
WHAT! THEY'RE JEWELS. JEWELS DON'T HATCH.
CHOMP!

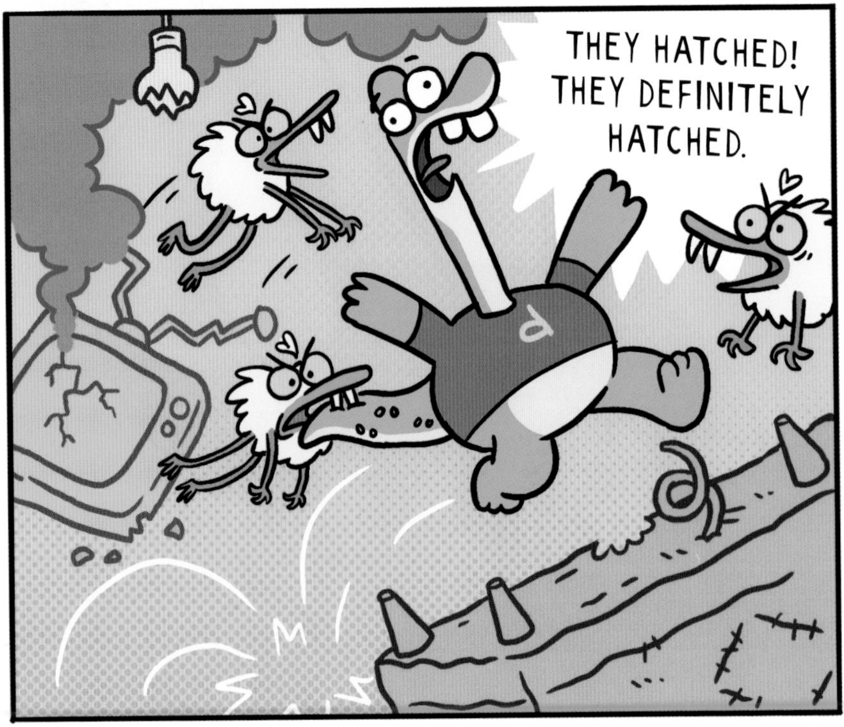
THEY HATCHED! THEY DEFINITELY HATCHED.

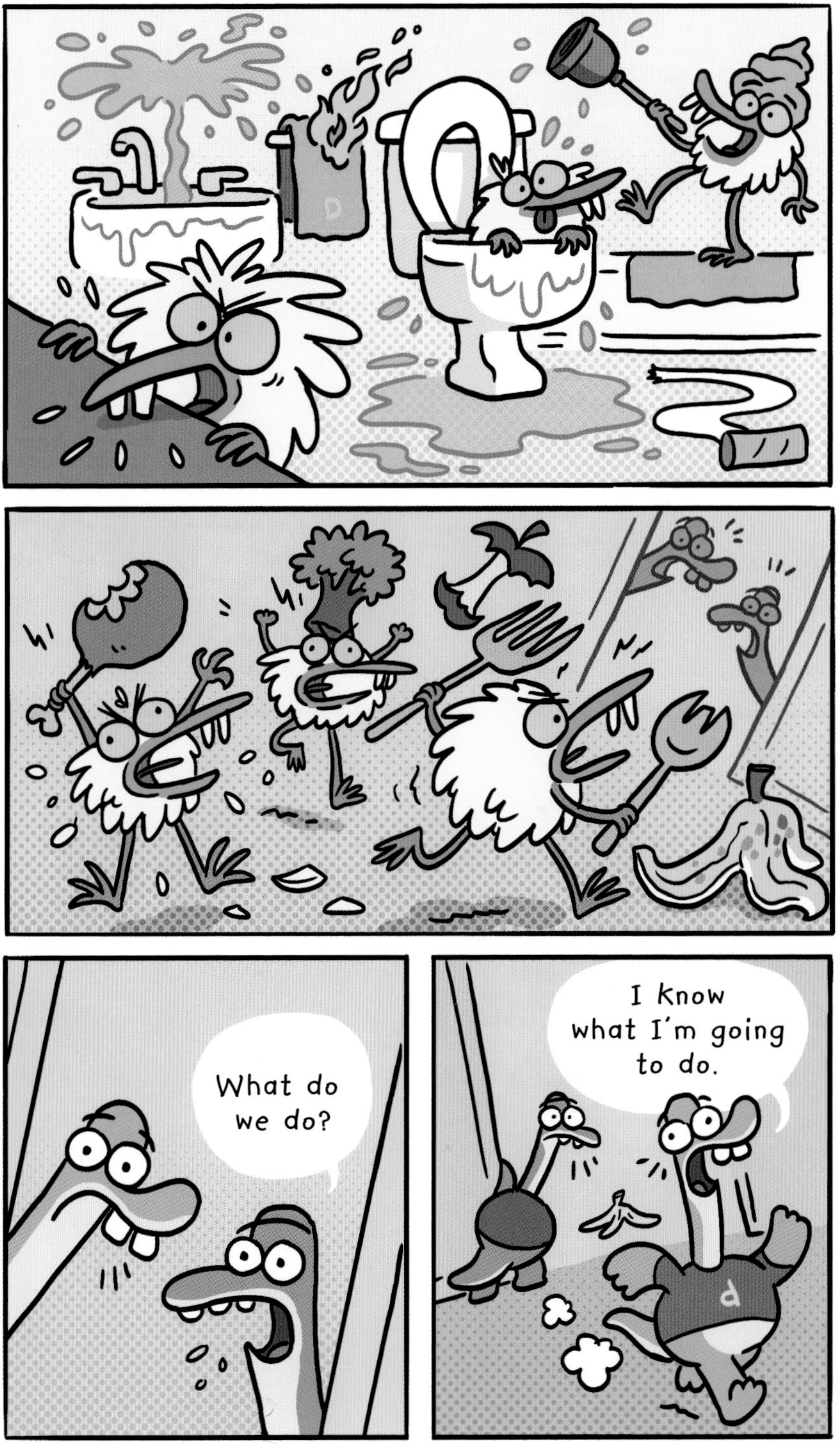
What do we do?
I know what I'm going to do.

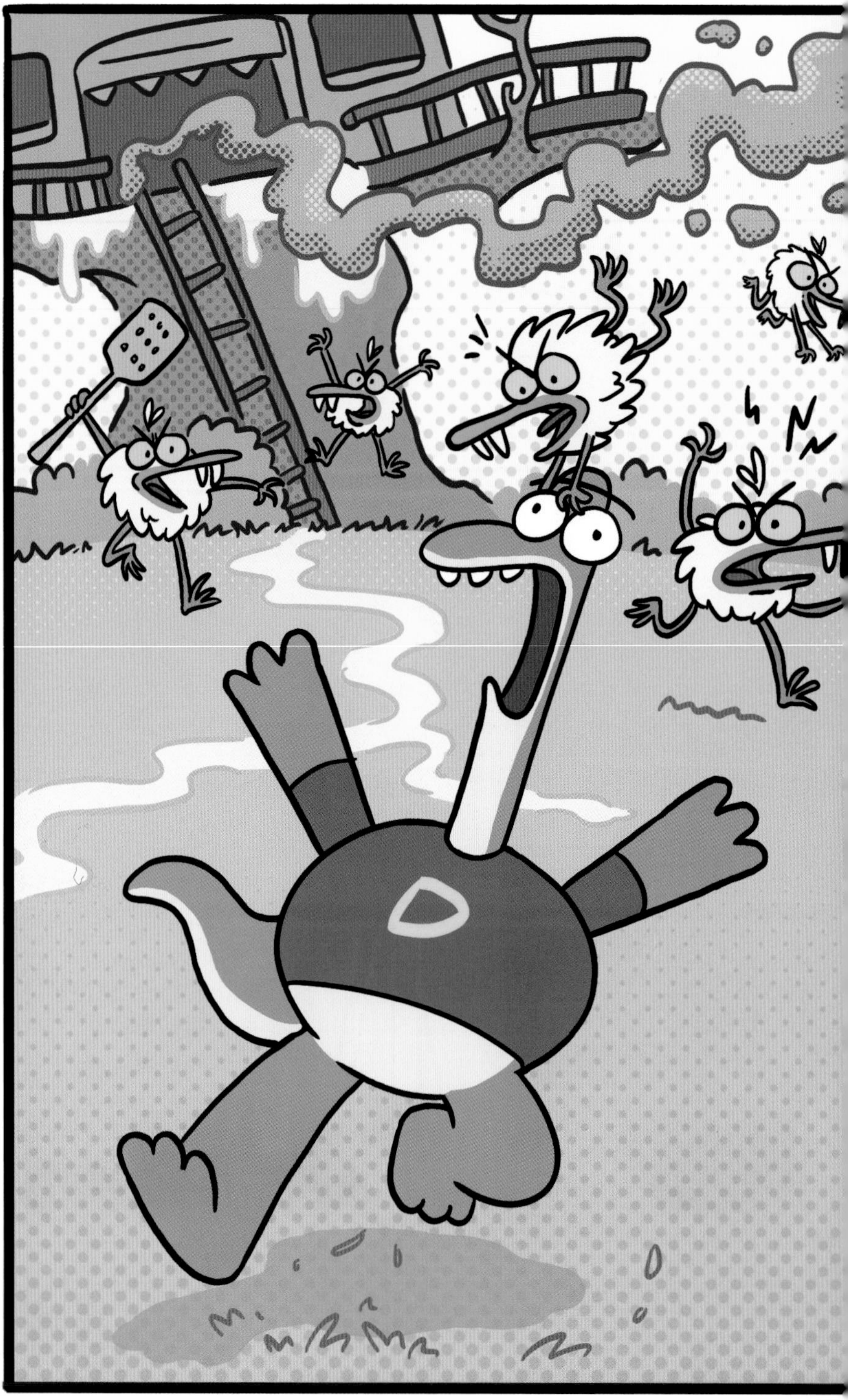

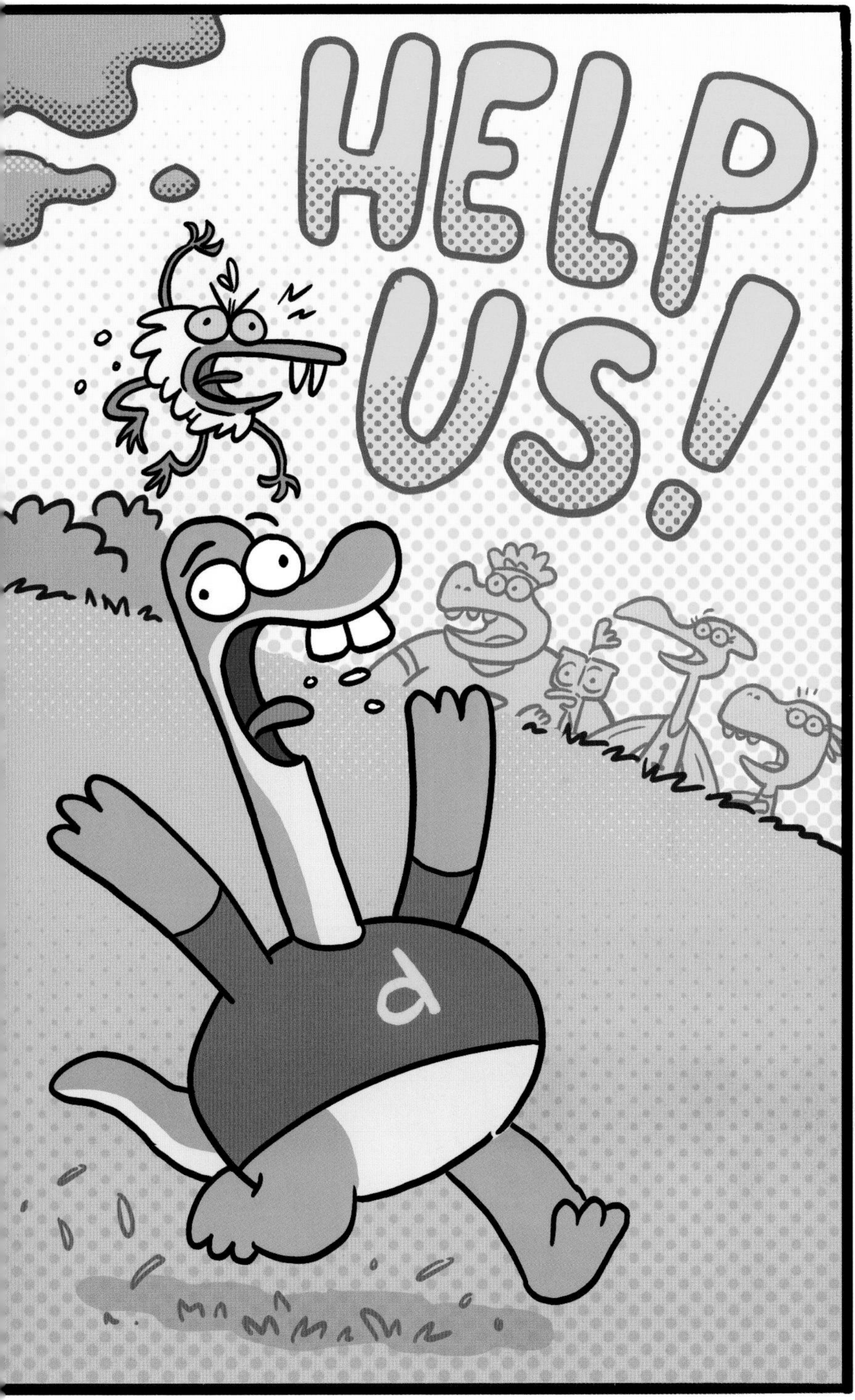
HELP US!

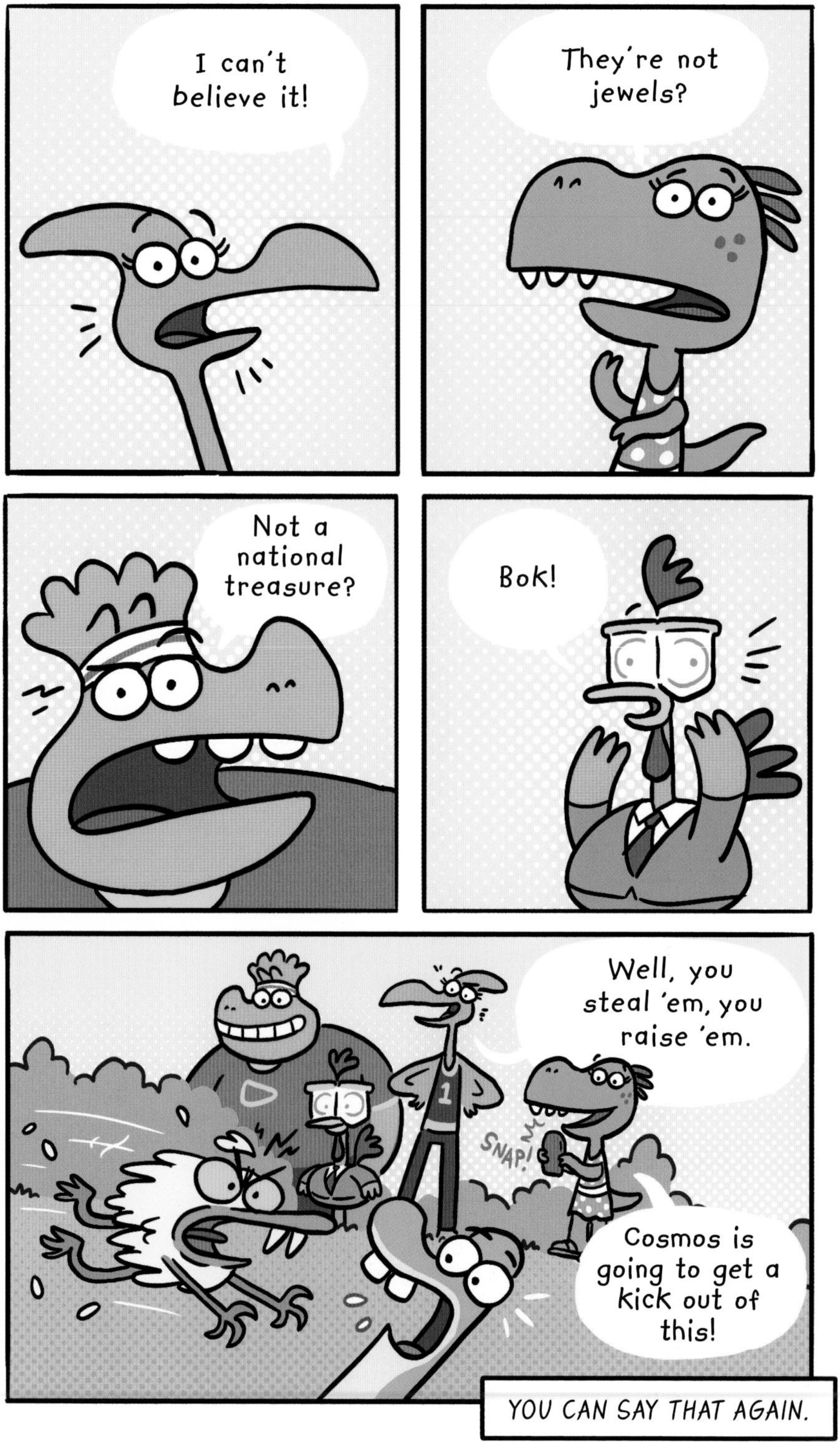
I can't believe it!
They're not jewels?
Not a national treasure?
Bok!
Well, you steal 'em, you raise 'em.
SNAP!
Cosmos is going to get a kick out of this!
YOU CAN SAY THAT AGAIN.

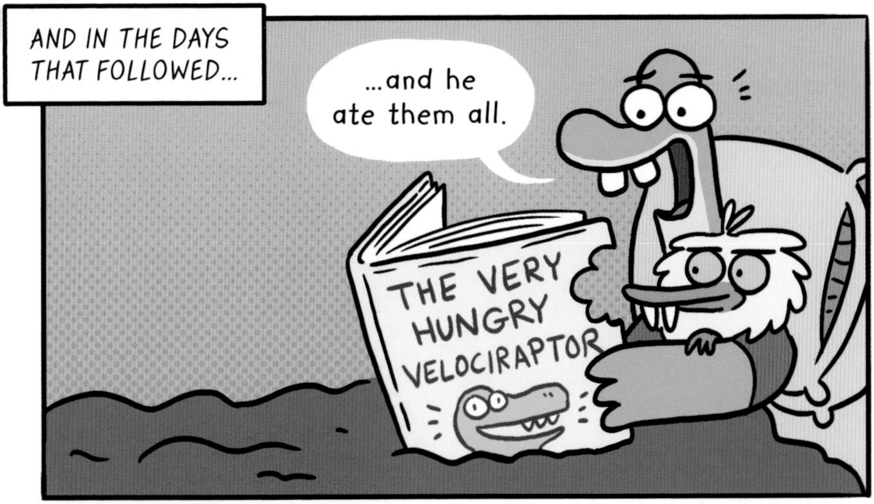
AND IN THE DAYS THAT FOLLOWED...
...and he ate them all.
THE VERY HUNGRY VELOCIRAPTOR

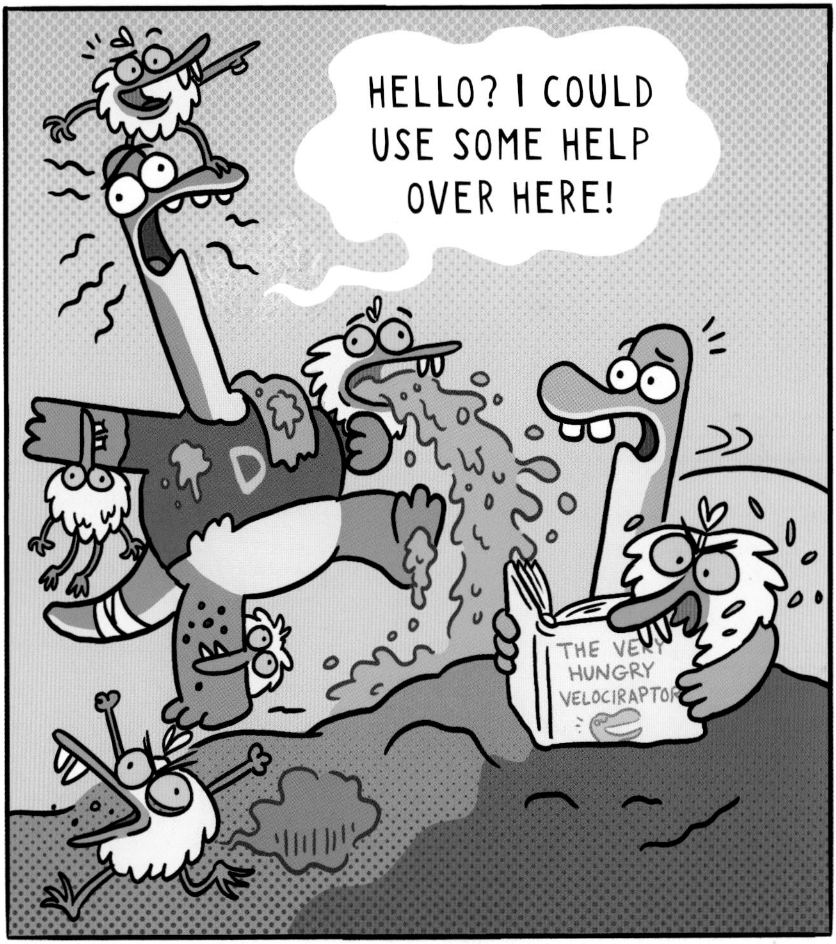
HELLO? I COULD USE SOME HELP OVER HERE!
D
THE VERY HUNGRY VELOCIRAPTOR

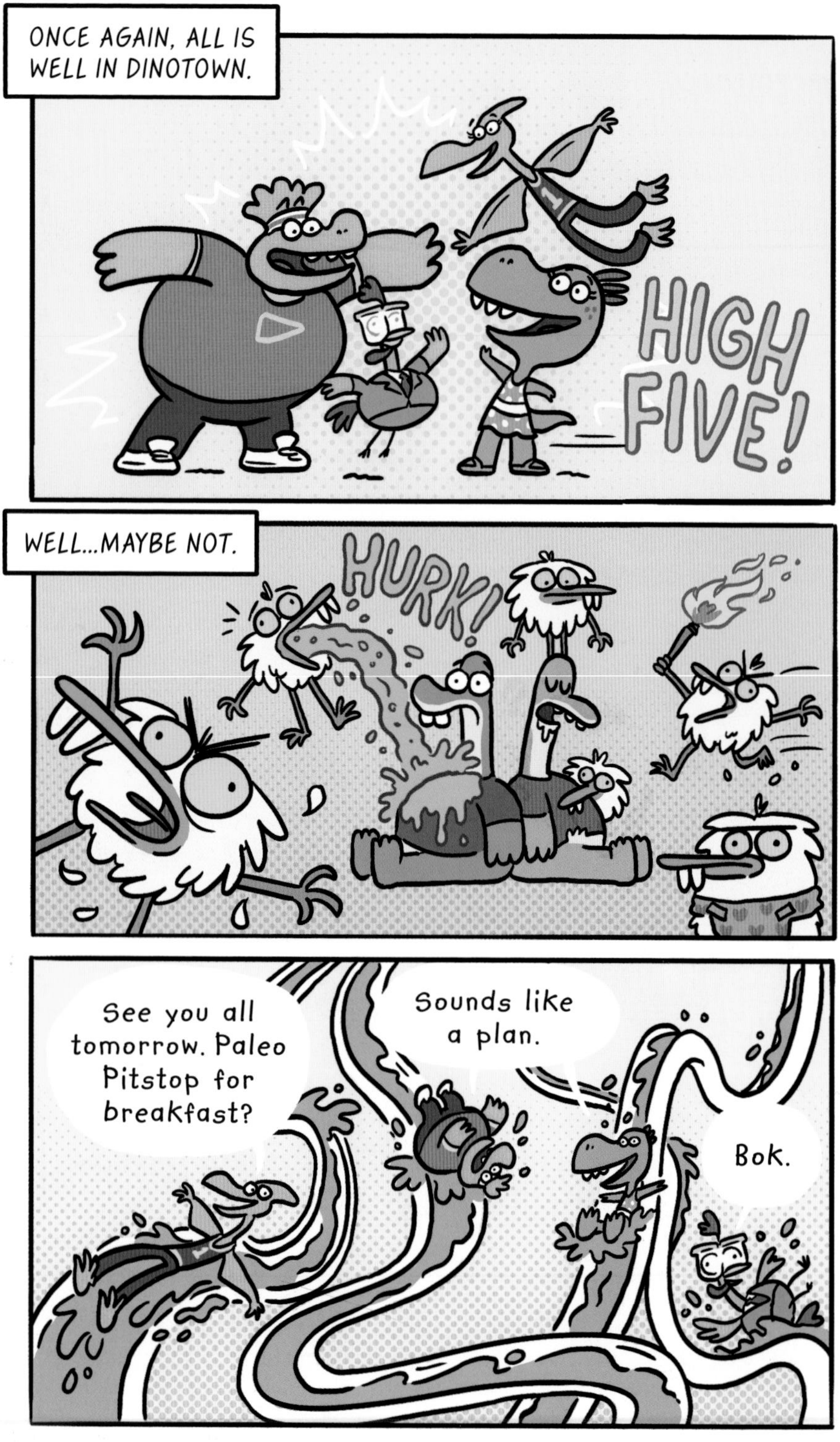
ONCE AGAIN, ALL IS WELL IN DINOTOWN.
HIGH FIVE!
WELL...MAYBE NOT.
HURK!
See you all tomorrow. Paleo Pitstop for breakfast?
Sounds like a plan.
Bok.

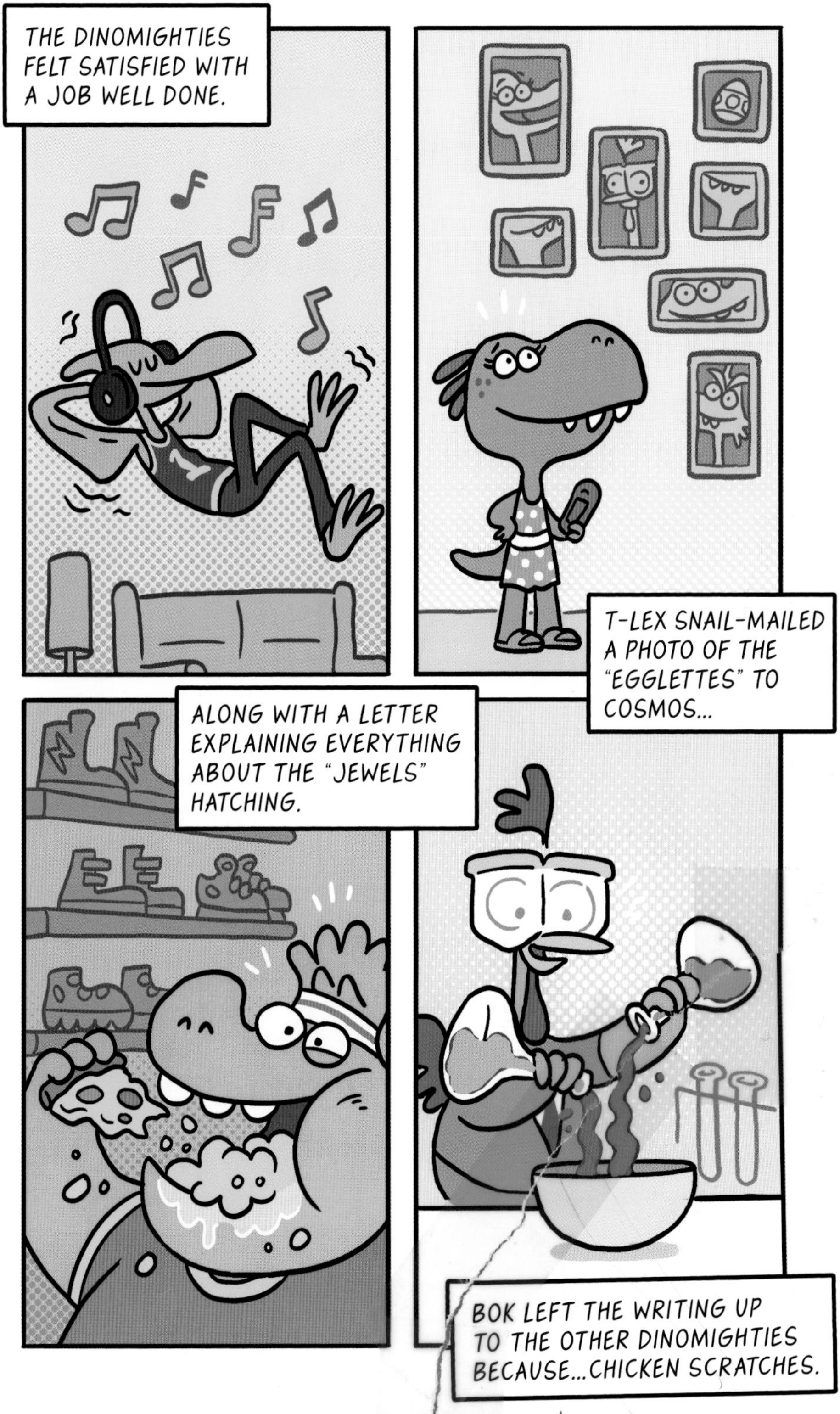
THE DINOMIGHTIES FELT SATISFIED WITH A JOB WELL DONE.
T-LEX SNAIL-MAILED A PHOTO OF THE "EGGLETTES" TO COSMOS...
ALONG WITH A LETTER EXPLAINING EVERYTHING ABOUT THE "JEWELS" HATCHING.
BOK LEFT THE WRITING UP TO THE OTHER DINOMIGHTIES BECAUSE...CHICKEN SCRATCHES.

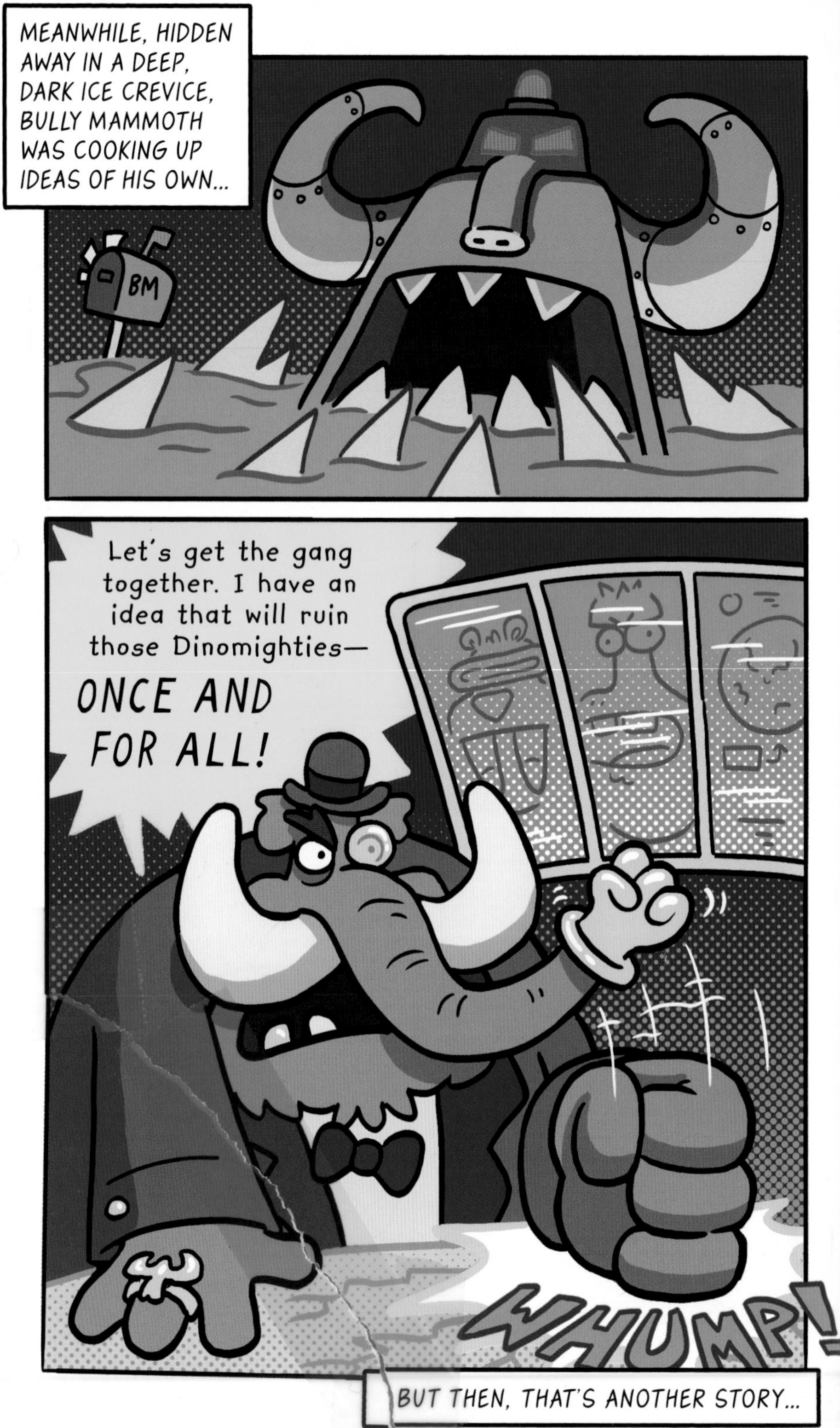
MEANWHILE, HIDDEN AWAY IN A DEEP, DARK ICE CREVICE, BULLY MAMMOTH WAS COOKING UP IDEAS OF HIS OWN...
BM
Let's get the gang together. I have an idea that will ruin those Dinomighties—
ONCE AND FOR ALL!
WHUMP!
BUT THEN, THAT'S ANOTHER STORY...

HANG ON...

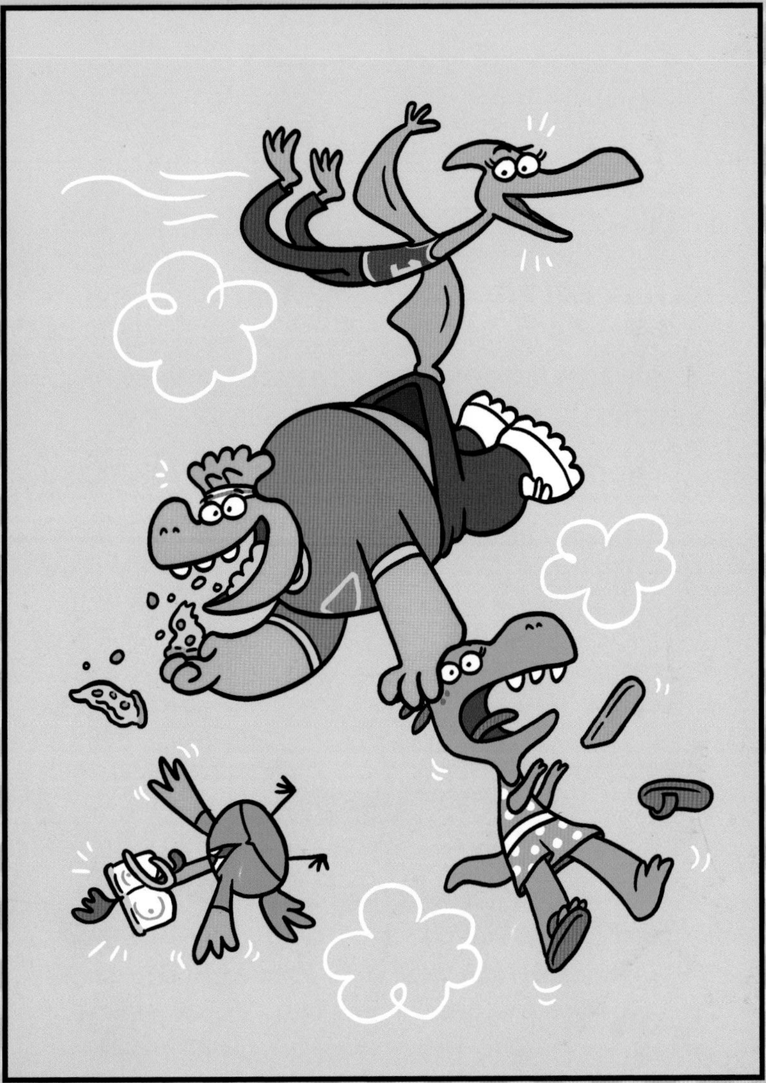

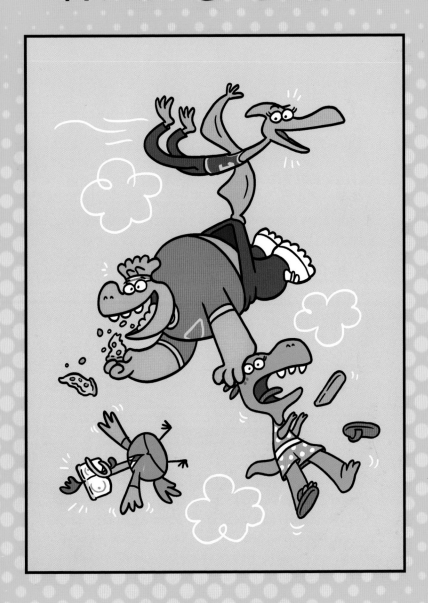

BOOK 2 IS COMING SOON!

DOUG PALEO IS A DINOMITE AUTHOR OF HILARIOUS BOOKS FOR YOUNG READERS. STONE IS HIS PREFERRED MEDIUM FOR ETCHING GRAPHIC NOVEL SCRIPTS. IN HIS FREE TIME, HE ENJOYS CAVE PAINTING, GOING ON LONG HIKES TO GATHER WILD BERRIES, AND OPEN-FIRE COOKING.

AARON BLECHA IS AN ARTIST AND AUTHOR WHO DESIGNS FUNNY CHARACTERS AND ILLUSTRATES HUMOROUS BOOKS. HE HAS WORKED ON SEVERAL POPULAR MIDDLE GRADE SERIES, INCLUDING GEORGE BROWN, CLASS CLOWN AND SHARK SCHOOL. AARON LIVES WITH HIS FAMILY ON THE SOUTH COAST OF ENGLAND. FIND HIM AT MONSTERSQUID.COM.